SHORT STORIES

by Luigi Pirandello

TRANSLATED FROM THE ITALIAN BY
LILY DUPLAIX

INTRODUCTION BY FRANCES KEENE

SIMON AND SCHUSTER • NEW YORK

LIBRARY OF CONGRESS CATALOG CARD NUMBER: 58-13756
MANUFACTURED IN THE UNITED STATES OF AMERICA

CONTENTS

Tales of Frustration

Tales of Anguish and Hope

Note on Bibliography

Note on Italian Pronunciation

INTRODUCTION

Before Pirandello ever wrote a play, he wrote poetry and short stories. The form his thoughts took at their grandest and most expressive—as in *Six Characters in Search of an Author* and *Henry IV*—was clearly foreshadowed in the dramatic juxtapositions which characterize his stories, and the tone of the plays at their best has the thin, pure echo of poetry. Thus to know and not merely to skim the works of this uniquely thoughtful dramatist a reader should have access to a fair cross-section of the short stories.

Easier said than done, for Pirandello wrote over three hundred and sixty-five short stories (he once told French critic Benjamin Crémieux that there was "a fair choice of extras for Leap Year"). Collections have been made and will continue to be made since the *opera omnia* remains untranslated. This book gives an organically sound, perceptive choice and, while not pretending to offer any final distillation, includes stories representative of Pirandello's major themes.

"Obsession" is not too strong a word to describe Pirandello's concern with the nature of reality. But if this, the dominant theme in all his work, is obsessive, it is the kind of obsession a suspended prism exerts on the curious eye of the beholder: the sides turn without the viewer's intervention and the surfaces reflect sun or shade, refract this or that sudden gleam of light in inexhaustible kaleidoscopy. Pirandello was the viewer; the prism was man's nature, his identity, turning apparently at will its many facets toward the beholder. But was the prism truly moving "at will"? Remember that it was suspended. Just so does the individual move before the author in apparent freedom, yet conditioned by who knows what cord that suspends him in his particular situation, his appointed place. Pirandello never sought to alter the movements of his prisms: there is no finger smudge on the clear planes, for the characters are never pushed or prodded by the author's nudge. Their motivation lies in the nature of *das Ding an sich*. Thus they turn and sway of their own momentum, yet within limits prescribed by their particular unalterable situation.

And by what casual interaction do the beams of light intertwine as two or more suspended prisms move in relation to each other! How transitory this tangled, indistinguishable light! From which prism comes the dominant glow? Who is to say which is the "perfect," the "right" reflection? What is the "truth" of this strange interplay?

Understanding and accepting this view of the relationship between author and subject, the reader at once sees clearly why Pirandello never overtly expresses compassion in either stories or plays. Can the viewer in all conscience feel compassion for the prism? By extension, this explains too why the writer never tells reader or audience which side he wishes taken. How can you choose one side when man is, by his very nature, multiform, no less different to different individuals than to his different selves?

Yet human nature craves certainty, and certainty implies choice. Thus we see exposed the root conflict of the human drama in these two antithetical and indeed mutually exclusive "truths": the prismatic nature of man and his devouring need for certainty. Am I what my wife sees, what my child "knows" is me, what my associate rubs elbows with daily, what my priest hears at Confession, what I understand me to be as I keep my journal by night? What manner of creature am I and of how many faces?

Does my beloved know if even I cannot know which of these faces is the "right," the "true"—and to which of these is he or she, in fact, *the beloved?* (This question of identity is treated par excellence in *Right You Are* . . . and is most theatrically plausible in *As You Desire Me.*)

Certain conclusions inevitably result from Pirandello's preoccupation with the nature of man, chief among them that the human being is nearly always uncomfortable in time and place but that, given his "suspension cord," there is little if anything he can do about it. These two unwelcome conditions of place and time are interwoven to form the background against which the character is pinioned. In the short masterpiece "The Soft Touch of Grass" (p. 167), Pirandello takes a bereaved and lonely man presumably in his early sixties and observes him in circumstances that twist a casual action into a gesture of apparent lewdness. The supposed intent is less stunning for the reader than is the appalled man's realization of what, by an accident of time and place, the young girl thinks he is up to. Wickedness in the eye of the beholder has seldom been more nakedly portrayed nor has an aging individual's plight seemed more poignantly unbearable.

"Cinci" (p. 173) goes to the other end of the chronological scale. Here Pirandello portrays a boy in early adolescence whose loneliness, natural at that age, is compounded by the wretched circumstances in which he and his mother live. Just as a young caged lion may pause before his bars and, for kicks, send up a frightening roar into the faces of his gaping, apprehensive oglers, so Cinci goes into the little church opposite the hospital and unleashes the frightening thunderclap of his dropped books. Having petrified the old people, he sees "no further need [sic] to gall the patience of those poor scandalized worshipers" and wanders on his way just as the young lion resumes his pacing. But the bars are still there.

Some measure of peace, a peace so restless that it can be broken at the slightest intrusion, settles on Cinci at the top of the hill where he lounges against a wall. He is not a violent boy, a lover of violence for its own sake, and this is made clear by his stifled cry of protest when the farm lad kills the lizard. He is not so much animated by pity as affronted by the wantonness of the gesture which does not even permit the boys to indulge human curiosity about the creature's darting looks and antics. The fight which this act unleashes and the controlled fear it awakens in Cinci give the silent struggle there in the white moonlight on the newly harrowed field a classic simplicity and terror. Cinci kills almost inadvertently; he fights for his life instinctively, kills, and frees himself as if it were happening to someone else. He "awakens" from the act as from a dream and leisurely resumes his return to loneliness, having tasted in that instant's action the bitterness of death—a recognition he will carry with him all his days. In that moment of truth he has passed from adolescence to manhood and there is no going back, although he has wilfully obliterated from his consciousness the events which precipitated the change.

"The Rose" (p. 197) takes the theme of human frustration to still another level. Signora Lucietta, the young widow, is caught like a fly in amber in the alien town where she has gone to earn her living. The elements in this story which bring it to the verge of tragedy are not of the spectacular, easily recognizable kind but are of an infinitely subtle, almost evanescent nature. Lucietta senses all that she is foregoing in turning down the one man who might have rescued her from perpetual exile in the narrow provincial world and who might have brought her, through his intelligence, to some sort of spiritual and emotional maturity. That her "suspension cord" forces her to complete the gesture which closes the escape hatch forever is as inevitable as the news of the fall of kings in Greek tragedy. Lucietta's true widowhood begins then.

Pirandello shared Thoreau's view that nearly all of us "lead lives of quiet desperation" and, again like Thoreau, he found that the epitome of man's self-torture was most often achieved in cities. There everything seems to conspire to thwart man's reaching for the sun and light, for warmth, and the simple relief of unsuspicious communion both with others and with nature. The cliché that man is nowhere more alone than in a crowd has, when examined in single instances of desperate isolation, elements in it which range from the grotesque to the terrifying.

Although from different social strata, Signor Bareggi in "Es-

cape" and the grandfather in "The Footwarmer" know equally
well the bleak, cheerless streets of the Roman periphery at night.
Though the news vendor would never seek physical escape as does
Bareggi, the old man's withdrawal into the womb of warmth and
silence that is his kiosk is as complete an immolation as is Bareggi's inevitable destruction in the mad chase that spells his deliverance. Not only is the situation in "Escape" magnificently
ludicrous, but the key character is never allowed to become so.
The power of the story lies in the fact that Bareggi's life is indeed
so unbearable that we tacitly agree to his own estimate of it, and
find his choice of a Pegasus perfectly in keeping with the hideous
monotony, the bleak vulgarity of his round of days. His escape is
no less grand for being accomplished in a milk wagon. And the
very coherence of the solution precludes in both writer and
reader any trace of pity or sentimentality.

In all his work, including the ironic and humorous, Pirandello underscores the inevitability of this human frustration—
human discomfort and discontent with place or time or both.
The human drama implies frustration, thanks to the irreconcil-
able dichotomy we talked of earlier, and, since Pirandello recog-
nizes it as endemic to life itself, he pulls it from the shadows and
places it where it belongs. This is no backwater, the author as-
serts repeatedly, but an essential part of the main stream: no
man can pursue his life and be ignorant of it.

The Sicilian tales have a place of their own in Pirandello's
work, for in them physical atmosphere is more an integral part
of the story than props and background are otherwise allowed to
be. In "Fumes" (p. 20) and "A Mere Formality" (p. 70) we
feel at all times the threatening presence of the sulphur mines,
the acrid stench of the burning stuff and the peculiar devastation
its extraction from the earth wreaks not only on the land but on
the lives of those who seek to exploit that land. We may see the
mines only from a distance, hear of the rigors of plant manage-
ment in an office adjacent to a bank, but the crude, uneven struggle of man against nature is as present as if it were played out an
arm's length away. Gabriele's ruin in "A Mere Formality" has
been brought about by the unwise assumption that he could step
into his father's shoes and acquire, by will power and dedication

alone, sufficient expertise to wrest a living from the pits for himself, his family, his employees. He is in pitched battle with the natural forces of his native island, and Nature, with blind unconcern for the affairs of men, has slapped him down. We see him on the verge of disaster, brought to this pass by the apparent vengefulness of a world which has refused to yield up its secrets to one who has never truly become a part of it. Gabriele is one of a series of protagonists in the author's many Sicilian tales and plays who hate the métier they must perform yet who, for reasons of middle-class solidarity and family duty, tempt fate by allowing themselves to be maneuvered into a family profession. Pirandello felt that this was a particularly frequent exploitation in Sicilian middle and upper bourgeois life. Sons who were sent to the mainland, to the Universities of Naples, Rome, Bologna, Milan—even as far afield as Paris or Bonn, where he himself went—risked returning strangers to their homeland, deracinated, unfit to consider confidently living out their lives there and yet unable, because of the matrix of Sicilian society, to cut the cord entirely.

Yet another aspect of the difficulty of being Sicilian is exposed in "Bombolo." This story of knight-errantry on behalf of the downtrodden peasant proves its perennial validity if one remembers the late highwayman, Giuliano, who, like Bombolo, took from the rich to give to the poor. A Sicilian by birth, Bombolo returns to his native island after successful years presumably as an illicit trader in the Levant. Disquieted and eventually goaded to action by the terrible inequities he sees all about him, Bombolo decides to bring "justice" at least to his own area. The tale reveals conclusions Pirandello must have found hard to swallow: the man who seeks to bring relief to the peasants is fighting a losing game, and the reasons why he can't win lie within the distorted nature of the peasants themselves. The *why* of this distortion is self-evident, nor has the recent creation of a World Bank altered its immediate relevance.

The sharp contrast between the intelligence of some of Pirandello's female characters and the roles society allows them to occupy is reminiscent of Ibsen. Nowhere is this closeness more apparent than in "The Rose." Signora Lucietta trying vainly to rally her strength sufficiently to compete for a living in the world of men finds that, though she may win employment and even respect, she is inevitably defeated on the social plane. This is Nora in more contemporary situations—but underlying such situations is the great, timeless question: has she, Lucietta, any more right than Nora or Williams' Blanche, for that matter, to her own complex identity?

Pirandello presents us with a somewhat similar case in the slighter story, "The Umbrella." Ostensibly, this tender little story tells of a young widow and her two small daughters, of her inability to buy a full complement of winter clothes for both children, and of the elder girl's yearning to possess the single new umbrella the mother can afford. But behind this thin veil of tear-jerking plot—complicated by the child's believable death—lies the writer's perpetual probing into the emotional motivation of human behavior: the mother is brusque with the elder child because she senses that it is this child, with her brooding, speculative glance, who will prevent her remarriage. The young widow is desperately lonely, insecure. In every sense, she admits the frustration the presence of Dinuccia causes her; she even admits that she yearns for her "not to die, God forbid," but simply not to have been born. Her consequent guilt at the child's coincidental death can only be imagined, for Pirandello will not trim his sails to a particular readership: the mother never reappears after she sends the maid for the doctor. The inclusion of this story in Mme Duplaix's collection is important, for it shows the range of Pirandello's appeal. Even the superficially trite situational story has its flashes of depth and perception, the same glow which so totally illumines the greater work. As many writers eke out an insufficient income by popularizing certain themes they treat more profoundly in their major productions, so Pirandello popularizes—and pinpoints—in this little story the theme of woman's fate. That this theme preoccupied him all his life is given monumental proof in one of his key works, "Such Is Life."

Frustration, encroaching age, perpetual loneliness, misunderstanding, death—*la condition humaine*—are, then, the recurrent subjects. The forms range, as we know, from the wildly, hilariously burlesque through the ironic, the gently satiric, the quasidocumentary, to the dramatic and, in the classic sense, tragic.

Details, too, run like cues for action through the gamut of the stories. There are cricket sounds at night, the play of moonlight on steel, the great sound of silence (which Leopardi caught so well), the pointlessness, the hopelessness, of hope. Over all, there is man's boundless inhumanity to man.

Is there, then, no end to man-inflicted, self-inflicted pain? There is, the author believes, but it lies in no faith, in no "right," in no assurance from within; it lies in patience, tolerance, maturity and compromise. "The Wreath" is the only example in this collection of Pirandello's personal formula for a fit survival. In it the husband wins grandeur and purity in his wife's eyes by acting above, beyond the formulas of the day, by dropping all the recommendations society would have given him and by acting, indeed, like a clement and loving god.

But a god's love—even if our gods are made in our own best image—is impersonal, benign—above all, unpossessive. And there it is, Pirandello's answer, arrived at with infinite greatness of spirit, infinite patient scrutiny of the poor whirling prisms with their irrevocably separate identities, their apparently autonomous gyrations. To the earlier question "Can one feel compassion for a prism?" the author would answer, "Yes, and even love, for strife-torn, strife-inflicting life is bearable only if love—not possessiveness—rule."

FRANCES KEENE

New York University
New York, 1958

Sicilian Tales

LOST AND FOUND

Crickets trilled all through the calm September evening along the narrow beach cluttered with heaps of sulphur. Until the middle of the last century, this had been an inlet and the sea pounded against the walls of the expanding town. When the inlet filled in, forming a narrow, sandy strip of beach, it was quickly appropriated and loads of sulphur were dumped there.

Who could tell what would become of Vignetta a hundred or two hundred years from now? Meanwhile, for the inhabitants it was almost a city. The port handled most of the commerce of the island, though it still had no dock. Two long stony arms curved into the sea and were joined in the middle by a slender wooden bridge, called the Old Jetty. This modest span had the honor of accommodating a kind of harbor office and the white tower of the main lighthouse.

All day long the place was in a hubbub. Every morning at dawn the town crier woke everyone with a roll on his drum: "Men of the sea! To work!"

Carts loaded with sulphur had already begun to screech on their axles. They had only iron mountings and no springs and they jolted over holes in the big, dusty road, crowded by teams of skinny donkeys harnessed and loaded with sulphur in two baskets balanced on either side.

Sicilian boats with big triangular sails half raised crowded into shore where scales were set up to weigh the sulphur before it was loaded onto the backs of the men of the sea. Sacks fastened to bands around their foreheads hung down and protected their backs. Barefoot, in duck pants, they waded into the water up to their waists to transfer their loads of sulphur to the waiting boats. When these were full the sails were hoisted high and the boats conveyed their cargoes of sulphur to the merchant ships anchored inside or just outside the harbor.

All this activity took place on the beach.

In the town, on the main thoroughfare, other carts arrived laden with sacks of barley, wheat and beans.

"Ho there! Weighers!" the porters hailed.

Sacks from each cart were taken down and emptied onto large burlap drop cloths spread out on the road. Barley and wheat were measured by *tomalo,* a Sicilian measure used especially for dry grain. The sacks were then refilled and carried into a warehouse, always well protected against humidity. Five *tomali* made one sack, and twenty *tomali* made a *salma.*

"Count one! Count two!" the weighers cried with every twenty *tomali,* in trailing singsong voices.

So it went until sunset, with only a brief respite at noon. In the evening, after all that noise, quiet reigned over the town. The crickets took over and thrummed their song along the beach among the heaps of sulphur; occasionally a watchdog barked. Meanwhile the surface of the harbor lay quiet as a lake and a dark forest of masts huddled under the protecting light of the beacon, whose green flash was reflected in the black water.

Beyond the little port, the open sea extended all the way to the horizon in the moonlight, forming a wide semicircle with Punta Bianca to the right and Monte Rossello to the left.

Overlooking the quiet sea from the terrace of the Prinzi villa, Signorina Rita listened to the avowals of her friend, Anna Cesaro. Her eyes wandered over those pale lips and slightly uneven teeth, causing Anna to lower her own eyes as she spoke and her voice to sound more muted and tremulous than ever. Sometimes Rita's eyes narrowed a little in sympathy, which disturbed Anna even more, and her trembling fingers plucked at the lace on her sleeve. Rita gave a little sigh and turned up her eyes.

"This morning, at last, I had my revenge," said Anna.

"Yes? What did you do to him?" asked Rita without the slightest curiosity.

"I closed the window in his face," Anna replied.

Rita sighed. In her heart she felt very sorry for her friend, who was so hopelessly in love with Mondino Morgani, the young doctor of Vignetta. Morgani was tall—six feet two at least—and as thin as a rail. He had hair the color of straw, and bright blue eyes. His nose was thin but so prominent that every time he laughed it went white and the skin stretched so tightly it nearly split.

Poor Dr. Morgani, how could he return Anna's passion when he did not even suspect it? Or so Rita thought, and the timid confidences of her friend made her suffer for her. The poor girl was so mislead that she did not realize how ridiculous her gestures must look to someone she wanted as a sweetheart—closing the window in his face, indeed! Poor thing—whatever for?

Being tied to the small town of Vignetta because of her father's sulphur business had altered Rita's naturally gay, easygoing disposition. The contrast here between the vastness of nature, the sky, the sea, and the depressing insignificance of the inhabitants was too strong. Her father was occupied all day with his business affairs, her mother with her housekeeping, so that Rita, left entirely to herself, fell into the habit of daydreaming. She had no friends in Vignetta except Anna, who was insignificant too, in her way. She found nothing and no one to interest her in this town. Aimless, almost lifeless, she consciously allowed the best days of her life to slip away one by one.

Anna lived in more modest circumstances than Rita. Her father, Rosario Cesaro, a strange sort of man, had died four years ago. He had thrown his all into sulphur holes in his mania to discover sulphur in the surrounding hills. He opened up those hills, dug holes as deep as six hundred feet and found nothing but water—water, which meant the installation of pumps to drain it off, then subterranean tunnels to deviate the stream. He fed thousands and thousands of lire into those gluttonous holes without ever realizing any return.

Anna met Dr. Morgani at the unfortunate time of her father's last illness. After his death, her mother, her sister and her brother-in-law were in mourning and paid little attention to Anna. She was now eighteen and had been in delicate health since childhood.

Mondino Morgani had been practicing medicine for only three months and Signor Cesaro was his "first death." It was true, he had been carried off by an incurable disease, but nonetheless Mondino felt a kind of remorse over his death.

During her father's illness Anna grew so thin that her small nose and slightly receding chin seemed to shrink back in alarm beneath those extraordinarily large green eyes under the flame of her thick, unruly red hair. Because of her long, slender neck, she seemed almost as tall as the doctor. When she coughed, Mondino glanced at her narrow chest and bony shoulders.

My God! he thought. That girl is tubercular.

He immediately took her under his care. He himself went to the kitchen to order broth and carried it up to the young girl's bedside.

"No, it's impossible," she said. "I can't, Doctor."

"Do me this favor. Look, just this little cup! Make an effort and it will go down."

"I swear to you—it's impossible."

"Do it for me. See, we'll try one spoonful . . . this little one."

"Oh, goodness."

"Another one, like a good girl."

"Enough. I can't take any more."

"Listen, I don't intend to budge from here until you drink this cup of broth."

Anna gave him a look with those big green eyes which said clearly, "I will do it just for you." Then she closed her eyes and swallowed.

"Good! That was fine. Now I can go feeling a lot happier! See you this evening, Signorina."

From her little bed, Anna followed him all the way to the door with her eyes, then she dived under the covers, sighing happily, completely carried away, kissing the pillow with yearning lips.

Mondino even went so far as to sample some bitter medicine himself first, to get his new patient to take it. What doctor would ever do a thing like that? And the way he talked to her—and coaxed her!

Rita hinted to her friend that she doubted he could be in love with her. Poor Anna! She fished around in her memory. No, no. She was not mistaken—not at all. Those carnations in full bloom—yes, the beautiful plant of red-streaked carnations she kept on the window sill of her room! Dr. Morgani liked flowers very much, and during his calls he could never take his eyes off that plant.

"What beautiful carnations! May I, Signorina?"

"Of course, Doctor."

He picked a flower with his long, thin fingers and put it in his buttonhole.

When Anna was up and around again, in gratitude to the doctor she presented him with the luxuriant pot of carnations. Dr. Morgani never wore any other flower in his buttonhole as long as the carnations were in bloom.

Was this not significant, too?

Rita thought to herself: That precious fool of a doctor; he's been basking in it. And on the whole she was right.

However, it should be said straight off that Mondino had no intention of hurting Anna. He really considered himself the most irresistible young man in Vignetta. By nature courteous and polite, he was without affectation, so what could he do about it? All the girls lost their hearts to him, thinking he was courting them. But, on his word of honor, there wasn't a word of truth to it. If they lost their hearts, they were free to do so—he even liked it—but he . . . Moreover, Signorina Cesaro—a charming girl, no denying it—should realize that he had a very noble, lucrative profession in hand, that his parents were rich and that she, poor little thing, had no dowry. Of course, when one is in love one does not consider such things; however, parents usually did. He would not mention her figure—let that pass. Mondino had his own ideas on the subject: "Beauty is not important in a wife. It is enough that she be intelligent and virtuous." But what was the use of discussing it? For the moment, he had no intention whatever of getting married.

Every time he was called to the Cesaro house, he snorted like a tired horse.

"Ouf! That girl takes sick just so she can have me near her."

But once there, beside Anna's narrow bed, the provocative touch of that slender wrist trembling between his fingers, the burning look in those big green eyes pleading for mercy troubled even Mondino Morgani. He was embarrassed and could hardly put two words together—two words of Greek from that store of medical terminology in which he excelled.

"Has she any fever, Doctor?" her mother asked.

Mondino wanted to reply in exasperation, "There's one thing certain: If she hasn't, she soon will have."

II

"Look . . . Look. He's turning around!" Anna nudged Rita's elbow on the railing of the terrace.

"Do be sensible, Anna," Rita chided, pretending not to see him.

Below, Mondino Morgani passed slowly along the beach, looking up deliberately at the terrace of the Prinzi house where the two friends were leaning. He passed like that every day at the same hour, always looking up at the terrace even when Anna was not there.

His look made Anna very happy. She thought it was directed at her.

"See . . . See . . . Now do you believe me?"

"No, I don't," said Rita dryly, looking out to sea.

"Why not? I assure you . . ." Anna insisted timidly.

"I am suspicious. I believe only facts. If I were you, I'd be wary."

"You know something? Have you heard something by any chance?"

"No, nothing. I speak from experience."

"And yet . . ." Anna sighed, on the verge of tears.

Rita, looking at those pale, trembling lips and large bewildered eyes, was sorry she had put her thoughts into words.

"Pay no attention to what I say. I'm feeling depressed today. No one knows about this better than you do, and if you say . . ." She interrupted herself to suggest, "Let's go down and play the piano. Come on."

Mondino Morgani passed by the terrace again.

Anna caught sight of him just as she was about to follow Rita, and she stopped with one hand on the railing, looking at him deliberately.

Mondino went by as straight as a stick without acknowledging her glance.

Did he see me or didn't he? Anna asked herself tremulously. Or was there someone in a window nearby?

She looked around but saw no one, and thought of what Rita had said. Suffering torment, she went down the steps of the terrace.

Rita was playing Coop's "Longing" fervently. Anna had hardly come into the room when she looked around, but kept on playing.

"He came back, didn't he?"

"Yes . . . but he didn't see me."

"Ah, he didn't turn around!" Rita remarked with a strange little smile at the corners of her mouth. She took her hands from the piano to pick up Anna's hands, looking into her eyes.

"If this is meant as a joke, he'll have to deal with me," said Anna, interpreting her friend's look and biting her lower lip.

"What can you do to him?" asked Rita with a shrug, the same smile still hovering on her lips.

"Oh, if he thinks I'm anything like the harbor captain's

daughter, that big flirt with all her carrying-on, or that fish, Sarina Scoma, who bills and coos on the public square with the officers, or—"

"My dear," Rita cut in, "where men are concerned, *they* are always right. You love him, don't you?"

Anna went on biting her lower lip.

"All right, then, suppose he starts flirting with someone else, suppose he even marries her, leaving you flat. What can you do?"

"We haven't come to that yet," Anna objected. "In any case, I must rid myself of this uncertainty."

Rita sighed. Unfortunately, she was not at all uncertain.

Mondino Morgani felt perfectly sure that at the flick of his finger all the girls of Vignetta would throw themselves out the window crying, "Take me! Take me!" Only one resisted him: Rita Prinzi. And there was no doubt, at least in Dr. Morgani's mind, that she was the most beautiful, the most intelligent of them all. Educated as a lady, she played the piano, embroidered, spoke French, came of a respectable family, and had a reasonable dowry.

And so back and forth he passed beneath her windows.

Rita saw very well what was going on. He thinks he has only to open his mouth like a frog, she thought, looking after him. Well, this fly won't fall in, my dear!

She went indoors so as not to give the fool any illusions. Oh, poor Anna!

At last Mondino was convinced that he was only wearing out good shoe leather and decided to take the plunge. "I'll pluck the loveliest rose of Vignetta! Goodbye, bachelor life! Goodbye, little secret affairs!"

But her answer was a curt "No!"

No? Why no? Why? Mondino asked himself. It gave him no peace. How can it be no? In despair, he walked up and down in his bedroom, hands behind his back, quite forgetting the cold, wearing only his shirt and slippers. That "no" was unexpected. How could it be? Their ages were right. Let's see, he thirty and she twenty-two—just eight years' difference. He was not deformed, nor so unpleasant to look at, really. For a man, he was of a good height, had a noble, lucrative profession, a good family from every point of view. "I don't understand it!" And he scratched his white, hairless chest under his shirt with cold, nervous fingers.

"I don't under . . . Ah-choooo! Ah-chooo!"

"God bless you, Mondino," his aunt called from the next room.

"Thank you," he called back.

He was catching cold. He put on his coat and began walking up and down again.

Could Signorina Rita be setting her cap for some prince? *For the moment, my daughter has no intention of getting married!* A fine excuse! At twenty-two . . . When would she make up her mind?

He blew his nose loudly. For three days he did not leave the house.

"Mondino, a patient."

"Say I'm in bed with a cold."

"Mondino, they are calling for you from the Cesaro house."

"Signorina Anna? Be damned!"

He rolled over in his bed and pulled up the covers.

"The doctor has a cold."

III

It was a mortal blow for poor Anna. She learned about his proposal to Rita from her friend's own lips through a trick of which no one would have thought Anna capable.

She had noticed a shade of bitterness pass over Rita's face and creep into her words whenever she referred to the doctor, where before there had been only pity. Why?

"I know that Dr. Morgani asked for your hand," she said to Rita, as if in answer to her friend's accusations against him.

"Who told you that?" demanded Rita with a frown.

"So then it is true!" exclaimed Anna, her face aflame.

"How did you know? Who told you?" Rita repeated in her embarrassment.

"No one. It was clear from what you just said."

"That I refused him?"

"Yes. Why? Because of me?" asked Anna, so emotionally upset that she looked as if she would faint any minute. "Oh, but if you did it because of me . . ."

"No," Rita put in haughtily. "In the first place you know that I never liked him, the old stick. But in any case I *would* have turned him down because of you."

Anna struggled in her heart with shame, love, jealousy and humiliation. On the one hand, she felt like lashing out at the doctor with every kind of insult, and on the other it hurt her to hear Rita say anything against him. She wanted to stop her friend from belittling the one she had so long deemed worthy of her heart, but pride restrained her.

"I have no dowry; that's the reason."

Rita tried to comfort Anna as best she could, deflecting all the ridiculous notions of revenge Anna proposed out of hurt feelings.

"Where men are concerned, as I already told you, they are always in the right. It is better not to love—"

"Yes . . . yes. It's far better," Anna agreed, sobbing.

Finally, when she had regained her composure somewhat, Anna went home. She wandered through the rooms all day in a daze, as if it was the menacing storm, whose clouds were rolling darkly above the iron-gray sea, that kept her from helping her mother with the household chores.

That night there was a downpour over Vignetta. Lightning flashed across the sky and immediately afterward there was the crashing roll of thunder.

Anna stood before the open window, bewitched by the violence of the storm. Rain lashed her face and drenched her clothes. She started with every flicker of that sinister light through the darkness over the raging sea. Crying, burning with fever, she imagined her unhappiness at this moment greater than that of any other living creature. She was wracked, trembling and convulsed by her misery. Out at sea, in the middle of the storm—how fortunate were those sailors facing imminent death. To die . . . to die . . . a thousand times better to die!

The next day when her mother came into her room she found

Anna in bed, the window open and the floor still wet from the rain.

"Did you sleep like this? Are you crazy, Anna? Are you ill? Oh, Lord God! How do you feel? Are you feverish?"

In alarm the poor mother sent for the doctor.

"The doctor is in bed with a cold and cannot come," the servant said when she returned.

But he did come the following day.

Anna received him as though he were a stranger. She would not answer any of his questions, possibly because she feared her voice might betray her emotions.

Mondino turned to her mother. "Why did she stand in the rain? The window open all night! How idiotic!"

Anna clenched her teeth and closed her eyes, drawing a long breath through her nostrils. Then she coughed.

"Horrible weather! Look at me, and I did nothing foolish, Signora."

To underline the fact that he was suffering from a cold, Mondino blew his nose. Then he wrote out a prescription and left. "I will be back this evening."

IV

Following Rita Prinzi's refusal, Mondino Morgani had an unforeseen series of utter failures. In quick succession he was refused by:

(1) The daughter of the harbor captain, Nannina Vettoli, rival of Rita Prinzi. She was twenty-four years old (twenty-one, she said), dark-haired, not pretty but winning, with a twelve-thousand-lire dowry, her mother dead; she spoke good Italian— not only the regional dialect—spoke fair French, and played the piano.

(2) Carmela Ninfa, eighteen years old, rather ugly—looked a little like a monkey—but had a twenty-five-thousand-lire dowry; both parents intact; French zero, Italian zero, piano zero.

(3) Sarina Scoma (even she!), twenty-seven years old, of dubious complexion under a pasty layer of make-up; fifteen-thou-

sand-lire dowry; no education at all; spoke Italian by ear, though in her native dialect she was voluble enough.

(4) Giovanna Merca, the niece of Lawyer Merca. Her father was a leather dealer, but she always referred to herself as "Lawyer Merca's niece." No dowry, only her trousseau; she embroidered beautifully, played the piano, read trashy novels from morning till night, talked like a man and was ugly—*but* she was Lawyer Merca's niece.

Nannina Vettoli refused him, or so he understood, because Rita Prinzi had refused him first; Carmela Ninfa because she was very short and he looked too tall beside her; Sarina Scoma because (at the moment) she was taken with an officer of a detachment stationed in Vignetta; Giovanna Merca, because she was carrying on a feverish correspondence with a port official who had recently been transferred to Leghorn.

Mondino was almost driven out of his mind.

Apart from his person, apart from his family, was he a doctor, yes or no? Is a doctor of medicine, by rights, an important figure in a little town like Vignetta, or isn't he? Oh, it was quite evident that those girls had talked one another out of it—because, of course, apart from his person, apart from his family, where could they ever hope to find a better match? The girls' plot was all too plain in the marked displeasure shown by the fathers and the lawyer-uncle when they had to bring him a negative reply. He seemed fated to remain a bachelor.

"Good riddance!" Mondino would have cried, no doubt, if it were not for the fact that he *was* a doctor and was therefore obliged to call again and again at the Scoma house, or the Mercas', at the Vettolis' or the Ninfas'. To make the best of his amorous misfortunes, Mondino decided to look on the whole thing as the hand of fate turned against him and, using this excuse as a shield to hide his true humiliation, he would appear to harbor no grudge against any of the families concerned. But he was very gloomy.

Meanwhile Anna grew worse every day. Mondino's fears, based on her weak constitution, proved only too true. Sitting at her bedside, he felt more depressed than ever without knowing why.

Anna had brightened a little during her illness, as her tempestuous feelings settled into passive acceptance of her lot. However, from time to time a thought would return to stir them up.

She replied now briefly to Mondino's questions.

"How do you feel today, Signorina?"

"Better, Doctor."

She said "better," but he well knew . . .

As the days passed, Mondino's visits grew longer and were more and more friendly. He talked with her mother and even managed to get Anna to say a few words.

After uttering a sad reflection on life or on the wrong concept we are apt to form of men or of society, he would smile bravely and sigh. Anna did not seem to be listening—but she was, most attentively.

Ah, the injustice of human nature, Mondino thought to himself. Here is this girl, dying because of me—and she really is dying, for there is no hope of saving her now. Yet I was unable to fall in love with her, the only one in the whole town I wouldn't have had to ask twice.

Suddenly he conceived the idea of asking her now; his spirit was low at the moment and then he believed that, if nothing more, it might help her to die happy.

It would be an act of charity, he told himself.

Moreover, he owed it to her, because at one time he knew he had been a little too encouraging to the poor girl.

Rita Prinzi watched over Anna like a sister. She never left the sick girl's side, reading softly to her so as not to tire her and talking gaily to keep her spirits up. However, every time the doctor came she fled so she would not have to meet him.

One morning she was not quick enough, and as Mondino turned the doorknob he heard a chair fall, yet he found Anna alone in the room.

"Am I disturbing you, Signorina?" he asked from the doorway, leaning forward on his long, straight legs.

"No," Anna replied dryly.

"I thought I heard someone run out."

"Yes, Rita," said Anna.

"Oh," Mondino said with a wry smile. "Why does she run away? Am I so frightening?"

He sat down and took Anna's frail wrist between his fingers.

"I was wrong, Signorina," he said, still holding her wrist, "to knock at certain doors where I should not have knocked, and I am sorry. If you could only know how deeply sorry I am, you would believe me. I wandered like a blind man, Signorina. Now my eyes are opened, I hope not too late—if you will only believe in my repentance and forgive me."

His words took Anna's breath away, and little by little she drew her wrist from his hand.

"You should not be saying these things to me," she said without looking at him and in a voice that tried to be firm.

Anna's mother, called by Rita, now opened the door and came into the room.

"To your mother, then?" he asked, smiling toward her mother.

"What is it?" she asked, sitting at the foot of her daughter's bed.

"We were saying—or, that is, I was saying to your daughter— that she must get well soon because we need her—I especially. I even more than you, Signora. I lost my way like a blind man, I told her, and I have found it again, here, beside this little bed. You do understand me, Signora? Here beside Signorina Anna— what do you say to that?"

Her mother understood neither his words nor the bittersweet tone of his voice. She looked at him in surprise. Then finally she understood from the look he directed at her daughter as soon as he had finished speaking, and from the strained expression on her daughter's face.

She blushed and replied, almost stammering, "What? But I never imagined. I . . . I . . . I'm very happy. But you must have her answer from her own lips. Isn't that right, Anna?"

Anna, her face like wax, half closed her eyes.

"Then it's up to you, Signorina," said Mondino, smiling, leaning over the bed expectantly.

"Well, then, *no!*" Anna said, opening her eyes with a frown.

At that "no" Mondino drew back, his face pale, a resigned smile on his lips.

"No!" he exclaimed. "You, too, *no?* Ah, you repay my sincerity badly, Signorina. I did not believe . . ."

He broke off, passing his hand over his forehead and his eyes. Then he resumed, with a long sigh: "Never mind, Signora Cesaro, you have nothing to fear. This will not in any way affect my care of her. I will try to win, if not her affection, at least her esteem. Insofar as I am able, I will do my duty."

He immediately changed the subject with great tact, or at least that was Rita's opinion as she listened at the door.

V

Jesus—an authentic portrait taken from an emerald cut by order of Tiberius, Roman Emperor in the thirtieth year of the Christian Era. This gem, the inestimable value of which does not exceed its artistic merit, came, after many vicissitudes, to enrich the treasure of the Turks, whose Emperor later gave it to Pope Innocent VIII to redeem his brother who had been taken prisoner by the Christians.

Absorbed in thought, Rita sat at the foot of Anna's bed and involuntarily reread this inscription under a picture of Jesus hanging above it.

After her "no," Anna had taken a turn for the worse. Her condition rapidly declined.

"You should not be here, Rita," she said. "If I were you, I would be afraid to stay here."

"Of course not, Anna. You must be joking! You are better."

"Yes, of course—better."

She no longer had the strength to lift her arms and, with a bitter smile, called her friend's attention to this weakness.

Rita's parents had also advised her—nay, begged her—not to go to Anna's house any longer.

"Nonsense," Rita replied. "When the doctor himself tells me it is no longer safe to go there, I will not go. We have not reached that point yet."

Anna's illness had quickened her senses and especially reinforced her innate suspiciousness. She spied on her friend, con-

vinced in her heart that Rita disapproved of her sharp refusal of
the doctor's offer. Mondino's reaction was now one of brotherly
attention—even in front of Rita. Why was it that Rita no longer
ran from the room when Dr. Morgani came in? Instead, she
turned to him with questions and asked his advice about Anna's
care. Mondino evidently took some pleasure in answering her
questions in his usual polite manner. And Anna gathered from
Rita's expression that she no longer found him either displeasing
or foolish.

Ah, how good, how very good he is, thought Anna deep in
her heart, and how well he expresses himself.

At the same time, Rita confessed to herself: He is not as silly
as I took him to be. And he certainly must have a good heart!

Mondino, on his side, was aware of these favorable reactions
and carefully fostered them. Following this course, he felt certain
of being safely maneuvered into port.

Anna foresaw it too and if, on the one hand, she had a feeling
of jealous resentment against Rita, on the other hand she forgave
Mondino. She enjoyed hearing him talk so beautifully to her
friend and noticed how he had already won her over. She wanted
to say to Rita, "You see, he *is* worthy of being loved after all.
Ah, now you think as highly of him as I did! Very well, go away.
You do not stay here because of me any longer but only to see
him and talk to him twice a day—I understand, perhaps even
more clearly than you do yourselves. You show so much pity for
me, both of you, because in that shared pity lies the path of your
own love. Go away, Rita—for my sake and for yours—go."

But Rita did not go. She was impatient if the doctor was five
minutes late, and went to look out the same window from which
Anna had once leaned to watch Mondino go by. Rita, meanwhile,
sincerely believed that her impatience was due only to her solici-
tude for her friend.

To discover just how far the understanding between them
had gone, Anna pretended one day to be asleep at the time the
doctor usually came to call.

That day her mother was not in the room because Anna had
begged her to go to bed and rest after the long hours she had
spent at her bedside during the previous night.

Finally Mondino arrived and Rita quickly made a sign for him to come in on tiptoe.

"She's sleeping," she whispered when he was beside the bed.

Mondino looked down at his patient, then turned toward Rita and sadly shook his head.

"She already looks as if the end had come." Rita sighed.

Mondino nodded assent and then, a little embarrassed, said softly, "Now, Signorina, listen. It isn't right for you to continue coming here. I understand that she is your dear friend. I am aware of your warmhearted impulses, but you must realize that . . . I am uneasy when I am away thinking of you here, constantly exposed to this danger. Do you understand me? Please go away after today—and don't come back. Will you promise? It is so unwise."

"I have already told her that!" cried Anna, suddenly opening her eyes wide on the two of them.

Rita and Mondino were startled.

"I said it was unwise," Mondino stammered, embarrassed, "not because of your condition, Signorina Anna, but because . . . because Signorina Rita is not well. She is worn out—and she suffers to see you like this."

"Ah, is that why? If that's all, then leave her alone, Doctor, because she is not suffering," said Anna, smiling bitterly. "I suffer—yes, I am the one who suffers. For pity's sake, let me die in peace. Don't either of you come back again. What joy can you have in loving each other here in the presence of death?"

Rita burst into tears, burying her face in her hands, and Mondino, confused, unnerved, could find no words to answer Anna. He went out hastily without daring to say goodbye.

About two weeks later Anna died.

For seven years now she has lain in the high-perched, lonely cemetery of Vignetta, among its bright flowers and its many cypress trees. It is as well for her peace of mind that she cannot know that Mondino Morgani and Rita Prinzi were married five years ago and now have two children, Coco and Mimi, as blond and blue-eyed as their father.

FUMES

As soon as the miners came up from the bottom of the pit, dead tired and gasping for breath, their eyes sought the distant green of that hill which closed off the wide valley to the west.

Here, on these parched slopes of burnt shale, not a blade of grass had grown for some time. Sulphur mines rose like anthills and seared the surrounding ground with their fumes.

The green hill soothed their eyes, smarting in the daylight after so many hours spent in darkness.

For those whose job it was to feed the furnaces or the huge melting pots with chunk sulphur, for those who watched over the molten sulphur, or for those who worked under the furnaces catching the slow-moving mass of burnt sulphur which dropped into their hods of damp wood, the very sight of all that green in the distance eased the pain of breathing—the bitter curse of the fumes which clung to their throats, causing grim spasms of suffocation.

The little Sicilian boys let their loads fall from their bruised, skinned backs and sat down on the sacks for a breath of air. They were caked with slimy clay from the walls of the tunnels and the sides of the slippery stairs with their broken steps which led up from the "hole." Scratching their heads, they peered through the glassy sulphurous vapor, which shimmered in the sunlight as it rose off the melting pots. Sometimes they thought about life on those farms, a happy life in the open air without risk or drudgery, and they envied the farmers.

"They are blessed."

That far-off hill was a land of dreams for all of them. From over there came the oil for their lanterns which barely pierced the utter darkness of the mine. From there came their coarse, black bread which kept them going through the long day's grind. From there, wine, their only comfort—wine to give them courage and strength to endure this cursed life, if one could call it life: underground they looked like ghosts at work.

The farmers on the green hill spat when they looked across the valley at those parched slopes.

There, in those devastating fumes, they saw their enemy. When the wind blew in their direction carrying the stench of burnt sulphur, they gazed helplessly at their trees and cursed the fools who went on digging graves to bury their fortunes. Not content with drying up the whole valley, they were envious of the little spot of green, and wanted to destroy those beautiful farms with their pickaxes and furnaces.

For it was rumored that there were sulphur deposits under the hill. Those ridges of siliceous limestone at the top, with crystal outcroppings at the base, made it very plain, and mining engineers had often confirmed it.

Although courted by rich offers, the farm owners not only refused to lease their subterranean soil for exploitation but would not make the most superficial test, if only out of curiosity.

The country lay there spread out in the sunshine for all to see, subject of course to bad years but compensated by the good ones. As for the sulphur mines, they were blind holes, and woe to him who slipped and fell in. He is no wise man who will give up a certainty for an uncertainty.

Every landowner on the hill hammered the alternatives into the others' minds, like a pledge of unity against temptation. They knew that if one capitulated, and a sulphur mine should rise in their midst, all would suffer. Once destruction began, other yawning mouths of hell would open and in a few years the trees and plants would die, poisoned by the "fumes." Then, farewell, green hill.

II

Among those most often approached was Don Mattia Scala, the owner of a little farm with a fine stand of almond and olive trees. His land was halfway down the slope of the hill, and here, to his disgust, all indications pointed to the richest deposit of minerals.

Several engineers from the Royal Mining Corps had come to study these outcroppings and make tests. Scala received them as a jealous husband would receive a doctor who came to his house to examine his wife for a secret illness.

He could not close the door in the face of men sent out by the government on official business. But he got his own back by shooing away others who came—either on behalf of rich mine owners or from mining companies—with proposals to lease the rights to his land.

"Lease! Nothing doing!" he cried. "Not if you offered me the riches of Croesus! Not even if you said: Mattia, scratch here with one foot like a chicken, and you'll find enough sulphur to make you as rich as—who shall I say?—as Midas with all his gold! I swear, I would not scratch!"

If they still persisted, he would shout, "Now, go away, or I'll call the dogs!"

He was obliged to repeat this threat quite often because the gate to his farm was on a *trazzera,* or mule track, across the hill, which was used as a short cut by men who worked in the mines: miners, overseers, engineers, on their way to and from the valley. The engineers took pleasure in goading him, and if they caught sight of him in his garden, they would stop by the gate to call out, "Changed your mind yet?"

And Don Mattia, to scare them away, would call up his dogs.

"Here, Scampirro! Here, Regina!"

He too had had the sulphur mania at one time, but it had sucked him dry. Now the sight of sulphur, even at a distance, turned his stomach.

"What is it? The devil?" they teased him.

"Worse! Because the devil may damn your soul, but if he chooses he can make you rich, whereas sulphur makes you poorer than Job and damns your soul into the bargain!"

Tall, lean, pale, with a white hat pushed back on his round head, he looked like a telegraph pole. He wore little gold rings through his ears, which stamped him as half middle-class, half peasant, a fact he took no pains to conceal.

He was liked by all the landowners on the hill.

They remembered that he had once been very rich and they were glad that, after losing almost everything, he had come there to live on those few acres bought with money he was able to realize on the sale of his house in town. For the town house had gone with all its furnishings, and he had had to sell the jewels of his wife, who had died of a heart attack. They remembered too that, at first, he had shut himself up in the four rooms of the little farmhouse and refused to see anyone. Iana, a child of about sixteen then, lived there with him, and they thought she was his daughter until they discovered she was the young sister of Dima Chiarenza, the scoundrel who had tricked him and brought about his ruin.

There was a long story behind it.

Mattia Scala had known Dima Chiarenza since he was a boy. Both of his parents were dead and his sister was much younger than himself. Scala helped him, gave him a job and, when he saw how industrious and bright the boy was, made him his partner after he had leased a sulphur mine. Scala assumed the financial burden of the operation and Dima Chiarenza was to stay on the job in order to direct and supervise the work.

Meanwhile Iana (Ianuzza, they called her) grew up in Mattia's house, with his only son, Neli, about her own age. Mattia and his wife soon noticed that the attachment between the two children was not one of a brother for a sister. Not to keep the straw too near the flame, they wisely decided to send Neli away for a while until he was at least eighteen. The boy went to the sulphur mine to lend Chiarenza a hand and to keep him company. They contemplated a wedding in another two or three years, if everything went on smoothly.

How could Don Mattia Scala ever have suspected Dima Chiarenza, whom he trusted as he did himself, whom he had taken in off the street and treated like a son? Dima Chiarenza had betrayed him as Judas betrayed Christ.

That was the way it happened. Chiarenza was in league with the chief engineer of the mine, he plotted with the overseers, made deals with the weighers and carters. He stole with impunity from administration expenses, from the sulphur extracted, and even cheated on the coal used for the engines that pumped water out of the mine. And one night the pit was flooded, completely destroying the ramp which Scala had built at a cost of three hundred thousand lire.

Neli was on the spot that infernal night. He had helped in the desperate, futile efforts to prevent disaster. Foreseeing his father's hatred for Chiarenza, a hatred which might extend to Iana, Dima's innocent sister, Neli thought that he too might be held responsible for this havoc because he had not denounced the thief who was soon to be his brother-in-law. He fled in panic in the midst of the furor, and disappeared without leaving a trace.

A few days later, his mother died, devotedly nursed by Iana. Scala found himself alone, without funds, his wife and his son gone, too. Only the girl remained, almost out of her mind with shame and grief. She clung to him, refusing to leave, and threatened to jump out the window if he sent her back to her brother. Won over by her insistence, Scala swallowed his repugnance and agreed to take her with him to his little farm.

Gradually, as time passed, he emerged from his brooding silence. He began to exchange a few words with his neighbors, telling them about himself and the girl.

"So, then she is not your daughter?"

"No, but it's just as if she were."

At first he felt ashamed to say who she really was. He never mentioned his son; the pain went too deep. And, for that matter, what news had he to give? None! The police, after a long search, had found no trace of him.

Several years later, Iana grew tired of waiting hopelessly for her fiancé's return and decided to go back to town to live with her brother. He had married a rich old woman, a notorious usurer, and he too had turned moneylender. In no time, he became one of the richest men in town.

Scala lived on alone at the farm. Eight years went by and, outwardly at least, he appeared to be himself again. He made friends with all the landowners on the hill who often gathered at his place in the evening.

Nature seemed to be trying to make up to him for all he had suffered. He was lucky to acquire those few acres because Butera, a rich landowner on the hill, had taken it into his head gradually to acquire all the land. By lending money, he extended the boundaries of his domain. He had already swallowed half of Nino Mo's farm, and, by advancing money on dowries for five daughters, had reduced Labiso's holdings to a corner of ground no larger than a handkerchief. He had eyed Lopes' land for some time, when the owner, after a series of bad years, took it into his head to sell off a piece at a lower price to a stranger—Don Mattia Scala.

In no time, by throwing himself into his work completely, trying to numb his sorrow, Don Mattia improved the land so much that his friends were amazed, and Lopes most of all. Actually he was consumed with jealousy. A slovenly man, his face florid and freckled, he wore his hat tilted far forward as if to avoid seeing anyone or anything. But occasionally from under the brim of that hat, an unexpected sidelong glance would flash out of his sleepy green eyes.

After a turn about the farm, the friends would come back to the little clearing before the house.

There Scala would invite them to sit on the low wall buttressing the steep slope on which the house stood. At the bottom of the slope behind the house rose a few tall, dark poplars, much to Don Mattia's annoyance. He could not figure out why Lopes had planted them there.

"What good are they? Tell me that. They don't bear fruit and they're in the way."

"Chop them down for charcoal," Lopes replied indolently.

But Butera advised, "Not so fast. First see if you can get someone to take them off your hands."

"Whoever would want them?"

"Woodcarvers, perhaps, for statues of saints."

"Saints? Oh, now I understand," Don Mattia concluded, "why saints no longer work miracles if they are made out of wood like this!"

Toward evening, those poplars were the meeting place of all the sparrows on the hill. Their incessant, noisy twittering disturbed the friends who lingered below to discuss the sulphur mines, as usual, and the havoc they wrought.

Nocio Butera generally opened the discussion. He was by way of being a big fish in that little pond because of his landholdings. He had studied to be a lawyer, but only once in his life had he exercised his profession—just after he had taken his degree. The poor young man had memorized his speech and believed he would be able to reel it off without a hitch for his first court case. However, in the middle of his address to the jury, he lost the thread of what he was saying and could not go on. Tears welled up in his eyes as if he were a baby and, before the whole court, he shook his clenched fist in the face of Justice, standing aloft, scales in hand.

"And then what? Good God!" he groaned aloud in exasperation.

Sometimes they reminded him of that famous fiasco: "Eh, *and then what? Good God!*"

Nocio Butera pretended to chuckle with them, muttering through his teeth, "Yes . . . yes . . ." as his plump fingers scratched the black whiskers on his ruddy cheeks, or adjusted the gold-rimmed glasses on his lumpy nose. He could have afforded to laugh wholeheartedly with them because, despite his bad start as a lawyer, he now carried the flag as farmer and property manager. But men are never content with what they have. Nocio Butera seemed to take delight only in other men's failures. When he came to Scala's farm it was usually to announce the current or imminent downfall of this one or that one and to string off the reasons behind it, proving how such a thing could never have happened to him.

Tino Labiso, very tall and already gone to seed, drew a large red-and-black checked handkerchief from his pocket and blew a blast from his nose which sounded like a sea trumpet. Then, carefully folding the handkerchief again, he passed it several times under his nose before returning it to his pocket. Like a prudent man not given to rash judgment, he would hazard, "Could be!"

"Could be? Is . . . is . . . is!" Nino Mo burst out, unable to abide Labiso's apathy.

Lopes showed signs of life under the big hat tipped over his nose, and mumbled, "Let Mattia do the talking. He understands these things."

But always, before Mattia would settle down to talk, he went to the cellar for a jug of good wine to offer his friends.

"Here's some vinegar. Poison yourselves!"

He drank too, then, sitting down and crossing his knees, he asked, "Well, what's the matter?"

"The trouble is that they're a bunch of fools," Nino Mo exploded as usual. "All of them together and each one separately."

"Who?"

"Those sons of bitches, the mine owners! They dig and dig and the price of sulphur goes down, down, down. Why can't they understand they bring about their own ruin as well as ours by pouring money into those pits—those greedy hellholes which will swallow all of us!"

"What's to be done?" asked Scala.

"Limit production," replied Nocio Butera calmly. "Restrict the production of sulphur. As I see it, that's the only solution."

"Madonna! What nonsense!" Don Mattia exclaimed, rising to his feet in order to gesticulate more freely. "Forgive me, dear Don Nocio, but you're out of your mind and I'll prove it to you. Tell me, out of, say, a thousand mines, how many do you think are directly exploited economically by the owner? Barely two hundred. All the others are leased. Do you agree, Tino Labiso?"

"Could be," Labiso repeated guardedly.

And Nino Mo: "Could be . . . is, is, is!"

Don Mattia raised a hand to silence them.

"Now, Don Nocio, what is the tenure, do you think, that the greed and power of these mine-owners—all as paunchy as yourself—allow in leasing a mine? Tell me seriously."

"Ten years . . ." Butera hazarded, with a condescending smile.

"Twelve," Scala conceded, "sometimes twenty. Now what can be done in that time? What profit can be dug out in so few years? However speedy and lucky they may be, there is no possible way of amortizing the costs of operating a mine even in twenty years. I'm saying this to show you that, given a slump, the owner-operator might conceivably slow down his production to steady the market. But for the short-term tenant-operator, that's impossible. He would only be sacrificing his interests for the benefit of his successor. Therefore he is bound to produce as much as he can under existing circumstances. Do you follow me? If he is caught short, as generally happens, he is forced to sell his sulphur for whatever he can get to keep going, because if he shuts down, you know, the owner can repossess the mine. The result of all this—as Nino Mo says—is that the price of sulphur goes down, down, down, as if it were no better than common gravel. For that matter, can you, Don Nocio, an educated man, and you, Tino Labiso, tell me what the devil sulphur really is and what it's used for?"

At these direct questions even Lopes gaped. Nino Mo thrust restless hands in his pockets as if searching for an answer. Tino Labiso again pulled out his handkerchief to blow his nose, taking his time like a cautious man.

"Oh, that's a good one!" exclaimed Nocio Butera, also embarrassed. "It's used . . . it's used for . . . for spraying the vines."

"And . . . and also . . . in making matches . . . I think," added Tino Labiso, refolding his handkerchief.

"*I think. I think.*" Don Mattia scoffed. "What do you think? That's just the point. Ask anyone you like. Those are the only two answers they will give. They couldn't tell you of anything else. Meantime we slave, we knock ourselves out digging for it, and carrying it down to the sea where all the big ships are anchored—English, American, German, French, even Greek—their holds open and waiting to suck it in. Then they give a fine blast on their whistles and—farewell! What use do they make of it out there in all those countries? No one knows. No one bothers to find out. Our riches, or rather our would-be riches, are drained from the veins of our gaping mountains while we stand by like so many blind men or simpletons, our bones aching from toil, our pockets empty. And what do we have left? These slopes, which once were farms, now completely parched by fumes from the sulphur which has been carried away."

After this poignant account of the way industry and commerce, with all the attendant merciless quarrels and money clashes, were exploiting their treasure—a treasure bestowed on them by nature—the four friends were speechless, as if sentenced to perpetual misery.

Then Scala returned to his first subject and began to enumerate the burdens a tenant-operator had to bear. He knew them all only too well, after years of bitter experience. Besides the burden of the short-term lease, he had to pay a tithe, or share in kind, of the gross amount of sulphur extracted. The owner was not interested in knowing whether the deposit was rich or poor, whether the nonproductive zones were rare or frequent, whether the subterranean levels were dry or flooded, whether prices were high or low—in brief, whether or not it was a paying venture. And, besides this tithe, there were all kinds of government taxes to be paid. In the mine itself, not only ramps had to be built, but shafts for ventilation and for the evacuation of water, roads and huts, furnaces and melting pots—all that was pertinent to the exploitation of a mine. Then, at the expiration of the lease, everything became the property of the owner, who even demanded that it be turned over to him in good working order—as if he had been the one to bear the expense of all these installations! It did not end there. The tenant-operator could not mine the sulphur the way he deemed best, but was obliged to follow the dictates of the owner and to construct arches, supports or trusses, often contrary to the specific requirements of the terrain.

One had to be desperate or out of his right mind to accept such conditions—presenting one's throat like that to the knife. Who were these tenant-operators anyway? A penniless lot of poor devils who, in order to operate their rented mines, had to incur more debts and submit to more abuse, soliciting loans from the sulphur traders down by the sea.

And when it was all added up, what was left for the operator? Could he possibly pay a more miserable salary to the poor wretches who slaved underground, constantly exposed to death? Life was a struggle—hatred, starvation and poverty for all: the operators, the miners and the young boys, crushed under their heavy loads, toiling up and down the slippery stairs and along the dark tunnels of the pit.

When Scala stopped talking and his neighbors rose to go back to their farms, the moon, high and seemingly lost in the firmament, appeared to belong to a time long past, after the recital of so much misery. Under its light the desolation of the valley looked more sepulchral, more evil.

Each was thinking as he went along that beneath those moonlit slopes, five or six hundred feet underground, people were breathlessly digging, digging. It made no difference to the poor miners buried down there whether it was night or day because, for them, it was always night.

III

Judging from Scala's words, everyone was convinced that he had all but forgotten his tragic past and no longer cared about anything save his little piece of land which he had not left in years, even for a day.

If someone brought up the subject of his son, lost in the great world somewhere, he eased his loss by speaking harshly of the boy's ingratitude and callousness.

"If he lives," he said, "he lives only for himself. For me, he is dead and I no longer think about him."

He talked that way, yet in all the outlying district there was not a peasant leaving for America who did not receive a furtive visit from Don Mattia on the eve of his departure. He came secretly to entrust him with a letter for his son.

"Not that I think anything will come of it . . . but if you should, by any chance, happen to run into him or even hear tell of him over there . . ."

Many of those letters, crumpled, yellow, almost illegible, came back again when the immigrant returned four or five years later. No one had seen Neli or even heard of him, either in Argentina or in Brazil or in the United States.

Don Mattia would listen and shrug his shoulders: "What difference can it make, after all? Give it back to me. I don't even remember sending it . . ."

He wanted to hide his grief from strangers, deluding himself with the hope that his son was in America, in some remote place, and would come back one day to discover that his father had made a new life here in the country and was waiting quietly for his return.

Perhaps his land did not amount to much, but for several years Don Mattia had secretly nursed a dream of enlarging it. He had already come to an agreement with his neighbor and a price was fixed on that adjoining land. There was no limit to the privations and sacrifices he made to accumulate the necessary funds. He fell into the habit of leaning on the balcony of his little house, letting his eye vault the low wall which separated his land from that of his neighbor, and regarding it as his own. The money was ready. All that was needed was for his neighbor to sign the deed and clear out.

It seemed like a thousand years to Scala, but unfortunately he had to deal with an eccentric, a good enough man, mind you, but odd. Don Filippino Lo Cicero was quiet, polite and meek, but without doubt not all there in the head. He read Latin from morning till night and lived all alone with a monkey he had received as a present.

The monkey was called Tita. She was old, and tubercular to boot. Don Filippino took care of her like a child. He caressed her, giving in to her whims without complaint. He talked to her and was convinced she understood him. When she was depressed because of her illness, she would perch on the canopy of his bed, a favorite spot of hers, while he sat in his armchair reading aloud passages from the *Georgics* or the *Bucolics*.

"*Tityre, tu patulae . . .*"

The reading would be interrupted from time to time by exclamations over a phrase, an expression, sometimes a single word of which Don Filippino savored the sweetness or appreciated the exquisite fitness. He would place the book carefully on his knees, half close his eyes, and repeat rapidly, "Beautiful, beautiful, beautiful," as he slowly sank back against the chair, swooning with pleasure. Then Tita would come down from the top of the bed and anxiously climb up on his chest. In his ecstasy Don Filippino would often embrace her and say, "Listen, Tita, listen . . . beautiful! Beautiful!"

Don Mattia Scala grew tired of waiting. He wanted that land. He was in a hurry and he was right. The price was set, the money ready, and Don Filippino needed that money. But, dear God, how could he ever find the same pleasure in reading the pastoral poetry of his divine Virgil in the city?

"Be patient, Don Mattia."

The first time Scala heard this, his eyes opened wide in astonishment.

"Are you joking or serious?"

Joking? Not in the least. Don Filippino was most serious. It seemed to him that Scala could never understand certain things. For instance there was Tita, accustomed to living in the country, who might not take to living in the city, poor little thing.

On nice days Don Filippino went for a walk with her. He allowed her to walk alone very, very slowly for a while before he picked her up in his arms and carried her like a baby. When he sat down on a stone to read under a tree, Tita would climb up through the branches and, hanging by her tail, swing back and forth trying to grab the tassel of his cap or snatch off his wig or whisk Virgil out of his hands.

"Be good, Tita! Please do me this favor, my poor Tita."

Yes, the dear little thing might die any day now and Mattia Scala would just have to wait.

"Wait," Don Filippino told him; "wait at least until this little beast is no more. Then my land will be yours. Is that agreeable?"

Yet more than a year had passed, and the ugly little beast refused to die.

"Would you like me to give you a cure for her?" Scala asked one day. "I have an excellent remedy."

Don Filippino smiled apprehensively and asked, "Are you making fun of me?"

"No. Not at all. A veterinarian who studied in Naples gave me this cure and he knows what he is talking about."

"Would to God, Don Mattia!"

"Well, then, take about a quart of good oil. Do you have *good* oil? Really good oil?"

"I'll buy it, whatever the price."

"Good. About a quart. Bring it to a boil with three cloves of garlic."

"Garlic?"

"Three cloves. Pay attention. When the oil comes to a boil, mind you, not just bubbling, remove it from the fire. Then take a good handful of flour from Majorca and throw it in."

"Flour from Majorca?"

"From Majorca, yes, sir! Stir it to a soft paste, the consistency of thick salve, and apply it while it is still warm to the chest and over the back of that ugly beast. Cover well with cotton, plenty of absorbent cotton, and bind with gauze. Understand?"

"Oh, yes. Absorbent cotton, then gauze. And after that?"

"Then open the window and toss her out."

"Ohoooooooooo!" Don Filippino groaned. "Poor Tita!"

"Poor farm, I say! You take no care of it. And I'm forced to sit over there looking on from a distance and thinking, the vines are all but gone; the trees have been waiting ten years to be pruned; the fruit trees haven't been grafted, and suckers shoot up unchecked, draining life from them. On all sides, things seem to be begging for help. The olive trees now are only good for firewood. In the end, what will I get for my money? Can I afford to let things drag along like this?"

Don Filippino looked so depressed by these just reproaches that Don Mattia did not have the heart to add any more. What was the use of talking, anyway? The poor man did not live in this world. The sun, our sun, never rose for him; for him, the sun of Virgil's day never set.

Don Filippino had always lived on that farm, first with his uncle, a priest, who had left it to him when he died, then alone ever since. He had been orphaned at the age of three and his uncle, a lifelong Latin and hunting enthusiast, had taken him in. But Don Filippino had never liked to hunt. Perhaps this was due to his uncle's accident: the poor man shot off two fingers of his left hand one day while loading his gun. Don Filippino chose to devote himself entirely to Latin, content to swoon with pleasure several times a reading. Whereas his uncle, who had a fiery temper despite his calling, would leap to his feet in transports of rapture, his face flushed, the veins on his forehead bulging until they looked as if they would burst, and read Latin passages aloud. Then he would hurl the book to the floor or into the astonished face of Don Filippino, shouting, "Sublime, God damn it!"

He died of a stroke, leaving Don Filippino in possession of the farm, but it was possession in name only.

The uncle also owned a house in town which he willed to another sister's son, Saro Trigona. Taking into account his position as a hapless sulphur broker and ill-starred sire of a large brood, Trigona had hoped that his uncle would leave everything to him—house and farm as well. He knew, of course, that this would entail taking his cousin, Cicero, to live with him for the rest of his days. Although Cicero had been reared in the country by their uncle, he would never be able to run that farm. However, since his uncle had not shown this consideration and since Trigona had no legal right to the farm, he made every effort to profit from his cousin's inheritance, pitilessly mulcting Don Filippino. He took over everything the farm produced: wheat, beans, fruit, wine and vegetables. If Don Filippino dared market any of it secretly, as if this were not his lawful right, his cousin Saro managed to find out about it and would descend on the farm in a rage, feeling cheated. Don Filippino would then humbly explain that he needed the money to pay the running expenses of the farm, but all to no avail. Saro would then demand the money.

"I'll kill myself. That's what I'll do!" he cried, pretending to pull a revolver out of his pocket. "I'll kill myself right here before your eyes, Filippino! I can't go on this way. Nine children, Holy God, nine children all crying to me for bread!"

It was not so bad when he came to the country alone and made these scenes, but sometimes he brought his wife and string of children. This fairly drove Don Filippino out of his wits, accustomed as he was to living alone. Those nine boys, the oldest not yet fourteen, all supposedly crying for bread, took over the peaceful country house like unbridled demons. They turned it inside out. The rooms shook with yells and screams in a wild stampede which inevitably ended in a collision and a terrible crash. Saro Trigona would then jump up and threaten, "I'll fix them!"

He ran off, chasing after the young rowdies. When he caught up with them, he distributed kicks, slaps, blows and spankings. Their yells rose in every key as he lined them up according to height. That was how he "fixed" them.

"Hold still . . . ah, what a sight! Look, Filippino, aren't they a picture? What harmony!"

Don Filippino stopped his ears, closed his eyes and stamped his small feet in despair.

"Take them away! They break everything; they ruin the house, the trees, everything! For pity's sake, take them away and leave me in peace."

Don Filippino seemed to forget that his cousin's wife never came empty-handed. She brought either an embroidered cap with a beautiful silk tassel—the one he was wearing, for instance—or slippers, those on his feet, which she had made herself. And his wig? A present from his cousin to prevent him from catching colds, to which he was exposed by his premature baldness. A wig from France! It had cost Saro Trigona a pretty penny. And what about Tita, the monkey? Was she not a present, too, from his cousin's wife, as a surprise, to amuse him and keep him company on his lonely farm?

"Jackass! Excuse me, but you're an ass!" cried Don Mattia Scala. "Why keep me waiting any longer? Sign the deed and free yourself of this yoke. With the money I'll hand over, you can live peacefully in the city for the rest of your days—given your simple needs and habits. Are you weak-minded? If you go on this way, you'll end by begging in the streets out of love for that Tita and your Virgil!"

Mattia Scala considered the farm as good as his and, not wishing to see it deteriorate further, made Cicero an advance payment.

"We will deduct so much for pruning, so much for the grafts, so much for manure, Don Filippino."

"Go ahead and deduct," Don Filippino sighed. "Just let me stay on here. In the city, with those nine devils close by, I'd be dead in no time. I'm not in your way here. You are the master, dear Mattia. You can do whatever you please and I won't say a word. All I want is to be left in peace."

"All well and good," Scala replied, "but meanwhile your cousin enjoys all the benefits."

"What can that matter to you?" Cicero pointed out. "You were to have paid the money in a lump sum. Instead, you give it to me little by little, and in the end with one deduction today, another tomorrow, I will be the loser because you will have paid for all the land and I . . . will have nothing."

IV

Don Filippino's reasoning was convincing, no doubt, but meanwhile what security did Scala have for the money he paid out? If Don Filippino should suddenly die—God forbid—with no time for signing the necessary papers acknowledging receipt of the money already paid against the sale, would Saro Trigona, his sole heir, honor those payments and agree to the sale?

From time to time this doubt arose in Don Mattia's mind, but then he reasoned that, if he should try to force Don Filippino to give him possession of the farm, using the money already advanced as a lever, he might retort, "Who obliged you to give me the money? As far as I'm concerned, the farm might have stayed as it was; it didn't matter to me. You can't put me out of my own house if I don't want to go." Besides, Scala thought, he was dealing with an honest man who wouldn't hurt a fly, and there was little danger of his dying suddenly with the sober life he led. Healthy and vigorous as he was, he could last another hundred years. At any rate, a time had been set: at the monkey's death. She couldn't keep them waiting much longer.

It was such a piece of luck for him to get the land for that price that he decided to be quiet and wait. Meantime, he was

glad to have a string attached to it, as it were, by putting down
small payments from time to time, whenever he chose. He felt
like the master, and spent more time over there than he did on
his own farm.

"Do this . . . Do that . . ."

He gave orders and watched the farm improve. Meanwhile
he had no taxes to pay on it. What more could one ask?

Poor Don Mattia! He might have been prepared for anything but that the cursed monkey, who had already given him
so much trouble, would play such a final trick.

Scala had the habit of rising before dawn in order to supervise the preparations for the day's work, which he had laid out
the previous evening with the farmhand. For example, if pruning
was to be done that day, he wanted no running back and forth
to the house for tools, ladder or grindstone to sharpen a sickle
or a hatchet, water or even lunch. The boy must leave, provided
with everything he needed so as not to waste time.

"Got your jug and a bite to eat? Here, take an onion, too.
And now get a move on!"

Thus before sunup, Don Mattia was generally on his way to
Cicero's farm. But that day, because he had to light a fire in the
charcoal kiln, he was late. It was after ten when he arrived and,
oddly enough, Don Filippino's door was still closed. Don Mattia
rapped. There was no reply. He rapped again—got no answer.
He looked up to the balcony and found the shutters still closed
as if for the night.

That's strange, he thought, going around to the farmer's
house to talk to his wife. But her door, too, was closed. The farm
looked deserted.

Scala put his hands to his mouth like a megaphone and called
out to the farmer across the garden. He was answered a moment
later from the bottom of the slope. Don Mattia called back asking the man if Don Filippino was with him. The farmhand replied that he had not seen him.

Alarmed, Scala returned to knock on the door once more,
calling several times, "Don Filippino! Don Filippino!"

There was no reply. He did not know what to think, and
started pulling at his big nose. Only the evening before, he had

left his friend in good health, so he could not now be so sick that he was unable to get out of bed. Perhaps he had merely forgotten to open the windows at the front of the house and had taken the monkey for a walk. Or perhaps he had closed the front door since there was no one at the cottage to look after the house.

Having reassured himself, Scala began looking for Don Filippino around the farm, stopping occasionally here and there to glance about with the watchful eye of an experienced farmer and make a mental note of any repairs that were needed. He called out as he went along, "Don Filippino! Don Filippino!"

In this manner he finally came to the far end of the property, where the farmer, helped by three hired hands, was digging up the earth for the new vines.

"What's happened to Don Filippino? I can't find him."

The farmer looked stunned. He too thought it strange that the villa was still closed at this hour, and Don Mattia's apprehension returned. He suggested they all go back to see what had happened.

"This morning's starting off on the wrong foot."

"I don't understand," the farmer said. "It's not like him! He's always up so early!"

"Maybe the monkey is sick," one of the hired men suggested. "Maybe he's holding her in his arms and doesn't dare move for fear of disturbing her . . ."

"Not even when he hears his name called the way I've been calling him?" said Don Mattia. "Not likely! Something must have happened."

When they reached the clearing in front of the house, the five of them, one after the other, called him but in vain. They took a turn around the house. On the west side they found one window with the shutters open.

"Ah!" said the farmer. "He has finally opened up. That's the kitchen window."

"Don Filippino!" shouted Mattia. "What's the matter with you? Do you want to drive us crazy?"

They waited, looking up, and they called again at the top of their lungs. Finally in desperation Mattia decided to investigate.

"Get me a ladder."

The farmer ran to his own place and was soon back with a ladder.

"I will go up," Mattia said, pale and distraught, pushing him aside.

At window level, he took off his hat to cover his fist and smashed the glass. Then he opened the window and jumped inside.

There was no fire in the kitchen hearth. Not a sound could be heard through the house. It was like the dead of night inside, except for the light which filtered through the shutters.

"Don Filippino!" Scala called out. The sound of his own voice in that strange silence sent a chill down his spine.

Groping his way, he came to the darkened bedroom and stopped short. He saw, or thought he saw, in the dim light, a shadow creep across the bed and disappear. His hair stood on end. He could not find his voice to call out. Rushing to the window, he threw it open and turned around. Aghast, eyes popping and mouth agape, his hands waving helplessly, he ran back to the kitchen window, trembling all over and cringing with terror.

"Up . . . up . . . come, come up. Killed! Murdered!"

"Murdered? What do you mean?" exclaimed the men below. They all rushed for the ladder, but the farmer, who wanted to go first, cried, "Mind the ladder now. One at a time."

Lying across the bed, his head thrown back and half buried in the pillow as though violently jerked into that position, Don Filippino lay with his throat ripped open. His hands were raised, those little hands which no longer seemed themselves, livid and grotesquely stiffened as they now were.

Don Mattia and the four terrified peasants stood staring. Suddenly, they were startled by a noise under the bed. They looked into one another's eyes before one of them stooped to investigate.

"The monkey," he sighed with relief, almost laughing.

Then the others bent down.

Tita was crouching under the high bed, her arms crossed over her chest. Seeing those five faces staring upside down at her, she took hold of the bed slats and sprang back and forth on her buttocks. Then she rounded her mouth and made a menacing noise: "khththth . . ."

"Look!" cried Scala. "Blood . . . blood all over her hands and chest! She killed him!"

Then he remembered the shadow he had seen move across the bed when he first came into the room, and he was convinced.

"Yes, she did it! I saw her with my own eyes! She was on the bed."

He pointed to the scratches on the cheeks and chin of the dead man.

"Look at that!"

But why in the world? The monkey who had been close to him for so many years, night and day . . .

"She may have rabies," one of the workmen cried.

At that, they all moved back from the bed.

"Wait! Get a stick!" said Mattia glancing around the room for something that could be used as a weapon.

The farmer picked up a chair by the back and stooped down but the others, unarmed and defenseless, took fright.

"Wait! Wait!" they cried.

They picked up chairs too and the farmer then pushed his under the bed several times. Tita sprang out from the other side of the bed, swung herself up by the bedpost and went to squat on the canopy. She peacefully scratched her belly as if nothing had happened and played with the corners of a handkerchief which Filippino had tied around her neck.

The five men stood there stupidly gazing up into the indifferent face of the beast.

"And now, what's to be done?" asked Scala, looking down at the corpse and quickly averting his eyes at sight of that bloody throat. "Let's cover him with the sheet."

"No, sir!" said the farmer flatly. "We will leave him just as we found him. I'm part of this household and I don't want to get into trouble with the police. And you're all my witnesses."

"What's that got to do with it?" exclaimed Scala, moving toward the bed.

But the farmer insisted, putting out his hand to restrain him.

"You can never tell with the police. We're poor folk, the rest of us . . . I know what I'm talking about."

"That may be," Mattia cried in exasperation, "but this poor

fool died like a simpleton, a victim of his own stupidity. Meanwhile I'm even crazier and more stupid than he. I'm completely ruined! Ah, but all of you can bear witness to the fact that I poured my own money into this farm, and my own sweat too. You can tell them. Now go and inform that fine gentleman, Saro Trigona, and tell the magistrate and the police . . . let them come and see the doings of this—accursed animal!"

In a burst of temper, he tore off the hat he was wearing and threw it at the monkey.

Tita caught it in mid-air, examined it attentively, rubbed it across her face as if she were wiping her nose, then stuck it under her and sat on it. The four peasants burst into uncontrollable laughter.

V

There was not a trace of a will, not a mark in a ledger, not even a scrap of paper.

Because of the loss he had suffered, Don Mattia Scala was the laughingstock of his friends. In fact, Nocia Butera said he had easily foreseen that Don Filippino Cicero would wind up that way. He had known that the monkey would finish him off somehow.

So long as his cousin remained unburied, awaiting the certificates of the doctor and the magistrate, Saro Trigona refused to listen, on the excuse that his bereavement made it impossible for him to talk business.

"As if the monkey hadn't made him a present of that farm—in cold blood," muttered Scala, giving vent to his feelings.

He thought Trigona should have coined a gold medal in the monkey's honor instead of having her shot the next day, notwithstanding the pretty explanation given by the young doctor who came out with the magistrate to investigate the case. According to him, Tita, suffering from tuberculosis, probably had difficulty breathing. Then there was the handkerchief poor Filippino had tied around her neck which might have been too tight and, in trying to get it off, she might have pulled it even tighter. She had jumped on the bed, according to the doctor, in an effort to make her master understand that she could not breathe. Possibly she had taken hold of his throat to show him and, exasperated by her suffering, she could have tightened her grip—and the deed was done! After all, she was only an animal. She did not know any better.

Frowning, the magistrate approved the young doctor's rare insight by repeatedly nodding his big, sweaty, bald head.

Then, at last, with his cousin buried and the monkey shot, Saro Trigona put himself at the disposal of Don Mattia Scala.

"Dear Don Mattia, now we can discuss it."

There was little to discuss. Scala, in his jerky fashion, briefly explained his agreement with Cicero and how—waiting from day to day, from season to season, in the hope that the beast would die so he could take over the farm—he had spent several thousand lire on it, with Cicero's full consent, of course. This sum was to be deducted from the price agreed upon for the farm. Was that clear?

"Very clear," replied Trigona, listening attentively to Scala and nodding his head as the magistrate had done. "Very clear. And I, for my part, dear Don Mattia, am disposed to respect this agreement. As you know, I am a broker. These are hard times. To place a cargo of sulphur one needs the helping hand of God. Profits are swallowed up in taxes and portage fees. I tell you this because, with my professional responsibilities, I could not look after a farm; besides, I don't know a thing about it. Then, too, as you know, dear Don Mattia, I have nine sons all in school. One may be dumber than the other, but they all go to school. Therefore I must live in the city. Let's get down to ourselves. There is only one difficulty. Ah, dear Don Mattia, unfortunately it is a big difficulty. Nine children, as we were saying: you can have no idea what that costs me in shoes alone. But there's no point in my adding it up for you. You'd go out of your mind. It's just to show you, dear Don Mattia . . ."

"For pity's sake, don't keep saying *dear Don Mattia,*" Scala broke in, irritated by Trigona's interminable speech. *"Dear Don Mattia . . . dear Don Mattia . . .* Get to the point! I've already lost too much time with the monkey and Don Filippino."

"Well, then," Trigona said calmly, "I wanted to tell you that I've been forced to turn to a certain gentleman—God forbid—do I make myself clear? He has a knife at my throat, you understand? You know who the big moneylender is around here . . ."

"Dima Chiarenza!" exclaimed Scala, jumping to his feet, very pale. He threw his hat on the ground and ran his fingers furiously through his hair. Then, his eyes wide, he pointed the index finger of the other hand like a gun at Trigona.

"You . . ." he said. "You went to that brigand? That cutthroat who devoured me alive? How much did you borrow?"

"Wait, I'll tell you," replied Trigona with agonizing calm. "Not I! Because that brigand, as you so aptly put it, would lend nothing against my signature . . ."

"Then what . . . Don Filippino?" groaned Scala, covering his face with his hands as if he wanted to hide his own words.

"And as security . . ." sighed Trigona, shaking his head sadly.

Don Mattia turned about the room, crying, "I'm ruined! I'm ruined!"

"Wait," said Trigona. "Don't despair. Let's see if we can't remedy it. How much did you intend to pay Filippino for the land?"

"I?" cried Scala, halting, his hands on his chest. "Eighteen thousand lire, all told. There are about six acres of land, at three thousand an acre—spot cash. God knows how hard I worked to get the money together, and now I see the deal fall through, the very ground under my feet—ground I already considered my own!"

While Don Mattia unburdened himself, Saro Trigona frowned and counted on his fingers.

"Eighteen thousand . . . that is to say . . ."

"Easy . . ." interrupted Scala. "Eighteen thousand if the poor soul had turned over the farm to me then and there. But more than six thousand have already been spent on the farm, as you can see for yourself. I have witnesses: this year I put in two thousand American vine shoots; exorbitant! And then . . ."

Saro Trigona stood up to cut the conversation short, saying, "But twelve thousand isn't enough, dear Don Mattia. I owe that brigand more than twenty thousand. Just imagine!"

"Twenty thousand lire!" cried Scala. "Do you *eat* money, you and your children?"

Trigona drew a long sigh and said, giving Scala a slap on the arm, "My hard-luck Don Mattia! Not a month ago I had to pay nine thousand lire to a merchant in Licata on the difference in price of a shipment of sulphur. Never mind! They were the last notes poor Filippino signed for me, God rest his soul!"

After many useless protests, they agreed to go to town that same day, twelve thousand lire in hand, and try to come to terms with Chiarenza.

VI

Dima Chiarenza's house stood on the main square of the town.

It was an old two-story house, blackened by time. English and German tourists who came to visit the sulphur mines used to stop in front of it to take pictures. The natives of the town stared at them with scorn and pity because, for them, the house was no better than a hovel, dilapidated and gloomy. It spoiled the harmony of the big square with the Town Hall opposite, all white, shining like marble, and so stately too with its eight columns forming a portico. Then there was the Mother Church here and the Commercial Bank there, with the imposing coffeehouse on one side and the Club on the other.

According to the members of the Club, the municipality should do something to make Chiarenza give his house at least a good coat of whitewash. It would do him good too, they said. It would brighten his face, which had taken on the same color as his house. However, they amended, just to be fair, this house had come to him with his wife as part of her dowry, and perhaps, in taking his marriage vows, he had felt obliged to respect the antiquity of each.

Don Mattia Scala and Saro Trigona, standing in the dim light of the huge waiting room, found some twenty peasants, all roughly dressed alike in heavy suits of dark blue cloth, big hobnail shoes of raw leather and, on their heads, black stocking caps with pompons at the end. Several of them wore earrings and, since it was Sunday, they were freshly shaven.

"Tell him I'm here," said Trigona to the manservant seated by the door before a little table, the top of which was all marked up with figures and names.

"Just be patient a moment," the man replied, staring stupidly at Scala, well aware of his enmity for his master. "Don Tino Labiso is inside."

"He, too! Poor fellow," murmured Mattia, looking at the waiting peasants who were as dumfounded as the servant to see him in this house.

After a while Scala could easily tell from their expressions which had come to settle their debts, which had brought only part of the sum due, and which already had in their eyes the plea they meant to turn on the moneylender to beseech his patience until the end of the following month. Then there were those who had come with nothing, not even a reasonable plea. They looked crushed beforehand at the prospect of starvation, knowing Chiarenza would ruthlessly strip them of all they possessed and throw them out in the street.

Suddenly the door of the "bank" opened and Tino Labiso, his face flaming, almost purple, his eyes bright as if he might have wept, ran off without seeing anyone, holding his red-and-black checked handkerchief in his hand—an emblem of his unfortunate prudence.

Scala and Trigona were shown into the "banking room." It was dark, with only one window protected by iron bars looking onto a narrow passageway. In full daylight, Chiarenza had to keep a light burning on his desk, covered by a little green shade.

He was seated in an old leather armchair before a desk with pigeonholes crammed full of papers. Chiarenza wore a shawl over his shoulders, a skullcap on his head, and wool mitts on his hands which were cruelly deformed by arthritis. Although he was not yet forty, he looked more than fifty. His face was yellow, his hair gray and dry, and it hung down over his temples like that of an invalid. His glasses were pushed up on his narrow, wrinkled forehead, and he gazed before him with almost lifeless eyes shadowed by heavy lids. Evidently he had to make an effort to quell his agitation and present a calm front before Scala.

The knowledge of his infamous reputation only inspired him

with hatred, a gloomy hatred against everybody but particularly against his old benefactor and first victim, Mattia Scala. Chiarenza did not yet know what was wanted of him but he was determined to agree to nothing, not to appear in any way to repent the crime he had always scornfully denied, passing Scala off as a fool.

Don Mattia had not seen him in many years even from a distance, and he was stunned by Chiarenza's appearance. He would not have recognized him had he met him on the street.

God's punishment, he thought, frowning, because he immediately realized that the man, altered as he was, would consider that he had expiated his sin and that no further reparation was due.

His eyes lowered, his face stiff with pain, Dima Chiarenza put one hand over his kidneys to hoist himself out of his chair. But Saro Trigona insisted that he remain seated and immediately launched into his habitual entangled phrases to explain the purpose of their visit: he by selling the farm inherited from his cousin to dear Don Mattia, there present, would then be able to pay at once twelve thousand lire against his debt to *caro caro Don Dima,* who, in return, would then agree to take no judiciary action against the Cicero estate, as pending . . .

"Easy there, son," Chiarenza interrupted at this point, pulling his glasses down over his nose. "I've already taken steps this very day to recall the notes signed by your cousin, now long overdue. One can't be too careful."

"How about my money?" Scala broke in. "Cicero's farm was worth no more than eighteen thousand lire. But now I've sunk more than six thousand into it, so if an honest appraisal were made, you would not get it for less than twenty-four thousand."

"Good," Chiarenza replied calmly. "As Trigona owes me twenty-five thousand, it means that in taking over the farm I stand to lose one thousand lire plus the interest."

"Twenty-five!" exclaimed Don Mattia, turning to Trigona, his eyes popping.

The latter twisted around in his chair as if it were an instrument of torture, and stammered, "How . . . how is that?"

"Well, son, I'll show you," Chiarenza said calmly, again placing his hands over his kidneys as he rose. "Here are my ledgers. They speak for themselves."

"Leave the ledgers out of this!" cried Scala, starting forward. "It's a question of my money . . . the money I put into the farm."

"How does that concern me?" said Chiarenza, hunching his shoulders and closing his eyes. "Who made you put it in?"

Furiously Don Mattia repeated the story about his understanding with Cicero.

"Too bad," Chiarenza remarked, scarcely breathing and again closing his eyes to hide his difficulty in controlling himself. "Too bad. I see that, as always, you know nothing about business."

"You dare throw that in my face!" cried Scala. *"You!"*

"I'm not throwing anything in your face but, good God, before laying out your money you should have had enough sense to find out if Cicero was in a position to sell his farm. He had already signed it away in notes that exceeded its value!"

"And so," continued Scala, "you'll also profit from my money."

"I don't profit from anything," Chiarenza was quick to reply. "It seems to me that I already pointed out that, according to your estimated value of the land, I stand to lose at least a thousand lire."

Saro Trigona tried to interrupt, flashing the twelve thousand lire Mattia had in his portfolio before Chiarenza.

"Money is money!"

"And how it flies!" retorted Chiarenza. "The best investment for money today is land. I will have you know, my friend, that notes are double-edged weapons. Interest rises and falls, but land remains stable."

Don Mattia agreed and, changing his tone and manner, told Chiarenza of his long love for the adjoining farm. He said that, after all the privations he had endured, he did not know how he could ever bear to lose it. If Chiarenza would be content, for the moment, with the sum he had with him, he would pay him the balance down to the last cent. He would give him the money, not Trigona, and he would hold to the price of twenty-four thousand lire, as though he had not already put six thousand into it. He would even go up to twenty-five thousand if Chiarenza would agree to wipe out Trigona's debt.

"What more can I say?"

Dima Chiarenza listened, his eyes shut, while Scala talked. Then he said in a solemn voice, "Listen, Don Mattia. I see that this land is close to your heart, and I would gladly let you have it if it were not for my health. But the doctors have ordered rest and country air . . ."

"Aha!" cried Scala, trembling. "Then you would go there to live next to me?"

"Moreover," Chiarenza continued, "you would not be giving me half the amount I should have. Who knows how long I would have to wait for the rest of the money? Meanwhile, by accepting a small loss, I can recover both my money and my health by taking possession of the land. I want to leave everything in order for my heirs."

"Don't give me this talk!" Scala interrupted indignantly. "You speak of your heirs. You have no children. Are you thinking of your nephews? You're a little late. You never thought of them before. Tell the truth for once: Say, 'I mean to persecute you forever.' Isn't it enough that you ruined me, caused the death of my wife and caused my only son to run away out of despair? Is it not enough that, in return for the good I did you, you made me a pauper? Must you now take this land away from me, land into which I have put my life's blood? Why, why this hatred for me? What have I done to you? When you betrayed me like a Judas, I did not open my mouth. I was too busy thinking of my wife who was dying because of what you had done, and of my son who fled because of you. Proof, material proof of your theft, to send you to jail, there was none. While the whole town with one voice cried: *Thief! Traitor!* I went quietly to that little farm. I said nothing. But there is a God and he has punished you. Look at those hands—the hands of a thief! See how deformed, how rapacious they are! Ah! You hide them? You are dead . . . dead! Still you persist in doing me harm. But this time you won't succeed. I told you the sacrifice I was prepared to make for that land. Answer me: Will you accept my offer?"

Chiarenza, twisted and grim, shouted furiously, "No!"

"Then, if I can't have it, neither will you."

Scala turned to leave.

"What will you do?"

Scala raised his hand menacingly and looked him straight in the eyes.

"Burn you out."

VII

Once Don Mattia had left Chiarenza's house, and had rid himself of Trigona, who sorrowfully tried to explain his good intentions, he first went to see a lawyer friend of his to consult him on this affair. He wanted to know if he could legally prevent Chiarenza from taking possession of the farm.

At first the lawyer could understand little or nothing from Scala's emotional account and tried instead to calm him, but without much success.

"In conclusion," he said, "you have no proofs, no documents?"

"Nothing at all."

"Then what the devil do you expect me to do?"

"Just a moment," Mattia said as he was leaving. "Can you tell me, by any chance, where Scelzi, the engineer, lives?"

When he had the address, Mattia decided to go to him right away.

Scelzi was one of the engineers who passed Scala's villa every morning, going along the mule track to the sulphur mines in the valley. He had been the most insistent in nagging him to lease the rights to his land. How many times Scala had threatened him with his dogs to get rid of him!

Although it was Sunday, a day when Scelzi usually saw no one on business, he lost no time having this unusual visitor shown into his study.

"What wind blows you here, Don Mattia?"

Scala frowned, planting himself in front of the younger man, and looking him squarely in the eyes, he said, "I'm ready."

"Ah! Excellent! You will lease?"

"Lease, nothing. I want to sell outright. What are your terms?"

"Don't you know?" exclaimed Scelzi. "I've repeated them to

you so many times."

"Will you have to make more tests?" Mattia asked, gloomy and reckless.

"No! Look here," said the engineer, pointing to a geological map on the wall carefully marked by the Royal Mining Corps of the region. He put his finger over a place on the map, adding, "It's right here. No need to go any further."

"All right. Draw up the contract immediately."

"Now? Tomorrow . . . tomorrow morning first thing, I will talk with the Administration Council. Meanwhile, if you wish, we can write out an agreement now which will certainly be accepted—unless you want to insert other conditions?"

"I need to tie it up right away," Scala said abruptly. "Everything, all of it will be destroyed, will it not?"

Scelzi looked at him in astonishment. He had heard a little about this man's impulsive nature but he was not prepared for this.

"The damage done by the 'fumes,' " he said, "is foreseen by the contract and an indemnity is allowed."

"I know. I don't care, just so the farms are destroyed—all the farms."

"What . . ." Scelzi began, puzzled.

"That is what I'm after . . . that's what I want," Mattia went on, bringing his fist down on the desk. "Here, engineer . . . write, write. Neither I nor he. Everything will be burned up. Write. Pay no attention to what I'm saying."

Scelzi sat before his desk and began to write out the agreement, after first slowly explaining the advantageous conditions which Scala had so often scorned. Now the farmer sat there frowning darkly and nodding his consent.

When the agreement was drawn up, Scelzi could not resist asking the reason for this unexpected right-about-face.

"Bad year?"

"Bad year? The year to come, you mean," said Scala, "when the mine opens."

Scelzi supposed that Don Mattia had received sad news about his son. He knew that, a few months earlier, he had made a petition to Rome through the consul asking that another search be made, but he did not want to bring up that delicate subject.

As he left, Scala again urged him to put the business through as speedily as possible. "At once," Don Mattia said, "and see to it that you tie me up well!"

But just the same, it had taken two days for the deliberations of the Council, the writing of the contract by a notary and the registration of the deed itself: two awful days for Mattia Scala. He neither ate nor slept, but followed Scelzi here and there as if he had lost his mind, repeating over and over, "Tie me up well . . . tie me up well."

When the contract was duly signed and witnessed, Don Mattia Scala rushed out of the notary's office like a man who has taken leave of his senses. He ran to the store on the outskirts of town where he had left his mare three days earlier, and rode away.

The sun was setting. An endless string of sulphur carts jolted along the dusty road toward the railroad station in endless succession. Astride his mare, Don Mattia looked with hatred on those springless carts loaded with sulphur from the far-off mines in the valley, beyond the hill which was not yet visible.

The wide road was flanked by two rows of prickly-pear cactus, their fleshy leaves dusted with sulphur from the carts in their incessant shuttling back and forth.

Don Mattia's aversion increased as he watched them. There was nothing to be seen but sulphur in this place. The very air you breathed was laden with sulphur: it hurt your throat and burned your eyes.

At a turn in the road, the green hill finally came into view, touched by the last rays of the sun.

Scala feasted his eyes on it and clenched his fist over the bridle until it hurt. To him the sun seemed to be kissing the green of that hill for the last time. Perhaps he himself would never see it again as he now saw it from the crest of the road. In twenty years, at this very turning, those who came after him would look upon a bare mound, dried and gray, pocked by sulphur mines.

And where will I be then? he thought with a feeling of bitter loneliness. This instantly brought his missing son to mind, roving the world somewhere, if he was still alive. Overcome with emotion, his eyes filled with tears. It was for the boy's sake that he had found strength to rise above the poverty into which Chiarenza had plunged him. And now his tormentor had deprived him of his farm.

"No! No!" he roared between clenched teeth. "Neither he nor I!"

He spurred the mare on as if he would fly there to destroy the farm which could never be his. It was evening when he came to the foot of the hill. The road followed around for a while before it joined the mule track. The moon came up, shining so brightly that it seemed like daybreak. The crickets all around wildly saluted this lunar dawn.

As Scala passed the neighboring farms, he was stung with violent remorse. He thought of his friends, fellow-landowners, who were as yet unaware of his betrayal.

All those dear farms would go before long. Not a blade of grass would be left and he, he, would be guilty of laying waste the green hill. In his thoughts, as he drew near home, he was once more seated on his little balcony, and was looking at the low wall that bordered his own small farm. He reflected wretchedly that his gaze should have stopped there . . . and not leaped over that wall onto his neighbor's land. Without the freedom of that little field—and with his enemy living there beside him—he would feel like a prisoner deprived of air. No! No!

"Destroy it . . . destroy it! Neither he nor I! Let it burn!"

He looked around at his trees, his throat gripped in anguish. The centuries-old olive trees with their mighty, gray, twisted trunks stood motionless in a mystical reverie under the moonlight. He imagined those living leaves, furled by the first biting fumes from the sulphur mine. They would soon fall. Then the naked trees would blacken and die, poisoned by the hot breath off the furnaces. Finally the ax. Firewood . . . all these trees.

A light breeze came up with the moon's ascent. All the leaves stirred as if sensing their approaching doom, and their shivering rippled along Don Mattia's spine as he stood there bowed over the neck of his white mare.

BOMBOLO

Bombolo sat in the café all day long, a red fez on his big curly head, his legs straddling the table base, one commanding fist on the marble top and the other on his hip. He would look around, not defiantly but with a stern expression that said flatly, "Make no mistake about it: here you deal with me!"

Landowners came one after another, not only from Montelusa but from all the surrounding countryside. Even the old Marchese, Don Nicolino Nigrelli, who always carried an ebony cane and held the round ivory ball of the handle against his puckered lips as if he were playing a flute. Then there were Baron Don Mauro Ragona, Tavella, too—all of them respectfully baring their heads.

"Don Zuli, please do me a favor."

Before this deference, Bombolo would jump to his feet, pull off his fez and stand at attention, head high, eyes lowered.

"At your service, Excellency," he would say.

The usual complaints, on the one hand, and exhortations, on the other, would soon follow. Nigrelli had lost four head of cattle on the hill; Ragona eight from the sheep fold; Tavella five from the stable. One came to tell him that the boy watching over his herd had been tied to a tree. Another said his cow had been taken and the newborn calf left to die of starvation.

Bombolo would, at first, show indignation over such outrages, exclaiming, "The villains!"

Then lifting clasped hands, he would go on: "But, sir, we call them villains, yet in all conscience, how much do these poor villains earn a day? Three tari—one lira and a quarter! That's what they're paid, isn't it? And what's three tari for a man? One of God's poor creatures baptized like you—not like me, a heathen Turk, as you can see," he would say, pointing to his fez. "Tell me, sir, isn't it a moral crime to pay three tari a day to a man who wields a shovel and sweats blood from sunrise to sunset, without pause except at noon, when he takes time out to munch a crust of bread with saliva for a chaser, and then returns to work still chewing his last mouthful? Look at Cosimo Lopes. Since he's been paying his peasants three lire a day, has he had anything to complain about?" Quickly, he pulled a hair from his head and held it up as if it were a talisman. "Three lire, sir, is only right! Do as I say and if tomorrow *any*one mistreats you or your animals, you may come and spit in my face. I'll be here."

In the end, changing both his manner and tone of voice, he would ask, "How many head did you say? Four? Leave it to me. I'll go saddle my horse now."

For two or three days he would pretend to scour the countryside for the missing cattle, riding all night, or so he said, in the rain or under the stars. No one believed it, of course. He well knew that they didn't believe it. But when, upon his return, he would reappear before old Marchese Nigrelli, or Ragona, or any of the others, he was received with the usual exclamations: "Poor Zuli, what a hard time you've had of it!"

"Never mind, never mind. It was not easy, but I tracked them down. You needn't worry; the animals are stabled and well cared for. They are all right where they are. The cattle rustlers themselves aren't so well off. If their lives weren't so hard, you can be sure they'd never resort to this kind of thing. . . . Well, that's all there is to it. They're willing to return the cattle—but, as usual, you understand, in dealing with a gentleman like yourself through my good offices, without agreements or conditions, they leave it entirely up to your conscience. . . . Don't worry! Tonight, without fail, your animals will reappear on the hill, better-looking than ever."

He would have taken it as an affront to himself as well as to the landowners had he so much as suspected that the rustlers might be ambushed by the police that night. He knew only too well that if the gentry appealed to him, it was because they had no faith in the authorities. They would never get their cattle back that way. But working through Bombolo, any thought of treachery was ruled out.

Bombolo received the money—five hundred, a thousand, two thousand lire, according to the number of animals sequestered— and every week on Saturday night he brought the total sum to the peasants of the League, who assembled in a store near the top of San Gerlando. There he saw that "justice was done." That is, by computing each peasant's wages at three lire a day, those who had worked for only three tari that week received the difference. Those who, through no fault of their own, had "sat it out" without work were paid seven lire for the week or a lira a day. However, first of all, deductions were made for the small weekly pensions allotted the families of three members—Todesco, Principe and Barrera—who had been arrested one night by a scouting patrol and sentenced to three years in prison. They had not "sung." Another share was set aside as dues to the watchmen who co-operated by allowing themselves to be bound and gagged. If anything was left over, it was put aside as cash reserve.

Bombolo kept nothing for himself, not a cent. The rumors going around Montelusa were malicious lies. He really had no need for the money. He had made a fortune in the East, where he had lived a long time. No one knew exactly where, nor how, but it was certain that he had money and was not interested in the relatively small sums that passed through his hands. They said you could see what he was by that fez, by his lazily watchful expression, his colorful speech, and the special odor given off by his whole person—spicy, exotic—thanks perhaps to the little leather pouches and small wooden boxes he always carried about him or from the Turkish tobacco he smoked. Because tobacco was a state monopoly, the foreign leaf had to be smuggled off boats in the nearby harbor. Some said he was engaged in shady business. They saw him, they said, sitting there hour after hour with that bright-red cylinder on his head, looking out to sea for all the world as if he were waiting for a sail to appear off Punta Bianca.

He had married into the Dimino family, rich landowners, with holdings so vast you could walk all day and not come to the end of them. Even though their daughter had died four years after her marriage, old Dimino and his wife were so fond of Bombolo that, it was said, they would give him their last cent!

He was a kind of Robin Hood working for justice, happy in the respect, love and gratitude of the peasants, who looked on him as their king. He held them all in the palm of his hand. Experience had taught him that open meetings, in protest against the tyrannical avarice of the property owners, would only be broken up by the police and the ringleader carted off to jail. That was the way they had always administered justice in Sicily. Even the landowners took no stock in it. But in the store up there on San Gerlando, Bombolo meted out justice in his own way.

If those gentlemen-farmers insisted on paying no more than three tari a day—well, what they didn't give freely, they would have to give by force. Peacefully, without bloodshed or violence, and with all due regard for the welfare of the animals.

Bombolo had a notebook in which he listed all the proprietors of the district, their names, the extent and location of their lands, as well as their livestock, large and small. Each week he would call a secret meeting of his most trusted henchmen to decide, from the open notebook, who would "pay the tax" and which peasants were to make the raid. They would be chosen because of their familiarity with the place, their friendship with the watchmen or their daring.

"A small touch never hurt anyone" was one of his favorite sayings.

But he went wild when one of the members of the League was reported for leeching, or idling. He would go after him and shake him with both hands so violently that the culprit's beret would fly off and his shirt and pants would part company.

"Snake in the grass!" Bombolo would shout. "What do you take me for? A champion of thieves and vagrants? Down here you must sweat blood! Down here, on Saturday nights you must report with your back breaking with fatigue, or this will quickly become a den of thieves. If you don't work, I'll crush you underfoot. I'll tear you apart! *Work is the law!* Only by work do you win the right to lead a beast by the horns from the stable of its owner and proclaim, 'Until I am paid what I have rightfully earned by the sweat of my brow, I will keep this animal.' "

In those moments he was frightening. Everyone in the dark store would listen, silent as shadows, staring at the flame of the candle butt melting over the dirty table. After such violent outbursts, Bombolo would gasp for breath, his mighty chest heaving and croaking like an old frog. If one of them had dared look up, he would have seen real tears of rage glisten in Bombolo's eyes. At those moments, he saw his austere concept of justice abjectly compromised. He felt the weight of responsibility and a certain scorn and bitterness for his undertaking. The peasants did not seem to appreciate the salary of three lire a day which he had managed to wring from the landowners by harassing them day after day.

It fed his pride to hear the farm gentry themselves say that they had never seen the peasants work harder or more willingly. This alone, in his eyes, purified and exalted the task he had set himself. For him, all those who heeded his constant preaching and granted a fair wage were sacred, and he wanted them to be just as sacred to every other member of the League. When money was needed and he could not turn up a name in his notebook to "pay the tax"—all those listed having already paid up—Bombolo would turn white with rage if a member timidly suggested one of the sacred few. They were untouchable.

Then what?

"Then," Bombolo would explode, tossing the notebook into the air, "*then* we bleed my father-in-law."

Two or three peasants would be assigned to go to the Luna domain, under cover of darkness, and to make off with six or seven big animals owned by Dimino—one of the first landowners to pay his men the equitable three lire a day.

By bleeding his father-in-law, Bombolo was robbing himself, because his son was Dimino's only heir. But he preferred to rob himself or his son rather than to go against what he knew was right. And what torment it was for him every time his father-in-law—dressed "old style" in knee breeches, black stocking cap with a pompon on the end, and little gold chains through his ears—sought him out and said, "What's the matter, Zuli? Is this the way they respect you? What's come over you? Have you lost your hold on them?"

"Spit in my face," replied Bombolo, eyes closed, drinking down the gall of Dimino's rebuke. "Spit in my face. What else can I say?"

He was only waiting until the three League members—Todesco, Principe and Barrera—were released from prison to dissolve the League itself. There were days when those three years seemed to him like a million.

When the day finally came, there was a big celebration in the store on top of San Gerlando. They drank and they danced. Bombolo beamed when he got up to make the final speech. He recalled their deeds and sang their praises. As a reward—the highest reward for those three who had suffered imprisonment—an honest wage had now been firmly established throughout the area. His task was accomplished, he said, and he could retire in peace and contentment. He brought down the house when he added that he had sent his red fez to his father-in-law, who had never been able to stomach the "crown." In giving up the fez he gave up his reign, and hereby declared the League dissolved.

Two weeks had not passed before the old Marchese, Don Nicolino Nigrelli, sauntered by the café as usual with the white ivory ball of his ebony cane held to his lips.

"Don Zuli, please do me a favor."

Bombolo went white as the marble table top and turned to look at the poor Marchese in such stupefaction that Don Nicolino backed away in fright and fell into a chair.

Bombolo stood over him, roaring between clenched teeth, "Again?"

Half fainting, although he was trying to smile, the Marchese lifted four fingers of his trembling hand and said, "Four, yes, as before. What's so new about that?"

Bombolo snatched the new hat off his head and tore it to shreds. Trembling, he moved between the tables, banging into them and upsetting the chairs. Then he turned on the Marchese, who still sat among the astonished customers, and cried, "Don't give them a single lira. By the Blessed Virgin! Don't give them *any*thing. I'll have to think this thing over."

Couldn't those three—Todesco, Principe and Barrera—be content with that "highest reward" of which Bombolo had boasted at the last meeting of the League? If Bombolo himself, toward the end, had allowed them to bleed his own father-in-law, known to be among the first to concede the higher wage, then why couldn't they, in all fairness, continue to bleed the other landowners?

That evening, when Bombolo found them on San Gerlando after an all-day search, he attacked them like a wild beast. They let him strike them and knock them about. They even said he could kill them if he cared to: they would not lift a finger to defend themselves, out of respect and gratitude for all he had done. However, if he did this, he would be killing them unjustly, for they knew nothing at all about the theft. Their consciences were clear. League? What League? There *was* no more League! Hadn't he dissolved it? Ah, so he threatened to denounce them? What for? For their past? Then they were all in it, and he the ringleader. As to a raid on Marchese Nigrelli, they knew nothing about it. But they might well scout the countryside for two or three days and question the brigands, as he had done before them, riding all night in the rain and under the stars.

Hearing them talk like this, Bombolo bit his hands in rage and frustration. He said he would give them just three days. If at the end of that time the four head of cattle had not been returned without a lira of ransom—well, what would he do? He didn't yet know.

What could Bombolo do? Even the landowners themselves—Nigrelli, Ragona, Tavella and all the others—tried to convince him that there was nothing he *could* do. Where did he come in? Hadn't he always acted as a disinterested party? What was so different today? Why did he now refuse to help anyone? Go to the police? Where would that get them? The police would not bring about the return of their cattle, nor would they find the guilty party who had made off with them. The proprietors themselves said it was simple-minded to expect the cattle to be returned without compensation. They had to make a deal, they said—without agreements or conditions. Just so long as Bombolo would act as go-between!

And from the tone in which these things were said, Bombolo understood that they mistook his present indignation for playacting, just as before they had misinterpreted his sympathy for the peasants.

In rage and despair he shouted that they should go back to paying the peasants three tari a day; they could at least do him that favor. Word of honor, they didn't deserve more than three tari! Shameless thieves! Dogs! Jailbirds! What then? Was he to burst his liver as well as his gall bladder because of these buzzards?

He sent his son to his grandparents up at the big Luna estate to ask them to return his red fez. Turk he was and Turk he would remain!

Two days later, bag and baggage, he went down to the harbor and boarded a Greek ship for the Levant.

WHO PAYS THE PIPER . . .

For three nights Uncle Neli Sghembri had slept out in the open on straw left on the ground after the threshing, to watch over his mule and two donkeys as they cropped the stubble close by.

The straw was bathed in dew—"the tears of the stars," as Uncle Neli called it. Crickets chirped softly all about him. Their concert was refreshing and cheerful after the rasping, monotonous din of locusts the livelong day. Yet the old man, stretched out there on his back, felt sad. He gazed at the stars and sighed from time to time, his eyes half closed. Fate had cheated him, he thought. It had given him none of the things he had longed for as a young man. Now, in his old age, it had even stripped him of the little he had managed to put by. Then too, he thought, though his wife was dead four years now, he still needed her. He was ashamed to go in quest of love at his age, with his gray hair and stooped back.

As he lay there, his thoughts rambling under the misty, diaphanous light, a firefly suddenly flashed its green lamp past his eyes and alighted beside him on the straw. With that flicker of light, the old man had the impression that the sky was close to him and yet at the same time far, far away. He sat up, startled, as if waking from a dream. But the dream was all around him in the blur of night, in his shack, cracked and smudged by smoke, in the mule and donkeys moving about in the stubble, and far down below in the wavering lights of his pretty little village, Raffadali.

The firefly was still there on the straw beside him. He lifted it into the hollow of his big calloused hand and looked closely at its feeble, pulsing light. This little "shepherd's candle," he thought, had come to him from his long-lost youth. It might even be the same one which caught in Trisuzza Tumminia's black hair that June night—it must be forty-five years ago. She had come up to glean with the other young girls from Raffadali, and, after the harvest, they had danced to the sound of the tambourines in the moonlight.

Youth! How terrified Trisuzza Tumminia had been of that little insect caught in her hair! She didn't know that it was a "shepherd's candle"! With two fingers he had delicately plucked it out of her hair.

"See, a little light like a star on your brow so white!" he had told her, making a rhyme.

That was how he had fallen in love with Trisuzza Tumminia, when the world was indeed an altogether different place. But their parents had opposed the marriage because of an old family feud, and Trisuzza had married someone else. And he had married too. Now he was a widower. She had been a widow for about ten years. Why had that little firefly come back? Why had it flashed past him just when he was feeling sad and lonely? Why had it settled there beside him on the straw bathed in the tears of the stars?

He took a piece of paper out of his pocket and carefully wrapped the firefly inside.

He lay there most of the night thinking and smiling to himself. Next morning, as a little girl came along the mule track leading to Raffadali, he called to her over the hedge.

"Nicu, little Nicu. Come here."

There was laughter in his eyes and his mouth longed to laugh too.

"Tell me," he said, passing the back of his hand over the bristles on his lip. "Do you know Aunt Tresa Tumminia?"

"The one with the sow?" asked the child.

The old man frowned, offended. But in Raffadali, that was precisely what they called her—"the one with the sow." For many years she had raised a sow, lavishing on it such care and tenderness that it had become so monstrously fat it could no longer stand on its feet. With her husband dead and her sons married, Trisuzza Tumminia had only the sow for company. Woe unto anyone who proposed butchering it! When she bent down to scratch its head, that rosy, mud-caked sow with its belly hanging loose on the straw enjoyed the tickling and grunted blissfully. Stretching all over, the sow twisted its snout in a would-be smile and turned up its loose throat. Such gratification didn't seem right. Everyone resented a sow being fed like that for no reason at all. If it was not intended for the slaughterhouse, why did she go on fattening it?

"Aunt Tresa, yes," Uncle Neli told the child. "That's the one. Now listen. There is a 'shepherd's candle' in this piece of paper. Mind it doesn't fly away, and don't squash it. Take it to Aunt Tresa and tell her that Uncle Neli Sghembri sent it. It's the same one, tell her, as many, many years ago! Don't forget: the same one as many, many years ago. Bring me her answer tonight and I will give you some bean flour as a reward. Run along now!"

After all, he was sixty-three but still strong and solid as the bole of an olive tree. Aunt Tresa herself was as fresh as an unpicked fruit, full of life and vigor.

That evening the child returned with her answer.

"Aunt Tresa said that her hair is white and the little candle gives no more light," she repeated, smiling.

"She said it like that?" asked the old man.

"Just like that," said the little girl.

Next day Uncle Neli, shaved like a bridegroom and wearing his best clothes, went to Raffadali and presented himself before Tresa Tumminia to say that the little "shepherd's candle" still glowed in his heart, bright and green as when he first saw it shine like a star on her brow.

"Let's get married and kill that fatted sow!" he proposed.

"Go along with you, old fool," she said, laughing, and gave him a push with both hands.

There was no question of killing the sow, but as for the wedding—well, why not?

It was fate. First their parents and now their children opposed the marriage. But this time the old couple paid them no heed. They made their own financial arrangements. They pretended to be offended, but actually they were pleased by the piquant touch of youth this opposition gave their union. It was amusing to hear their own children talk of "good sense" and "suitability."

Both had had four children by their first marriages. Tresa Tumminia had four boys, and Uncle Neli two boys and two girls. All four of Tresa's children were married and their patrimony equally divided between them. Uncle Neli still had one daughter living with him, but she too was of marriageable age.

To settle all these claims before the wedding, the two old people drew up papers with a notary, protecting their children's interests in case of death. They hoped in this way to dispel the antagonism which flared on both sides from the beginning, but in vain. Although Uncle Neli's children received the larger share —for the old man had stripped himself not only of his dead wife's possessions but of his own as well—they were the more bitter. He decided to work for a living as long as he could, and enjoy the produce of his second wife's land as well as that of his daughter Narda for whatever time she should continue to live with them.

His oldest daughter, Sidora, whose married name was Peronella, fairly frothed at the mouth with rage.

"May my tongue be eaten by worms if that old witch doesn't see to it that Narda stays a spinster! The son of the King himself could ask for her hand and she wouldn't find it a suitable match," she told her husband, her sisters-in-law and her brothers, Saru and Lazzu. She talked this way because she was convinced that Tresa Tumminia would never allow her husband to make his living on her property if he turned over all he had to Narda as a dowry.

Sidora snapped at the neighbors who came to tell her of all the nice things Aunt Tresa did for Narda. She could do no more for her own daughter, they said, showering her with gifts, gold earrings, a gold ring, a coral necklace, silk handkerchiefs for her head, a silk shawl with fringe four fingers wide, calf slippers with high lacquered heels—so many things, in fact, that it was all but incredible!

But Sidora would not be mollified. "Fools! Can't you see she's baiting her? She just wants to fatten her up and keep her there like that sow!"

But she stopped at last when they came to tell her that Narda was getting married. And what a match! All arranged by Aunt Tresa herself with Pitrinu Cinquemani, no less! A young man of pure gold, the brother-in-law of Tresa's oldest son, so big and handsome he stood out like a flag! Pitrinu Cinquemani, with all his property, houses and cattle!

"Ah, indeed!" Sidora sighed, determined not to give those gossips a chance to gloat over her. "Pitrinu Cinquemani? How nice for poor Narda."

Neither she nor her brothers had gone to see their sister since she had lived at her stepmother's, yet Saru's farm was no more than a gunshot away. So close was it, in fact, that from the side of his house, through the fig and almond trees, Saru could not only see the little roof of Aunt Tresa's courtyard shelter with its feeding trough for the animals but could count the chickens scratching there in the dung. They no longer wanted to hear anything more about Narda. By now she had been won over to her stepmother and to her half-brothers, who, never having had a sister, rivaled each other for her attention, showing their affection in every possible way.

The day before Narda's wedding, Uncle Neli went over to Saru's farm. Scowling and scratching the bristles on his cheeks, he spoke to his eldest son so he could relay the conversation to the others. Saru listened with his eyes cast down.

"These are lean years, my son, and we are all poor," he began. "God knows I would like to have all of you with me and make a big celebration for your sister Narda's wedding. But the bells of Raffadali's church chime a single refrain. They repeat, 'With what? With what? With what?' I've stripped myself of everything for you all until I'm as bare as Christ on the cross. I can do no more. I must keep things to a strict minimum, that's all. If the bride's family is invited, then Pitrinu Cinquemani will want to have his family, of course. After all, they are partly Tresa's family too, you know—and you've made bad blood between you. So we have decided not to invite either family. There will be just myself and Tresa for the bride, and the father and mother of the groom. The strict minimum—no more!"

Saru stood there and heard his father out with averted eyes, obviously thinking.

"Papa, take care!" Saru said finally. "You're the head of the family. We're of your blood and we'll do as you say. But make sure that we're not the only ones left out! I'm warning you, Papa; if we are, it will end badly!"

Without looking his son in the face, the old man stood there bathed in sweat and waited a moment longer, scratching his cheeks.

"As for me, my son, I've sent them word not to come just as I'm telling you not to come," he said. "What more can I do?"

"And if one of them should come?" asked his son.

The old man did not reply. His silence made it clear that if one of the others should come, he wouldn't know how to handle it.

"Very well, Papa," Saru said. "Go along. We'll think it over."

He followed his father with his eyes as Uncle Neli went off pulling at his left ear with two fingers. Then Saru went into his little house and drew a long knife—the kind known as a ham knife—from the bottom of a knapsack hanging on a nail. He picked up the whetstone off the floor under the table, wet the blade of the knife, and went to sit in the doorway with the stone between his knees. He began carefully to sharpen the knife.

His wife, terrified, called him three times without getting any reply.

"Holy Mother!" she implored him, clutching her hair, her eyes brimming with tears. "Saru *mio,* what do you intend to do?"

"In God's name!" cried Saru, leaping to his feet like a tiger and brandishing the knife, "Don't bother me, woman, or I'll begin with you!"

She threw her apron over her head to smother her tears and went to sit in a corner. Saru took up the stone again and slowly set to sharpening the knife under the eyes of his three young sons, who sat around him in silence. A cock crowed in Aunt Tresa's courtyard and was immediately answered by the rooster in their own yard, raising one foot and shaking its blood-red comb.

"One . . . two . . . three . . . four . . . five . . . six!"

Already six harnessed mules stood around the trough under the little roof of the courtyard shelter opposite. They stood out clearly in the moonlight, all six of them ranged neatly one beside the other.

From his doorway Saru counted them again, bending his head this way and that to see through the trees. He shuddered.

There were six already and maybe more to come. It would be a big banquet. All his stepmother's sons, their wives and children had been invited. Only they, the closest relatives, the brothers and sisters of the bride, were left out. Maybe right now they were feasting over there, and later on the music would begin, and the dancing.

He took off his jacket and placed it over his arm to hide the sharp knife. Inside the house, his wife and their oldest son, Niluzzu, trembled with fear as they spied on him, openmouthed. Earlier he had ordered his wife to light the fire and put the big cauldron on to boil. Numb with terror, she had obeyed, not daring to guess what he meant to do with all that boiling water.

"Holy Mother," she prayed, "send us your help! Oh, Holy Mother, cool his hot blood and soothe his wounded spirit!"

Outdoors in the bright moonlight crickets chirped softly—a long, thin thread of almost luminous sound.

"Niluzzu," Saru suddenly called to his son, "run to your Aunt Sidora and then to your Uncle Luzzu. Tell them to come right over, all of them. Understand? Now go."

But Niluzzu did not move. He stood there gazing at his father in terror, one arm raised over his head as if to ward off a blow.

"Papa, I'm frightened. Pa—"

"Frightened? Blockhead!" cried his father, shaking him. He

turned to his wife. "You go with him. And come back quickly, all of you together."

"But, Saru *mio,* what are you going to do, for pity's sake?" his wife ventured, tears in her voice.

Saru put a finger to his lips, then motioned imperiously to her to obey him.

Soon after, he began to move cautiously toward the farm opposite, taking cover from the bright moonlight first behind one tree, then another, until he reached the last fig tree right beside the courtyard. His heart beat wildly and his temples were pounding. It gave him a start when one of the mules standing by the trough snorte The hot, rich stench of manure rose to his nostrils, while from within came a confused sound of voices and laughter and the clattering of plates of those who were feasting in his stepmother's house. He poked his head through the branches of the fig tree to peer around. There were only the six mules in the courtyard and the gigantic sow lying over by the door. Stretched out there, her snout resting on her forefeet, her ears back and her eyes half closed, she seemed lost in languid contemplation under the soft light of the moon. Secure in the fullness of her bliss, she heaved a contented sigh from time to time.

Crouching low, Saru came up quietly behind the sow and, slowly reaching out his hand, began to scratch her head. Responding to her mistress' customary caress, the beast stretched, twisted up her snout in ecstasy and exposed her throat. Saru was ready with the other hand and soundlessly plunged his sharp knife in to the hilt.

Returning to his house dragging the immense carcass, Saru arrived almost at the same time as his wife, followed by the rest of his alarmed family.

"Sshh!" He motioned to them, gasping and panting, covered with blood from head to foot.

"We'll have a feast, too, right here, and a better one than theirs," he announced. "A quarter for Sidora, one for you, Luzzu, and two quarters for me—which I well deserve. But wait. First help me slit this beast open. Luzzu, take a firm hold there. You, Sidora, here. And you, Niluzzu, go fetch me a large plate, the round one from the closet. I want to send the liver to the old woman as a little surprise. Not a word from any of you! The liver goes to the old woman."

He drew the knife down the length of the carcass, deftly removed the liver, and ran to wash it in the bucket. Then he arranged it all shining, whole and quivering, on the plate and handed it to his son.

"Here, Niluzzu, go over to Grandpa's and say, 'Papa, Saru sent me with this present for Mama Tresa. And his greetings to the sow.' "

A MERE FORMALITY

In the spacious offices of the Orsani Bank, the old clerk, Carlo Bertone, wearing a skull cap and with glasses clamped to the tip of his nose as if to squeeze little tufts of gray hair from each nostril, leaned on his high desk and worked over a difficult computation in a big ledger. Pale, hollow-eyed, Gabriele Orsani stood watching the operation over his shoulder, spurring him on from time to time when Bertone seemed to despair of coming to the end of the ever-mounting sum.

"Wretched glasses," complained the old man, impatiently flipping them off his nose with one finger.

Gabriele Orsani laughed. "What good do those glasses do you, my poor Carlo? They won't make things any clearer."

Annoyed, Bertone picked up the ledger and said, "Allow me to go into the next room. With you carrying on in here I can't accomplish a thing. It takes peace and quiet."

"Bravo, Carlo," Orsani mocked. "Peace and quiet . . . with that maelstrom you have in your hands?" he said, pointing to the ledger.

He threw himself into an easy chair near the window and lit a cigarette.

The dark-blue curtains gave the room a restful half-light. They swelled occasionally with a light breeze from the sea. With the sudden glare of light, the noise of the surf could be heard breaking on the beach.

At the door, Bertone suggested that his chief receive an odd character who was waiting in the anteroom. Meanwhile, he would try to unravel the intricate account.

"Odd?" Gabriele repeated. "Who is he?"

"I don't know, but he has been waiting half an hour. Dr. Sarti sent him."

"Then show him in."

A small man around fifty, with gray hair waved and parted artfully down the middle, was ushered into the room. He looked like a puppet whose strings were controlled by invisible hands jerking his jointed limbs into bows and other comical gestures.

He had only one good eye, but seemed to think that, by wearing a monocle over the artificial eye, the defect would pass unnoticed.

He handed Orsani his visiting card:

LAPO VANNETI
Inspector
London Life Assurance Company, Ltd.
Subscribed Capital £4,500,000—Paid-in Capital £2,559,400

"Mozt exzellent zir," he began, and after that there was no stopping him.

Just as he used a monocle to disguise his glass eye, so he brought out an odd little laugh after every unfortunate "z" to hide the defect in his speech.

Orsani tried to interrupt him several times, but to no avail.

"While pazzing through thiz highly ezteemed provinze," the undaunted little man went on with rambling eloquence, "thankz to the meritz of our company, the oldezt, most reliable of itz kind, I have clozed a number of exzellent contractz covering all the zpecial combinations offered to our clientz, not to mention the exzeptional advantagez which I will briefly zum up for you . . ."

Gabriele Orsani felt limp; Signor Vannetti did all the talking, putting the questions and giving the answers himself, raising doubts only to swoop them aside.

"Mozt kind zir, I know you might object and zay to me, Yes, dear Vannetti, of course I have every confidenze in your company, but what can I do? (Zuppozition). The rate is too zteep, or I haven't that much extra cash in the bank (everyone knows hiz own affairz bezt). My dear Vannetti, you might zay, there is nothing to dizcuss. But here, most kind zir, I will take the liberty of pointing out the zpecial advantagez our company haz to offer. Ah, I know, you zay—all the companiez offer them more or lezz. No, no, excuze me, Signore, if I dare queztion your ztatement. The advantagez . . ."

Orsani, seeing him pull a batch of printed matter out of his briefcase, held up his hand as if to defend himself.

"Excuse me," he said hurriedly, "but I read something somewhere about a company insuring the hands of a famous violinist for I don't know how much. Is that right?"

Signor Vannetti was momentarily taken aback, then he smiled. "American nonzenze. We, of courze . . ."

"I asked you," Gabriele rushed in quickly, "because I also used to . . ." And he resorted to the pantomime of playing a violin.

Completely disconcerted, Vannetti seemed to think that congratulations were in order.

"Wonderful . . . wonderful . . . but really we don't go in for that kind of buzinezz."

"It's an idea, nevertheless." Orsani sighed, rising to his feet. "You might insure everything subject to loss or damage over an average lifetime—hair and teeth, for instance. And what about the head! One so easily loses one's head. As the violinist insured his hands, so a dandy might insure his hair, a sportsman his teeth, a businessman his head. Think it over. It has possibilities."

Crossing the room, he now pressed a button on the wall near his desk, adding, "Please excuse me for a moment."

Embarrassed, Vannetti bowed. He imagined that, in order to get rid of him, Orsani had made a most unkind allusion to his glass eye.

Bertone answered the bell, entering the room with a bewildered look.

"In the filing cabinet on your desk, under the letter S . . ." Gabriele began.

"The sulphur-mine report?" asked Bertone.

"The last report, after we built the shaft with the ramp . . ."

"That has already been taken into account," said Bertone, nodding.

Worried and frowning, Gabriele sought the old man's eyes and asked, "Well, what then?"

Bertone, ill at ease, looked at Vannetti, who at last realized his presence was an intrusion and ceremoniously begged to be excused: "With me, a zuggeztion iz enough: I catch on right away. I wizdraw. That iz, I mean, with your permizzion I will go negzt door for a little znack, then I'll come back. Pleaze don't dizturb yourzelvez. I know the way. Goodbye!"

With another jerky little bow, he went out.

II

"Well?" Gabriele Orsani repeated as soon as Vannetti had gone.

"The expense of that last construction job, coming just when it did," Bertone said hesitantly.

Gabriele flew into a rage.

"God alone knows how many times you have said the same thing! What else was there for me to do? Cancel the contract? For my creditors, that mine represents my last hope of solvency— I know it. And I know better than you that a hundred and thirty thousand lire have been sunk there without a cent of return. Don't make me shout!"

Bertone pressed his hands over his tired eyes a moment. Flicking imaginary dust from his sleeve, he said softly, almost to himself, "If only there were a way to get hold of enough money to set the machinery in motion—the machinery we still have to pay for. Then there are the notes about to fall due at the bank . . ."

Pacing back and forth, his hands in his pockets, Orsani frowned and stopped. "How much, all in all?"

"Ah . . ." Bertone sighed.

"*Ah!*" mimicked Gabriele, furiously. "Give me a round figure! Tell me frankly—is this the end? Am I ruined? Praised be the blessed memory of my father! He pushed me into this and I did as he wished. Let's wipe the slate clean and say no more about it."

"Don't give up now," pleaded Bertone. "Of course, the way things look at the moment . . . but let me explain."

Gabriele put his hands on the old clerk's shoulders. "What can you explain, my good friend? You're trembling all over. Now is not the time to get upset. You should have opposed my plans from the very beginning, with all the authority of your years of service. You knew how unfitted I was for this business and you should have advised me. Why do you put me off like this? I feel sorry for both of us."

"What could I have done?" Bertone asked, tears in his eyes.

"Nothing," replied Orsani. "And neither could I, but I must put the blame on someone. Don't mind what I say. How has all this happened? How have I let myself be trapped here, in this business? I still don't know what my mistakes were—apart from building that shaft where I floundered like a drowning man. What other mistakes did I make?"

Bertone shrugged, closed his eyes and raised his hands as if to say: What's the use of talking? "Better try to find a way out," he said tearfully.

Again Gabriele laughed. "A way out? What can I do? Take up the violin I used to play before my father wished this fine business on me? Go from door to door like a blind man, a beggar, to earn my children's bread? Is that what you suggest?"

"If I may say so," Bertone ventured, "all in all, if we manage to meet the payments as they fall due, and cut down on everything—excuse me, your household expenses included—I think that for the next four or five months, at least, we can swing it. Meantime . . ."

"*Meantime* is a word that can no longer deceive me," Orsani said sadly, shaking his head.

Bertone insisted that it could be done and started out of the office to finish the work on his balance sheet.

"I will show you just where we stand in a moment," he said over his shoulder.

Gabriele again slumped into the easy chair by the window. He clasped his hands behind his neck and started to think.

No one suspected the gravity of the situation as yet, although he himself had no more illusions. A few more months of desperate expedients and then the inevitable crash would come.

For almost three weeks now he had stayed in the office, as if there he might stumble across a solution in one of the pigeonholes of his desk or hidden away in one of the ledgers. Little by little his violent tension had relaxed, his will had weakened and he now found his thoughts drifting away from this relentless torture.

He deplored his blind, spiritless obedience to his father's wishes which had cut short his studies of mathematics and music to plunge him into the maze of business. He still resented the wrench he had felt on leaving Rome to return to Sicily, bringing with him a doctor's degree in physics and mathematics, a violin, and a nightingale. Ah, blissful self-delusion! He had fancied he could study in his spare time. Only once, three months after his return, had he taken his violin from its case, and then it was to enclose the embalmed remains of his dead nightingale in what he considered a fitting sepulcher.

He never understood why his father, so able himself, should fail to recognize how unsuited he was for business. Perhaps his reasoning had been clouded by a desire to carry on the old Orsani name in its established milieu, and he had been led to believe that, with time and the inducements of wealth, his son would adjust to this new life and grow to like it.

How could he blame his father now when he himself had never raised the slightest objection, accepting everything as though it were a pact concluded at his birth, the conditions of which were never to be reviewed? And then, to avoid the temptations of the very different life which had been his dream, he had agreed to marry the girl long destined for him—his orphaned cousin, Flavia.

Like all the women of this accursed region where the men, enmeshed in the intricacies of endless, risky business ventures, never found any leisure to dedicate to love, Flavia took up the modest role of housekeeper without bitterness, as if this were understood between them. When he came home exhausted from the mines, or the bank, or the beach where he sometimes spent the whole day under the hot sun supervising the loading of sulphur, she saw to it that he had every material comfort.

Before he had time to understand the business, his father suddenly died, leaving him to head the firm. Alone, without a mentor, he hoped for a while to sell everything and retire early. But it was not so simple. All the capital was tied up in the sulphur mines. He had to follow along in the groove and chose as his guide good old Bertone, whom his father before him had trusted implicitly.

He felt utterly confused by the weight of responsibility suddenly dumped on his shoulders, a weight rendered even more unwieldy by the fact that the future of his three children was at stake. Never before had he felt so like a blindfolded animal hitched to a bar, turning a millstone round and round.

Embittered by regrets over the life he might have had, he saw his wife and children as the living destruction of his ideal. His heart was burdened with resentment that found no release. Flavia, seeing him sad, brooding, silent, assumed that he was obsessed by business worries. She had never tried to draw close to him, wounded perhaps by his neglect of her, and she dared not remonstrate now with a man so beset by overwhelming responsibilities.

Some evenings he watched her leaning over the balustrade of the large terrace, looking at the sea as it slapped against the wall below. It was as if she stood on the quarter-deck of a ship gazing off into the star-studded night, a night filled with the restless movement of that vast stretch of water. At times, the deep, hoarse whistle of a ship weighing anchor came up to them from the harbor. What was she thinking? Did the moan of the sea convey to her any obscure forebodings?

It never occurred to him to disturb her, convinced as he was that she could never enter his world. His eyes slowly filled with silent tears. Would it continue like this until death, with no hope of change? On such gloomy evenings his emotion was so intense that the static condition of his existence seemed intolerable to him. Sudden mad impulses flashed across his mind. With only one life to live, how was a man to continue along the same unhappy path forever? The thought of others eking out harder, more materially ungrateful lives did not soothe his sorrow.

He was sometimes brought back to himself by the familiar cry of one of his children. Flavia would stir too, but it was he who would jump up, saying, "I'll go." He would pick up the child from its crib and, cradling it in his arms, walk up and down the room, quieting his own grief as well as the baby's unrest. After putting the child to sleep, he would stand for a moment by the window, looking up at the brightest star.

Nine years had passed like that. At the beginning of this year, just when his financial position took a turn for the worse, Flavia grew extravagant. She even asked for a carriage of her own and he had not known how to refuse her. Now, here was Bertone pressing him to cut down all expenses, even those at home!

On the other hand, Dr. Sarti, his closest friend, had recommended a change for Flavia to counteract the nervous depression brought on, it seemed, by her monotonous life. Gabriele rose and began to pace back and forth, thinking of Lucio Sarti with mixed feelings of envy and scorn.

They had been students together in Rome. At that time, it would have been impossible for either of them to get through the day without seeing the other. Until recently, this bond had remained unchanged. But during the illness of one of his children, Sarti's concern for Flavia appeared excessive to Gabriele. It was no more than an impression because he had complete confidence in the loyalty of his friend and of his wife.

However, there was no denying that Flavia now agreed with whatever the doctor said. Lately she had taken to nodding her head when Sarti spoke—she who, as a rule, never opened her mouth about anything to him. He was annoyed. If she approved of such ideas, why hadn't she spoken out before? Why had she never discussed the children's education with him if she shared the doctor's more rigid opinions in preference to his own? He even accused her inwardly of not loving the children. What other conclusion could he draw if she disagreed with him and yet said nothing until a third person put her views into words?

For that matter, Sarti had no right to meddle. Gabriele thought that for sometime now his friend seemed to forget certain things—for instance that all, or almost all, he had was thanks to him.

Who, if not he, had extricated Sarti from the squalor in which he was born? Sarti's father, convicted of robbery, had died in jail. Then, when the boy was old enough to understand how his mother made her living, he ran away. Gabriele had found him working as a waiter in a third-rate coffee house, and it was he who had wheedled a small job for him in his father's bank. He lent him his own books and classroom notes to study. It was solely through Gabriele's help that Sarti had been able to make a career. Gifted and a hard worker, Sarti had built up a secure position for himself without having to renounce his own dreams. Sarti was a man, while he—he now stood on the brink of disaster.

Two knocks on the door which led from the office to his private apartments now interrupted his thoughts.

"Come in," he said.

Flavia entered.

III

Her lovely figure was enhanced by a navy-blue dress which set off her blond beauty, and on her head she wore a smart but simple dark hat. She was buttoning her gloves.

"I wanted to ask," she said, "if you were going to use your carriage, because the bay cannot be hitched to mine today."

Gabriele looked at her, as lovely and flowerlike as if she had stepped out of a misty dream world whose language was unintelligible to him.

"What?" he asked. "Why?"

"It seems the poor thing has picked up a nail. He limps."

"Who?"

"The bay. Didn't you hear?"

"Ah," said Gabriele, rousing himself. "Too bad!"

"I'm not playing for sympathy," Flavia said resentfully. "I was just asking for your carriage. I'll walk."

And she started to leave.

"Please take it. I have no need for it," Gabriele hurried to say. "Are you going alone?"

"With Carlo. Aldo and Tina are being punished."

"Poor little things." Gabriele sighed, almost unaware that he had spoken.

Flavia mistook his tenderness for reproof and asked him please to leave those decisions up to her.

"Of course, if they were naughty," he said, "they should be punished. I was only thinking that, through no fault of theirs, a much greater punishment will be meted out to them before long."

Flavia turned to look at him. "And what may that be?"

"Nothing, dear. Nothing heavier than your veil or one of the plumes on your hat. Ruin, that's all!"

"Ruin?"

"Poverty, yes—and possibly even worse for me."

"What are you talking about?"

"Does it surprise you?"

Flavia, deeply troubled, came up to him and fixed her eyes on his as if she doubted his seriousness.

With a smile, Gabriele answered her halting questions calmly, gently, as though it no longer concerned him, until he noticed how upset she was.

"Ah, my dear!" he exclaimed. "If, in all these years, you had paid the slightest attention to me, if you had tried to understand how little pleasure this hypothetical business gave me, you would not be so shocked now. There is a limit to what a man can do, and when he is forced beyond his capacities—"

"*Forced!* Who forced you?" Flavia interrupted, noting the emphasis he had put on the word.

Gabriele looked at his wife as though her interruption and the defiance with which she now faced him were confusing. He felt a bitter taste rise in his throat and his mouth went dry. Opening his lips in a grotesque exaggeration of the same nervous smile, he asked, "Did you think it was spontaneous?"

"I never forced you," Flavia shot back. "If it was for me, you might have spared yourself the sacrifice. I would have preferred a thousand times the most abject poverty—"

"Don't!" he cried, beside himself. "Don't say it. Since you can't know what you are talking about . . ."

"Poverty? What have I had out of life?"

"*You?* How about me?"

They faced each other, trembling with anger, almost frightened by their deep-rooted hatred which now flared up after smoldering in secret for so long.

"Why blame me?" cried Flavia. "If, as you say, I paid no attention to you, when did you ever pay any attention to me? You throw your sacrifice in my teeth, as if *I* hadn't been sacrificed, condemned to atone for the dream-life you gave up. Was this the life I was meant to have? Had I no right to dream of a different life? Who made you love me? Me, the chain that bound you to forced labor. Can anyone love a chain? Meanwhile, I was supposed to be content with your work and not expect anything more from you. I have never complained, but now you provoke me!"

Gabriele buried his face in his hands, repeating, "This too, this too . . . Next," he broke out, "my children will throw my sacrifice in my face like a useless rag."

"You distort everything I say," she answered with a shrug.

"No . . . no," Gabriele went on with biting sarcasm. "I deserve no other recognition. Call them! I've ruined them and they have a right to accuse me."

"No!" said Flavia, softening at the thought of her children. "Poor little things, why should they blame you?" Then with fluttering hands she cried, "How will they ever make out, brought up as they have been?"

"How?" snapped Gabriele. "Without a father's guidance, you mean? That's another thing they can taunt me with. Go and prompt them! And to cap it all, Lucio Sarti will blame me."

"What has Lucio Sarti to do with it?" said Flavia, stunned by his last remark.

"You repeat every word he says," Gabriele went on, very pale.

"All you need to do is to put his thick-lensed glasses on your nose."

Flavia drew a long sigh and, half closing her eyes, said with undisguised scorn, "Anyone who has ever known us as a family could see—"

"Only he," Gabriele interrupted with increasing violence. "He alone! He grew up knowing how to take care of himself because his father . . ."

He stopped, regretting his words, and then continued: "I don't hold it against him, but it explains why he lives as he does —apprehensive, austere, mindful of every little thing, hoping people will forget the stigma of his parents. But why should I be a tyrant to my children?"

"Who said anything about your being a tyrant?" Flavia tried to cut in.

"Free . . ." he said. "I wanted my children to grow up free, since I was condemned to this torment by my father. As a reward, I promised myself the joy of seeing them free—the only reward I asked for my wasted life. All in vain . . . now."

Sobbing convulsively, he broke off and, raising his trembling arms, sank unconscious to the floor.

Terrified, Flavia called for help. Bertone and another clerk ran in from the bank. They lifted Gabriele to a couch, and Flavia, seeing the deathly pallor of his damp face, began raving incoherently: "What's the matter with him? Oh God, help me! Help! It's all my fault. It's all my fault!"

The clerk ran to call Dr. Sarti, who lived nearby.

"It's my fault . . . it's my fault," moaned Flavia.

"No, Signora," Bertone said, gently supporting Gabriele's head. "Since this morning—actually for some time now . . . Poor boy . . . if you could only know . . ."

"I know. I know . . ."

"Then what did you expect? It was bound to happen."

What could she do? Bathe his temples? Yes, perhaps a little ether. Flavia rang a bell and the butler entered.

"Ether. Get a small bottle of ether. Be quick."

"What a blow! Poor boy," Bertone murmured bitterly to himself, gazing through his tears at Orsani's face.

"Are we actually ruined?" Flavia asked him.

"If he had only listened to me," sighed the old clerk. "But he was never cut out for this business."

The butler hurried in with a bottle of ether.

"A little on a handkerchief?"

"No, it's better right from the bottle. Here," said Bertone. "Put your finger like this and let him breathe it in slowly."

Lucio Sarti rushed in all out of breath, followed by the clerk. Tall, his stern expression hardening the beauty of his fine, almost feminine features, Sarti wore spectacles very close to his myopic eyes. He hardly noticed Flavia's presence, brushing past her to the side of the sick man.

"Please, let me examine him," he said, turning to Flavia. "Don't carry on like that."

Opening Gabriele's shirt, he pressed his ear to the heart. After listening for a moment, he stood up and felt carefully over the entire chest as if he were searching for something.

"Well?" asked Flavia.

Taking up his stethoscope, he asked, "Is there any caffein in the house?"

"No . . . I don't know . . ." Flavia said. "I have some ether."

"That's no good."

He went over to the desk and wrote out a prescription, handing it to the clerk.

"Here. And hurry."

Then he also sent Bertone to the pharmacy for an injection syringe which he had forgotten to bring with him.

"Doctor," implored Flavia.

But Sarti ignored her and went back to the couch. Before auscultating the patient, he gave orders without looking around: "Make arrangements for him to be moved upstairs."

"Go . . . go . . ." Flavia told the butler.

The man had hardly closed the door before she grasped Sarti by the arm and pleaded, looking him in the eye, "What is wrong? Is it serious? I must know."

"I don't know myself yet," Sarti replied with enforced calm.

He placed the stethoscope on Gabriele's chest and bent down

to listen, closing his eyes, his face contracted as if to shut out any distracting thoughts.

At one time, he had set his heart on Flavia Orsani, who had been taken in by her uncle when she was orphaned. He did not know then how rich she was nor that her father, at his death, had entrusted her inheritance to his brother. Sarti had worked hard to overcome the memory of his parents' disgrace, and had counted on Flavia's sympathy as well as the affection which the Orsani family had always shown him. But soon after he returned to Sicily with his doctor's diploma and established himself in the community, Flavia became Gabriele's wife. Gabriele, in all the time they had spent together in Rome, had never given him the slightest intimation that he was in love with his cousin, but nevertheless he had taken her from Sarti without either making her happy or himself. It was a tragedy for all three of them.

Over the years, as if nothing had happened, he attended Gabriele's growing family as a doctor, trying to hide the distress he suffered every time he entered that loveless household. He sensed the wealth of affection locked in Flavia's heart which Gabriele, neglecting her as he did, probably never even suspected, and the fact that the children were left to grow up without a father's guidance. He wondered if Flavia had ever known he loved her. The answer came during a moment of supreme anguish when one of the children was critically ill. Painfully alone, almost delirious in her anxiety, Flavia had turned to him and opened her heart, saying she had always, always understood, right from the beginning.

And now, at this moment, with Gabriele unconscious before them, she turned to him. "I beseech you to tell me," Flavia insisted, unable to bear the suspense any longer. "Is it serious?"

"Yes," he said briefly.

"Is it his heart? It happened so quickly. Please explain."

"What good would that do? You do not understand the scientific terms."

But she was not content until he explained them.

"Then, is there no hope?" she asked.

He removed his glasses, blinking his eyes. "I would never have

had it happen like this, believe me. I wish that I might give my
own life to save his."

Flavia turned pale. She stared at her husband and made Sarti
a sign to be quiet.

"I would like to say so many things," he went on, unheeding,
"but then you understand me so well already, don't you? You
know I will do everything I can, without thinking of myself
or of you."

"Hush!" she said, terrified.

"Trust me! Why should we reproach ourselves? He never suspected the harm he did us, and he will never know. I will give
him all the care a devoted friend . . ."

Breathless, trembling, Flavia could not take her eyes off her
husband.

"He has come around," she said.

Sarti turned to look at him. "No."

"Yes, he moved," she said softly.

They hung there a moment in suspense, eying him. The doctor bent down to take the patient's pulse and called to him:
"Gabriele . . . Gabriele."

IV

Ashen and weary from the effort of holding himself in check for
so long, Gabriele opened his eyes and asked his wife to leave
the room.

"I'm all right now. Take the carriage and go for a drive," he
said to reassure her. "I want to talk with Lucio. Go!"

Flavia did not wish him to suspect the seriousness of his illness, so she accepted his suggestion, urging him, however, to keep
as quiet as he could. Then she said goodbye to the doctor and
went out.

After staring at the door through which she had disappeared,
Gabriele put his hand to his chest and asked, "Is it the heart?
During the auscultation, a funny thing happened. It seemed to
me that that little man—what's his name, Lapo?—yes, that little
man with the glass eye had tied me up and I couldn't free my

self. You laughed and said, 'Failure—' wasn't that it?—'failure of the aortic valve'?"

Sarti blanched when he heard him repeat the technical term he had explained to Flavia.

Gabriele smiled. "I heard you, you know."

"What . . . exactly what did you hear?" Sarti asked, a painful smile on his lips as he struggled to control himself.

"What you said to my wife," Gabriele replied calmly, staring before him with sightless eyes. "I saw . . . it seems I could see through closed lids. Tell me, please, without beating around the bush, without any silly lies—how long do I have to live? The less, the better."

Sarti observed him, astonished and frightened, especially by his extraordinary calm.

"What has come over you?" he asked.

"An inspiration!" Gabriele exclaimed, his eyes flashing. "Ah . . . by God!"

He pulled himself up and went over to the door leading in to the bank where he buzzed for Bertone.

"Listen, Carlo," he said as the clerk appeared. "If that little man who was here this morning should come back, have him wait. Better still, send someone or go find him yourself right away. He said he was going to the café next door."

He closed the door and turned to Sarti, rubbing his hands together as if in gratification.

"You sent him! Now I'm going to grab him by that wavy hair of his and plant him between us. I want to take out some insurance. Tell me just how to go about it. You are the company doctor, aren't you?"

Tortured by doubt as to how much Orsani had overheard, Lucio Sarti was taken aback by his sudden decision, which did not seem to make any sense. For the moment he felt relieved.

"What foolishness!" he exclaimed.

"Why?" Gabriele replied quickly. "I can pay the premiums for three or four months anyway. I know I won't live longer than that."

"You *know?*" said Sarti, forcing a laugh. "And who set this inflexible time limit? Go along with you!"

Somewhat reassured, he thought it was just a subterfuge to find out the truth about his condition. But Gabriele was quite serious and began to talk about his inevitable financial ruin. Sarti turned cold. He now saw that this sudden decision had a reason behind it and he felt cornered. Having sent the inspector to Orsani that morning, how could he in all conscience fail to approve Gabriele's application without betraying the gravity of the illness which had struck him so suddenly?

"But you can live a very long time, my friend, if you take the necessary precautions," said the doctor.

"Precautions? How?" Gabriele cried. "I've lost everything, I tell you! You still insist I can live a long life? So much the better. If that is true, there is no moral difficulty for you to approve."

"How about your own calculations?" asked Sarti, suddenly remembering what Gabriele had said. "If you can afford to honor the premiums only for the next three or four months . . . ?"

Gabriele thought for a moment. "Take care, Lucio. Don't deceive me. Don't raise this question to try to dissuade me from an action of which you don't approve, something you don't want to be implicated in—although it would involve little or no responsibility on your part."

"There you are mistaken!" Sarti said before he could check himself.

Gabriele smiled bitterly. "Then it's true," he said. "Then you know I'm doomed, perhaps even before the time I've allowed. I heard you, you know. It's all a question now of trying to save something for the children. And I mean to provide for them! Don't worry, if there's any mistake in the timing, I'll know how to die, and no one will be any the wiser."

Lucio Sarti rose, shrugging his shoulders, and glanced around for his hat.

"Since you won't listen to reason," he said, "allow me to leave."

"Reason?" cried Gabriele, grasping him by the arm. "Come here! I tell you I'm going to provide for my children, understand?"

"But how do you mean to provide for them? Do you seriously think you can do it this way?"

"By my death."

"Nonsense! Excuse me, but do you expect me, as your doctor, to stand here and listen to such talk?"

"Yes," said Gabriele violently, still holding him by the arm, "because you are going to help me."

"To kill yourself?" asked Sarti wrathfully.

"No. That, if necessary, will be my concern."

"What, then? Cheat. Steal?

"Steal? Steal from whom? We are dealing with a company which exposes itself to such risks. Don't interrupt. What they lose on me they gain from a hundred others. But call it stealing—it is still my concern, not yours. I'll make it straight with God. You don't enter into it!"

"You're mistaken," Sarti repeated emphatically.

"Will you benefit from this money?" Gabriele asked, staring pointedly at him. "It will be paid to my wife and three children. So what risk is there for you?"

Under Orsani's look, Lucio Sarti realized that his friend had really heard everything he had said to Flavia. Gabriele was now only controlling himself to accomplish his purpose, to place an insurmountable obstacle between his friend and his wife by making Sarti an accomplice to this fraud. Acting for the insurance company, he could not declare Gabriele in good health today and hope to marry Flavia if she was the beneficiary of this insurance. The company would most certainly suspect him. But why this intense hatred even beyond the grave? The things he had overheard should prove beyond a doubt that he had nothing with which to reproach either of them. What was the reason, then?

Sustaining Orsani's look, he determined to defend himself until the very last, but his voice wavered when he asked, "What risk do you mean?"

"Wait," said Gabriele abruptly, as though surprised by his own perception. "Don't forget I was your friend long before you became associated with this company. Wasn't I?"

"Of course . . . but . . ." Lucio stammered.

"Don't worry. I'm not going to throw anything up to you. I'm only trying to point out that you are not putting *me* first at this moment, but the company."

"But fraud . . ." said Sarti heavily.

"So many doctors make mistakes," Gabriele retorted. "Who can accuse you of anything? Who can say at this moment that I'm not perfectly fit? I'm the picture of health. I may die in five or six months, but what doctor could foresee that? In any case, so far as you and your conscience are concerned, you are duty-bound, as my friend, to deceive me."

Crushed, his head bowed, Sarti took off his glasses and rubbed his eyes; then, in a trembling voice, he tried to make a last stand.

"I would prefer to find another way to accomplish what you call dutifully deceiving you."

"How?"

"Do you remember where and how my father died?"

Gabriele stared at him, bewildered, whispering to himself, "What's that got to do with it?"

"You are not in my position, so you cannot judge," Sarti went on, replacing his glasses, his jaw set. "Remember how I grew up and allow me to act decently now, with no regrets."

"I do not understand" said Gabriele coldly, "what regrets you could possibly have in insuring my children's future."

"At the expense of others?"

"I have no such intentions."

"But you know that will be the result."

"I know something else which means far more to me and should to you. There is no other way. Because of this scruple of yours which I cannot share, you would have me refuse an opportunity which you have laid at my door."

He went over to the door to listen, making a sign to Sarti to be quiet.

"There, he's come in."

"No. It's useless, Gabriele," Sarti cried in desperation. "Don't force me."

Orsani once more seized his arm. "Mind you, Lucio! This is my only chance of saving myself."

"Not this way, ' protested Sarti. "Listen, Gabriele: by all that's sacred I promise that your children . . ."

"Charity?" he sneered.

"No," Lucio replied quickly. "I will only be repaying you what you have given me."

"By what right? How could you provide for my children? You? They have a mother. By what right? It's not only gratitude, is it? You lie! You refuse for another reason which you dare not admit!"

As he spoke he took Sarti by the shoulders and shook him, commanding him at the same time to lower his voice and asking how far his deceit had gone. Sarti, refusing to submit to violence, tried to free himself, to defend himself and Flavia.

"We'll see," Orsani said between clenched teeth.

He went to the door and called Vannetti in, masking his agitation with enforced gaiety.

"A prize!" he cried as he returned with the ceremonious little man. "A big prize for our friend, Dr. Sarti, the company's most eloquent advocate. I was about to give up the idea, put it out of my mind, but he convinced me. He overcame *all* my doubts. Hand him the medical declaration to sign immediately. He is in a hurry. He has to leave. Then we'll work out the whys and wherefores between ourselves." And he clapped him on the back.

Vannetti, delighted, took a printed form out of his briefcase and handed it to Gabriele in a burst of congratulations, repeating, "A mere formality . . . a mere formality."

"Here, sign this," commanded Gabriele, putting the form down in front of Sarti, who looked as if he were in a trance, his eyes riveted to the ridiculous, jerky little man—the personification of his unlucky fate.

Tales of
Humor and Irony

WATCH AND WARD

'Are you all here? Anyone missing?" San Romè asked, leaning out a low window of the charming blue villa with its turrets and balconies of sculptured marble.

"All here," they chorused from the green lawn still wet and glistening with dew. The vacationers were buoyant after their walk uphill from the neighboring town of Sarli in the cool of the early morning.

"Pepi did not come," someone sang out.

"Oh, he's the dish that ran away with the spoon," said the General's wife, opening the folding stool she carried with her.

They all laughed, not so much at her quip as at the broadside view of her enormous derriere as she bent down to adjust the stool on the uneven lawn.

"Why didn't Pepi come?"

"Headache. When I went over to wake him," Biagio Casoli replied, "he said he thought he had a little fever, too."

At this, the young girls immediately started to whisper. San Romè could see it all from the window and bit his lip as he caught Tani, the little snake, winking at Bongi.

They asked him to hurry up. Having risen before dawn in order to make the slow climb to Gori, they were impatient to set out for Roccia Balda—a good three hours' walk—before the sun was too high.

"I'll be down in a moment; Dora must be ready by now," he said as he left the window.

He ran upstairs and rapped on the door of his sister-in-law's room. She was stretched out on a chaise-longue in her white dressing gown, looking for all the world like Beatrice Cenci, with her beautiful blond head bound in a large, wet towel.

"What!" he exclaimed. "You're not ready yet! They're all waiting out on the lawn."

"I'm sorry," Dora said, her eyes half closed, "but I can't come."

"What!" he repeated. "Why not? What's the matter?"

"Can't you see?" she said, lifting a listless hand to her head with a sigh. "I have *such* a headache I can barely stand."

"You too!" he exploded, pale with rage. "You haven't a little fever too, by any chance? Quite a coincidence. Signor Pepi . . ."

"What has Pepi to do with it?" she asked, frowning.

"Headache. He has such a bad headache he couldn't come." San Romè informed her with emphasis, "Take care, Dora! His sudden illness has already been commented on downstairs. I beg you not to give their idle tongues something to wag about."

Dora crossed her beautiful hands, covered with rings, over her head, allowing the full sleeves of her robe to slip back.

"I don't understand," she said with an imperceptible smile. "Isn't one permitted to have a headache in your house?"

"*Our* house," San Romè began angrily, but controlled himself and changed his tone. "Come now, Dora, please get up and stop this play-acting. You're keeping all those people waiting, and I warn you I'm about at the end of my patience."

Dora burst out laughing. Holding the towel around her head with one hand, she got up and came over to him.

"Not even my husband would talk to me in that tone of voice," she said. "Did he leave instructions I was to obey you to the letter? Dear Warden, dear Guardian, dear Mr. Policeman, I really have a headache. Now let it go at that!"

She went into the next room, slammed the door behind her and shot the bolt, sending him a final peal of laughter.

Instinctively Roberto San Romè had taken a step forward as if to stop her, but now stood stock-still before the closed door with a hand to his cheek, as if he had been slapped by her laughter. The impression was so real that it infuriated him. All of a sudden, he realized what a ridiculous role he had been playing for the last three months—ever since his brother had left his young wife in Gori and returned to Milan, supposedly, to attend to some unfinished business.

He had done everything to make her stay in the little Alpine village a pleasant one. Almost every morning he took her to Sarli, where there were more summer people, and he had arranged parties, excursions and picnics for her amusement. At first his sophisticated, capricious little sister-in-law was bored and plainly showed it. She wrote her husband many times that she had had more than enough of Gori and would he please come for her immediately. But Cesare was having a good time in Milan and did not even bother to answer her on this score. Out of spite, then, she had taken up with Signor Pepi, who flirted with her outrageously.

That had been the beginning of San Romè's torment. What duty could be more absurd than looking after a sister-in-law who seemed to do things on purpose to arouse his suspicions? At his wits' end, he was often on the verge of shouting, "Dora, one of these days I'll poke that turtledove of yours right in the jaw! If you don't believe me, I'm ready to prove it!"

But he knew his anger made her smile all the more impudently. She had a way of smiling that cut like a knife and showed only too clearly how foolish she considered his constant watchfulness.

He flattered himself that, thanks to his tact and *savoir-faire,* he had headed off a scandal. But, given his sister-in-law's temperament, he was never quite sure but that his vigilance had not made things worse. He gave her to understand that he was on to everything, that he could tell from what she said, from the way she looked or acted, whether she had seen Pepi or not. She appeared to accept the challenge behind his dark, determined glance and armed herself with that maddening laugh of hers, refusing to admit that he had the slightest authority over her. For example, one morning all alone she left the cottage at a very early hour, obliging him to run all over the place like a bloodhound until he found her in the chestnut grove halfway between Sarli and Gori. Alone, yes; he always found her alone. But more than once he thought he saw Pepi at night through the slats of the venetian blinds—Pepi there, outside the villa in Gori; Pepi, who was summering down in Sarli.

Until today probably nothing serious had happened. But now, in spite of all his precautions, he had to admit he was trapped. It was perfectly clear that the two of them had an understanding. But it was too late now for him to pull out, having proposed the trip to Roccia Balda in the first place, and having already sent the lunch on ahead for the whole party. Besides, they all might have taken an easier, more direct route from Sarli had they not wanted to go out of their way to pick up Dora and himself. What excuse could he find to back out at this point? It couldn't be done. Ah, his poor brother!

And how could he bring himself to tell those people out there that Dora, like Pepi in Sarli, had a headache? As a last resort, he decided to ask the ladies to persuade Dora to join them. But at this announcement, he was showered with questions: "Why? What is the matter? Doesn't she feel well? Really, poor little thing! What could be the matter? Since when? What ails her?"

He was careful not to mention what ailed Dora, but she told them herself a few minutes later and added deliberately, "I'm afraid I have a little fever too."

San Romè had an impulse to send her flying through the window. It would have done his heart good to unleash all the accumulated irritation of the last three months.

"Fever . . . really, my dear?" said the General's wife, as if she believed the story of a headache. "Let me feel your pulse—very fast, very fast. You need rest, dear. It's probably nothing but a little cold coming on."

They advised this and they advised that—she should be very careful that it didn't get any worse. Poor Dora! Dear Dora! Those hypocrites whom he had counted on for help gave him a pain with their loving ministrations.

"She looks a little pale," they said. "The fever shows in her eyes. A little rest will do her good. Too bad, too bad. Roccia Balda is much too far. She could never walk all that distance."

Kisses, reassurances, admonitions, goodbyes. They took their leave regretfully, as it was getting late, and carried off dear, good San Romè, who had had the bright idea of this delightful outing in the first place.

Nor did they let it drop there. Crossing the meadows, bordered by tall poplars, which lay beyond the last group of houses on the outskirts of Gori, they noticed San Romè's pallor and silence, and vied with one another in urging him not to take it so hard. To the accompaniment of the sound of water coursing through ditches and gullies, they chattered on, assuring him that Dora was only slightly indisposed and would soon be well. The poor man had to smile, bravely telling those good, dear ladies that he wasn't in the least worried about his sister-in-law, that in fact he was most happy to find himself in such pleasant company for the whole day!

With that clear sky, there was no danger that a sudden downpour would break up the party. Nor was there any probability of freeing himself before evening—not when that doughty Signor Bortolo Raspi of Sarli, who weighed no less than two hundred and fifty pounds, was busy boasting what a great walker he was! He was beginning to wheeze, though, and was quick to second the General's wife, still carrying her folding stool, when she declared that she needed a brief pause every so often not to overstrain her heart. Tired? No, the General's wife was never tired, but then of course as one gets on, one slows down, doesn't one? Her husband, the General, knowing this only too well, had wisely stayed behind in Sarli. But then he had not only slowed down but had come to a full stop these past seven years.

"Nandino! Nandino! Don't run ahead like that, child. You'll get all overheated. San Romè, please come up here, and then maybe those dear girls won't go so fast."

To keep him by her side, she began to tell him the story of her life as she had already told it to all the summer visitors in

Sarli: her papa, she said wistfully, had had a fine position and earned a good living; in fact, she was a *marchesa,* yes, indeed she was, but she had never boasted about it. When she was eighteen—a beautiful girl to be kept under double lock and key—her papa had married her off to a *marchese.* That one had put her through the mill, all right; then she had had to nurse him for eight years, with his spinal trouble. Widowed and beautiful—even though she said it herself—she met the General at one of her soirees. He was a handsome officer and they fell in love at first sight. It ended, you know, as it was bound to end. When Nandino was born, she did what was only right and proper: she put the child in care of a nurse and married her General.

"One must always know the right thing to do, my dear."

"Ah, yes, indeed," San Romè replied with a smile, burning inwardly to snap back at her that he had heard all the gossip, how she had worked first as a servant girl for the *marchese* and then for the General. But he had to admit that she didn't give that impression at all, or at least not before a certain hour. Despite her corpulence, she was always poetic in the morning. Later in the day she would fall to talking about food, because, she said, she liked to look after the house herself and was always glad to show her friends how to make toothsome little dishes. She cooked the General's meals, yes indeed, because the dear man was such a delicate eater. Never, but *never* would he touch a thing prepared by other hands than hers!

"How beautiful!" she cried, stopping to admire a meadow covered with myriads of straight, fragile stems like a thin veil festooned with dark-red plumes. "What is the name of that beautiful flower?"

"Good-for-nothing," grunted Signor Raspi. "Even the cattle won't touch it. It's called *scaletta.* Good-for-nothing."

What a look the General's wife turned on Raspi, whose big round face and little pig-eyes reflected the beatitude of utter stupidity. How could he possibly understand that, in a poetical mood, one did not admire things only for their usefulness?

"Not that I'm tired, San Romè," she said, "but tell me how much farther it is to Roccia Balda so that I can estimate the time it will take."

"Oh, we still have quite a way to go, dear Signora," he replied. "From five to six miles, I'd say, but we'll soon enter the woods."

"Beautiful, beautiful!" she repeated.

Unable to put up with her any longer, San Romè left her with Raspi. Up front, the little gossips Bongi and Tani had their heads together whispering and giggling, and now glanced back to make sure he was not within earshot.

On the last sloping pasture at the edge of the woods, several oxen grazed, guarded by two ugly old women, wrinkled and gaunt, who sat spinning under the shade of the trees.

"Where is the Third Weird Sister?" Biagio Casoli called over to them.

As they didn't understand, he started to recite:

> *"Beautiful square-chested oxen,*
> *Their crescent horns erect,*
> *Sloe-eyed, snow-white*
> *Beloved of the gentle Virgil . . ."*

At this Signor Raspi laughed in his special way, as though whimpering, and called out to Casoli, "What did Virgil love, the horns?"

"That's right, horns!" said the General's wife.

And they all burst out laughing at this reference to cuckoldry. San Romè had seen those horns from a distance. He would have been surprised had his friends missed the chance to make some such allusion.

When they entered the wood, all those dear people might have admired the foaming waterfall, a glen of low-growing alders in deep shade, or a moss-covered stone in the river where the water broke like a shower of crystal. Certainly the General's wife and Raspi did so almost perfunctorily in order to stop and catch their breath. But not the others! Not one of them sensed the delight of that sudden cool shade pungent with sharp fragrance, or the silence tremulous with the chirr of crickets and the babbling of small streams.

Chattering among themselves, they were making approximate

calculations. From the ground they had covered, they figured just about where Pepi would be by now on the road from Sarli to Gori. Poor San Romè was doing the same thing, but growing more and more gloomy and nervous at everything. No doubt Dora had gone down leisurely from Gori to meet him. Then, of course, when they caught sight of each other—she from above, he from below—they would wander off the road and meet in the wooded valley of the Sarnio. There, well protected by trees, both would have forgotten their headaches by now.

These visions danced so clearly before San Romè's eyes that he actually saw the two of them going to their tryst, laughing at him first by themselves, then together. He angrily opened and closed his hands, sinking the nails into his palms. Then, noticing that the others were aware of his ill-humored preoccupation, not even speaking to him as though they understood, he went over to them and forced himself to talk, putting those vivid pictures out of his mind—pictures which seemed to betray him more than his brother, who was far off and knew nothing. But, a little later, unable to bear their empty chatter, he sank back into his own black thoughts again. He felt he was the laughingstock of them all who knew only too well what torment this outing was for him. They smiled to show how much they appreciated this excursion, and asked such questions . . . For instance, that girl Tani had wanted to know if the tree over there had been felled by lightning. Why? Because its forked trunk looked like a pair of horns. Then later, when they finally reached Roccia Balda and had admired the view of the Valsarnia, why did the General's wife want to know the name of those gray-blue peaks rising sharply above the wide valley? Only to point out that those two peaks of Monte Merlo rose like horns in the distance. After lunch, why did Signor Raspi take out his linen handkerchief, knot the corners, and cap his big perspiring head with it, if not to show the two delicate little horns just above his forehead?

Horns! Horns! Horns! San Romè saw nothing but horns in all directions that day. He almost touched them with his hands when, in the evening, after he had accompanied the group all the way back to Sarli by the shorter route, he was climbing up the road to Gori. Below, in the valley, he caught a glimpse of

Pepi through the trees, sitting there absorbed, no doubt, in his recent joy.

San Romè stopped, pale, trembling, his teeth and fists clenched. There were two alternatives: on the one hand, prudence; on the other, his impulse to give that imbecile a going over and thus revenge himself for the long day's torment. Just then, around a bend in the road, he heard a serene, warm voice humming a tune he knew very well. Turning, he saw his sister-in-law, her head resting lovingly on the shoulder of a man whose arm encircled her waist.

Roberto San Romè felt his legs go limp. "Cesare!" he cried.

His brother was gazing ecstatically at the first stars in the sky as his languid little wife sang. At first he was startled when he heard his name called, then he walked up with Dora, who broke into one of her peals of laughter.

"You here!" San Romè exclaimed. "When did you arrive?"

"Why, this morning at nine. Didn't you see my telegram last night?"

"No," Dora interrupted, her eyes shining. "He'd already gone down to Sarli to organize the excursion to Roccia Balda; I didn't want to spoil their fun. I'm sorry I upset you—because of the headache—but I needed an excuse not to go. It's gone now, Roberto—the headache."

She slipped her arm through his, walking between the two men as they climbed slowly back to Gori.

"Tell me, Roberto, did you have a nice time?" she asked affectionately.

THE EXAMINATION

The few guests of the Hermitage, isolated up there on top of the mountain, had been listening for some time to the donkey driver's voice as he made the exhausting climb up the slope to their retreat.

"Skee . . . brr! Skee . . . brr!"

In that stifling heat, the continuous scraping of the locusts and shrill of the crickets was annoying enough without this. The guests wondered if that lopsided fellow, Natale, was bringing up a long-term fellow sufferer or just a passing visitor, and from time to time they leaned out the windows of the former convent which had been converted into an inn.

The convent was little changed. There were the same small cells, provided with a wretched cot so narrow it was impossible to turn over, a crude wooden table, a washbasin, and three or four rush-bottom chairs. The old refectory was still in use and so were the long, dark, resounding corridors with their worn, gray stairs. But the little chapel adjoining the main building was always closed.

The guests tolerated this lack of comfort because living in a cloister had a piquancy all its own, and when this wore off they did not want to admit it. It was Signor Lanzi who had had the bright idea of opening this so-called hotel; every year he promised that new quarters would be ready for the following season—built according to the Swiss plan, with a funicular railway.

"Yes," everyone agreed. "This would make a delightful place to spend a vacation."

"But when I've put my all into it and can offer you every convenience," Signor Lanzi would say with a sigh, scratching the top of his head, "you gentlemen will tell me that the prices are too high and you won't come, or you will think: If we have to pay that much, we might as well go to Switzerland! It'll make a better impression! And then where will I be with all my conveniences?"

Was there never to be a new building, Swiss-style, then?

Of course—the following year, for sure.

To entertain his guests, Signor Lanzi pointed out the exact spot where the new hotel was to be built, and described it down to the smallest detail. It would be magnificent! They could almost see it there already, and each one came forward with advice and suggestions. Signor Lanzi also told them of the discussions now under way for the construction of a funicular railway. The work was to begin next October.

"Bravo, Signor Lanzi! Natale with his good-for-nothing donkey is really a disgrace."

"Skee . . . brr! Skee . . . brr!"

Meanwhile, Natale's voice was coming closer.

Signor Lanzi with Quagliola, the former deputy, as bald and round as a barrel, and the redheaded professor, director of his own Tancredi Picinelli School, a thin, freckled, nervously polite young man, were walking on the terrace in front of the convent. Looking up, they saw the four other guests half leaning out their windows, waiting. There was blond Signora Ardelli, whose husband—"such a fine man"—came up every Saturday evening from town where he was employed; Signor Mesciardi, the lawyer, who was flirting with the Signora; then Quagliolino, the son of the deputy, who had also tried to flirt with her like a silly schoolboy, to the detriment of his health; and last of all there was the little priest, Don Vine, who fled before temptation.

The donkey, reasonably enough, was the first to appear—then collapsed, ears dangling, eyes closed, his sides heaving as if he were all in. Natale rushed up, furious as a devil from hell, brandishing his stick.

"Up, pig! Up!"

A donkey should, it seems, feel insulted by being called a pig. But this one didn't. Realizing this, perhaps, Natale tried clubbing some sense into him. However, the donkey acted as if the blows were not meant for him. He only tried lifting one skinned ear to find out from which direction they came.

Finally, the new guest trudged into view, all out of breath. Lawyer Pompeo Lagumina, a nearsighted giant, was vexed because his glasses kept slipping off of his sweaty nose. The wide brim of his white canvas hat was limp with perspiration and flapped against his big face. Rushing up to the donkey, he shouted at Natale, who shrank back.

"I'll carry him myself, you brute, the way Morgante carried the monastery's horse!"

He really tried to lift the little donkey, to the general amusement of the onlookers.

"The man is a *mountain,* I tell you," whined the donkey driver apologetically to Signor Lanzi, indicating Lagumina.

"*I* came all the way on foot," Pompeo Lagumina shouted to Natale. "Why won't this donkey of yours stand up? He's even more of an ass than you are!"

"With that case full of lead," growled Natale.

"*Science,* idiot. They're books!" retorted Lagumina, shaking Natale by the shoulders.

"Ah, science! No wonder the donkey is weighed down," Quagliola observed, as Lagumina said harshly to Natale, "I won't pay you. You'll get no tip from me."

Signor Lanzi quickly interposed, "Do as you wish, Signore, but please come inside. You are in a sweat and might catch cold."

"Thank you. There's no danger of that," replied Lagumina, swelling his mighty chest. "Are you the proprietor?"

"At your service."

"Very kind, thank you. I would like to point out that I have not touched this donkey. I tried to mount it but my feet dragged on the ground. The beast simply collapsed under me."

"He broke the donkey's back," grumbled Natale.

"I'll break every bone in your body," thundered Pompeo Lagumina, turning on him with clenched fists. "Now, hold your tongue!"

From her window, Signora Ardelli burst out laughing. Lagumina looked up irritably and, seeing a lady, tried to pull the hat off his moist head, grinning like a big baby.

"I will say no more, Signora, and leave everything to your good graces."

But Signora Ardelli had already disappeared from the window.

"I have come here especially to study," said Lagumina, turning once more to the hotel proprietor. His face suddenly grave, he commanded, "I require a room quite removed from the rest of the guests."

"Ah, here there are only poor monks' cells, made for study and meditation, Signore," replied Signor Lanzi. "Come, I will show you."

"Gentlemen," said Lagumina with a bow, before stepping out like a grenadier and going stiffly off behind Signor Lanzi.

Signor Quagliola and Professor Picinelli glanced up to the windows where the others were taking in the scene. Mesciardi was rubbing his hands together, as if to say, Cheer up, the fun has just started.

"Did you say *lead*, Natale?" Quagliolino called down. "You were right."

"He killed my donkey for me, God damn his soul," Natale cursed, using his teeth as well as his hands to undo the cord around the load of books attached to the pack saddle.

Picinelli tried to urge the donkey to rise, but the poor beast knew only the language of a stick. Though he pricked up his ears at this friendly persuasion, he let them fall again, thinking, no doubt, He can't be talking to me!

A little later, the guests at the Hermitage met under the trees to the east of the mountain for their midday meal.

Pompeo Lagumina, much refreshed after copiously dousing himself with cold water, his big face wreathed in smiles, sat down at his own table placed between that of Professor Picinelli and the table shared by the Quagliola. He was carrying a big book under his arm.

"Ah," he sighed, almost inaudibly, as he closed his eyes and placed the book on the table. "I really haven't a minute to spare."

All the guests were seated at separate tables, except for Quagliola and his son. Mesciardi, the lawyer, tried to listen to what the newcomer had to say, because he did not want to miss anything, but at the same time he wanted to keep his place near Signora Ardelli. He soon had an inspiration and, getting up, went over to Lagumina to present him with his visiting card.

"Since you are now a fellow monk . . ."

"Quite right. Thank you very much," Lagumina said.

Then he rose to distribute his cards all around with a great show of politeness. Names were exchanged. and Lagumina returned to his table.

Although I am the senior member of this group," said Quagliola, "your stature entitles you to the priority of the convent, lawyer Lagumina!"

"How happy I would be to accept it, Lagumina replied sadly. "And you may rest assured that—always with our Don Vine's consent—I would found a new order of Hermits, a band of jolly good fellows! But my time is precious. I am preparing for a difficult civil-service examination for Chief Clerk of the Council of State."

"No less!" exclaimed Mesciardi.

"Unfortunately, what can I do?" Lagumina sighed. "It's of vital importance to me. If I succeed—but there, I refuse to entertain a doubt as to the outcome. I have only a month at my disposal. When I think of it, my courage fails me."

But not his appetite. He devoured everything in sight, neatly putting away a large dish of risotto and talking uninterruptedly about his examination. His food disappeared so quickly that, foraging in his empty plate with his fork, he looked up with surprise at the guests, then at the waiter.

"If I'm not mistaken, this was very good. Shall we repeat it? Bring me some more. Ah, this mountain air! Too bad I cannot enjoy it—but it's a comforting thought that, for me at least, study has always been a consuming passion."

"Not to mention risotto," Quagliola remarked under his breath to Picinelli.

In fact, cutlets, chicken, salad and the rest followed in quick succession. Don Vine, thinnish and fastidious, was simply amazed.

And the book? Patience . . . the end of the meal was at hand.

"How enchanting it is here!" Lagumina remarked as he got up, both hands under his belly, gorged and content. "Now, I think a little shade is what I need. Excuse me." Beaming, he took up his book and sauntered a short distance away to stretch out at the foot of a beech tree.

Today is Saturday. I've just arrived, he thought to himself, blissfully lighting a cigar. Tomorrow is Sunday. Best begin on Monday and give myself some time to get accustomed to the place and satisfy my curiosity.

He gazed into the distance at the ethereal blue chain of the Apennines.

"Ah, the spinal column of our Fatherland!"

What excellent ideas he had sometimes, without even thinking about it—in his moments of leisure—and what a strong picture that metaphor conveyed! He certainly had nothing to worry about for the forthcoming examination. He was nobody's fool. *The Apennines, spinal column of our Fatherland!* Had that thought ever occured to anyone before?

His head was not quite comfortable against the trunk of the tree. Slipping down a little, he rested it on his book and in no time was snoring loudly. At a signal from that terrible Quagliolino, worthy son of such a father, the other guests approached on tiptoe to gaze down at him.

"Shhh! He's studying," whispered Quagliola, holding a finger to his lips. "We won't disturb him. He's already before the Council of State!"

But Lagumina's sleep did not last long. Every Saturday after-

noon the little group at the Hermitage gave the Honorable Ardelli a noisy greeting when he arrived from town. They made
such a racket that Lagumina awoke with a start and, since he had
been dreaming about the examination and was frightened, he
immediately took the book from under his head and started to
read, his eyes still puffed and red from sleep. Those idlers came
over to him, bringing Ardelli, mounted triumphantly on the
donkey. He was as round as Quagliola, but with the head of a
Goliath.

"Here's our latest," said Mesciardi, pointing to Lagumina.
"Ardelli, we would like to present our new Father Prior."

Lagumina got up, smiling. "I told you that I could not accept. You see me here wracking my brains. Good heavens, it's almost dark! I was so busy reading that I hadn't noticed."

"I must warn you, you'll ruin your eyes," said Quagliola with
a show of sympathetic concern.

Sunday: true, he was determined not to lose a day, not even
a single minute. But had he not promised himself, the evening
before, to begin on Monday? Yes, first he needed to adjust himself to the mountain air. But, heavens, how late it was! Nine
o'clock, already.

What a heavy sleeper! Tomorrow, Monday, I'll be up at five.

He dressed and, taking his big book under his arm, went
down to the terrace.

What a crowd! So many women and girls, all in a holiday
mood! They had arrived on little donkeys from the nearby vil-
lages. A swing had been strung between two trees. The girls
were taking turns on it and every time a young man gave a harder
push, they let out joyful squeals of fright, feigning not to notice
their flying skirts, but prettily displaying their legs in colored,
openwork stockings.

Pompeo Lagumina turned away, frowning. He no longer had
the right to look at girls. The one in his heart was enough. A
responsible man, once he has given his promise, respects it. Near
or far, it was his duty to be faithful even in thought. He invoked
the thought of his modest little Sandra, who was eating her heart
out for love of him at this very moment. She had waited two long

years for their wedding, all the while contending with her sulky mother, who wanted her to marry her rich, stupid cousin Mimmino Orrei. Sandrina did nothing but laugh at him. Poor, poor Sandrina! But what else could he have done? His heart was as big as the ocean, so far as that was concerned. But as for money . . . Ah! Diogenes, yes, it was Diogenes who threw away the cup to drink out of the hollow of his hand. Perhaps Diogenes was not the right comparison. What would really fit him like a glove right now was that clerkship with the Council of State. Then her mother would consent, all right. But how could he study and prepare for the examination in the city when he had to spend so many hours a day at the Ministry of Industrial and Commercial Agriculture, and was always distracted in his free time by that terrible urge to see his sweetheart? Impossible. He needed to get away for a month, away from everything, off in a remote corner by himself. But then, he also needed the wherewithal!

When he thought of what Sandrina had done for him, it was a miracle Pompeo Lagumina did not burst into tears in front of all those people. The hard time she had, the things she went without to save a thousand lire, which she insisted on giving him so he could go away from her to study. Now everything depended on the outcome of the examination.

At this point, Pompeo Lagumina quickly opened his book.

"Surely not here, with all this noise!" exclaimed lawyer Mesciardi, coming up to him, pointedly staring at the girls on the swing to annoy Signora Ardelli, who was all eyes for her husband that day.

"You're right," said Lagumina. "It's impossible here. Our convent seems to have been invaded with demons today."

And he laughed. There! Another beautiful phrase with a classical ring. Decidedly, he had a flair for words. They came to him just like that, as spontaneous as lightning. He thought he would take refuge in the bush which covered the steep slopes of the mountain.

What beauty! What shade! How refreshing!

"Ohhh . . . Ouch!"

Nothing much. He had taken a tumble, that's all. But he

had to be careful with that mess of leaves all over the ground like a slippery carpet. It hurt a little at the base of his spine. The book? There it was, over there by that tree. It had slithered all the way down.

Lagumina was too frightened to let go of the bush. He hung on with both hands while he stretched out one foot toward the trunk of a tree below. Ah! Lucky thing his glasses were not broken, banging against the tree like that. All right, he would be more careful, but it was fun sliding down in little spurts—whee!—another . . . and another . . . down . . . down . . . from trunk to trunk . . . almost to the bottom of the hill.

Good for you, Pompeo! Now up you go!

Ah, the book? Heavens! He had forgotten it on the ground up there—but where? How was he ever going to find it again among all those trees?

If I don't find it, I'm ruined. Up . . . up.

He found it, fortunately, after searching frantically for three hours. It lay open there on the dry leaves at the base of a tree, bearing the visible token of a little bird.

"Dirty little thing!"

Pompeo climbed the rest of the way to the top, his face aflame, dripping sweat, his clothes torn and disheveled, but his appetite was unimpaired.

Monday: First of all, set up the books. It was five o'clock on the dot, exactly the hour he had decided on. Pompeo Lagumina rubbed his hands in satisfaction.

But that little table, it could never hold all the big books he needed to have within easy reach. Still, a larger table would never fit into the cell. What could he do? Ah! He had an idea. He would set his packing case on two chairs beside the table. There!

He diligently arranged the books according to subject matter, laid out paper to make notes, sharpened lead pencils as well as red and green pencils for his particular signs, a memorizing device. Then, at last, he sat down to begin his assignment.

"Lawyer Lagumina! Lawyer Lagumina!"

Oh, those idlers again!

Pompeo Lagumina huffed and shook his fist furiously in the air. Let them sing out. They were a nuisance. Didn't they know he had not come here to amuse himself?

"Father Lagumina!"

"Father Prior!"

That prior business again. Yet if he didn't answer them, they might go on calling indefinitely, they might even imagine that he was still asleep.

He went to the window.

"Please excuse me, gentlemen. I've been at it since five! You know very well—"

"I know nothing of the kind," cried Honorable Ardelli, getting on the donkey. "I'm going back to town and I want all of you to come with me part of the way."

"Excuse me, I cannot come," Lagumina replied. "You have a very fine escort as it is. Leave me to my studies."

"I'll accept no excuses," said Ardelli. "We can't do without our prior."

"But Quagliola is the honorable prior."

"Then I, as prior, order you to come down and accompany our brother hermit," said Quagliola.

"Excellent," they all approved.

Mesciardi added, "Come on, Lawyer Lagumina. Don't forget that a little walk early in the morning is good for the mind. It clears the head."

"That's true," Lagumina agreed courteously—also because there was no doubt that a little walk . . .

He never should have said it.

"Come on down, then," they chorused.

He couldn't refuse now. He left the window, snorting, and went down.

"On one condition," he told them. "That we make it quick. I'll rely on you."

"Just the time to go and come back," they replied.

But all the way down as well as all the way back, they encouraged him to talk about the difficulties of his examination.

He discussed it willingly. When they reached the top of the hill, it was time for the midday meal. Pompeo Lagumina looked forlorn. He said he could not eat.

"A whole morning wasted!"

"What can you do about it now?" asked Mesciardi. "Be patient. You can always study later on."

"But as you know, the morning is the best time for study," Lagumina argued irritably. "Let me go. Don't keep me."

"If you refuse to take a little nourishment," Quagliola said with his usual placidity, "I'm telling you, you won't have the strength to study. Isn't that true, Signora Ardelli?"

"He must eat," she said. "I hope he will excuse us for not wanting to do without his pleasant company."

"Don't talk that way, Signora!" Lagumina exclaimed, deeply flattered. "I would be so happy . . . if only I didn't find myself in this . . . situation."

"We promise not to disturb you again," replied Signora Ardelli. "Is that all right? Now please eat. Do me this little favor."

In order to please the charming signora who pleaded so insistently, Pompeo Lagumina ate. Eating and chatting, he forgot his annoyance and did honor to his appetite. In fact, after the meal he had difficulty getting up from his chair. But now to work! No more excuses!

"Are you gentlemen going to sleep? I must go back to my books. I hope you rest well."

And he went back to his cell. With all the good will in the world he set out to study. But his eyelids were heavy and he felt himself overcome by sleep. He tried to resist, but he found it more and more difficult to concentrate on the page before him. Little by little, as his resistance weakened, he lost consciousness until his eyes closed of their own accord. With a sudden jerk of his head, he sat up in a daze. Looking around him, he spied the bed. It was no use. There was no holding out against such a meal in that heat. Just a short nap—only for an hour.

When he woke up, it was evening.

"Lord! Look at that gloomy expression!" cried Quagliola from the terrace as he caught sight of him at the window. "What are you trying to do, kill yourself with work?"

"As a matter of fact, yes," muttered Lagumina, rubbing his eyes and forehead as if he had really been hard at it until then— not so much that he wanted to convince them as that he wanted desperately to convince himself.

"Come on down. We've already had supper."

"No. I'll be down later . . . if I come," Lagumina said. "Now I must write a little letter."

He wrote his dear Sandra that he was alone up here with a huge dog who refused to follow the monks when they left the old hermitage. It was cold here in this Alpine solitude. He too felt cold in his spirit so far from her and, to console himself, he studied without interruption. He even studied during his frugal meals, which were brought to him every morning by a boy from the nearby village. He ate in the old refectory, now completely deserted, while outside the wind howled through the trees on the mountaintop. The big dog watched him intently, his kind eyes deep as silent pools.

After rereading his pathetic letter, Pompeo Lagumina wept. His lies were sincere because with all his heart he wanted everything he wrote to be true. Bundled up against the evening chill, with a lump in his throat, he went down to supper a little later.

Tuesday: That treacherous bed so filled him with fear after his experience of the previous day that he decided to go outside and study peacefully in the shade. No one would bother him there in the woods.

He selected a book and picked up his notebook and pencil to take along.

When he had installed himself, a stifled cry made him jump. Red in the face, his eyes glistening, Quagliolino suddenly rolled over on his stomach and looked up at him anxiously.

Lagumina smiled but his voice was harsh. "Did I surprise you?"

"No. It's nothing," the boy said, lowering his eyes. Then he asked, "Did you see them . . . over there?"

"No. I didn't see anything."

"Well, wouldn't you like to see the fine sport certain people around here have together?"

"Ah . . . who?"

"Over there," the boy said, pointing.

His curiosity aroused, Lagumina crept over, and Quagliolino joined him.

"Shhh! Softly. Watch out for the branches. I don't know if they're still there."

"But who?" asked Lagumina.

"Don't you know? Mesciardi and Signora Ardelli!"

Pompeo Lagumina's eyes widened. "Are you serious? Has it gone that far?"

The young man sighed and nodded. Alas, yes.

"Ah, poor Honorable Ardelli," Lagumina remarked. "That's why they had a party yesterday to see him off."

"Oh, they have one every day," retorted the boy.

"Well . . . after all," said Lagumina, heaving a deep sigh, "it's a tempting spot, very treacherous. With nothing to do . . . in this season . . . man—*hic et haec*—is a beast, you know. A vile beast. He yields. There's not a man in the world who can resist. Take me. I came here purposely to study. Now with this news you have thoroughly upset me. It's terrible—not so much the betrayal, which we have accidentally discovered, as the confirmation it gives of man's common plight. The weakness of our natures exposes us to the mercy of chance. Propitious circumstances develop the germs of evil to a degree ranging from the smallest fault to the most monstrous crime. Ah, the evil in us is truly without end!"

He rambled on and on in this vein, dazzled by his own brilliance, intoxicated by the sound of his own voice, delighted with the profound ideas which sprang effortlessly to his lips.

The boy stared at him in astonishment, wondering what he had said to deserve all this. Swallowing his surprise, he asked finally, "Shall we go look for them?"

Pompeo Lagumina wanted to think over what he had said and tried to recapture his words, but was unable to. He felt discouraged. His mind seemed to work in flashes. Here he was standing before this boy who was staring at him like an owl, and there were times when he knew he was capable of stunning the whole world.

"Coming?"

"Oh, all right."

They combed the bush for several hours like two bloodhounds, stopping here and there, alert and suspicious of the slightest sound. Pompeo Lagumina felt moved by a heroic spirit, as if it were his duty alone to protect mankind from dishonor.

"Poor Ardelli!"

They searched far and wide but they did not find the guilty lovers. So another morning passed and it was again time for dinner before Pompeo Lagumina had time to open his books.

Wednesday, Thursday, Friday . . .

As the days passed, all of them wasted for one reason or another, Lagumina was beset by humiliation and remorse on one hand and a mounting fear of the approaching examination on the other. On certain days, his anxiety was so great that he could no longer remain alone in his cell. He had to escape and talk to someone to distract him from his torment. The sight of all those books, several of which he should have digested by now, became intolerable. All this information of legal, political, juridical or administrative nature added up until it loomed like a mountain before his eyes. He escaped to the terrace, where the others sat gossiping idly under the trees.

"I need a breath of air. My temples are throbbing. My head is fairly steaming."

He rattled on for a while to numb his pain, then he fell silent, frowning. A few minutes later he went back upstairs to study, his jaw set. He opened his books and began to read, but at the first difficulty he encountered after only a few pages, he was plunged into despair. He fell prey to a restless remorse which gnawed at him like an irritating pain in his stomach; he turned an unreasoning anger brutally inward on himself. He wanted to slap his own face, claw it with his nails. With his elbows on the table, his head sunk in his hands, he moaned.

"It's not his fault, poor fellow," Quagliola remarked on the terrace below, first making sure that his son was nowhere about. "It's not his fault if Nature has endowed him with a body that demands only to eat and sleep. When he has eaten, come what may, he cannot absorb knowledge of any kind. His eyes close and—good night! Can he force them to stay open? When you can't, you can't."

Out of fellow feeling, he led the group under Lagumina's window and called to him, so that he might at least blame them for his lost time and so give him a pretext to steal from his martyrdom without compunction.

"I should study," the unhappy one told them every time he leaned out of the window.

"Yes, of course," answered Mesciardi, Quagliola and Picinelli from the terrace, "but meanwhile come on down for a moment. Relax a little! Besides, we need you here to settle an argument."

Pretending to believe Lagumina when he told them of all he had accomplished that day, they said encouragingly, "Bravo, lawyer! Your goal is already in sight. Now take it easy."

Pompeo Lagumina was grateful for their kind words and the momentary relief. His heart swelled with tenderness, and a few tears glistened in his eyes behind their thick glasses. He could have kissed them. On the other hand, if he were forgotten and left alone in his cell, without being disturbed, he would grow angry and hate them. When he was not called, he leaned out the window to attract their attention and pricked up his ears, trying to catch a few words of their conversation.

"They might lower their voices," he muttered. "Beasts! Egotists! Amusing themselves—only right, of course, during vacation—but just the same, they could go farther off to do their talking. Must they be right here where they know a man is trying to work?"

And so the third Sunday of the month came around. The game of the Graces, a sort of lacrosse, was played on the hilltop with hoops and sticks which that tempting demon, Honorable Ardelli, had brought up with him—an innocent pastime for the poor brothers at the Hermitage. None of the young girls who came over that day seemed to catch on to the game, and even Signora Ardelli was unable to teach them how to throw the hoop with the two sticks and catch it again in mid-air. Pompeo Lagumina, whose attention was continually diverted from his book by squeals of excitement, leaned out of his window to glare at the girls. He would not even take a Sunday off from his books.

"I just want to see who is going to win," he said, going over to the window several times during the morning.

They made too much noise. He could not resist leaning out again at least to take part in the game with his eyes. His hands itched because, although nearsighted, he excelled at this game.

At last he cried out to one of the girls, "Not like that—no. Excuse me."

They all turned to look up at the window. Signora Ardelli sweetly begged him to come down and teach them how to play.

"Just for five minutes . . . I warn you," he replied.

When he had been showing them how to toss that little circle of the Graces—ooop-la . . . ooop-la—for about an hour and was perspiring freely, all the gay young girls burst into a round of applause.

It came like a bolt out of the blue!

Pompeo Lagumina, his hand half raised holding the sticks, was petrified. The hoop which had already been tossed landed like a crown on his head. They all laughed and he tried to laugh, too. He walked stiffly to the edge of the terrace, where Sandrina and her mother were standing quietly.

"What a wonderful surprise!"

"Liar!"

"Cheat!"

"What? No? Why?"

"Puppet!"

"Buffoon!"

"Sandrina, my own, listen . . ."

"Go away!"

"For shame!"

They didn't give him a chance to speak. As soon as he opened his mouth they fired point-blank, peppering him with insults. Then they turned and marched off down the mountain, without stopping for a moment's rest or even a sip of water.

Pompeo Lagumina closed himself in his cell and threw himself on the cot. He remained there for some time in a blank stupor which even frightened him at one point. Through that terrible nothingness, that suspension of consciousness, a grim idea occurred to him and, feeling lost and shamed, he did not know how to reject it. He thought that he had nothing to say in his own defense. He remembered Signor Lanzi telling them a few days before of the suicide of a poor *carabinière* the previous winter. He had thrown himself off one of the cliffs on the west side of the mountain. What a horrible death!

The laughing of the girls' voices on the terrace finally roused him and he was able to throw off the nightmare of that frightening thought. He rose from the bed and decided to write a long letter of explanation to Sandrina, in which he would propose to reconsider his drastic decision to kill himself if she would reply at once.

Naturally, the suspense of waiting made it impossible for him to study during those days. Under such conditions, who else could have done any better?

In dismal anguish, he went down to the table at every meal and was not conscious of eating. Then he threw himself on the bed; after all, it was only in sleep that he could find peace.

Two days later the answer came—but not from Sandrina. Her mother wrote to tell him that his indecent behavior that day had been enough to convince her daughter that she was mistaken. She had finally given her mother the satisfaction of accepting her wise advice: she would marry her cousin, Mimmino Orrei, whom she had so foolishly refused. Henceforth all relations between her daughter, Sandrina, and himself must cease.

Pompeo Lagumina rushed down to the terrace waving the letter in his hand. At first he felt drunk with resentment, but soon his enormous body triumphed in its newfound freedom, as if a big stone had been rolled away from his chest.

"Rejoice, gentlemen!" he cried to his idle friends. "I don't have to pass the examination! Now I can accept the office. Waiters! What can you offer me today as Father Prior to this band of jolly good fellows?"

And he sang lustily:

> *"Every Wednesday, a big turnout*
> *Of hare, partridge, pheasant and trout,*
> *Succulent beef and fat capon,*
> *Delicate fare to feast upon."*

MORTAL REMAINS

Signor Federico Biobin was the despair of his nephews. They must have loved him dearly to put up with so much after he had turned over to them everything he owned. They called him Uncle Fifo. He was a puny little man, completely bald, with a shiny pear-shaped dome and ten stiffly dyed bristles above either side of his ferretlike mouth.

He would get up at night, light in hand, and steal quietly through the house, rummaging into everything, sniffing and snorting and grimacing as if to keep his pointed nose constantly on the alert. Suddenly the whole house would be jolted out of a sound sleep by china crashing down from a kitchen shelf, or boxes hurtling pell-mell in the storeroom. Then everyone would come running, in their shirts, pajamas or nightdresses.

"Uncle, what have you done? What's happened?"

"Nothing. It fairly stinks of old furniture in here!"

He could always manage the most unexpected replies, as if he had not made any noise—in fact, as if he himself had heard nothing. With perfect calm, though somewhat testily, he would

speak of the sweet silence that had reigned in the house before
they had rushed in on him.

He did not let a day pass without some trick. The best of it
was that he called *doing them favors* all the trouble and annoyance he gave, driving his nephews and their servants almost out
of their wits. He had been known to spend whole days in the
kitchen clipping and pasting strips of paper to doctor a broken
pane in the door leading from it to a smelly water closet. It drove
the cook to distraction.

"You talk about old furniture stinking," she said. "What
about that privy?"

But apparently he didn't smell anything and went right on
sniffing, snorting and grimacing in his effort to mend the pane
with those strips of thin paper.

Or he would go down to the garden and get mad as a hornet
because one side of the gate was embedded in the ground and
refused to budge. Pale with rage, the veins bulging at his temples,
he would shake the gate so violently that his arms were almost
wrenched from their sockets.

"Give up, Uncle," a nephew would call from the window.
"Can't you see it won't open?"

"Give up!" he'd explode. "I'll open this gate if it kills me!"

He did not open it and it did not kill him, but he came up
all out of breath, inflamed and bathed in sweat, holding out his
little hands in a pitiful state to be oiled and bandaged.

When pestering his relatives no longer amused him, he would
go out to plague people in the street. For example, on days when
the rain came down in torrents, he would open his umbrella and
deliberately plant himself under a rain spout to annoy people by
blocking their way so that they were tempted to push him back
under cover, close against the wall. The malicious pleasure this
gave him curled the corners of his mouth so that he looked like
a surly little dog gnashing its teeth.

His latest was the gray alpaca duster he had bought to wear
in the house as a bathrobe. When his nephews pointed out that
it was intended to be worn for traveling, he cried, "For traveling? Well, then, I'll go."

"Go? But where will you go?"

"To Bergamo," he said. "To Ernesto's. I'll go and say good-bye before he leaves for Genoa to sail for America."

There was no dissuading him from this notion of leaving immediately. That his visit would be a hindrance rather than a pleasure for poor Ernesto in all the commotion of his imminent departure was yet another reason to go. And still another lay in the fact that the doctor had ordered him to be quiet and not overexert himself because of his heart. He *wanted* to die! "But not in Bergamo in the midst of all that upheaval!" Yes, sir, right there in the topsy-turvy house in Bergamo!

Off he went, then, in his gray duster. Unfortunately the threat of death—which his nephews had used without believing in it, just to keep him at home—was fulfilled. News of his death came like a thunderbolt the very hour he reached Bergamo, shocking his nephews in Rome because they had unwittingly predicted it and, having predicted it, albeit unwittingly, had allowed him to go.

This final ordeal meted out to his distant nephews was an even more bitter blow for the nephew in Bergamo. There Uncle Fifo lay in the midst of all the confusion of moving, stone dead on the narrow iron bedstead, in his fine gray duster, from which peeped his stiffly pointed toes. More than content, he seemed blissfully happy.

Among the scattered pieces of furniture pulled away from the walls, he lay comfortably on that bed which no one would dare touch as long as he was there. Four lighted candles stood, two at the head, two at the foot. Fifo's hands lay crossed over his already slightly swollen paunch. The slyboots, he really looked as if he were smiling through half-closed eyes, with those ten little spikes bristling on either side of his ferretlike face.

Uncle Fifo having fulfilled his mission of coming to die in Bergamo for the benefit of his nephew who was leaving for America, it was now up to Ernesto to remove him, either for burial in the cemetery at Bergamo or for shipment to Rome, if the others wanted him to rest in the family vault.

Ernesto decided it was quicker to ship him to Rome and let his cousins have the worry and expense of a funeral. For him every minute was precious. As things were now, he would just about make it to Genoa in time to embark. However, as luck would have it, in making out the shipment forms he had deemed the term *mortal remains* more respectful and dignified than the word *corpse*. He had sought in this way to make amends for all the curses he had heaped on poor Uncle Fifo, who had chosen such a crucial moment to fall dead at his feet.

In Rome, Uncle Fifo's nephews came to the station to collect him, accompanied by a magnificent hearse with four horses, wreaths of flowers, scores of friends and acquaintances as well as representatives of different societies with banners and standards, a priest for the absolution, followed by two long lines of nuns and choir boys carrying lighted candles. When they came for the coffin, the customs officials presented them with a bill amounting to a fine of several thousand lire.

"A fine? What for?" they asked.

"False declaration."

"False? How?"

"Do you think you can get away with calling a coffin containing a corpse 'mortal remains'? Mortal remains: a little pile of ashes and bones in an urn is one thing—as such it's charged at a specific rate. A coffin is something else. A different rate. No matter how small, this is still a coffin and you must pay the regular coffin rates plus the fine."

The nephews protested that there could be no question of fraud on Cousin Ernesto's part. But even admitting hypothetically that such could be the case, the fine, if any, should then be paid by the sender and not by the receiver. They offered to pay the difference in rate since this was definitely a coffin and was not mortal remains—though it did seem to them like splitting hairs. But as to the fine—no, no, no! They were not at fault. Cousin Ernesto had gone to America and if there had been a mistake—mind you, not a *fraud*—it was on the part of the customs office in Bergamo, which had received and shipped out a whole coffin, accepting the declaration as "mortal remains."

To placate the station master, called in to back up the customs official, the nephews were even ready to find excuses for the customs office in Bergamo. They explained that Cousin Ernesto must have shipped who knows how many boxes and, as it was well known in town that he was leaving Italy for good, the customs official in charge of shipments could easily have thought that he was shipping the mortal remains of a relative long-buried in the cemetery at Bergamo whom he did not want to leave behind. The fault, in this case, was reduced to a mere oversight. Were *they* to be fined for that? If anyone was responsible, it was the customs official in Bergamo. They did not enter into it at all.

While this discussion was raging in the customs office, outside on the square in front of the station the funeral party, dressed in black and wearing top hats, had lined up stiffly against the wall to take shelter from the sweltering August sun. The narrow strip of shade along the wall barely covered the toes of their shoes. All else before them shimmered in the blinding heat.

They looked like pickets of a fence as they stood there staring stiffly at the enormous hearse, which loomed, a black-and-gold nightmare, in the very center of the square. The nuns, bundled in heavy brown woolen habits, all deep-bosomed under starched white bibs, with peaked black wool hoods on their heads, stood impassively, their eyes lowered, lighted candles in their hands. The sunlight was so strong that it swallowed the candle flames and only wavering wisps of smoke could be seen.

What was going on? Why didn't they bring the coffin? What were they waiting for? The more impatient went inside. Then, little by little, all the mourners sought the delicious cool of the customs office, a vast warehouse whose four walls were piled high with crates, bales and bundles. Only the driver of the hearse, the nuns and the choir boys remained in the square.

The big place re-echoed with loud voices in the hot dispute between the nephews of the dead man and the station master and his officials. Everyone's blood was boiling. The station master was adamant: pay the fine or no coffin. Infuriated, the elder nephew threatened to leave the coffin there. A corpse was hardly the kind of merchandise to resell at auction! He'd like to see what the station master could do with it! The station master scoffed; he'd get permission to have two porters carry it off and bury it, and the bailiffs would then take care of collecting costs, duties and fine. A tremor of indignation met this retort and, encouraged by the common consent of the mourners, the younger nephew now dared him to do it. The administration, he said, would be held responsible for moral and material damage: their uncle was not a dog to be carted off and buried in this fashion. Why, several hundred people had gathered here to honor him as he deserved, with banners and standards, a first-class hearse, a holy priest, nuns and choir boys with more than forty candles!

The two nephews, red as lobsters, their white shirts bulging and showing beneath their vests in all the excitement, still trembling after their violent outburst, were led away, crying tears of rage.

Empty and swaying, the nightmare hearse rolled grandly away, back to the stables; the nuns and choir boys turned their candles over and snuffed them out on the flagstones. Everyone, even the nephews, had a strange feeling of relief over the outcome, as though Uncle Fifo had dismissed his funeral and was no longer dead.

Could he really be considered dead, Uncle Fifo, when he continued to do what he had always done in life: heckle and torment everybody?

Of course a dead man has never been known to uncross his hands and shoo a fly from his nose, but Uncle Fifo, doubly protected in a zinc and walnut coffin lying at the feet of the station master, left alone there in the customs warehouse to contemplate the long box and scratch his head, could well be imagined lifting his fine little hands and rubbing them together with glee.

MAN'S BEST FRIEND

Still in her slip, her arms and shoulders bare and one breast more than a little exposed, Giannetta sat before the mirror doing her hair. Don Giulio del Carpine, sprawled in an easy chair at the foot of the rumpled bed, was testily smoking a cigarette. He scowled at it as if he would like to tear it to pieces, and pulled on it desperately, exhaling the smoke in great puffs through his nose.

"No . . . I can't believe it," he exploded finally, shaking his head.

Donna Giannetta looked at him with a smile, her beautiful arms raised, her hands to her hair, with no fear of displaying her body.

"So you're still thinking about that?"

"It doesn't make sense," he burst out, getting up angrily. "Why would Livia choose what's his name . . . Sandro—when . . . well, it's not for me to say!"

Donna Giannetta bent her head to one side and watched Don Giulio from under her raised arm, as if to appraise him before she spoke.

"Ah, that depends," she said archly.

"Depends on what, if you please?"

"It depends . . . It depends, my dear," she repeated simply.
Del Carpine shrugged his shoulders and moved restlessly
about the room.

When he had worn a beard he'd been quite handsome, tall
and well built, she thought. But now that he was stylishly clean-
shaven, with that big nose and little chin, he was no longer as
good-looking as he seemed to think.

"Jealousy," he said pompously, "depends not so much on the
respect a man has for a woman, or vice versa, as on the respect
he has for himself. That being the case . . ."

He glanced at his fingernails and lost the thread of what he
was saying. Distractedly, he looked at Donna Giannetta as if she
had spoken, not he.

Giannetta, her back to him, continued to observe him in the
mirror. Then, with a little twinkle in her eyes, she asked, "That
being the case . . . ?"

"Well, that's the way it is. It all stems from—" he hurried
on— "a lack of self-respect, perhaps of self-confidence. We imagine, or we fear, that we can never measure up to the heart, mind
or whims of our beloved."

"Oh," she said with a sigh of relief, "you don't suffer from
that!"

"From what?"

"Why, from a lack of self-confidence!"

"No, I don't, especially if I compare myself with—what's his
name?—with Sandro."

"Poor Sandro," said Donna Giannetta, breaking into one of
her rippling laughs. "But to get back to your wife. Now you will
find out what respect she has for you."

"Listen," Don Giulio snapped, flushing with irritation. "You
can't seriously imagine she would prefer—"

"What's-his-name?"

"It doesn't make sense! My wife may be—whatever you like—
but she *is* intelligent. So far as I know, she has never suspected
a thing about us. So what would her motive be? Why Sandro?"

"On the whole," she said, rising, "you make sense . . . for

yourself. Hand me my blouse, will you? Yes, that one. Thank you. But not good sense for your wife, my dear. After all, Sandro is affectionate, discreet, thoughtful—and nobody's fool, you know. For example, I haven't the slightest doubt that he . . ."

"Come, come," Don Giulio said. "What do you know? Who told you?"

"What?" said Donna Giannetta, going over to him and taking him by the arms to make him look into her eyes. "Aren't you holding your head a little too high? Does it really upset you so? That's ridiculous, when we have been—"

"That has nothing to do with it," Del Carpine interrupted. "I just can't believe it. It seems impossible, absurd. Livia, of all . . ."

"Ah, really?" She turned her back to him. "Just a moment," she said as he buttoned her blouse. Then she crossed the room to get her purse and took out a small gilt-edged page torn from an engagement book. She handed it to him.

"If it interests you," she said, "just out of curiosity."

Don Giulio stared in astonishment at that little piece of paper with an address scrawled in pencil: *via Sardegna 96*.

"How . . . How did you find this?" he gasped.

"Ah," she replied, half closing her eyes maliciously, "Sandro is discreet. But I . . . for our own sakes, my dear. You pay too much attention to yourself, Giulio, and too little to others. For instance, I'm sure you haven't noticed how nonchalantly I come and go lately."

"Let me see," he said absent-mindedly. "Via Sardegna—doesn't that cross via Veneto?"

"Yes, number 96 is one of the last houses, just above a sculptor's studio which Sandro has also rented. Ha, ha! Can you imagine Sandro—a sculptor?"

She went on laughing as she finished dressing, highly amused by the thought of her husband, Sandro, as a sculptor with Livia del Carpine for his model. She glanced out of the corner of her eye at Don Giulio, who was again sitting glumly in the chair with the little page from the engagement book wrapped around his finger.

When she was ready and the veil on her small hat pulled in

place, she looked again in the glass, first full face, then from the side, and said, "You shouldn't be so conceited. I'm happy for poor Sandro, and for myself too—and you should also be pleased."

Again she burst out laughing at sight of his face, then ran to sit on his knees to caress him.

"Take out your revenge on me. You really are terrible. Remember the saying: One gets as good as one gives. Now that Sandro is amusing himself—"

"But first I want to be sure," he said roughly, and he half rose with an angry gesture, as if to push her away.

Donna Giannetta jumped up, offended, and said coldly, "Do as you like. Goodbye!"

He jumped up too, his eyes full of repentance. Although this surge of affection was quickly overtaken by a fit of temper, he managed to say, "Excuse me, Gianna. You have upset me. You're right. We must revenge ourselves—more than ever."

So saying, he grabbed her around the waist again and hugged her close.

"No, for heaven's sake. Now you've messed me up," she objected happily, trying to free herself from his arms. Then she kissed him through her veil, very, very softly, very tenderly, and ran off.

Giulio del Carpine frowned, staring into space, one hand across his mouth, idly scratching his cheek. As he pulled himself together, he had a feeling of irritation against the woman who had poisoned his mind against his wife just for the fun of it.

She was satisfied—but it was not their safety she cared about, as she had said. She was happy because now she was not the only one to be unfaithful. Why, she even said as much. Also she had taken him down a peg. The silly fool could not realize that, with Sandro for a husband, she had had every excuse for her infidelity, whereas Livia—by God!—she had none!

Now that the idea had been implanted in his mind, he knew no peace. He did not rank his wife's fidelity any higher than he did that of other women, but he had a high opinion of himself, his vigor, his masculine superiority, and was therefore still convinced that Livia . . .

Or perhaps she had taken up with Sandro out of spite! But, dear God, what kind of revenge was that? It was Sandro Sacchi who was revenged, not she, who had, after all, a superior husband.

True, he was having this foolish affair with a woman who certainly was no match for his wife. That was perhaps why Sandro was so little worried by Giannetta's infidelity. To be sure, in the exchange it was Sandro who came out ahead. Now there was nothing he could do because of his own liaison with Sandro's wife. The loss and ridicule were all his. No, oh, God! No!

He slammed out of the room, angry and full of hatred.

Somehow, he struggled through the day; the more he thought about the situation, the more unlikely it seemed. After six years of marriage, he felt he knew his wife, who, although not quite indifferent, certainly had never shown much inclination for love-making. Was it possible that he was deceived to that extent? He stayed out until late that night, only returning home when he was sure not to run into her. He was afraid of betraying his suspicions, although within himself he did not believe them.

Next day, when he awoke, he decided to go and find out. But he was soon assailed by irritation, bitterness and humiliation. Supposing he found out that she was unfaithful—what could he do? Suppose he met her in that street—what could he say? Before coming to a decision, it was best to go to via Sardegna and take a look around.

He dressed hurriedly and went out. On the ground floor of Number 96 he saw the studio which had made Giannetta laugh so. The accuracy of her information riled him, as if that alone were proof of his own betrayal. Stopping in a doorway opposite the house, he looked up at the windows of the apartment Sandro had taken. This entrance where no one could see him would be a good place to hide, he thought, when the time came to spy on them.

Knowing his wife's habits and the hours she usually left the house, he figured that her rendezvous with her lover would take place either in the morning between ten and eleven or in the afternoon around four. But it was more likely to be in the morning. Well, since he was here, why not wait? Perhaps this morning his doubts could be scuttled. He glanced at his watch and saw that it was barely after nine. He could not possibly wait in the doorway that long. As Porta Pinciana was nearby, he decided to walk in the Villa Borghese gardens for an hour.

It was a beautiful November morning, rather cold but bracing. As he entered the park, Don Giulio saw two artillery officers out for a canter with two young girls who appeared to be English and sisters, blond and lithe. They wore gray breeches and had long scarlet ribbons tied around the mannish collars of their riding shirts. As he watched, they all started to race as if taking up a dare. Don Giulio was amused. He went over to the bridle path to watch them and, with an expert's eye, noticed that the bay ridden by the girl on the right had something wrong with its hind leg. The four of them disappeared around a bend in the road. Don Giulio stood looking after them wistfully. In his mind's eye he saw his wife, Livia, mounted on a big, fiery bay. No other woman held herself as well as she in the saddle! It was a pleasure to watch her. She was a born horsewoman. With such a passion for horses, contrary to feminine inclinations, how could she have chosen that effeminate, foolish Sandro Sacchi? Well, that was still to be seen!

Absent-mindedly, absorbed in his thoughts, he wandered on. Suddenly he looked at his watch and turned back in a hurry. It was nearly ten and now he would have to hurry to reach the doorway on via Sardegna in time. He felt sure his wife would not come by via Veneto but from a cross street off via Boncompagni. However, by coming this way he ran some risk of meeting Sandro.

Meanwhile, Sandro Sacchi, standing in that same doorway, was caressing a little black dog who showed him great affection— a little dog all atremble, twisting, stretching and scratching at Sandro's legs with its paws, or jumping up in an effort to lick his face. Sandro was very pale, his eyes filled with tears. That good little beast, dear little thing, it loved him and was faithful. Yes, *he* was not like his fickle mistress; yes, yes, she was not to be trusted, but Liri was a good doggy. A woman who used the apartment of her lover, to receive a good-for-nothing, a real rascal, no doubt—yes, she was a bad, bad . . .

Sandro Sacchi, standing there caressing the little dog and talking to himself, wept tears of shame and anguish.

Pretending nonchalance, Del Carpine drew nearer. He let out a sigh of relief when he saw the doorway a few steps ahead. But slipping into the entrance, he caught sight of Sandro.

"What, you here!" he exclaimed.

Both men changed color. Sandro Sacchi forgot about his red eyes, but, as the tears continued to slip down his poor, flushed face, he instinctively brushed them aside with his fingers. Sandro might have expected anything but that Giulio del Carpine should have shown up here to surprise him in ambush.

Sandro had discovered Donna Livia's duplicity by a slip of the tongue of the maid who took care of the apartment. Finding Liri, Livia's pet dog, alone in the street was enough to confirm his worst doubts. He, too, had refused to believe her unfaithful because it was an unthinkable affront, but now he understood why she had not wanted him to have a key to the apartment and had always made him wait for her downstairs in the sculptor's studio. Oh, how stupid he had been—how blind!

"I'm just waiting," Sandro stuttered, his lips parting in a stupid grin as he looked at Don Giulio.

"What about Liri?" Del Carpine asked, glaring at the dog.

Sandro Sacchi looked down, as if he had not noticed the dog before.

"I don't know," he said. "I found him here."

Confronted with this foolishness, Don Giulio could hardly control himself. He stepped back into the street to look up at the number over the door.

"What number is this, anyway?"

"Huh?" Sandro grunted, looking as if all the blood was drained from his veins.

"Who are you waiting for?" demanded Giulio with a glassy stare.

"A . . . a friend," Sandro stammered. "He . . . went out."

"With Livia?" snapped Del Carpine.

"No. What do you mean?"

"Well, since Liri is here . . ."

"Yes, but I swear I found him here, right here in the street,"

Sandro blurted out, turning redder than a beet.

"Here? In the street?" repeated Del Carpine, stooping to the dog. "Do you know this street, Liri? How can that be?"

The little dog, hearing the unusually gentle tone of his master's voice, was overcome with joy and threw himself at his legs, shaking all over. He began to wave his paws, to yelp and roll on his back as if he had suddenly gone mad, turning round and round. He jumped first on his master, then on Sandro, barking louder and louder in his wild affection for both of them, as though he were unable to express all his joy and devotion.

The fidelity of the little dog for the two men, each deceived by the faithless Livia, was indeed touching. Both tried to conceal their embarrassment by a show of pleasure for the frantic attentions of the dog, laughing nervously and inciting him.

"Here, Liri!"

"Poor little doggie!"

Suddenly Liri sniffed and cocked his ears. He went to the doorway and sat on his tail, looking down the street, all attention, his head to one side. Then he shot out.

Don Giulio cautiously looked around the door and saw his wife turn into the street, the little dog at her side.

"Wait," said Sandro, pale and trembling, pulling him back by the arm. "Let me see who—"

"What?" exclaimed Don Giulio.

Liri stopped at the corner in a quandary, looking back toward the doorway. A moment later, a boy of about twenty, sporting an unbelievably large mustache, came out of the door of Number 96 and looked around, as proud as a peacock.

"Toti!" breathed Sandro Sacchi with a groan that twisted his face in a painful grimace. Still holding Don Giulio by the arm, he said, "It's Toti! He's just a boy, a student! You understand what your wife is up to? Let me take care of this. You saw? Now that's enough, Giulio—enough for all time!"

Don Giulio was dumfounded. So there were two of them! And now Sandro was out of the running? Then he too had been here to spy on her? No wonder the little dog was lost, confused, running hither and yon in the street. He felt shaken with disgust and at the same time he pitied Sandro, who had been so cavalierly treated by Livia, tricked and even openly flouted . . .

Don Giulio walked quickly away, pulling a handkerchief from his pocket to wipe his hands where the dog had licked them. He rubbed them so hard it seemed as if he was trying to remove the skin.

Then he noticed the dog running meekly beside him, ears down, tail between his legs. Poor Liri, after first trying to follow his mistress, then Toti, then Sandro, had finally caught up with his master.

Don Giulio flew into a rage. The faithfulness of that dumb animal seemed obscene to him. He lifted his foot and let fly a violent kick.

"Away with you!"

A BREATH OF AIR

Sparkling eyes, blond hair, bare little arms and legs, childish laughter escaping in muffled giggles—that imp of a Tina darted across the room to open the glass doors of the balcony.

She had started to turn the knob when a hoarse growl, like that of a wild beast surprised in his lair, quickly stopped her. Petrified with fear, she turned around to stare into the room.

Everything was dark.

The balcony shutters were open only a crack. Although her eyes were still blinded by the lighted corridor from which she had come, she was keenly aware of her grandfather's presence in the darkness, a huge mound propped up in his big chair heaped with cushions, gray-checked shawls, and rough, shaggy blankets, all smelling of stuffy old age stagnating in paralysis.

His immovable bulk did not frighten her so much as the fact that she had forgotten him there in the dark and had disobeyed her parent's strict order never to go into his room without first knocking and asking permission. What was it she was supposed to say? "May I come in, Grandpapa?" Then she must enter very, very quietly, on tiptoe, without making a sound!

The first impulsive laugh was quickly stifled by a gasp verging on a sob. The trembling child tiptoed toward the door not realizing that the old man, accustomed to the dark, could see her.

"Here!" he commanded harshly, just as she was about to step over the threshold.

She caught her breath and hesitantly tiptoed back toward him. Now that she too began to see in the darkness, the wicked look in her grandfather's piercing eyes made her quickly lower her own.

Those eyes, alert with inexorable terror and silent hate, showed between puffy, inflamed bags which reminded her of the sticky body of a tarantula. Already held captive by death, the old man's huge frame seemed to have banished his soul, which now rallied only in his eyes.

He could still move his left hand a little. After staring at it a long time with those implacable eyes, willing animation into it, he at last succeeded in lifting it ever so slightly above the covers. After a fraction of a second it fell back again inert. He persevered in this exercise because that flicker of movement was all the life left to him—"life" understood as movement in which others participated at will and in which he, too, could still take this infinitesimal part.

"Why . . . the balcony?" he faltered, his sluggish tongue struggling with the words.

Still trembling, the child did not answer. The old man immediately sensed something different in her. She trembled with fear every time her mother or father bade her approach him, yet this time it was not the same. She had been startled by his harsh, unexpected command, but there was something else which sent a thrill through her whole body.

"What's the matter?" he asked.

"Nothing," she replied, hardly daring to raise her eyes.

The old man still detected something unusual in the child's voice, even in the way she breathed.

"What is the matter?" he repeated resentfully.

She burst into tears and threw herself on the floor. She screamed and struggled with such convulsive violence that the old man was increasingly irritated, for here too he sensed a difference.

"Heavens, Tina, what's the matter?" cried her mother, running into the room. "What's come over you? Now, now, hush! Come to Mama. Why did you come in here? . . . What's that? Bad! Who is bad? . . . Ah! Grandpa! No, *you* are bad. Grandpa loves you. What happened?"

The old man, to whom the last question had been addressed, stared fiercely at the smile on his daughter-in-law's red lips, then at the lovely strand of golden hair the child pulled from her mother's head in her struggle to drag her from the room.

"Oww! My hair . . . Oh! Tina, you'll pull it all out. Mama's poor hair! Bad little girl! Look!" she said, opening the small hand and drawing the hairs, one by one, through the little fingers, repeating, "See . . . see . . ."

The child stared down at her fingers with tears in her eyes. She suddenly believed she had really pulled out all her mother's hair. But seeing nothing in her hand, and hearing her mother's happy laugh, she started to cry again, tugging at her mother to leave the room.

The old man breathed heavily. He was nettled by the question, which had rekindled his hatred.

"What's the matter with all of them?" he said to himself.

Their eyes, their voices—even his daughter-in-law's laugh, and the way she drew those hairs, one by one, through the child's little fingers—had something unusual about them. No, neither of them behaved the same as on other days. What was it all about?

His resentment soared when he lowered his eyes and saw a golden hair resting on the blanket over his knees. Wafted there by her carefree laugh, it had settled on his dead legs. He tried doggedly to urge his hand along little by little toward the hair which mocked him so bitterly. When his son came in, as was his custom before leaving the house to go to work, he found the old man exhausted from the effort he had been making in vain for half an hour.

"Good morning, Papa!"

The old man looked up, his eyes dilating with fear and surprise. His son, too?

Understanding his look to mean that the child had annoyed him, the son hastened to say, "Tina is a little devil! Did she disturb you? Listen, she's still crying because I scolded her. So long, Papa. I'm in a hurry. See you later. Nerina will come in to you shortly."

The old man's eyes followed him all the way to the door.

Yes, his son, too! Never before had he used that tone. "Good morning, Papa!" Why? What had he expected? Were they all in league against him? What had happened? First the child came in all a-flutter, then the mother laughed because her hair was pulled, and now his son with his cheerful "Good morning, Papa!"

Something had happened or was going to happen today and they all wanted to keep it from him. What could it be?

They had taken the world for themselves, his son and daughter-in-law and grandchild—*his* world that he had created and into which he had placed them. Not only that, but they had also appropriated time—as if he no longer existed in time! As if time were not his also—was he not to see, nor breathe, nor think in it? He still breathed, and he saw everything—more than all of them put together.

A stream of impressions and memories ran riot in his mind, like lightning flashing in a storm. La Plata, the pampas, the salt marshes of lost rivers, innumerable pawing herds bleating, whinnying, lowing. Out there, he had built a fortune from nothing in forty-five years, always keeping his eye on the main chance, forever hatching schemes with patient cunning. Beginning as a herdsman, he had gone on to become a small-holdings settler, then an employee of big railroad contractors, and finally a contractor and builder on his own. He had come back to Italy after the first fifteen years and married, but immediately after the birth of his only son he had gone back there alone. His wife died without his having seen her again, and his son, raised by his mother's relatives, had grown up without knowing him.

Four years ago he had returned, a sick man near death, his body horribly distended by dropsy, suffering from hardening of the arteries, his kidneys ruined and a bad heart. But although his days and even his hours were numbered, he didn't stop. He bought land in Rome and started building, having himself transported to and from the site in a wheelchair, enormously swollen but rugged as a rock. Every fifteen days or so they would drain quarts of fluid from his belly, and then he'd be right back in the thick of things again. That is, until two years ago when he was felled by a stroke of apoplexy—but not quite finished off. No, he had not been granted the good fortune to die in harness. For two years now he'd been completely paralyzed, smouldering in resentful anticipation of the end and hating his son, who was so unlike himself, a stranger to him. His son had voluntarily liquidated the whole business, about which he knew nothing, and had prudently invested the paternal fortune, but he had chosen to continue his own modest legal practice—as if refusing to give the old man any satisfaction, thus avenging his mother and himself for their long abandonment.

He detested the son. They had nothing in common, either of thought or feeling. Yes, he detested his daughter-in-law too, and that child! He despised them all because they had excluded him from their life, refusing to tell him what had happened today to change all three of them.

Big tears slipped from his eyes. He let himself go and cried like a baby, forgetting the tower of strength he had been for so many years.

Nerina, the servant, paid no attention to his tears when she came in a little later to take care of him. The old man was so full of water that it did no harm if a little of it spilled out of his eyes. With this thought, she carelessly dried his face and took up a bowl of milk.

"Eat, eat," she told him, dipping a biscuit into the warm milk and holding it to his mouth.

He ate, peering stealthily up at her. She sighed, he thought, but not because she was tired or bored. He suddenly raised his eyes and stared at her. There! She was about to sigh again but smothered it. Instead of ignoring his gaze, she huffed and shrugged her shoulders as if she were cross. Then, for no reason at all, she blushed! What was the matter with *her*? They all had something strange about them today. What could it be?

He refused to eat any more.

"What's the matter with you?" he demanded testily.

"Me? What's the matter with me?" she repeated, surprised.

"Yes, you—everybody. What is it? What's happened?" he asked.

"Nothing . . . I don't know. What do you mean?"

"Sighs!" he mumbled.

"Did I sigh? Not at all! Well, if I did, maybe I did it unconsciously. I really have no reason to sigh," she said, and laughed merrily.

"Why do you laugh like that?"

"Laugh? I laughed because you said I sighed," she told him, laughing all the more.

"Oh, go away," the old man snapped.

Later, when the doctor arrived for his regular visit and they all gathered in the room—his son, daughter-in-law and their little girl—the suspicion he had nursed all day, even in his sleep, that they were hiding something from him became a certainty.

They were all in on the secret. They talked of other things in his presence just to put him off, but the understanding between them showed clearly in their glances. They had never before looked at one another in just this way. Their gestures, their voices, their very smiles did not match their words. And what about all that animated discussion about wigs? It seemed that wigs were coming into fashion again!

"Green, if you please, green, or mauve!" cried his daughter-in-law, turning pink with mock indignation, so feigned indeed that she couldn't help laughing outright.

Her mouth laughed of its own accord, and her hands rose instinctively to caress her hair—as if her hair needed that caress!

"I understand, I quite understand," the doctor said, his full-moon face wreathed in smiles. "When one has hair like yours, dear lady, it would be a crime to hide it under a wig."

The old man could hardly restrain his anger. He would have liked to bellow and drive them all out of the room. The doctor, accompanied by the daughter-in-law holding her little girl by the hand, was hardly through the door when his rage exploded against his son, left alone with him in the room. He shot the same questions at him as he had put in vain to the child and to the servant girl.

"What's the matter with all of you? Why are you all behaving like this today? What's happened? What are you trying to hide from me?"

"Nothing at all, Papa. What is there to hide?" his son replied in surprise and dismay. "We're all just about the same as usual, I think."

"It's not true! There's something different. I see it! I feel it in all of you! You think I don't see anything or feel anything because I'm like *this!*" he said thickly, trying to turn his head to the wall.

"But, Papa, I really can't think what you see new or different in us today. Nothing has happened. Believe me. I swear and double-swear it! Now, you must be calm."

The old man was somewhat mollified by his son's evident sincerity, but he was not yet fully convinced. He had no doubt whatsoever that something was up. He saw it; he felt it in all of them. What could it be?

When he was alone in the room, the reply came suddenly, silently, from the balcony. The knob, half turned by the child that morning, was released now in the early evening by a breath of air and the door onto the balcony swung open.

He did not notice it at first, but then he smelled a delicious perfume invading the room which came from the garden. He looked up and saw a strip of moonlight lying across the floor, a trace of luminous brilliance piercing the dark shadows.

"Ah, so that's it," he said, sighing.

The others could not see it. They could not even feel it in themselves because they were still part of life. But he who was almost dead, he had seen and felt it there among them. So that was why the child had trembled this morning. That was why his daughter-in-law had laughed and taken such delight in her golden hair. And that was why the servant girl sighed. That was why they had all behaved differently, without even knowing it.

Spring had come.

YESTERDAY AND TODAY

War had broken out only a few days before.

Marino Lerna, a volunteer in the first special course of Officers Training School, had received his commission as second lieutenant in the Infantry. He spent a week on leave with his family and then left for Macerata to join his regiment, the 12th Casale Brigade.

He expected to spend a few months there training recruits before being sent to the front. However, three days after his arrival his name was called out in the courtyard of the barracks. Going upstairs, he found eleven other second lieutenants from different platoons who had all come to Macerata at about the same time.

"What's up? Why? Where?"

"Upstairs, in the Colonel's office."

With his comrades Lerna stood stiffly at attention before a massive table cluttered with files and papers; he understood from the Colonel's first words that they had been ordered to the front. Still dazzled by the June sunlight in the courtyard, he could distinguish nothing clearly in the dark room except the shining emblems on the collar of the Colonel's uniform, the long, flushed, horse face barred by a large mustache, and the confusion of white papers scattered over the table.

His thoughts ran riot, and the Colonel's military jargon, snapped out in a hard, clipped voice, made no sense to him. But by listening attentively he soon discovered that he had guessed right: they were scheduled to leave the following evening.

It was common knowledge around the barracks that the 12th Brigade held a tough position near Podgora, where many young officers had already been wiped out in several unsuccessful attacks. Now they were rushing men forward to replace those casualties.

When the Colonel dismissed the twelve young men, their tension relaxed and for a few minutes they felt a kind of spurious hang-over. This was quickly replaced by a show of nonchalance as each tried to impress the other with his *sangfroid*.

They all decided to go to the telegraph office and wire their families, bravely announcing their departure. That is, all except one—the very one out of eighty officer candidates in Rome who had been assigned with Marino Lerna to the 12th Regiment, a man named Sarri. It was just Lerna's luck that Sarri would be paired off with him—the only one of his comrades he disliked.

Sarri had no one to whom he could telegraph the news of his departure. In the three days the men had spent together in Macerata, Lerna had come to feel less hostile toward him, although he had not radically changed his opinion. Perhaps this was because, when they were alone, Sarri dropped the contemptuous attitude which had made him so unpopular with all his comrades in Rome. It was now Lerna's opinion that this haughty manner was prompted by Sarri's determination never to appear to share his feelings with anyone else. To this end, he felt obliged not only to take a different stand from the others but exactly the opposite, without caring what people thought of him. He was proud of the antipathy he inspired, more because of this need for detachment than because of a cantankerous nature. He could get away with it because he was rich and all alone in the world.

He brought a young woman along with him to Macerata whom he had been keeping in Rome for the last three months.

All the members of the platoon knew her well. Sarri, too, had counted on staying there a month or more during which time he had wanted, he said, to gratify his appetites, or at least the simpler one for the opposite sex. He was convinced he would be killed at the front, and, besides, the idea of living after the war in the wake of a countryful of heroes was intolerable!

"Aren't you coming?" Lerna asked when Sarri did not make a move to follow the others to the telegraph office.

Sarri shrugged.

Lerna, embarrassed, tried to cover up his mistake. "No . . . that is . . . I want to ask your advice."

"Really? Why mine?"

"I don't know. You see, three days ago when I left Rome I promised my father and mother—"

"Are you an only son?" asked Sarri.

"Yes. Why?"

"I pity you."

"Oh, I know, it's hard on them. I assured them I wouldn't leave for the front for a couple of months, and that before leaving I would go back and say goodbye . . ."

He was about to say "for the last time," but caught himself.

Sarri understood and smiled. "Go ahead, say it: 'for the last time.' "

"No. Let's hope not. I'll keep my fingers crossed. To greet them, let's say, once again before leaving."

"Good. And then?"

"Wait! My father made me promise that if my leave were canceled, I would let him know in time so that he could come here with Mama and say goodbye. Now we are leaving tomorrow at five."

"But if they caught the ten-o'clock train tonight," Sarri suggested, "they could be here tomorrow morning at seven and spend almost the whole day with you."

"Is that what you advise me to do?" asked Lerna.

"Not at all!" Sarri protested. "Here you have the good luck of being able to leave without tears . . ."

"No, for that matter, Mama has already cried."

"Isn't that enough for you? Do you want to see her cry again?

Wire you're leaving tonight and say goodbye now. It's better for you, and for them too."

Seeing that Lerna was still undecided, Sarri added, "So long. I'm going to tell Nini we're leaving. That'll be a laugh. She loves me, but if she cries I'll slap her."

And he left.

Still wondering whether or not to follow Sarri's advice, Marino Lerna walked to the telegraph office. He found that all his comrades had sent their farewells, so he decided to do the same. Then, as he thought it over, it seemed like a betrayal of his poor father and mother, so he sent another telegram marked *urgent,* explaining that if they took the ten-o'clock train they would arrive in the morning in time to see him off.

Marino Lerna's mother was an uncompromising little woman of the old school whose like can now be found only in the provinces. Erect in her whalebone corset, a little stiff and angular without being thin, overanxious, she wavered between doubt and suspicion, her mousy little eyes darting restlessly to and fro.

She adored her only son to such a point that, not wishing to be separated from him during his university days, she had forsaken the comforts of her old home, with all the hereditary customs of village life in the Abruzzi, to go to live in Rome, where for the past two years she had felt completely lost.

The following morning she arrived in Macerata in such a state that her son quickly regretted having told them to come. She was hardly off the train before she started protesting, "No, no, no . . ." and she hung on his neck, crying against his chest.

"Oh, don't tell me, Rinuccio . . . don't tell me."

Meanwhile, his father's face was grave as he patted him on the shoulder. He was a man, and men do not cry.

Just before leaving Rome he had had a conversation with an unknown gentleman whose eldest son had been on the field of battle from the first day of the war, and he still had two younger sons at home. A conversation between fathers—that's all. "Without tears."

However, his effort to restrain his tears at all costs—an effort which showed clearly in his feverish, gleaming eyes—gave his thin, small, well-cared-for person an air of ridiculous solemnity, more pathetic perhaps than the uncontrolled grief of his wife.

He was evidently wrought up, alluding to that mysterious conversation with the unknown gentleman as if he had something to hide. The effect on him was curious: it made him aware of his own agitation under his mask of calm; this both annoyed and humiliated him when confronted by the frank, strong, silent emotion of his son, who was upset by his mother's tears and tried to reassure her more with caresses than with words.

It was just as Sarri had foreseen—a useless ordeal.

After taking his parents to the hotel, Marino Lerna had had to rush off immediately for the barracks, where he was kept until noon. He just had time to eat lunch with them in their hotel room—his mother's eyes were too red and swollen to go down to the dining room and she was barely able to stand—before bolting back to the base for his final instructions. His parents did not see him again until just a few minutes before the train left.

Alone with his wife in their room, the father embarked on a beautiful speech, a long, logical speech in which, swallowing frequently and passing a trembling little hand over his lips, he said she should not cry like that, because nothing indicated that their Rinuccio—God forbid—so many things could happen. The regiment might even be sent back to the rear lines, since, as everyone knew, it had been at the front from the first day of the war. Then if all the soldiers were to be killed at the front . . . Was it likely? They were more likely to be wounded. Some little wound—in the arm, for example. God would look after their son. Why put the evil eye on him with all those tears? She must remember that it was bad for Rinuccio to see her carrying on like that—surely it upset him.

But his wife said that it wasn't her fault. Her eyes . . . her eyes . . . What could she do? It was the effect of her son's words, everything he did—a cruel sensation of *remembrance*.

"Each word, you understand, has the effect not of being said now, but of *having* been said. It remains stamped there as if he were already no more. What can I do about it? Oh, God!"

"Isn't that an ill omen?" asked her husband.

"No! What are you saying!"

"I say it's a bad sign! As for me, I'm going to laugh. You'll see, I'm going to *laugh* when he leaves."

If it had gone on like that much longer there would have been an argument. Their anxiety became even more acute with their son's prolonged delay. God! Why couldn't his superiors understand that these last moments belonged to his poor mama and papa?

Their impatience reached the breaking point when Marino's comrades began to arrive, one after the other, running into the hotel, leaving the carriages waiting outside for their luggage, ready to set off immediately for the station. An orderly carried out a dressing case; another was loaded down with a knapsack, an overcoat and a dress sword. Then they all climbed in and the vehicles rolled off at a great clip.

Marino, the last to leave the barracks, ran to the shoemaker's to pick up a pair of hobnail boots he had ordered the previous day. And so he was late.

It was more than a separation; it was a wrenching apart, with hysterics at the last moment. In fact Marino arrived with his parents just as the doors of the train were being closed. He leaped into a carriage where his çomrades hung out calling to him to hurry, and the train began to move amidst the hubbub of voices, tears, goodbyes, with handkerchiefs flying, hats and hands waving.

Signor Lerna waved his hat until the train disappeared. He was annoyed with himself that he had not had time to do it properly. When he turned around to his wife, he couldn't find her. They had carried her away to the waiting room in a faint.

Now the station was calm and deserted. In the dazzling light of the long, drowsy summer afternoon there were only the shining rails and the distant monotonous scraping of the locusts.

All the carriages had gone off to town with people who had come to the station to say goodbye. When Marino Lerna's mother finally came to and could be taken back to the hotel, there was not a single conveyance left. A station attendant kindly offered to run over to the garage nearby to see if the bus had returned from its trip to town.

At the last moment, when Marino's mother had been helped, almost carried, to a seat in the bus and it was about to start, a blond young girl ran up out of nowhere and climbed in. She was wearing a large straw hat covered with roses, a very low-necked dress; her eyes and lips were painted. She was weeping as though her heart would break.

A beautiful young girl.

In one hand she clutched a small blue embroidered handkerchief, and the other, sparkling with rings, she held over her right cheek to hide the burning red mark of a slap.

It was the same Nini who had come to Macerata with Sarri three days before. Marino Lerna's father knew what kind of girl the little blonde was, but his wife did not. Seeing another woman in tears like herself, she couldn't resist asking, "Are you a wife, Signora?"

Holding the doll-sized handkerchief before her eyes, the girl quickly shook her head.

"Sister?" the mother insisted.

But at this point her husband intervened, giving his wife a discreet nudge with his elbow.

Perhaps the young girl noticed his maneuver; in any case, she knew that the old lady would soon find out about her and she did not reply. But she also sensed something else which made her cry even harder: she knew that the old woman would stop crying now because she would be ashamed to mingle her tears with those of a girl like herself.

But *her* tears were real too, she thought—and tears shed from a sorrow were more unusual than the everyday, natural tears of a mother. In Rome, toward the end, Nini had gone not only with Sarri but with many of his comrades as well—perhaps even with this boy for whom the old woman wept.

Today, at noon, she had sat with ten of the boys at table—a tableful of devils! They teased the life out of her like a bunch of giddy fools and she let them have their way—poor boys leaving for the front. They insisted on baring her breasts right there in the restaurant. Her little breasts were famous among them,

looking almost virginal with those upturned nipples. Like idiots,
they had wanted to christen them with champagne. She let them
do whatever they liked—touch, kiss, press, pull and fondle her—
so that they might have a living memory of her flesh, made for
love, out there where one by one all those handsome young men
of twenty might be killed. She had laughed with them so much
and—yes, dear God!—had kissed each of them for the last time
and . . . Sarri was the one who had slapped her when her eyes
had filled with tears, yet she didn't hold it against him.

So now why couldn't that old mama let her cry her heart out
without taking offense? Of course the old lady did let her cry,
but she stopped crying herself and there was no telling how
badly she needed to cry, poor old soul.

So the young girl tried to hold back her tears to allow the
mother's to flow freely, but all in vain. The more she tried to
stop crying, the more uncontrollably her tears flowed down her
cheeks. She was depressed to by the disapproval she felt. At last,
unable to bear the scowl on the face of the old woman who
stared at her with all the jealous hatred mothers feel for such
girls, she burst into sobs.

"Have pity," she moaned. "I can't help crying, Signora. They
are *my* tears. I can cry too. You for your son, and I . . . well, not
really for your son, but for one who left with him and who
slapped me because I was crying. You cry for one, I for all of
them. I *can* cry for them, even for your son, Signora. All . . .
all of them."

Lerna's mother was so stricken over her son's departure that
she needed to quiet her nerves, but this girl disturbed her and
was offensive as well. The thought that her son would not be
exposed to danger for another two days had given her a respite,
so now she could be hard, and hard she was! Fortunately the
distance from the station back to town was not great. When the
bus stopped, she got out without so much as a glance at the girl
sitting there.

The following day, on their way back to Rome, Signora Lerna
stood beside her husband when the train stopped in the station at
Fabriano. As they leaned out the window of their first-class carriage, she recognized the young girl of the bus running along

the platform with a very young man and looking for a place in the train. She was laughing, and in her arms she carried a bunch of flowers.

Signora Lerna turned to her husband and said in a voice loud enough to be heard, "Look, there's the one who was crying for 'all of them.'"

The girl turned, without anger or scorn, and her eyes seemed to say, "Poor foolish old mama, don't you understand that is the way of life? Yesterday I cried for one, so today I must laugh for another."

Tales of Frustration

ESCAPE

This fog is the last straw! Bareggi thought as its icy needles stung his face and neck. Tomorrow I'll feel it in all my bones—head heavy as lead, eyes swollen shut between watery bags. It's enough to drive a man out of his mind.

Signor Bareggi, worn out by nephritis at fifty-two, squelched along the avenue with his cheap cloth shoes oozing as if there had been a downpour. His feet were so swollen that if a finger were pressed to them it took a full minute for the skin to come smooth again, and the pain in his kidneys never let up.

Morning and evening, wearing the same cloth shoes, Signor Bareggi trudged from home to office and from his office, home. (Hadn't his doctor told him to exercise "within reason"?) As he dragged himself along, moving slowly because of those tender, aching feet, he nursed a dream: he would run away some day, run away to hide from it all, run away forever.

His home life drove him to desperation, too. The thought of having to go back day after day to that house—on its remote cross street off the long avenue where he was now walking—had become unbearable. It was not the distance he minded, though, with his feet, it was no small matter. Nor was it the isolation, which, in fact, he cherished. The cross streets were little more than lanes with no street lamps, and as yet there were few signs of "civilization." There were only three small houses to the left, and, on the right, a country hedgerow shielded vast truck gardens. In the midle of the hedge was a weather-beaten sign reading LOTS FOR SALE.

His was the third little house, with four dark rooms on the ground floor. There were shutters at the windows. In addition the glass panes had been screened to shield them from the stones thrown by the hoodlums in the neighborhood. But on the upper floor there were three small cheerful bedrooms and a little veranda with a view over the truck gardens, which was his delight in good weather.

As soon as he entered the house he was plagued by the anxious attentions of his wife and daughters, a fluttering hen followed by two peeping chicks. They ran here, flew there, getting his slippers or his cup of milk with the egg yolk in it. One of them would be down on all fours untying his shoes, another asking, in a whining voice, whether he was soaked from rain or sweat, according to the season—as if he could be dry when he had walked all the way home without an umbrella, or as if in mid-August he would not be bathed in perspiration!

All this coddling would be the ruination of his stomach. They only treat me this way so I can't give free rein to my feelings, he thought ruefully. How could he complain before those eyes melting with pity, before those eternally ministering hands?

And how he yearned to complain—about so many things! He had only to turn his head to left or right to find a reason for complaint, a reason they never even dreamed of. Take the big old kitchen table, for instance. They all ate there and, with his diet of bread and milk, its smell of good raw meat and beautiful onions in their golden skins was a downright offense! Could he chide his daughters because they ate meat which their mother prepared deliciously with those onions? Or could he reproach them because they did the laundry at home to save money and threw the water, reeking of strong soap, out the door, thus spoiling that breath of fresh green from the vegetable gardens he so enjoyed in the evenings?

How unjustified such a reproof would seem to them who drudged all day long, stuck away there like exiles, little dreaming that, in other circumstances, each of them might have led a far different life.

Fortunately, his daughters were a little simple-minded, like their mother. He pitied them, but, seeing them reduce themselves to the state of old dish rags, his pity turned to sour vexation.

For he was not good-natured. No, no. He was not even good, as those poor women—and for that matter most everybody else— seemed to think. He was bad. At certain times the bitterness he felt deep inside must have burned in his eyes. It would come out as he sat alone at his desk in the office, unconsciously toying, perhaps, with the blade of his penknife. Insane impulses, like slashing the canvas sheathing of his desk top or the leather of his armchair, would almost overcome him. Instead, he would spread out his swollen hand, fingers splayed on the desk, and look at it while tears welled up in his eyes. With the other hand he would pluck furiously at the reddish hairs on the backs of his distended fingers.

He was bad, yes, but he was desperate too, for he would probably wind up one of these days in a wheelchair, paralyzed down one side, completely at the mercy of those three tiresome women. It was this longing to escape while there was yet time that drove him wild.

That evening, as he was nearing the house, the longing suddenly rushed into his hands and one foot before it reached his head. His foot rose automatically to the step of the milkman's cart and his hands went to the seat, as it stood there untended at the corner of his lane.

What! Signor Bareggi, a serious man, sedate, respectable, a professional man, on a milkman's cart?

The impulse came over him when he had spied the cart through the thickening fog as he had turned off the avenue into the cross street; when his nostrils had caught that fresh odor of hay in the feedbag and the goaty smell of the milkman's coat thrown across the seat; when smells of the distant countryside far, far beyond Casal dei Pazzi—vast and free—had assailed him.

The horse, stretching his neck and cropping grass at the roadside, wandered a step at a time away from the three little houses at the end of the lane. The milkman tarried, as usual, to chat with the women, well knowing that his horse would wait patiently before their door. Tonight, when he came out, empty bottles in hand, and didn't find the horse in its usual place, he started to run toward the corner.

Bareggi's eyes were fever-bright. He tingled all over with pleasure and apprehension. Whatever happened, he no longer cared about the consequences for himself, the milkman, or his womenfolk. In the confusion of his troubled mind, all was dismissed as he seized the reins in one hand, the whip in the other, gave the horse a mighty slash on the rump—and they were off!

The startled horse looked old, but he wasn't. Bareggi had not counted on the beast's flying leap, which set up a din of clattering cans and jugs, racks and bottles, in back of him. The reins flew out of his hands when he tried to brace himself after the jolt, and his feet were knocked off the shaft as he was thrown backward. He scrambled to his feet again and recovered the reins, but scarcely was one danger over when another loomed. He held his breath as the maddened beast launched out on a wild race through the fog which had closed in with the coming night.

No one ran up to head them off or called out to anyone else to waylay them, even though all those milk cans banging around must have made a frightful racket. Perhaps there were no longer any people on the avenue or, if there were, their cries were not heard above the din. The streetlights must certainly have been lit by now, but Bareggi could not see them through the dense fog.

He let go of the whip and reins to hang onto the seat with both hands. The horse was either as fear-crazed as himself or not accustomed to the whip. Then again it might have been joy at the quick end of his evening's rounds that set him off, or his relief at no longer feeling the restraining reins. He neighed and neighed. Signor Bareggi was terrified by the violent backward thrust of his flanks in that race that seemed to gain momentum with every lunge.

The risk of crashing into something as they turned off the avenue crossed his mind and he tried to retrieve the reins, but when he let go of the seat to stretch out a hand he was thrown forward and banged his nose. Blood now spurted over his mouth, chin and hands, but he had no time to stanch it. He could only clutch the seat and hang on for dear life. God, oh God, how that milk was swishing and sloshing around in those overturned cans, splattering all over his back! Blood before and milk behind! Signor Bareggi laughed aloud as his bowels twisted in terror. He was laughing wildly at his own fear, instinctively rejecting the certainty of imminent disaster and hoping that, after all, this might turn out to be a magnificent joke—a mad prank to tell at the office tomorrow. He went on laughing desperately as he tried to recall the calm of the farmers watering their vegetable gardens while he watched them from his little balcony across the street. He thought next of things like the patches peasants wear on their clothes, as if to say, Yes, poverty covers my buttocks, knees and elbows, as bright and defiant as a flag. Meanwhile, beneath such thoughts, the threat of turning over at any moment lay vivid and terrifying. At any moment the cart would surely crash into something and scatter all over the place.

They flew past the Nomentana gate, past the Casal dei Pazzi, on and on into the open country, dimly visible through the fog.

When the horse finally stopped in front of a small farmhouse, the cart was battered and not a can or jug was left inside.

Hearing the horse pull up unusually early, the milkman's wife called out a greeting. When no one replied, she went to the door with an oil lamp and saw the wreck. Again she called her husband's name. Where could he be? What had happened?

But these were questions which the horse, still panting and happy after his wonderful gallop, was unable to answer. Snorting and stamping, his eyes bloodshot, he could only shake his head.

THE FOOTWARMER

In the wintertime, what good were those black oaks planted in a double row around the large square to give summer shade? After a rain, every little gust of wind shook water from the leaves onto the people walking below. And this dampness hastened the decay of Papa-rè's poor kiosk.

Apart from these difficulties in winter, the shade those trees gave in summer was surely a blessing. Well . . . men take things for granted when they go right, accepting them as their due, but let the slightest thing go wrong and their tempers flare. Irritable, ungrateful beasts, men! Good Lord, why did they have to walk under those trees right after a rain anyway?

It was true, however, that Papa-rè did not really enjoy their summer shade in his kiosk either. Actually he could never enjoy it because, winter or summer, he was not there during the day. What he did and where he went were a mystery. He always came back along via San Lorenzo looking very tired, as if he had walked a long way. Although the kiosk was closed most of the time and Papa-rè hardly turned a penny there, he had to pay taxes just like everyone else.

It was ironical that Papa-rè's kiosk was considered "*immovable* property," when it was likely to walk off by itself at any moment, what with the termites that occupied the premises in place of the owner. But termites were no concern of the tax collector. If the kiosk had taken a turn around the square or ambled up the street, it would still have been taxed the same as any other piece of real estate.

In back of the kiosk was a self-styled music hall, built of wood. To be exact, it was a barracks painted with flowery ostentation where so-called singers held forth to the accompaniment of a honky-tonk piano. How they managed to perform, poor things, was a mystery, for they barely had breath enough to say, "I'm hungry." Yet, reeking of tobacco smoke, the place was jammed every night with customers in carnival mood. They were highly entertained by the clumsy antics of the poor girls, who, when their voices couldn't make it, waved their arms or, more often, their legs.

"Hurrah! Bravo! Encore!" the men shouted, taking sides for this girl or that, and applauding or booing so violently that the police had to come settle their brawls.

Every night Papa-rè waited until after one for these distinguished customers. Half dead of cold, he dozed behind his wares: cigars, tallow candles, matches, tapers and the few evening papers left over from his usual rounds.

In the early evening he waited for his little granddaughter to bring him the big earthenware footwarmer. Taking it by the handles and holding it at arms' length, he waved it back and forth to fan the coals. Then he banked them with ashes kept in the kiosk for that purpose, and, without bothering to lock the door, left the little stove smoldering there untended. Old and decrepit as he was, Papa-rè could never have withstood those cold nights without his footwarmer.

And without a good pair of legs and a shrill voice, how was he to go on selling papers? Years alone had not weakened Papa-rè, nor was it age that made his legs do foolish things, but rather the weight of so many misfortunes. It had all begun when the Holy Father lost his temporal power, and was followed soon after by the death of Papa-rè's wife, and then that of his only daughter

—a disgraceful death in a miserable hospital, giving birth to this little girl for whom he went on living and toiling. Ah, if he hadn't the little one to look after . . .

Papa-rè wore an immense, battered old hat, much too big for him, which sank below his eyebrows. It seemed like a symbol of fate weighing on his old age. Who had made him a present of that hat? Where had he ever found it? Standing under it, there in the middle of the square, he seemed to say, "Here I am. If I'm to go on living, I must wear this wretched hat, which is so heavy I can hardly breathe!"

Go on living! But he didn't in the least want to go on living! He was bone-tired and hardly earned anything any more. He used to get hundreds of papers; now the distributor gave him a few copies out of pity—and then only after all the other newsboys had been supplied. They fought their way ahead of each other to be the first on the street with the news. Papa-rè now hung behind. He even waited until the women had theirs. When some roughneck shoved him aside, he bore it patiently, withdrawing into a corner, letting them all shoot by like rockets.

"For you, Papa-rè—have fun. Two dozen all for you tonight. Revolution in Russia!"

Papa-rè shrugged, blinked and picked up his pack. He was the last to leave. Then he too tried to run and strain his hoarse voice to a shout:

"Tribu-u-une!"

Then a notch lower:

"Revolution in Russia!"

And finally, almost to himself:

"Read all about it!"

Fortunately there were two porters in via Volturno, one in via Gaeta and another in via Palestro, who were faithful and waited for him. The other copies he disposed of as best he could, wandering all through the Macao district. Around ten o'clock, tired and spent, he went back to his kiosk, where he waited, dozing, until the customers came out of the café. He was fed up with this god-forsaken business. But when you are old, what choice is there? Rack your brains and you'll find none. The only alternative was to jump off the high wall of the Pincio.

At sunset, seeing his grandchild arrive almost barefoot and in rags, wrapped in an old woolen shawl given her by a neighbor, Papa-rè regretted the small cost of that fire which was so essential to him. He had no other comfort in life now but the child and the footwarmer. He smiled as he saw her coming, and rubbed his hands together. He kissed the child's forehead and shook the little stove to stir up the embers.

But one evening—either because his hands were colder than usual or because he felt weaker and more tired—as he started to wave the footwarmer back and forth in the middle of the square, it flew out of his hands and broke into pieces. People passing by greeted the crash with howls of laughter, provoked by Papa-rè's expression when he saw the faithful companion of his cold nights fly from his grasp, and by the simplicity of the child who ran forward as if to catch the stove in mid-air.

Grandfather and grandchild looked dully into each other's eyes. Papa-rè's arms were extended as if they were still in the act of swinging the little stove. But this time he had swung it too far. The live coals hissed there among the shards of pottery in a puddle of rainwater.

"Cheer up!" he said finally, rousing himself and shaking his head. "Laugh! Laugh, dear, and I will too. Go, my Nena, go on home. Who knows? Perhaps it's for the best."

And he went off to get his newspapers.

That evening he roamed the streets of the Macao neighborhood instead of returning around ten to the kiosk. He knew it would be deathly cold sitting in there. But soon he grew tired. Before going into the kiosk, he stopped at the place on the square where the footwarmer had shattered, as if he might still find a little warmth from its charred remains. The jarring sound of the battered piano came to him from the café, broken by scattered applause and cat-calls from the customers. Papa-rè had turned the collar of his shabby overcoat up to his ears, and he clutched the few remaining newspapers tightly to his breast as he stopped a moment to look through the frosted glass door. Must be good and warm in there, with a little hot punch in your stomach! That west wind had started to blow again, lashing his face and whitening the cobbles on the square with frost. There was not a cloud in the sky; even the stars looked shivery-bright.

Papa-rè sighed as he turned to the dark kiosk under the black oaks; then, stuffing the papers under his arm, he was about to shoot back the bolt when a harsh voice called from within, "Papa-rè!"

The old man was startled, and leaned down to peer inside. "Who's there?"

"Rosalba. Where's your footwarmer?"

"Rosalba?"

"Vignas. Don't you remember me? Rosalba Vignas!"

"Ah," said Papa-rè, who had only a confused recollection of the names of the café singers, past and present. "Why don't you go in where it's warm? What are you doing here?"

"I'm waiting for you. Coming in?"

"What do you want with me? Let me take a look at you."

"I don't want you to see me. I'm in here under the counter. Come on in. We'll be fine and warm."

Papa-rè, bending down, went in through the low door and shut it after him.

"Where are you?"

"Here," the woman answered.

She could not be seen, hidden there under the counter where Papa-rè displayed his papers, cigars, boxes of matches and candles. She filled the space where Papa-rè usually put his feet when he sat on his high stool.

"Where's the footwarmer?" she asked again from below. "Don't you use it any more?"

"Hush! I broke it today. It slipped from my hands as I was swinging it."

"What a pity! You'll die of the cold in here. I'd counted on your footwarmer. Sit down. Let me warm you up, Papa-rè."

"You? Warm me up? How? I'm old, child. Go on with you. What do you want of me?"

The woman broke into a shrill laugh and took a firm hold of one of his legs.

"Now, be quiet," said Papa-rè, pushing her away. "You smell of liquor. Are you drunk?"

"A little. Please sit down. You'll see there's room for both of us. Up . . . up . . . on the stool, like that. Now let's warm up your legs. Want another footwarmer? Here it is."

She put a bundle on his knees. How nice and warm it felt!

"What's this thing?" asked the old man.

"My baby girl."

"Your baby . . . You brought your baby here too?"

"He turned me out of the house, Papa-rè. He left me."

"Who?"

"Him, Cesare. I'm out in the cold with this baby in my arms!"

Papa-rè got off the high stool, bent down in the dark toward the woman crouching there and held out the baby.

"Take it, child, take it and go away. I have my own worries. Leave me alone."

"It's cold," said the woman hoarsely. "Are you going to throw me out, too?"

"You can't expect to live here," he said sharply. "Are you crazy or just drunk?"

The woman did not reply nor move. Perhaps she was weeping. The faint sound of a mandolin, titillating the silence, moved gradually closer from the end of via Volturno, and then suddenly turned and was gone, fading away in the distance.

"Please let me wait in here," the woman said.

"Wait? For whom?" asked Papa-rè.

"Him. I told you—Cesare. He's there in the café. I saw him through the window."

"Then go find him if you know he's in there."

"I can't with the baby. He's left me, I tell you. He's there with somebody else. You know who? That Mignon! She starts singing there tomorrow night. He's introducing her, fancy that! He even had her take singing lessons from a teacher at so much an hour! I just want to say a couple of words to him as soon as he comes out. To him *and* to her. Ah, let me wait here. I'm not in your way. Besides, I keep you warmer too. Papa-rè, with this cold outside and my poor little baby . . . It won't be long now, a half hour, more or less. Come on, be nice, Papa-rè! Sit down proper and take the baby on your knees. I can't hold her under here. You'll both be warmer. The poor mite's asleep; she won't be any trouble."

Papa-rè settled himself and took the baby back on his knees, muttering, "Just look at the new footwarmer I've found for myself. . . . What do you want to tell him?"

"Nothing. Just a couple of words," she repeated.

They were silent quite a while. From the station nearby came the mournful whistle of an occasional train, arriving or departing. A few stray dogs crossed the big, deserted square. On the other side, two night watchmen passed wrapped in their cloaks. In the silence, even the hum of the street lamps could be heard.

"You have a grandchild, haven't you, Papa-rè?" the woman asked, settling herself further under the counter with a sigh.

"Nena? Yes."

"No mama?"

"None."

"Look at my little girl. Isn't she pretty?"

Papa-rè did not answer.

"Isn't she pretty?" the woman insisted. "Now what is to happen to her, dear little thing? But I can't go on like this any longer. Someone will have to take her in. You see, I can't find work with her in my arms. Where can I leave her? Then, too, who would hire me? They won't take me on even as a servant."

"Do be quiet!" the old man said nervously and began to cough.

He remembered his daughter, who had left him a little baby so like this one on his knees. He hugged the child to him tenderly, but the caress was not for her; it was for his own grandchild, who had been small and good and quiet like this one.

A loud burst of applause and shouts rang out from the music hall.

"That bastard!" the woman cried through clenched teeth. "He's having a time for himself in there with that ugly monkey. She's as withered and dried-up as an old stick. Tell me, does he still stop here every night like he used to for a cigar as soon it lets out?"

"I don't know." Papa-rè shrugged.

"Cesare, from Milan, you know him perfectly well! That blond, tall, big fellow with his beard parted on his chin. He's a handsome devil and he knows it, the rat. He makes use of it, too.

Don't you remember last year when he took me off with him?"

"No," replied the old man dryly. "How do you expect me to remember if you won't let me see your face?"

The woman gave a laugh that sounded like a sob and said, "You wouldn't recognize me any more. I'm the one who used to sing duets with that fool, Peppot. You know Peppot? Monte Bisbin? Yes, that's the one. But it doesn't matter if you don't remember. I'm so changed. He finished me off, used me up in a year. And you know what? At first, he even said he wanted to marry me. That's a good joke! Imagine!"

"Imagine," repeated Papa-rè, starting to doze off.

"Of course, I never believed him," the woman continued. "All I wanted was to stay with him because this little creature was on the way. I don't know how that happened; perhaps it was because I was so much in love with him that God wanted to punish me. Later on, it was worse. So I had a daughter. Seems like nothing! Gilda Boa—you remember Gilda Boa? Well, she told me, 'Get rid of it!' How do you like that? He'd have agreed to get rid of it, all right. He had the nerve to say it didn't look like him! But look at her, Papa-rè—if she's not his spit and image! Ah, the brute! He knew very well it was his; I couldn't have made it with anybody else, because there was never anybody for me but him. I loved him so. I was like a slave to him. He beat me, and I didn't complain; he let me almost die of hunger, and I didn't complain. How I suffered, God knows, Papa-rè. But not for me, you understand; for this little one here. I had no milk for her unless I ate. Now . . ."

It went on that way a while longer, but Papa-rè was not following. He was tired and, comforted by the warmth of that little baby he had found there in place of his footwarmer, he had fallen asleep as usual. He was roused with a start when the door of the café opened and the noisy customers began pouring out into the night while the last applause still rang in the room. Where had the woman gone?

"Hey! What are you doing there?" Papa-rè asked sleepily.

She was hiding on all fours behind the legs of the high stool on which Papa-rè was seated. She had opened the little door with one hand and lurked there, panting like an animal.

"What are you doing?" Papa-rè repeated.

A pistol shot rang out just outside the kiosk.

"Lay low, or they'll arrest you too!" the woman cried as she rushed out, banging the door after her.

Papa-rè, frightened by the shouts, curses and all the dreadful confusion around the kiosk, cowered there trembling as he bent over the little one, who had jumped at the sound of the shot. A carriage pulled up and soon after rattled off toward the Hospital of Saint Anthony. A knot of excited people went past the kiosk, shouting and gesticulating, then disappeared in the direction of the Piazza delle Terme. There were others who still stood about heatedly discussing the incident, and Papa-rè strained his ears to listen. He didn't move, however, for fear the baby might start crying. Then one of the waiters from the café came up to the kiosk to buy a cigar.

"Did you see what happened, Papa-rè?"

"I . . . heard . . . it . . . all," he stammered.

"And you didn't move?" said the waiter, laughing. "Always cozy in there with your footwarmer, eh?"

"With my footwarmer, yes," Papa-rè said, leaning over, his toothless mouth open in a wan smile.

THE SOFT TOUCH OF GRASS

They went into the next room, where he was sleeping in a big chair, to ask if he wanted to look at her for the last time before the lid was put on the coffin.

"It's dark. What time is it?" he asked.

It was nine-thirty in the morning, but the day was overcast and the light dim. The funeral had been set for ten o'clock.

Signor Pardi stared up at them with dull eyes. It hardly seemed possible that he could have slept so long and well all night. He was still numb with sleep and the sorrow of these last days. He would have liked to cover his face with his hands to shut out the faces of his neighbors grouped about his chair in the thin light; but sleep had weighted his body like lead, and although there was a tingling in his toes urging him to rise, it quickly went away. Should he still give way to his grief? He happened to say aloud, "Always . . ." but he said it like someone settling himself under the covers to go back to sleep. They all looked at him questioningly. Always what?

Always dark, even in the daytime, he had wanted to say, but it made no sense. The day after her death, the day of her funeral,

167

he would always remember this wan light and his deep sleep, too, with her lying dead in the next room. Perhaps the windows . . .

"The windows?"

Yes, they were still closed. They had not been opened during the night, and the warm glow of those big dripping candles lingered. The bed had been taken away and she was there in her padded casket, rigid and ashen against the creamy satin.

No. Enough. He had seen her.

He closed his eyes, for they burned from all the crying he had done these past few days. Enough. He had slept and everything had been washed away with that sleep. Now he was relaxed, with a sense of sorrowful emptiness. Let the casket be closed and carried away with all it held of his past life.

But since she was still there . . .

He jumped to his feet and tottered. They caught him and, with eyes still closed, he allowed himself to be led to the open casket. When he opened his eyes and saw her, he called her by name, her name that lived for him alone, the name in which he saw her and knew her in all the fullness of the life they had shared together. He glared resentfully at the others daring to stare at her lying still in death. What did they know about her? They could not even imagine what it meant to him to be deprived of her. He felt like screaming, and it must have been apparent, for his son hurried over to take him away. He was quick to see the meaning of this and felt a chill as though he were stripped bare. For shame—those foolish ideas up to the very last, even after his night-long sleep. Now they must hurry so as not to keep the friends waiting who had come to follow the coffin to the church.

"Come on, Papa. Be reasonable."

With angry, piteous eyes, the bereaved man turned back to his big chair.

Reasonable, yes; it was useless to cry out the anguish that welled within him and that could never be expressed by words or deeds. For a husband who is left a widower at a certain age, a man still yearning for his wife, can the loss be the same as that of a son for whom—at a certain point—it is almost timely to be left an orphan? Timely, since he was on the point of getting married and would, as soon as the three months' mourning were passed, now that he had the added excuse that it was better for both of them to have a woman to look after the house.

"Pardi! Pardi!" they shouted from the entrance hall.

His chill became more intense when he understood clearly for the first time that they were not calling him but his son. From now on their surname would belong more to his son than to him. And he, like a fool, had gone in there to cry out the living name of his mate, like a profanation. For shame! Yes, useless, foolish ideas, he now realized, after that long sleep which had washed him clean of everything.

Now the one vital thing to keep him going was his curiosity as to how their new home would be arranged. Where, for example, were they going to have him sleep? The big double bed had been removed. Would he have a small bed? he wondered. Yes, probably his son's single bed. Now he would have the small bed. And his son would soon be lying in a big bed, his wife beside him within arm's reach. He, alone, in his little bed, would stretch out his arms into thin air.

He felt torpid, perplexed, with a sensation of emptiness inside and all around him. His body was numb from sitting so long. If he tried now to get up he felt sure that he would rise light as a feather in all that emptiness, now that his life was reduced to nothing. There was hardly any difference between himself and the big chair. Yet that chair appeared secure on its four legs, whereas he no longer knew where his feet and legs belonged nor what to do with his hands. What did he care about his life? He did not care particularly about the lives of others, either. Yet as he was still alive he must go on. Begin again—some sort of life which he could not yet conceive and which he certainly would never have contemplated if things had not changed in his own world. Now, deposed like this all of a sudden, not old and yet no longer young . . .

He smiled and shrugged his shoulders. For his son, all at once, he had become a child. But after all, as everyone knows, fathers are children to their grown sons who are full of worldly ambition and have successfully outdistanced them in positions of importance. They keep their fathers in idleness to repay all they have received when they themselves were small, and their fathers in turn become young again.

The single bed . . .

But they did not even give him the little room where his son had slept. Instead, they said, he would feel more independent in another, almost hidden on the courtyard; he would feel free there to do as he liked. They refurnished it with all the best pieces, so it would not occur to anyone that it had once been a servant's room. After the marriage, all the front rooms were pretentiously decorated and newly furnished, even to the luxury of carpets. Not a trace remained of the way the old house had looked. Even with his own furniture relegated to that little dark room, out of the mainstream of the young people's existence, he did not feel at home. Yet, oddly enough, he did not resent the disregard he seemed to have reaped along with the old furniture, because he admired the new rooms and was satisfied with his son's success.

But there was another deeper reason, not too clear as yet, a promise of another life, all shining and colorful, which was erasing the memory of the old one. He even drew a secret hope from it that a new life might begin for him too. Unconsciously, he sensed the luminous opening of a door at his back whence he might escape at the right moment, easy enough now that no one bothered about him, leaving him as if on holiday in the sanctuary of his little room "to do as he pleased." He felt lighter than air. His eyes had a gleam in them that colored everything, leading him from marvel to marvel, as though he really were a child again. He had the eyes of a child—lively and open wide on a world which was still new.

He took the habit of going out early in the morning to begin his holiday which was to last as long as his life lasted. Relieved of all responsibilities, he agreed to pay his son so much every month out of his pension for his maintenance. It was very little. Though he needed nothing, his son thought he should keep some money for himself to satisfy any need he might have. But need for what? He was satisfied now just to look on at life.

Having shaken off the weight of experience, he no longer knew how to get along with oldsters. He avoided them. And the younger people considered him too old, so he went to the park where the children played.

That was how he started his new life—in the meadow among the children in the grass. What an exhilarating scent the grass had, and so fresh where it grew thick and high. The children played hide-and-seek there. The constant trickle of some hidden stream outpurled the rustle of the leaves. Forgetting their game, the children pulled off their shoes and stockings. What a delicious feeling to sink into all that freshness of soft new grass with bare feet!

He took off one shoe and was stealthily removing the other when a young girl appeared before him, her face flaming. "You pig!" she cried, her eyes flashing.

Her dress was caught up in front on a bush, and she quickly pulled it down over her legs, because he was looking up at her from where he sat on the ground.

He was stunned. What had she imagined? Already she had disappeared. He had wanted to enjoy the children's innocent fun. Bending down, he put his two hands over his hard, bare feet. What had she seen wrong? Was he too old to share a child's delight in going barefoot in the grass? Must one immediately think evil because he was old? Ah, he knew that he could change in a flash from being a child to becoming a man again, if he must. He was still a man, after all, but he didn't want to think about it. He refused to think about it. It was really as a child that he had taken off his shoes. How wrong it was of that wretched girl to insult him like that! He threw himself face down on the grass. All his grief, his loss, his daily loneliness had brought about this gesture, interpreted now in the light of vulgar malice. His gorge rose in disgust and bitterness. Stupid girl! If he had wanted that— even his son admitted he might have "some desires"—he had plenty of money in his pocket for such needs.

Indignant, he pulled himself upright. Shamefacedly, with trembling hands, he put on his shoes again. All the blood had gone to his head and the pulse now beat hot behind his eyes. Yes, he knew where to go for that. He knew.

Calmer now, he got up and went back to the house. In the welter of furniture which seemed to have been placed there on purpose to drive him mad, he threw himself on the bed and turned his face to the wall.

CINCI

The dog sat patiently on his hind legs before the closed door and waited for it to open. Every so often he lifted a paw and scratched; every so often he let out a low whine.

Cinci, back from school with his books, strapped together, slung over his shoulder, found the dog still sitting there in the street. The boy was annoyed by this patient waiting and gave the dog a kick. Then he kicked the door for good measure, knowing that it was locked and that no one was home. Finally, he threw his books at the door, as if he expected them to pass right through it and land on the floor inside. But they came flying back at him with the same force with which he had hurled them. Surprised, as if the door were playing with him, Cinci threw the books back again. Then, as there were already three in the game —Cinci, the door and the books—the dog wanted to play too. He jumped at every throw and barked with each rebound.

People stopped to look. A few of them smiled, almost in spite of themselves, at the silliness of the game and at the dog's delight. Others were indignant to see expensive books treated with so little regard. Cinci soon tired of the sport and dropped his books on the ground, then lowered himself to a sitting position by scraping his spine along the wall. He had planned to sit on the books, but they slipped out from under him and he found himself coming down hard on the ground. He looked around with a foolish grin while the dog jumped back, eying him.

All the mischief that passed through Cinci's head showed clearly in that thatch of straw-colored hair and in his sparkling green eyes. He was at the awkard age, gawky and bristling. Having forgotten his handkerchief when he returned to school in the afternoon, he now sat on the ground snuffling, his long legs exposed because he still wore short pants though he was too big for them, his knobby knees pulled up almost level with his face. No shoes could withstand the treatment he gave them. The ones he had on were already done for.

He was bored. Above all, he was bored. Hugging his knees, he snorted, then dragged his back up along the wall again. Fox leaped up, expectant. Where are we off to? A walk in the country, perhaps, to swipe a couple of figs or apples? Cinci was not yet sure. He listlessly tied up his books and replaced them over his shoulder.

The paved street ended beyond his house where the dirt road began, and it led deeper and deeper into the open country. What a wonderful sensation it must be, when you're riding in a carriage, to feel the horse's hoofs and the wheels pass from the hard pavement onto the soft, silent dirt road! It must be a little like when the teacher, after being provoked and flying into a rage, suddenly speaks in a quiet, gentle voice once more and the dread of punishment decreases. To get into the open country, you followed the dirt road past the last houses of their stinking suburb until it widened out into the little square on the outskirts of town. A new hospital had just been built there, its whitewashed walls still so fresh and glaring that they blinded you in the sun.

All the patients had recently been moved from the old hospital in ambulances and on stretchers. It was like a parade when they filed by, the ambulances first, their curtains fluttering at the little windows, then the bed cases carried by on beautiful hammocklike stretchers.

By the time Cinci and his dog reached the square, it was

growing late. The sun had already set, and the convalescents in their gray shirts and white nightcaps no longer leaned out of the large windows to stare sadly at the old church opposite where it rose amid a cluster of dilapidated houses and a few straggling trees.

Cinci stopped, uncertain, then lounged against a paling, filled with helpless bitterness at so many things he could not understand. First there was his mother. How did she live and what did she live on? She was never at home and insisted on sending him to that school—that cursed school so far away. Every day he had to run for at least half an hour to get there on time; then at noon he came back only to rush again after bolting a couple of mouthfuls. His mother always said he was a loafer who wasted his time playing with the dog. She was forever reproaching him: he did not study, he was dirty, he always got cheated when she sent him to buy something, he brought back food that wasn't fresh . . .

Now where was Fox?

There he was, poor little dog, mutely waiting for him to make up his mind. Anyway *he* knew what was expected of him: follow your master! Cinci wanted to do something, but there was always the same problem—he didn't know what to do. His mother could at least have given him the key when she went out to sew by the day in gentlemen's houses—for that's what she gave him to understand she was doing. But no. She said he was not to be trusted and that, if she had not returned by the time he got back from school, she would not be long and he could wait. Where? In front of the door? Sometimes he had waited two hours in the cold and even in the rain. Then, instead of taking shelter, he would go to the corner and stand under the rainspout on purpose so that he would be wringing wet. Finally, she would appear, all out of breath, carrying a borrowed umbrella, her face flaming, her eyes very bright and shifty, so nervous she could never find the latch key in her purse.

"You're soaked! Now just be patient. I was kept late!"

Cinci frowned as he kept on walking uphill. There were things he didn't want to think about—his father, for instance. He had never known his father. When he was little he had been told that his father had died before he was born, but no one had ever said who his father was; now he no longer cared to ask or to find out. He might even be that cripple over there, paralyzed down the right side, who still managed to drag himself along to the saloon. Fox went up and barked at him. It was the crutch he didn't like.

All those women standing around in a circle, bulging in front but not pregnant—well, maybe one of them was, the one with the skirt hiked up in front and nearly dragging on the ground in back. That other one with the baby in her arms, reaching into her blouse—ugh! What a blob of flesh! His own mother was beautiful, still young and slender. She too had nursed him at her breast when he was a baby, perhaps in a house in the country or out in the sun on a threshing floor. He vaguely remembered a house in the country when he was little—if he had not dreamed it, or seen it somewhere. Who knows? When evening came and the oil lamps were lit, one could feel a shadow obscure those country houses as the lamp was carried from room to room and the light faded from one window only to reappear at another.

Beyond the square, the road meandered up the side of a hill and continued on into the country. He looked up and could see the whole vast expanse of the sky. The last rays of the dying sun had disappeared, and above the darkened hill there was the softest blue. Evening shadows fell across the earth, dimming the white glare of the hospital wall.

An old woman hurried toward the little church for evening prayers. Cinci suddenly made up his mind to go in too, and Fox stopped, looking up at him because he well knew he was not allowed inside churches. At the entrance, the old woman, who was already late, was panting and whimpering as she struggled to lift the heavy leather curtain. Cinci held it aside for her, but she frowned instead of thanking him, sensing he had not come there to worship. It was cold as a cave in that little church. On the main altar two candles burned fitfully, and here and there a few stray lamps glimmered. The dust of ages lay in the penetrating dampness. Echoes lurked in the gloomy silence, ready to spring out at the least noise. The pews were lined with devout old women, each in her accustomed place. Cinci felt an impulse to let out a howl to make them jump. Not a howl perhaps, but what about throwing down his heavy load of books, as if by accident! Why not? He let them drop and, like a shot, the echoes jumped out to his great delight, thundering and crashing about him. Cinci had often tried this experiment of raising echoes. There was now no further need to gall the patience of those poor scandalized old worshipers. He walked out of the church and found Fox ready to follow along the path uphill. He longed to bite into some fruit and climbed over a low wall to grope his way through the dark trees. But he could not be certain whether this impulse was prompted by hunger or by an urge just to do *something*.

The steep country road was deserted and full of little stones loosened by the hoofs of passing donkeys and sent rolling down over and over. Cinci kicked a couple into the air with the toe of his shoe. The slopes on either side were covered with long green, plumed oats, so pleasant to chew on. The little plumes came off and clung together like a bouquet in your hand. If they were thrown at someone, the oats that clung were counted as future wives or husbands. Cinci decided to try this out on Fox. Seven wives, no less! But then, nearly all of them stuck fast in Fox's fur, so it didn't count. Fox, the old stupid, just stood there with his eyes closed, not understanding the joke about the seven wives on his back!

Cinci did not feel like going any farther. He was tired and as bored as before. He went to the left of the road and sat on the wall. From there he looked up at the new moon, its pale gold just beginning to shine in the faint green of the sky. He saw it and he didn't see it—like things that slip through the mind, one flowing into another, then all receding farther and farther from his young body sitting there so still that he was no longer aware of it. If he had put his own hand on his knee, or on his foot hanging down in its dirty, scuffed shoe, it would have seemed like a stranger's. He was no longer *in* his body. He had joined the things he saw and did not see—the darkening sky, the brightening moon, that mass of dark trees which seemed suspended in thin air, the fresh, black earth so newly tilled, still exhaling the odor of damp rot of these last sunny October days.

All of a sudden, absorbed as he was, he was distracted and instinctively lifted his hand to his ear. A shrill little laugh had come from beneath the wall. A country boy about his own age had hidden himself on the side of the wall bordering the fields. He had picked and stripped a blade of oats too and, slipping a loose knot in one end, he was stealthily lifting up his arm to loop it over Cinci's ear. As soon as Cinci turned, the boy quickly signaled to him to be still. Then he moved the blade of oats along the wall toward the head of a little lizard peeping out from between the stones. The boy had been hoping to trap it for an hour. Cinci leaned down anxiously to watch. Without realizing it, the lizard had slipped its own head into the noose but not quite far enough to be caught. The head must advance a trifle more, and even now, if the hand holding the trap should tremble and alarm the lizard, it might escape. Yes, yes, but wait! Easy now! He must be prepared to give a jerk at just the right moment. It was the work of a second. There! The lizard was flashing like a fish at the end of that long blade of oats.

Cinci eagerly jumped down from the wall, but the other boy, holding the noose and probably fearing he would take the lizard from him, swung his arm around several times in the air and then brought the creature down with a dull slap on a big stone which lay among the weeds.

"No!" screamed Cinci, but too late.

The lizard lay motionless on the stone, its white stomach gleaming in the light. Cinci was angry. He too had wanted to see the lizard caught, prompted by the natural instinct of the hunter in all of us. But to kill it like that, without first looking closely at those quick little eyes, watching it up to the last convulsion, those twitching legs, that all-over quiver of its green body—no, it was too stupid and shameful! Cinci went up to the boy and punched him in the chest with all his might, sending him sprawling. The boy jumped right up again, furious, and grabbed a handful of dirt from the nearest furrow which he flung in Cinci's face, blinding him. Cinci was all the more outraged and infuriated by the taste of dirt in his mouth. He took a clod of earth and threw it back. The fight grew desperate. The country boy was quicker and had a surer aim. He never missed, moving in closer and closer with those missiles of dirt which did not wound but struck with a dull thud and fell like hail on Cinci's chest, in his face and hair, in his ears and even into his shoes. Suffocated, unable to protect or defend himself, Cinci leaped up with his arm raised to snatch a stone from the wall. Something scurried away—was it Fox? He hurled the stone and, all of a sudden, where before everything had been spinning around, striking his eyes, now nothing moved—the clump of trees, the thin crescent moon. It was as if time itself had stopped in stupefied amazement at sight of the boy stretched on the ground.

Still panting, his heart pounding, terror flooding him as he leaned against the wall in the unbelievable silken repose of the countryside under the moonlight, Cinci foundered in a backwash of man's eternal solitude from which he wanted to flee. He had not done it! He had not meant to do it! He knew nothing about it! Then, as though he were actually someone else drawing near only out of curiosity, he took a step, then another, and bent down to look. The boy's head was bashed in; blood still dripped from his gaping mouth onto the ground. Part of his leg showed between his cotton sock and his pants leg. He looked as if he had always been dead. It was like a dream. The lizard lay stomach up on the stone with the blade of oats still caught around its throat. Cinci knew he must wake up and go away. He quickly vaulted the wall, picked up his bundle of books and started off. Fox followed him, as usual.

On the way back downhill, Cinci's confidence increased as the distance lengthened so that he did not hurry at all. He reached the empty square. The moon shone here too, but it was another moon, unheeding, which lit up the white façade of the hospital.

Now once again along the road through the suburbs, back to the house—to which, of course, his mother had not yet returned. No need to give any explanation of his whereabouts; he had simply waited here for her. And this—which would be true for his mother—became the truth for him too. In fact, he stood with his shoulders against the wall beside the door just as before.

It was enough that he be found there, waiting.

THE UMBRELLA

"And wittle boats, wittle boats," Mimi repeated, toddling along, trying to step out in front of her mother, who held her firmly by the hand under the umbrella.

Dinuccia, her elder sister, walked along as prim and serious as a little old woman. She held an old, torn umbrella in both hands. It would be handed down to the maid as soon as the new umbrella was bought.

"Umbella," Mimi went on, "two umbellas, two waincoats, four wittle boats."

"Yes, darling, little boats and all, but hurry," her mother urged impatiently, trying to move more quickly through the shifting mass of people who pressed along the sidewalk in the drizzling rain.

Suddenly the store lights flashed on with a low hum, a blinding contrast of opalescent, glowing red and yellow.

The hard-pressed little mother, as she hurried along, was thinking that seasons should never change—above all, winter should never come! Such an expense! Every year new books were needed for school, and new clothes to protect the girls against the cold, wind and rain. Poor darlings, orphaned before the younger had had time to learn to say "Daddy!" How wretched she felt to see them going off some mornings without the proper things to wear.

Having been accustomed to comfort all these years, she found this sudden reversal all the harder to bear. Try as she might, she could not stretch the meager pension left by her husband any further.

Now that Mimi was enrolled in kindergarten, tuition cost six lire more a month—and she could not bring herself to take Dinuccia out of private school. But tuition was the least of her worries. She had to keep up appearances in that school where all the other students came from well-to-do families.

But she did not lose her head. Now that her husband—who was almost twenty years older than she—had died unexpectedly, leaving her with two children to raise, she went back to finish her schooling. Armed with a diploma and availing herself of her husband's connections, she made the most of her unfortunate situation to get appointed to a new class in a supplementary school. But even her salary added to the pension was barely enough to make ends meet.

Had she wished—but she never bothered to dress well, and now, combing her hair hurriedly every morning and pulling on an old hat to go off to school, without glancing to right or left . . . Still, had she wished—already two offers of marriage—and why did men turn to look at her, even tonight walking between the two children in this rain? What folly even to think that she would give Dinuccia and Mimi another father.

Meanwhile all those admiring glances—some impertinent, some languid and yearning—annoyed and irritated her, but deep within they excited her. They made her renunciation of worldly pleasures seem heroic. They made her daily sacrifice for the children seem light and beautiful.

Her pleasure was like that of a miser whose self-inflicted privations do not bother him so long as he knows he can have anything he wishes. But what if the miser's gold should lose its value from one moment to the next?

Some days, for no reason at all, or rather for no reason she cared to admit to herself, she felt restless and cross, taking advantage of the slightest pretext—and how many there were!—to flare up. Dinuccia became the target of her ill humor. The serious, inquiring look on the child's pale face provoked her mother's outbursts. She felt a reproach in those large, pensive eyes.

"Goose!" she cried, turning on the child.

Why goose? Could the little girl understand the reason for this irritation when even her mother refused to comprehend it? Dinuccia was surprised to see her mother less lighthearted than usual. But it was not at all surprising, with all the demands and worries and difficulties plaguing her.

However, she used them as an excuse to hide her remorse for speaking harshly to the child and making her cry. Although her troubles were real enough, her refusal to admit the reason for her nervousness made her all the more depressed and upset.

Fortunately there was the little one, Mimi, who with that winning way of hers performed the same miracle of restoring calm every time. She tried to put her simple, loving look into words, forming them with cherry-red lips.

"Pretty . . . Mama pretty."

Then she would bow with her hands behind her back, shaking all the black ringlets on her little head.

"You like?"

She never could manage "Do you like me?" but only "You like?" Her mother would open her arms and, almost before that little creature could fling herself into them, she would start to cry, hugging her close. Quickly she called Dinuccia and hugged her, too, very tenderly, especially after she had snapped at her. Her depression gave way to overwhelming joy at the thought of these two little girls to whom she was so willing to dedicate herself.

But this evening their mother was feeling gay.

"Come, Mimi, here we are."

The little one was staring wide-eyed into a dazzling shop window on via Nazionale. Pulled away by her mother, she went into the store, repeating, "Boats; first wittle boats."

"Yes, hush!" her mother told her as a clerk came over to wait on them.

"Boats . . . there, you see, you've made me say it too! I mean two pairs of—"

"Boats," prompted Mimi.

"Show me some rubber boots for these children. The baby calls them 'boats.' It really *is* a nicer word than galoshes."

"Overshoes," corrected the clerk dryly, raising his eyebrows with an air of self-importance.

"Little boats is cuter."

"Me first, me first!" cried Mimi, clambering up on a chair and waving her feet.

"Mimi!" her mother scolded with a severe glance.

Dinuccia instantly noticed the change and her grave eyes took on that questioning look which so irked her mother. Neither of them paid attention to Mimi's joy as the supercilious clerk tried on the first little boot: she wanted to get down immediately and walk, before the other one was put on.

"Sit still, Mimi, or we will go right home. It's too large; can't you see?"

The clerk would have liked to try this pair on the older child before going back to look for a smaller size, but Dinuccia warded him off, pointing to her little sister.

"Silly, what difference does it make?" said her mother, taking her roughly by the arms and lifting her onto a chair. To pacify Mimi, she told the clerk to go for another pair and meanwhile she would try these on the older child.

Dinuccia, with the overshoes on her feet, did not move from her chair. But as soon as she was fitted Mimi slipped nimbly down, clapping her hands and turning around and around like a top, uttering little squeals of joy. First she raised one foot and then the other to examine them. Dinuccia looked on, smiling wanly, but her expression clouded when she heard her mother exclaim, "Forty *lire!* Twenty lire a *pair!*"

"American-made, Signora," the clerk replied, meeting the customer's astonished expression with the cool dignity of one who knows the value of his merchandise. "An indestructible article. Look, you can roll it in your fist."

"I understand . . . but . . . for such small feet, twenty lire?"

"We have only two prices, Signora," the clerk retorted. "Twenty lire for the small size and thirty-five for the larger. A little longer or a little shorter makes no difference, you understand. It's the labor that counts."

"I was not prepared for anything like that," confessed the mother in distress. "I figured twenty lire for the two pairs at the outside."

"Impossible!" said the clerk, horrified.

"Look," said the mother, trying to bargain with him. "I have other things to buy: two raincoats, two umbrellas."

"We have everything."

"I know. That is why I came here. Will you allow me a discount?"

The clerk raised his hands in protest. "We have a fixed price, Signora. Take it or leave it."

The mother gave him a wrathful look: it was all well and good to say *leave* it. But how was she ever going to get those little boats off Mimi's feet now without a tantrum? She should have asked the price first. But who would ever have thought they cost so much? She had counted on spending a hundred and twenty lire for everything, and no more.

"Show me the raincoats," she said. "How much are they?"

"Step this way, please."

"Dinuccia! Mimi!" she called, annoyed. "Now be good, Mimi, or I will take off your galoshes. Come here, let me see. Aren't they still a little too large?"

She would have liked to take them off her feet and try to find a cheaper pair somewhere else. She felt like slapping the clerk.

"No . . . not too big . . . pretty," cried Mimi rebelliously.

"Let me see."

"Pretty, no, pretty. *Very* pretty!" Mimi said again and again, scampering off. She waved her little arms, toddled about, and puffed out her cheeks to blow like the wind, pretending she was paddling through water in her little boats.

Even the clerk deigned to smile at this, although he would have done better not to. The mother mistook the smile for pity and her blood froze. She thought of the hundred and thirty-five lire she carried in her bag, figuring that if raincoats cost forty lire each and forty for two pairs of overshoes, it left only fifteen lire—certainly not enough to buy two umbrellas. Maybe she could find one—a very cheap one.

But each child wanted to have an umbrella all her own, as well as the little boats. They were not at all interested in the heavy gray raincoats. When they found out that only one umbrella was to be bought the fight began.

Dinuccia reasoned that, as she was the elder, the new umbrella should belong to her, but Mimi had been promised an umbrella too and would not listen to reason. The mother tried vainly to make peace, saying the umbrella would belong to neither one of them, but that they could both go to school under it.

"Then I will cawwy it," Mimi announced promptly.

"No, I will," protested Dinuccia.

"You will take turns," their mother said sharply. To Mimi she added, "You could never hold it straight anyway."

"Yes, I *can* cawwy it, too."

"But it's taller than you are. Look!"

And her mother stood the umbrella beside her. Mimi quickly grabbed it with both hands. This seemed unfair to Dinuccia, who tried to snatch it back.

"Shame on you!" cried their mother. "What a scene! What well-behaved children I have! There, the umbrella is for me. Neither of you shall have it."

Back again on the sidewalk, although they were now wearing raincoats and little boats, both children were silent, brooding with hurt, angry eyes, thinking only of the umbrella. Once they got home the fight would start again. It was all very well to own one umbrella between them, but who would have the privilege of carrying it to school? That was the whole point: to hold the umbrella and walk under it in the rain. Dinuccia felt sure that she should be the one to carry it. Wasn't she proving right now how well she could carry an umbrella in the street? Having carried the old umbrella all the way to the store, why wasn't she given the new one to carry now? Why had it been bought? For her mother to carry rolled up under her arm? Her mother was walking with Mimi under her own umbrella, and she was left to struggle with the ugly old one. It was Mimi, tyrannical Mimi, who deserved to be punished. She was too little anyway to carry an umbrella. Let her just try it once!

Thinking of her grievances, Dinuccia stole a glance from under her umbrella, careful not to tilt it and hoping her mama would notice how well she was carrying it. But she saw a dark scowl on her mother's face such as she had never seen before. The umbrella wobbled between her little hands. A shiver ran down her spine. She thought that not only Mimi but her mama, too, was bad. Carefully shielding Mimi under her own umbrella, her mother was paying not the slightest attention to her, leaving her with that awful old umbrella which leaked and was so heavy it made her arms ache. She wondered how much longer she could manage to hold it.

The mother, having left the store angry and humiliated, now struggled to put a wicked thought out of her mind—a terrible thought which she knew would leave an ugly mark if she allowed it to reflect on her conscience. But there were times when she was faced with hard reality that the same thought had occurred to her: if only she did not have Dinuccia—not that she should die, God, no!—but if she were not there, if she had never been born! Mimi was always so gay and natural. With only Mimi, she might have remarried. Mimi would soon find her way into the heart of a new father. She would put her little arms around his neck, shake all her curls and ask, in that enchanting way of hers, "You like?" Who could resist her? But Dinuccia, with those serious, questioning eyes . . . Ah, she could imagine only too well those eyes turned pensively on a stepfather. No, never! With that child, she could never marry again. It was out of the question.

She glanced down at Dinuccia and, as usual, a flood of remorse and anxious affection swept over her. There she was, walking along intent on proving just how well she could carry an umbrella. It made the mother smile. If only some passer-by would remark, "Look at that little girl, how nicely she carries her umbrella!" That old umbrella, poor dear, how happy she would be if she could carry the new one. Yes, but Mimi . . . Mimi always got her way. She should never have promised her one in the first place when she could not afford to buy two. Mimi was selfish. It was only right for Dinuccia, who could carry an umbrella so well, to have the new one instead of that old thing.

At this, she gave the new umbrella to Dinuccia, but the child did not welcome it with as much enthusiasm as her mother had anticipated. Could she possibly have guessed her guilty thoughts?

The new umbrella felt so much lighter that Dinuccia looked up with a grateful little smile, but this did not satisfy her mother, who turned immediately to Mimi.

"Stay close beside me like a good little girl, under my umbrella. Dinuccia will carry her own umbrella. What would people say if they were to see her with that old thing? 'Ah, how poor she is,' they'd say. 'She must be somebody's little housemaid.' You wouldn't want them to say anything like that about your sister, now would you?"

Mimi did not answer. She was busy with her own concerns. As soon as they got in the door, she was going to tell her mama, "Me umbella . . . me cawwy umbella upstairs."

Once in her possession, the umbrella would be safe! And when they reached the top of the stairs she refused to surrender it, protesting that Didi had carried it for a long time in the street. Then the inevitable fight broke out. While their mother was in the next room taking off her things, Dinuccia tried to grab the umbrella away from Mimi, and it fell with a bang on the floor. Mimi screamed and immediately the umbrella was restored to her. Dinuccia was punished and went without any supper.

Later, when her mother went to look for her, she found her sound asleep, curled up on the floor in a corner beside the big wardrobe. She was burning with fever. Now her mother understood why she had not rejoiced when she gave her the new umbrella in the street, and why, always so patient with her little sister, she had made Mimi cry that evening.

"Oh, God, no," the mother cried in alarm, picking the child up in her arms. "My little Dinuccia . . . No . . . no . . . no."

She undressed her and put her to bed, sitting by her side

drained of all feeling, as though in a trance.

That night it poured and all the next day. The rain came down without a let-up for six days in a row.

Mimi's first thought when she awoke the following morning was about the umbrella which she had carefully placed beside her bed before going to sleep. She was delighted to see it was still raining so she could wear her little boats and her new raincoat, too. She would go to school with her feet in the boats and hold the umbrella proudly over her head in the rain.

No? She was not going to school today? Why not? Dinuccia was sick? Too bad, because it was such a lovely rainy day.

She wanted to ask her mother to send her to school with the maid, but her mother cried and paid no attention to her. She went to the kitchen to ask the maid, but found her about to rush out to call the doctor. She was in such a hurry she did not even turn around.

Mimi looked out the window for a while, watching the beautiful rain, then she put on her little boats and her raincoat before the looking glass. She pulled the hood up over her head and all the way down to her eyebrows. Then she opened the beautiful umbrella. It was a little difficult, but she managed, and she stood there looking at herself blissfully in the mirror, feet together, shoulders hunched as she laughed and shivered under the imaginary rain.

Every morning for five days Mimi rehearsed the same routine before the glass. Again and again she went back to look at herself before taking off the raincoat and overshoes and hiding the umbrella in a secret corner known only to her. Now the umbrella was hers, all hers, and she would never give it up, not even to Mama. What a pity all that nice rain was going to waste!

On the evening of the sixth day, the maid took Mimi to the apartment next door occupied by two old ladies, friends of her mama. They had been in and out of her house these last few days, going back and forth between the bedroom and the kitchen, but she was too occupied with her treasures to pay much attention. She was glad her mama was busy with her big sister and did not bother about her, so that she could play winter as much as she liked.

That night she ate at the neighbors' house and played and chattered about all sorts of things with the maid before she finally fell asleep.

She was awakened with a start, very late. The whole house shook with a violent clap of thunder which gradually diminished to a low rumble. The child looked around in bewilderment. Where was she? This was not her home. This was not her bed. She called the maid two or three times before wriggling out of the covers in which she was wrapped. She found she was still fully dressed. The bed beside her was unopened—and suddenly she realized where she was: this was the room where the two old ladies slept. She had visited this room many times. Slipping from the bed, she crossed the dark room and found the front door open wide. Out on the landing, she was terrified by the noise the rain made drumming on the skylight and by the sudden flashes of lightning. The door to her own apartment stood open.

Mimi rushed in and ran straight to the bedroom, calling, "Mama! Mama!"

One of the old ladies sitting by the side of the dying child ran quickly to meet her at door.

"Go, go, my darling," she said, a finger to her lips. "Hush! Mama is in there."

"Didi?" questioned the child as she caught sight of her sister's waxen face under the soft glow of the night light.

"Yes, dear," the old lady replied. "God wants to take her to Him. Didi is going up to Heaven."

"To Heaven?"

Mimi went away without another word. She stopped in the dark hallway, a little perplexed. Through the open door she could hear the rain beating against the skylight. A flash of lightning lit up the window, revealing the stormy sky. Mimi ran quickly down the long hallway.

A moment later the two old women watching by Dinuccia saw Mimi return with the new umbrella in her arms.

"Here, umbella . . . for Didi," she said falteringly. "It's waining up in Heaven."

THE NEW SUIT

The suit poor Crispucci had worn from time immemorial reminded everyone of the bedraggled, discolored fur of a stray dog. It could no longer be considered separate from his body, or susceptible to change. That was why his employer, lawyer Boccanera, never dreamed of passing on to him one of his own discarded but still wearable suits. From the lawyer's point of view, Crispucci was perfectly satisfactory as he was, as Boccanera's clerk-messenger at a hundred and twenty lire a month.

Usually Signor Boccanera had only to say with a wink, "Eh, Crispucci?" for Crispucci to grasp his meaning. But today the clerk apparently understood little or nothing of Signor Boccanera's long, friendly talk. He just stood there in front of the lawyer's desk, his long arms dangling, his body stooped and twisted into a letter S. From time to time he opened his mouth, but no words were uttered. His cheeks contracted, his yellow face puckered as he bared his teeth in a grimace of scorn or pain, but perhaps it was only a sign of concentration.

". . . And, my dear Crispucci, all things considered, I advise you to go. Your absence will mean serious difficulties for me, of course, but you should leave anyway. I will manage for a couple of weeks. It will take you at least that long to get through all the legal formalities and to clear things up. Then, too, I imagine you'll want to sell everything."

Crispucci raised his arms in a helpless gesture, his faded eyes staring fixedly into space.

"Yes," Boccanera went on, "everything should be sold—jewels, clothes, furniture. The jewels will fetch the most. At first glance, from the description in this inventory, you should get around a hundred and fifty to two hundred thousand lire. Maybe more. There is also a pearl necklace. As for her clothes, of course, your daughter couldn't possibly wear them. Who knows what they're like! But don't count on getting much for them. Clothes never bring good prices, no matter how fine. If you're clever, you might get something for the furs—she seems to have had quite a collection. Now, mind what you do about the jewels. Better find out where they were bought. The boxes may be marked. I can tell you that the price of diamonds has gone way up and there are a number listed here! Brooch . . . another brooch . . . ring . . . earrings . . . a bracelet . . . another ring . . . ring . . . a brooch . . . bracelet . . . bracelet . . . quite a few, really."

At this point Crispucci raised his hand as a sign that he wished to be heard. On rare occasions he made this gesture and twisted his face in an effort to bring his voice up from the depths of silence into which his spirit seemed permanently sunk.

"Could I . . . might I," he faltered, "might I be so bold as to . . . one of . . . just one of those rings . . . for your wife?"

"What are you saying, my dear Crispucci?" exclaimed the lawyer. "For my *wife* . . . one of *those* rings? What could you be thinking of?"

"Excuse me," Crispucci said, dropping his hand and nodding several times in belated agreement. His eyes filled with tears.

"No, on the contrary; I thank you very much for such a generous thought. Come, come, dear Crispucci! I didn't mean to offend you. I know. I understand; this is all very sad for you. But remember you are not accepting this inheritance for yourself. You have a daughter, and it will not be easy to find a husband for her without a dowry. Ah, yes, I know. I know. It's hard. But money is money, dear Crispucci, and therefore one must close one's eyes to many things. You have a mother, too! Besides, you are not in very good health, and . . ."

Crispucci, who had nodded approval of everything else, now opened his eyes with a look of annoyance when the question of his health was raised. Bowing, he turned to leave.

"Here, aren't you forgetting your papers?" the lawyer asked, holding them out to him across the desk.

Crispucci turned, wiped his eyes with a soiled handkerchief, and took the papers.

"So you'll be leaving tomorrow?"

"Signor Lawyer," replied Crispucci as if he had made up his mind to say something difficult, but then he stopped short. He struggled a moment to hold back what was already on the tip of his tongue, then shrugged slightly, raised his arms again and left.

He was about to say, "I'll go, if your honor will accept a ring for your wife from my inheritance."

The other clerks in the office who had taken pleasure in tormenting him these last three days, goading him cruelly about his inheritance, had been promised, through clenched teeth, one a silk dress for his wife, another a feathered hat for his daughter, the third a muff for his fiancée.

"May she wear it in health," he muttered. "And what about a couple of fine embroidered blouses, open down the front, for your sister?"

"Would to God!"

Crispucci wanted all of them to be sullied as he felt he was in accepting the inheritance. He could probably dress all the women in town, he thought, after reading the long description in the inventory of the dead woman's elaborate wardrobe—closets and closets full of lingerie alone. If a remnant of good sense had not checked him, he would have collared passers-by with "My wife just died in Naples. She was thus and thus . . . but she left me this and that. Would you like something for your wife, your sister, your daughter? Half a dozen of the finest silk net stockings, for example?"

A balding, jaundiced young man with a longing to be stylish

had been writhing these past days listening to all these fine offers in the office. He had been working there only a week, filling in as errand boy when he was not needed as a clerk. Mindful of his dignity, he scarcely spoke a word to anyone, but then no one ever spoke to him either. A slightly scornful smile played around the corners of his mouth as he listened to Crispucci. With a knowing gesture, he pulled on his yellowed cuffs, or pushed them back under the too-short sleeves of his jacket.

That day, Crispucci had hardly come out of the lawyer's office and taken his hat and cane from the rack to go out when the new clerk, unable to resist, followed right behind him. The others, laughing, called from the top of the stairs:

"Crispucci, remember that blouse for my sister!"

"And the silk coat for my wife!"

"The muff for my fiancée!"

"An ostrich plume for my daughter!"

In the street, pale with rage, the young man accosted him.

"Why all this foolishness? Why scatter your inheritance like this? Has it any mark to show where it comes from? You've had this piece of good luck and you don't even know how to make the best of it! Are you crazy?"

Crispucci stopped short and eyed him.

"*Good luck,* yes!" the young man harped. "Good luck before and good luck now! Years ago, to be freed when she fled your house . . ."

"Ah, so you found out about that!"

"Yes, I found out! Well, what troubles, obstacles, anxiety can you have now? Now she's *dead,* and you don't call that luck? Not only is she dead and gone, but she left you enough to begin a new life."

Crispucci stopped again to gaze at him.

"Perhaps you also *found out* that I have a daughter who is not married?"

"That's why I'm talking to you."

"You certainly speak frankly."

"Very frankly!"

"And you believe that I should accept the inheritance?"

"You'd be a fool not to! Two hundred thousand lire!"

"And with two hundred thousand lire, you would like me to give you my daughter?"

"Why not?"

"Because with two hundred thousand lire I could buy something less shameful and odious than your proposal."

"You insult me!"

"No, I respect you. I respect you just as you respect me. For a proposal like yours, I wouldn't pay more than three thousand lire."

"Three?"

"Five, if you like, and a little linen thrown in. You have a sister? Three silk blouses for her, open down the front. I'll give them to you, if you like."

And he left him standing there in the middle of the street.

At home, Crispucci said not a word to his mother or his daughter. For that matter, in the sixteen years since his tragedy, he had never allowed them to speak of anything except matters strictly relating to their daily life. If either of them so much as hinted at anything else, he turned such a look on her that her voice died on her lips.

He went to Naples the next day, leaving them not only in the most painful uncertainty about the inheritance but also in dread lest he do something rash.

Neighbors fanned their fears by repeating and commenting on all the queer things Crispucci had done during the past three days. One of them, wondering about the dead woman, asked idly, "How did she get to be so rich?"

"I heard her name was Marguerite," said another. "However, her linen, I understand, was marked 'R. B.'"

"Not 'B'—'R. C.'" corrected another. "Rose Clairon was what I heard."

"Ah . . . Clairon . . . Clairon . . . Wasn't that the name of a singer?"

"I don't believe so."

"Yes, of course it was, and what a singer! Not lately, of course, but she used to sing!"

"Rosa Clairon! Now I remember the name!"

The young girl, listening to all this, glanced at her grand-mother with a feverish light in her deep-set eyes and a flush on her thin cheeks. The old woman, her heavy, yellow face deeply lined, adjusted thick-lensed spectacles on her nose. Since her operation for cataracts, her eyes looked enormous and vague between the long sparse lashes like insect antennae. She answered the women's idle gossip with low grunts.

There were some among them who hotly maintained that Crispucci was not as crazy as he was made out to be and that he should not be blamed if he did not want a stitch of that under-wear to touch his daughter's pure young body. He would do better to give the clothes away if he did not want to sell them. Naturally, it was only right that they be distributed among the neighbors. In any case, a few presents at least! What a river of glistening silks, what a flow of foaming laces between banks of soft velvets and crests of bright feathers would come into the squalor of that hovel! Just the thought of it narrowed their eyes to slits. And Fina, the young girl, listening to them and seeing their intoxication, wrung her hands under her apron and finally jumped up and ran out of the room.

"Poor child," said one of them. "It's so hard for her."

"Do you think he'll make her wear mourning?" another asked.

The old woman grunted, signifying that she knew nothing about it.

"Of course he will; it's only natural."

"After all, she was her mother."

"*If* he accepts the inheritance!"

"You'll see, he'll wear mourning too!"

"No . . . not him!"

"Not even if he accepts the inheritance?"

The old woman squirmed on her chair and Fina tossed on her bed in the next room. That was the crux of the question: would he accept the inheritance?

The women had gone secretly to lawyer Boccanera at the first news of Rosa Clairon's death, in alarm over Crispucci's fury about the inheritance. They begged the lawyer, with clasped hands, to prevent a silly refusal. What was to become of his daughter if Crispucci died? She had never had anything since she was born, poor girl. He weighed the dishonor of the inheritance against his pride in honest poverty. Why question such good fortune? This girl had not asked to be brought into the world and had she not paid dearly for her mother's shame?

Their doubts and torment lasted an eternity—eighteen long days. Not a word did they hear in all that time. Finally, one evening, the two women heard stumbling steps and heavy breathing on the stairway. Porters were lugging up eleven heavy trunks and boxes which they had brought from the station.

Crispucci waited by the entrance door until the men had carried everything up to his apartment on the fourth floor. Then he paid them and, when all was quiet, he started up the stairs.

His mother and daughter, lamps in their hands, waited anxiously for him on the landing. At last they saw his bent head in a new green hat. He was wearing a new suit of rough brown wool, too, bought ready-made, no doubt, in a Naples department store. The pants covered the heels of his new shoes. The jacket gaped at the neck.

Neither one nor the other dared ask a question. The suit spoke for itself. Then, seeing her father go directly to his room, the young girl said just as his door was closing, "Have you had supper, Papa?"

Crispucci turned. With a new twist to his smile, and in a new voice, he replied, *"Wagon-restaurant."*

THE ROSE

The little train moved on through the darkness of the winter evening at a pace that left little hope of its arriving on time.

Signora Lucietta Nespi, Loffredi's widow, bored and tired as she was from the long trip in that dirty second-class carriage, was in no hurry whatsoever to arrive at Peola.

She thought and thought.

Though she was being carried along in the train, her thoughts were still back there in the empty rooms of the house in Genoa. Stripped of the handsome furniture which, almost new, had had to go for a song, the rooms had suddenly seemed very small. What a disappointment! She needed so much, on that last visit, to see them as big and grand, so that when she was poor she could say proudly, "The house I had in Genoa . . ."

She would say it anyway, but the insignificance of those bare rooms would haunt her always. She thought about the good friends to whom she had not even said goodbye at the last minute because they too had let her down, though they had pretended to outdo one another in helping her. They had helped all right, by bringing around all those honest buyers whom they had tipped off to the opportunity of picking up for a pittance things that had originally cost a small fortune.

Signora Lucietta tightly closed her beautiful eyes on these unhappy thoughts, then opened them wide again as she lifted her forefinger to pass it along her pert little nose in that unconscious, pretty little way she had.

She was really very tired and would have liked to sleep. Her two fatherless children, poor dears, were sleeping soundly, the older one stretched out on the seat under a coat, and the baby curled up beside his mother, his blond head on her lap. She might have slept too if only she could have found a way of resting her head on her hand without waking the child pillowed on her knees.

The seat opposite was still marked where he had propped his little feet until the man had chosen to sit in that place—with all the empty seats in the other carriages!—a big man around thirty-five, dark and bearded, with light-green eyes—big intense, sad eyes.

Signora Lucietta took an immediate dislike to him. For no reason, his large eyes gave her the feeling that no matter where she would go the world would always remain alien to her. She would be lost, vainly calling for help among eyes like those now looking at her, veiled with sorrow but essentially unconcerned.

To avoid them, she kept her face turned toward the window although nothing could be seen outside. There was only the reflection of the oil lamp in the carriage, its little red flame wavering high among the shadows, smoking up the curved glass chimney. The reflection looked like another lamp suspended outside in the night, following after the train with difficulty and giving both comfort and fright.

"Faith," the gentleman murmured.

Signora Lucietta turned to look at him in astonishment. "What?"

"The light that is not there."

Brightening, she looked at him and smiled, pointing to the lamp hanging from the ceiling of their compartment. "But there it *is!*"

The man nodded, then added with a little smile, "Yes, like

faith . . . we kindle a light here and we also see it there, without realizing that when it is put out here, there will be no light there either."

"You are a philosopher!" exclaimed little Signora Lucietta.

He raised a hand from the knob of his cane in a vague gesture and sighed. "I observe."

The train halted for a long time at a small junction. Not a voice could be heard. When the rhythmic noise of the wheels stopped the unbroken silence seemed eternal.

"Mazzano," the gentleman murmured. "Usually there is a wait here for the through train."

Finally, they heard in the distance the plaintive whistle of the other train arriving late.

"Here it comes."

In that oncoming train, rolling over the same tracks on which she would soon pass, Signora Lucietta could hear the voice of her fate condemning her to be lost for all the rest of her days with her two little ones.

She shook off this moment of despair and asked her traveling companion, "Are we far from Peola?"

"It's more than an hour away," he replied. "Are you going to Peola, too?"

"Yes, I am the new telegraph operator. I passed the State examinations. I was fifth on the list, so they assigned me to Peola."

"Oh, yes. You were expected last night."

Signora Lucietta brightened up. "As a matter of fact," she started to say but remembered the sleeping child on her lap. She opened her arms, indicating the two children with a look. "You see how tied down I am . . . and alone, with so many things to take care of at the last minute."

"You are the widow Loffredi, aren't you?"

"Yes." Signora Lucietta lowered her eyes.

"Did they ever find out anything more about it?" he asked after a short, weighty silence.

"Nothing. But there are those who know," Signora Lucietta said, her eyes flashing. "Loffredi's real murderer was not the hired killer who struck him in the back and then fled. They tried to imply that there was a woman involved, but I know better.

Reprisal! It was political vengeance, pure and simple. Loffredi had no time to think about women. The one he had already took up too much . . . What I mean is, I was all he needed. Just imagine! He married me when I was fifteen."

As she said this, Signora Lucietta's face turned bright pink and her restless eyes lit up as they darted back and forth; finally she lowered them as before. For a moment the man watched her, impressed by the rapid change from animation to sudden embarrassment.

How could anyone take this show of feeling seriously? Although the mother of two children, she looked no more than a child herself—a doll. She was ill at ease probably because she had stated so emphatically that, with a wife as young and sparkling as herself, Loffredi had no thought for other women.

She must realize that no one, seeing her and knowing the man Loffredi was, would believe her. No doubt she was influenced by him while he lived, and perhaps still was, in her memory. She could not bear for anyone to think that Loffredi had not cared for her or that, for him, she had been just a doll. She wanted to be sole heir to the sensation stirred up in all the Italian newspapers about a year ago over the tragic end of this fiery, irrepressible journalist.

Silvagni felt well pleased that he had guessed her character so exactly when, after a few well-placed questions, he succeeded in getting her to talk and unconsciously to confirm everything he had surmised.

He had a tender impulse toward this little meadowlark hardly out of its nest and just learning to fly who fancied it was already free, self-reliant and confident in its knowledge of life. No, no, Signora Lucietta would never be at a loss! To think that she had not lost her head through all the horror of that tragedy! She had run here, run there, done this and that, not so much for herself as for those little ones—and, yes, a little for herself, too. After all, she was only twenty—and at times she did not even look that! Her age was another obstacle for her, perhaps the most vexing of all. Everyone seeing her first rebel and then despair laughed as though she had no right to do either. The more furious she became, the more they laughed, each one promising her one thing or another, all of them wishing their offer might be coupled with a little caress which they dared not give. Well aware of their motives, she soon grew tired of their game and, in order to get away, applied for a civil-service job as a telegraph operator.

"Poor Signora." Her fellow traveler sighed, smiling—he too!

"*Poor.* Why poor?"

"Ah . . . because . . . you'll see, it is not very amusing in Peola."

And he told her a few things about the town.

Boredom was always visible and tangible, in all the streets and squares of Peola.

"How is it visible?"

"In the endless number of sleeping dogs stretched out on the cobblestones. They do not even wake up to scratch themselves; they do it in their sleep."

Anyone opening his mouth to yawn in Peola must beware— it might stay open for five yawns at least; their ennui took that long to come out! If there were anything specific to be done, everybody in Peola closed his eyes and said with a sigh, "To-morrow . . ."

Because today and tomorrow were one and the same—and to-morrow was as good as never.

"You will see, there is nothing to do at the post office," he concluded. "No one ever goes there. Take this little train; it moves along like a stagecoach. Well, even a stagecoach would mean progress for Peola. Life in Peola goes by at the pace of a wheelbarrow."

"Heavens, you frighten me!" said Signora Lucietta.

"Don't be frightened," he said, smiling. "Now I'll give you some good news. In a few days, we're going to have a ball at the Club."

"Ah . . ."

Signora Lucietta looked at him with the sudden suspicion that even this gentleman wanted to make fun of her.

"Do the dogs dance?" she asked.

"No, the good citizens of Peola dance. You must go. It will

amuse you. The Club happens to be right on the square, near the post office. Have you found a place to live?"

The signora said she had, in the same house where her predecessor had lodged.

"And, excuse me, your name is . . . ?" she asked.

"Silvagni, Signora. Fausto Silvagni. I am secretary at the Town Hall."

"Oh, really! It's a pleasure."

"Ahem . . ."

Silvagni lifted his hand in a weary gesture and smiled bitterly at her deference, a smile which reflected the melancholy of his large, light eyes.

At last the train greeted the little station of Peola with a plaintive whistle.

"Are we here?"

II

Peola lay ringed within a vast range of blue hills, cleft here and there by valleys of mist, darkened by oaks and firs, brightened by chestnut trees. The little town with its clusters of red roofs and its four bell towers, its uneven squares and narrow streets sloping between small old houses and a few new and larger ones, now had the thrill of welcoming the widow of Loffredi, the journalist whose tragic and mysterious death was still referred to in the country's leading newspapers. It was an uncommon privilege to hear directly from her mouth many things no one in the big cities knew, but it was almost enough just to see her and to be able to say, "When he was alive, Loffredi clasped that little thing there in his arms."

The good folk of Peola were very proud of her presence. As for the dogs, they would have gone on sleeping peacefully, stretched out in the streets and squares of the town unaware of this honor, had the rumor not been circulated that their torpor made a bad impression on the signora. Everyone, particularly the young men but the older ones too, began disturbing them, chasing them off with kicks or by stamping their feet and clapping their hands.

The poor animals got up from the ground more surprised than frightened, and cast sidelong glances, barely cocking an ear. Some of them, tripping off on three legs, the fourth benumbed and drawn up, went elsewhere to stretch out. What had happened? They might have understood had they been less dulled by sleep. They had only to glance at that one little square where no dog was allowed to lie, or even to run past.

The post office stood on that square!

They might have noticed—had they just a little more wit— that all who passed there, especially the young men but the older ones too, seemed to breathe a different air, more stimulating, which quickened their gait and their movements. The men's heads turned as if a sudden rush of blood made them uncomfortable in their starched collars, and their hands busied themselves pulling down vests and adjusting ties.

The square crossed, they behaved as if they were intoxicated, hilarious and nervous. And at the sight of a dog:

"Get along with you!"

"Out of my way!"

"Off with you, ugly little cur!"

They even threw stones at them. Kicks were no longer enough.

Fortunately, there were those who sided with the dogs. A window would fly up and a woman, her eyes flashing, her fists raised, would cry out furiously, "Ruffians! What do you have against those poor animals?"

Or else: "You too, Signor Notary? With all due respect, aren't you ashamed of yourself? What a treacherous kick! Poor little beast! Here, here, doggie. Look at his little paw! You've crippled it, and off you go with a cigar in your mouth perfectly unconcerned. How shameful! And you a decent family man!"

In no time a close bond of sympathy was established between the ugly women of Peola and the dogs, mercilessly persecuted by their men: husbands, fathers, brothers, cousins, fiancés and, by contagion, all the riffraff of the town.

The women, a little more alert than the dogs—some of them at least—immediately noticed a new air about the menfolk that made their eyes shine and stare into space. The red, moss-covered roofs were brightened and every corner of the sleepy old town was exhilarated—or so it appeared to the men, at least.

Yes, life so filled with worries, troubles, bitterness all of a sudden had smiled. God, how it smiled, for no reason at all! If, after days and days of fog and rain, a ray of sunlight shines through, doesn't it cheer the heart? Doesn't it draw a sigh of relief from every breast? No more than a ray of sunshine, and yet all life was suddenly changed. The heaviness lifted, the darkest thoughts brightened, and those who had not wanted to leave the house were out of doors again. Smell the good aroma of the damp earth. As good to breathe as the odor of fresh mushrooms. Plans for the future suddenly seemed so simple and easy. Everybody shook off the memory of bad moments, realizing that they had been given too much importance. Courage! Chin up! And up with the mustache too!

That was the effect of the ray of sunlight which had abruptly pierced the clouds hanging over Peola, brightening the post office on the little square. Besides persecuting the sleeping dogs, husbands began to ask their wives, "Dear, why don't you arrange your hair better?"

Never, certainly not for years and years, had the citizens of Peola hummed so much without realizing it—at the Club, in their houses, or walking along the street.

Signora Lucietta saw and felt all of this. Such obvious desire flashed from burning eyes following her every move, voluptuously caressing her with a look, enveloping her with such warmth of feeling that she too became quite intoxicated.

It didn't require much doing because Signora Lucietta was already aquiver, simmering inside herself. What a nuisance they were, those little curls on her forehead, tumbling down every time she bent over to follow the ribbon of dotted paper running through its little ticking machine on the office table! She shook her head and almost jumped with surprise as her hair tickled her neck. What sudden blushes, and catchings of breath, ending in a tired little laugh. Oh, but she cried too. At times she wept without knowing why. Hot burning tears, brought on by a strange longing which ran through her whole body. She could not control those tears, and then, out of the blue, she would laugh again.

She determined to pay strict attention to her work in order

not to dwell on anything else, not to let her fancy fly after every amusing or dangerous idea that came to her, not to lose herself in certain unlikely prospects. She must take hold of herself firmly with both hands, so that everything would proceed according to rules and regulations. She must always remember that her two poor little orphans were at home in the care of that stupid old bumptious servant. What a worry that was! Two children to raise all alone, by her own hard work and sacrifices. Today here, to-morrow there, adrift with them—and then, when they were grown and had a life of their own, maybe all the hardships she had suffered would be forgotten. No, now they were still very little. Why imagine such ugly things? She would be older then, her first youth past in any case, and when one is old it is easier to smile even over sad memories.

Who was talking like that? She was, but not because such gloomy ideas came to her spontaneously. *He* passed the office every morning, that gentleman she had met on the train, and sometimes in the evening too, when he came from the Town Hall. He would stand in the doorway a moment, or before her counter, talking of different things, even amusing things. For instance they laughed together about the war on the dogs, and about the ugly women rising to their defense. But she read mournful, depressing ideas there in his eyes, those large, clear eyes, and they remained with her long after he had gone.

It was he who had started her worrying about her children—who knows why?—and without even asking about them or referring to them at all.

She felt annoyed, and repeated to herself that they were still so small—why allow herself to be discouraged? She should not and would not! Courage! She was still young, very young, and then . . .

"Can I help you, sir?" Yes, count the words of the telegram and then add two cents more. Would you like a telegraph blank? No? Well, I just asked. I understand. Good day, Signore. Don't mention it.

How many came into the office just to ask silly questions! It was hard not to laugh. They were so comical, those Peola gentle-men. And the delegation of young men, members of the Club who came to the post office one morning with their nice old president to invite her to the famous ball Signor Silvagni had spoken of on the train. What a sight! They looked eager, ready to eat her up, and seemed to marvel that, at close range, she had such and such a nose, with eyes and a mouth like that—to mention only her head! But the most impertinent were also the most embarrassed. None of them knew how to begin.

"Would you do us the honor . . ." "It is a yearly custom, Signora . . ." "A little *soirée dansante* . . ." "Oh, quite unpretentious, of course . . ." "A family affair." "Let me speak . . ." "What are you trying to say? If you would be so kind as to do us the honor . . ."

They fidgeted, wrung their hands, and stared at one another in an effort to get their words out, while the president, who was also mayor of the town, fumed, turning purple with rage. He had prepared a speech and they did not even give him a chance to deliver it. He had also carefully arranged the long strand of hair over his bald pate before sticking it down and had worn yellow gloves, inserting two fingers of his right hand between the buttons of his vest.

"It is our custom every year . . ." he began at last.

Although she could hardly keep from laughing, she blushed at these pressing invitations, expressed more clearly in sly looks than big, uneasy words. At first she tried to get out of it: she was still in mourning, as they knew, and then there were the children . . . she could only spend evenings with them . . . she did not see them all day . . . she always put them to bed . . . and there were so many other things she had to do . . .

"Come now, just for one evening." "You could come after they were in bed." "Isn't the servant there?" "For one evening . . ."

One of the boys, in his enthusiasm, went so far as to say, "Mourning? What nonsense!"

Someone gave him a sharp poke in the ribs and he did not dare utter another word.

Finally Signora Lucietta promised she would go, or rather that she would do her best to go. Then, when they all had left, she stood there looking at her little white hand against her black dress and at her finger on which Loffredi had placed that gold ring when he married her. Her hand had been so delicate then, the hand of a child, and now that the fingers had filled out, the ring was too tight. She could no longer take it off.

III

In the bedroom of her little furnished apartment, Signora Lucietta was telling herself that she would not go, cradling in her arms—bye-bye—her blond angel dressed in black—bye-bye—the smallest one who wanted to fall asleep in her arms every night.

The older child, undressed by the heavy-handed old servant, had gone to bed by himself, and, yes, the darling was now fast asleep.

Very lightly, careful not to waken the sleeping baby in her lap, Signora Lucietta now undressed him. Very softly, first one, then the other shoe; the socks, one, two, and now the little trousers along with the underpants, and now—ah, now it was more difficult to slip the arms out of the sleeves. Up, very carefully, with the help of the servant—no, not like that; here, that's right . . . there! Now the other side . . .

"No, my darling . . . yes, right here with your mama. Mama is here. I will do it alone, then. Please turn down the bed? There now."

But why so slowly, all this?

Did she really want to go dancing, a short year after her husband's death? No, and perhaps she would not have gone had she not seen—all of a sudden, as she came out of the bedroom into the little hallway in front of the closed window—a miracle.

She had been in that rented apartment for days and had not noticed the old wooden flower box standing there in front of the window. In that flower box a beautiful red rose had just opened— a miracle at this time of year.

She stood there astonished, looking at it as it bloomed between the drab gray hangings of that dirty little entrance, and her heart quickened with joy. In that rose she saw her own burning desire to enjoy herself for at least one night. Suddenly freed from the dilemma which made her hesitate—the specter of her husband, the thought of the children—she picked the rose and looking into the mirror over the console, pinned it in her hair.

Yes, there! With that rose in her hair she would go to the ball—and with her twenty years, too, and her joy, dressed in black.

IV

It was rapture, delirium, madness!

When she appeared, just as everyone had given up the hope of seeing her, the three dark rooms of the Club, divided by large arches and badly lit with oil lamps and candles, suddenly seemed ablaze with light. Her face, a little drawn from inner excitement, was flushed, her eyes shone, and that red rose in her hair proclaimed her joy for all to see.

The men lost their heads. Throwing convention to the winds and taking no further notice of jealous wives, sweethearts, pining spinsters, young girls, sisters, cousins, they rushed over and crowded about her, with the excuse of welcoming their guest. The dancing had started and, without giving her time to look right or left, they nearly came to blows squabbling over her in their wild enthusiasm. Fifteen, twenty arms were offered, elbows crooked, all for her! But which one first? One at a time—she would take a turn with each of them. Make way, make way! What about the music? What were they doing, those musicians over there? Were they also lost in a spell of admiration? Music! Music!

And she was off, stepping out for her first dance with the old mayor and president of the Club, in full dress.

"Excellent!"

"Look at him go!"

"Oh, the tails of his coat. How they fly!"

"Great!"

"Heavens! His hair is coming unglued."

"What? Why, he's already leading her to a chair."

Again fifteen, twenty arms with elbows crooked appeared before her.

"With me! With me!"

"One moment!"

"She's promised me."

"No, I'm next."

What a sight! It was a wonder they didn't tear each other apart.

While waiting their turn, the unlucky ones wandered off dejectedly to ask other ladies to dance. The uglier ones accepted sulkily, but the others, furious, refused indignantly with a curt "No, thank *you!*"

The women exchanged baleful looks and some of them abruptly made a great show of leaving, signaling to their friends to follow.

"Come, let us go. Never have I witnessed such indecent behavior!"

Some cried tears of rage; others trembled with vexation, unburdening themselves to inconspicuous little men who sat stiffly in suits polished by long use and smelling of pepper and camphor. Not to be caught up in the swirl, these shy creatures clung to the wall like dried leaves sheltered by the honest silk skirts of their wives, sisters-in-law or sisters—fancy dresses indeed, puffed and flounced, in violent shades of green, yellow, red or blue, gowns which hermetically preserved their wearers' sullen provincial modesty in the musty smell of venerable wooden chests and which comforted both their nostrils and their consciences.

The heat of the rooms became stifling. A kind of haze rose from the steaming sensuality of the men. Panting, burning, their faces flushed purple, they took advantage of the brief pauses between the dances to paste down and smooth their wet and bristling hair, by slipping trembling hands over their heads, along their temples or necks. Their animal natures rebelled out of all reason against propriety. The ball came only once a year! What harm did it do? Let the women quiet down and stay put!

Fresh, light, filled with a joy that brushed aside any vulgar contact, laughing and escaping with a quick gesture, amusing herself, intact and pure in that moment of folly, an agile, flickering flame among those dark, burning, senseless logs, Signora Lucietta, triumphant, whirled like a top, dancing and dancing without seeing anything or anyone. The arches dividing the three rooms, the furniture, the yellow, green, red and bright blue dresses of the ladies, the men's black clothes and white shirt fronts—all spun around in flashing streamers. As soon as one dancer wearied and started to pant heavily, she broke from his arms to throw herself into those of another, and off she went again, swirling around and around in a frenzied confusion of lights and colors.

Seated in the last room against the wall in a dark corner, Fausto Silvagni, his hands on the knob of his cane, watched her for two hours, his large, light eyes warmed by a friendly smile. Only he understood the purity of that mad joy and delighted in it, as though his tenderness had made her a gift of this innocent exultation.

His tenderness? Still only tenderness? Wasn't this throbbing of his heart more than tenderness?

For many years Fausto Silvagni, his eyes intent and sad, had looked at everything as if from a long way off. To him all things were but fleeting shadows, even his thoughts, his feelings.

Misfortune and heavy obligations had doomed him to failure. His youthful dreams, kindled with so much spirit, had petered out and were now remembered only with bitterness. He fled reality, choosing to lose himself in painful isolation.

Now, in that exile, a feeling had come over him, an emotion he wanted to hold at bay, as yet unwilling to accept it but equally unwilling to reject it completely.

Perhaps, since they could not appear to him in any other form, this dear, mad little creature, dressed in black with a flashing rose in her hair, had brought the living incarnation of those long-lost dreams for him to clasp—living and breathing—in his arms. Could he not check her flight, hold her and, at last, return through and with her from his remoteness? If he did not stop her, who knows where and how she would end. She too needed help, guidance, advice, lost as she was in a world not of her choosing but which, alas, she wanted to enjoy. That rose said so, that red rose in her hair.

For a while, Fausto Silvagni had looked at that rose in dismay. He didn't know quite why. There it lay like a flame in her hair. She shook that foolish little head of hers so often, how was it that the rose did not fall? Was that what he feared?

Meanwhile, deep within him, his trembling heart was saying, "Tomorrow, tomorrow or one of these days, you will speak out. Meanwhile, let her dance on like a wild little sprite."

By now, most of her partners were ready to drop and breathlessly declared themselves bested as they looked about for their wives who had left. Only six or seven obstinately held out, among them two old men—who would ever believe it?—the mayor and the widower notary. Both were in a sorry state, perspiring, faces flaming and eyes popping, ties crooked and shirts rumpled, pitiful in their senile frenzy. They had been nudged aside by the younger men all evening and now came forward for a couple of turns only to collapse on chairs like empty sacks one after the other.

It was the last lap, the closing dance.

Signora Lucietta found herself surrounded by all seven of the survivors, aggressively exuberant.

"With me!" "With me!"

The sensual overexcitement in their eyes alarmed her, and the thought that her innocent gaiety could arouse such passion disgusted and shamed her. She wanted to flee, to escape from them. At a startled fawnlike movement of her head, her hair, already loose, slipped down and the rose fell to the floor.

Fausto Silvagni was pulled to his feet by a strange presentiment of danger. The men fell all over one another in an effort to pick up the flower. It was the old mayor who retrieved it, but not without having his hand scratched.

"Here!" he cried, running with the others to offer it to Signora Lucietta, who was putting up her hair in the next room. "Here it is! Now you—" he was so out of breath that his head wobbled—"now *you* must make a choice. Here . . . offer it to one of us!"

"Hurrah! Wonderful idea!"

"She must choose . . ."

"Who will it be?"

"The judgment of Paris!"

"Hush! Wait and see!"

Breathless, holding the still-lovely rose high over her head, Signora Lucietta looked around at her pursuers like an animal at bay. She knew instinctively that they wanted to compromise her at all costs.

"To one of you? My choice?" she cried unexpectedly, a light in her eyes. "Very well, I will. But first step aside. Everyone stand aside. I will offer it to . . ."

Her eyes flew from one to another, as if hesitating in her decision. The awkward men stared at her uncertainly, their hands outstretched, their coarse faces grotesquely reflecting undisguised supplication. With a quick feint, she slipped by the last two on her left and ran toward the farther room. She had found a solution! She would present the rose to one of those who had sat quietly looking on all evening, the first one she came to.

"I will give it to . . ."

Her glance met the clear eyes of Fausto Silvagni. She turned pale and hesitated, trembling and confused.

"Oh, God!" she breathed, "have pity." Quickly recovering herself, she held out the flower, "Here, for you, take it. Take it, Signor Silvagni."

Fausto Silvagni took the rose and turned with a wan smile to look at the seven men rushing after her.

"No! Why to him? Why not to one of us! You must give it to one of us!"

"That's not so!" Signora Lucietta said impatiently. "You said *to someone,* that's all. And so I offered it to Signor Silvagni!"

"But that's an out-and-out declaration of love!" they protested.

"What?" exclaimed Signora Lucietta, her face crimson. "Not at all! It would have been a declaration had I offered it to one of you. But I gave it to Signor Silvagni, who hasn't moved from here all evening and who certainly would not interpret it like that! And you mustn't see it that way either."

"We do. We certainly do. After all, you chose him deliberately."

She was completely upset by their persecution. It had long since ceased to be a jest. Resentment showed in the men's eyes and mouths, and their sly winks and knowing grunts clearly referred to the visits Silvagni had paid her at the post office and to all the attention he had shown her since she had arrived.

Meanwhile his own pallor and uneasiness, heightened their malicious suspicions. Why did he blanch and fidget? Did he too think that she . . . Impossible! Why should he? Perhaps because the others chose to believe it. Why did he not protest? Why did his eyes reflect such suffering?

With a pang she suddenly understood everything. In her perplexity she was still confronted by the defiance of those insolent, thwarted men, however, as they screamed in unbridled rage around her.

"There now, you see! *You* say it doesn't mean a thing, but he doesn't utter a word!"

"What do you mean?" she cried, allowing her scorn to dominate her feelings to the contrary.

Trembling from head to foot, she turned to Silvagni. Looking him straight in the eyes, she asked, "Do you seriously think that in offering you this rose I have made a declaration of love?"

Fausto Silvagni looked at her for a moment, a pale, sad smile on his lips.

Poor little fairy, she was forced by their crude insistence to flee the magic circle of her joy, the innocent delirium in which she had whirled all evening like a little fool. Now, to safeguard the simplicity of her gift of a rose from the relentlessness of the men—all the purity of her joy in a single evening—she was asking him to give up a love which would last a lifetime and to make a reply which would wither the rose in his hand.

Looking coldly at the men, he said, "Not only I do not believe it, but you may be sure, Signora, that no one else will ever think it. Here is the rose. Throw it away yourself because I cannot."

Signora Lucietta took the flower with a not too steady hand and tossed it into a corner.

"Thank you," she said, knowing full well what it was she was throwing away forever with that rose of a moment.

❧

Tales of
Anguish and Hope

CANDELORA

"It wouldn't do, believe me, dear, it wouldn't do," said Anton Papa, his plump hands clutching the brim of his old Panama hat.

"Then what *would?*" cried Candelora, furious. "Stick on with you? Croak here in a fit of disgust?"

"Yes, dear, stick on here, as you say, but without croaking," placidly replied Anton Papa, yanking the brim of his hat down farther and farther. "Look, just be patient, I will explain. Chico—"

"I forbid you to use that name!"

"Isn't that what you call him yourself?"

"That's just it, because that's my name for him!"

"Oh, well, I thought it would please you. Shall I call him 'the Baron' then? As I was saying, the Baron loves you, Candelora, and he is spending on you—"

"Ah! So it's on *me* he's spending? Fool! Wretch! Isn't he spending a lot more on you?"

"If you won't let me finish . . . The Baron is spending on me *and* on you. But, don't you see, if he spends more on me, what does it mean? Be sensible. It means that you are more desirable because you take on added shine from me. See?"

"Shine?" Candelora turned and screamed at him. "Yes, shine from these!" And lifting her foot, she pointed to her shoe. "*Shame* you mean. *Shame,* that's all I take on from you!"

Anton Papa smiled and, more calmly than ever, replied, "No, excuse me. If there is any shame attached to this, it is mine. I am your husband. That's the whole point, Candelora. If I were not your husband, and, above all, if you did not live here with me under this hospitable roof, there would be no zest in it, understand? As things are, they can all come here to honor you with impunity, and the more you—shall we say—dishonor and shame me, the greater their enjoyment. Without me around, Candelora, you would be less attractive and more of a risk for Chico—I mean the Baron. . . . What are you doing? Crying? Don't, I was only joking."

Anton went over to Candelora and was about to put his hand under her chin when she seized his arm and savagely sank her teeth into his flesh. She bit down hard and hung on. He ground his teeth with a mute smile of pain, turning pale, and tried to favor his arm by curving it up toward her mouth. His eyes became unnaturally sharp and bright.

Then, at last, she let go. Ah, what blissful relief! His arm felt as though it had been branded with fire. He said nothing.

Gingerly, he pulled up the sleeve of his jacket, but his shirt sleeve was caught in the wound. A bloody circle showed where Candelora's strong teeth had cut through the flesh. He had difficulty pulling out the cloth, but finally, still pale and smiling, he succeeded. Each tooth had left its mark, and inside the circle the flesh was bruised and dark.

"See what you've done?" said Anton, holding out his arm.

"I'd bite into your heart too if I could," cried Candelora from where she sat huddled on a bench.

"I know," said Anton. "That's why you'll decide to stay here with me. You'll see. Now, take off your little hat and go get some iodine and a bandage. You'll find them in my desk drawer, second on the right. I know what a little beast you are, and that's why I'm prepared for any emergency."

Candelora looked up, stealing a glance at his arm. Anton admired her in that moment. What a marvel of form and color, forever new and different—a real challenge to his painter's eye.

In the little garden of the villa, slashed with violent shadows under the noon sun of mid-August, she looked frightful. Just back from the beach, her skin coarsened and burned by the sun and salt water, with her clear eyes, receding chin and bleached-out yellow hair, she looked like a drowsy little goat. Her strong bare arms were peeling and every movement of her powerful hips threatened to burst that fragile clinging dress of blue voile.

Ah, how ridiculous that dress looked!

Candelora would swim whole mornings or lie naked in the sun on the deserted beach, sprinkling her firm flesh with burning sand, while cool, quivering sea foam licked the soles of her feet. How could she ever expect to hide her exuberant nudity now under that blue dress? Worn for the sake of decency, it made her appear far more indecent than if she were naked.

Through her rage she caught the look of admiration in his eyes and instinctively smiled, a smile of satisfaction which almost at once turned to exasperation. The smile became a sneer; the sneer broke off into sobs.

And Candelora ran toward the villa.

Anton Papa's face wrinkled with a certain amusement as he followed her with his eyes. He looked down at his wounded arm, which stung in the sun, and then, for no reason at all, his eyes filled with tears.

It was ghastly, in the middle of a sultry day like this, to be reminded of life's affliction and, with a sweating brow, to feel a yearning tenderness in a spirit so burdened with shame and loathing.

Drooping in all that torrid sunlight, Anton Papa now felt the depressing, alarming, almost frightening presence of so many things, strangely suspended around him: those tall acacias, the glassy green pool of stagnant water bordered by artificial rocks, the benches . . . What were they waiting for? Of course, he could move, go away, but he felt he was being watched by all those things, not only watched but held there by a hostile fascination, almost ironical, rising from their deathlike calm which made his power to leave seem futile, stupid, even ridiculous.

That garden was a symbol of Baron Chico's wealth. He and Candelora had been here for nearly six months, but only this morning, when she came back from the beach, had he felt the need of pointing to his own shame and hers, but jokingly, because Candelora had said she wanted to get away from that shame *now that we can*.

Yes, now that the critics had hailed his work, wealthy collectors were flocking to his shows. True, they had no real understanding of his art, but his paintings sold and sold well.

Critics? Reviews? Mere words! Words without meaning except in the pants of a critic. What about the critic to whom Candelora went in desperation one day, screaming in his face that it was unfair to let an artist like Anton Papa starve? That critic—the most influential of them all—chose to call attention to the new and very personal art of Anton Papa in a masterful review. *But* he had also chosen to have his recognition of the artist—we won't say paid for—graciously rewarded by Candelora's gratitude. And Candelora, intoxicated by her victory, lavished her gratitude not only on the critic but on all the fanatical admirers of her husband's art. She was grateful to them all, and especially to Baron Chico, who went so far as to lodge them in his villa to have the honor of sheltering this prodigy, this child of glory. What receptions and parties! And what presents they received!

Had this cost her nothing, then there was no harm done. Poor Candelora. She was afraid of poverty—that was it. But she said, no, it did not scare her, it made her angry—not the hardship and despair of poverty but its injustice. How? By accepting this villa, this car, boat, gold, jewels, trips, clothes, parties? She even scorned him because he remained impervious to joy or sorrow, as slovenly as before, finding no pleasure outside his work and wishing only to dig down into his art, never satisfied, always digging deeper so as not to see the ridiculous vortex of life swirling around him.

Perhaps this clowning fantasy symbolized his own fame: the jewels, the luxury in which Candelora now lived, the guests, the parties, his own glory and—why not?—his own shame. Or did the answer really matter?

All his life, everything that was alive in him he gave, spent, lavished on the joy of recreating a leaf; he put himself into the flesh, the fiber and veins of that leaf, into the hardness and bareness of a stone, which became a real stone on the canvas. That alone mattered to him.

His shame? His life? The lives of others? Irrelevant, fleeting things, unworthy of serious concern. Only his art lived and took overpowering form in the light and torment of his spirit.

What is to be will be.

This morning, as if it were someone else talking, he had mentioned to Candelora—oh, casually enough—that he sometimes longed for a life companion who would not have resented poverty so much, a humble, mild companion on whose breast he might have sought repose and whose suffering would have inspired him with the same tender pity as had his own unrecognized work. Naturally, Candelora had spat at him like an angry cat.

But what could be keeping her all this time? Wasn't she ever coming back with the iodine and bandage? She had gone off crying, poor girl.

Now she wanted to be loved. Candelora wanted him to love her, regardless of his indifference. Wasn't that preposterous? If he had really loved her, he would have had to kill her. Only this indifference made it possible for him to endure the shame she personified. Couldn't he get away from this shame? But how was that possible when they both had it inside, outside and all around them? The only thing was to give it no importance: he must go on painting and she must amuse herself, now with Chico, then with another, and also gaily, according to her fancy, with Chico and another at the same time. Life is like that—just foolishness. One way or another, it passes without leaving a trace. Meanwhile, laugh at the misbegotten who go on suffering in their ugly, indecent way until, with time, they crumble to dust. Everything carries its own misery: the distress of being what it is with no hope of ever being otherwise. That was exactly what was *new* about his art: suffering expressed through form. He well knew that every humpback must resign himself to his hump. Deeds, too, are like forms. Once a deed is done, nothing can change it. Candelora, for example, could never be pure again as she had been when she was poor. But, on second thought, perhaps she had never been pure—not even as a child—or she would not have done those things later and taken pleasure in them.

Why this longing for purity all of a sudden? Why did she want to be alone with him, peaceful, simple, loving? With *him*, after all that had happened? As if he could ever take anything seriously again. And love—a love as entangled as hers was with that comic image of Chico, the critic and so many others, spinning round and round the idyll of their embrace, like a ring-around-the-rosy.

By now the blood had clotted and formed a scab over the tooth marks as he stood there in the hot sun. His wrist, even his hand, had begun to swell.

Anton Papa roused himself and climbed back up to the house. He called out twice from the foot of the stairs, and then again from the hall: "Candelora! Candelora!"

The empty rooms echoed the sound of his voice, but there was no answer. He entered the room next to the studio and jumped back. In the bright light of that white room, Candelora lay stretched out on the floor, her dress half raised, exposing her thigh, as if she had rolled over. He ran to lift her head. Oh God! What had she done? Her mouth, chin, neck, breast were stained a dark yellow. She had drunk the iodine.

"It's nothing . . . nothing," he cried. "Candelora, darling, what silly thing have you done? My baby . . . it's nothing. It will burn your stomach a little . . . Come, get up."

Vainly, he tried to lift her. "Baby . . . baby," he scolded gently, because it seemed so childish that she would drink iodine. "Baby," he repeated, called her his little fool, and tried to pull down the blue dress over her bare thigh, turning his eyes aside from the sight of her black-stained mouth. The flimsy dress ripped under his frantic hand, baring even more of her twisted body.

He was alone in the house. Candelora had discharged all the servants before she left for the beach. There was no one to help him, no one to send for a carriage to rush her to the hospital. But, luckily, just then he heard the horn of Chico's automobile.

And a moment later Chico appeared in his too youthful, too elegant clothes, surprise showing on that stupid, sallow face.

"Oh! What's this?"

Automatically, he adjusted his monocle to run his eye over her exposed thigh.

"Help me lift her, for God's sake!" Anton cried in exasperation.

As they raised her from the floor, a revolver fell from the hand concealed under her hip, revealing a pool of blood.

"Ah! Ah!" moaned Anton as they carried her toward the bedroom.

Candelora was not unconscious but dead. Almost out of his wits, Anton Papa had barely laid the corpse on the bed before he screamed at Chico, "Who went to the beach with you? Tell me who was at the beach with you this summer?"

Chico, bewildered, mentioned a few names.

"Ah, dear God!" raged Anton. He turned on Chico, grabbing the lapels of his jacket and shaking him. "Is it possible that anyone can be as stupid as that—you fools with all your money!"

"Stupid? Us?" Chico mumbled more bewildered than ever, backing away at every shake.

"Yes! Yes!" Anton Papa pursued. "You're all so stupid you made that poor girl turn to me for love. Do you understand? Me, me! She wanted *me* to love her!"

He burst into tears and threw himself across Candelora's body.

THE BLACK SHAWL

W ait here," Bandi told d'Andrea. "I'll go in and talk to
her. If she still refuses to see you, come in anyway!"

Both were nearsighted and stood very close together as they
faced each other. Tall, thin, about the same age and build, they
might have been taken for brothers, especially in their straight-
laced look revealing finicky natures bent on doing everything
just so. When they talked together, one of them would usually
adjust the other's glasses on his nose, straighten his tie or, if nothing else, idly finger the buttons of his coat. But they talked little,
and their uncommunicative natures showed clearly in their
gloomy faces.

Raised together, they had helped each other with their lessons
right up to the time they entered the university—one to become
a lawyer and the other a doctor. Now separated during the day
by their professions, they met each sundown for a walk along the
road which led from town into the open country.

They knew each other so intimately that a sign, a word, a
look was enough for the one immediately to grasp the other's
thought. Their walk usually began with a brief exchange of

words and was followed by a long silence while they mulled things over. Walking along with heads lowered like tired horses, their hands clasped behind their backs, neither of them felt any desire to look in the direction of the low wall bordering the road where a view of the whole countryside opened out: hills, valleys, plains, with the sea in the distance, all aglow under the last rays of the setting sun. It was incredible that anyone could pass by such a magnificent panorama without giving it even a fleeting glance.

"Eleonora isn't feeling well," Bandi had told d'Andrea the day before.

"Would you like me to take a look at her?" d'Andrea asked, gathering from his friend's eyes that his sister's illness was nothing serious.

"She says no."

They both frowned, thinking almost with hatred of the woman who had mothered them and to whom they owed everything.

D'Andrea, still a child when his parents died, had been taken in by an uncle who was in no way able to provide for him. Eleonora Bandi, orphaned at eighteen and with a brother much younger than herself, was able to manage at first, with painstaking economy, on the small nest egg left by her parents. Then, by giving piano and singing lessons, she kept her brother as well as his inseparable friend in school.

Eleonora was enormous, but the gentle sweetness of her features gave her that seraphic look often seen in churches on the faces of marble angels in flowing robes. The expression in her beautiful black eyes, fringed with velvety lashes, and the harmonious sound of her voice softened the impression made by the size of her body.

She played and sang, not perfectly perhaps, but with much feeling. Had she not been born and raised among the prejudices of a small town and hampered by her responsibility for her little brother, she might have ventured into the theatrical world. It had been her dream at one time, but never more than a dream. Now almost forty, she was content with the tribute paid her musical talent by the townspeople and their admiration for her unswerving effort to secure the future of those two fatherless boys.

Dr. d'Andrea sat waiting in the little sitting room for his friend to come out and call him.

The room, flooded with light despite its low ceiling, with its worn, old-fashioned furniture, breathed an air of days gone by in the unchanging reflection of two large facing mirrors. Only Eleonora's piano, a baby grand, was new. The faces of the old family portraits hanging around the walls, the true occupants of the room, seemed to look down on it with a frown.

Finally, tired of waiting, the doctor got up and poked his head around the door into the hall. He heard crying in the next room and rapped on the closed door.

"Come in," said Bandi, opening the door. "I can't understand what makes her so stubborn."

"I tell you there's nothing wrong with me," Eleonora insisted through her tears.

Huge and pale, dressed all in black as usual, she sat in a big leather armchair, a strange look on her childlike face, perhaps more ambiguous than strange because of a certain hardness in her eyes—an almost mad fixity which she tried in vain to conceal.

"There is nothing wrong with me, I assure you," she repeated more calmly. "For pity's sake, leave me alone! Don't pay any attention to me."

"Very well," her brother concluded, in a ruthless, obstinate tone of voice. "Meanwhile, Carlo's here. You can tell him what ails you." And he went out, slamming the door furiously behind him.

Eleonora buried her face in her hands and sobbed.

D'Andrea looked at her with embarrassment; then he asked, "What it it? Can't you tell me, either?"

As Eleonora continued to sob, he went to her and gingerly tried to remove her hands from her face.

"Quiet down, now. Tell me what it's all about. That's why I came."

Eleonora shook her head, then suddenly seized his hand in

both of hers and, her face distorted as if in pain, moaned. "Carlo! Carlo!"

D'Andrea leaned over her, feeling that his customary impassive behavior was being compromised.

"Tell me . . ."

She laid her cheek against his hand and pleaded desperately in a low voice, "Help me die, Carlo. Show me how. Have pity on me. I haven't the courage, the strength . . ."

"Die?" the young man asked, smiling. "Why do you say that?"

"Die, yes!" she repeated, choked by sobs. "Show me the way. You are a doctor. Take me out of this agony. Have mercy. I *must* die. There's no other way out. Only death."

He stared at her in bewilderment. She too raised her eyes to look at him but quickly closed them, her face twisted again in sudden despair.

"Yes, yes," she said firmly. "Carlo, I am lost."

Instinctively d'Andrea withdrew the hand she was still holding in both her own.

"What . . . what are you saying?" he faltered.

Without looking at him, she put a finger to her lips and pointed to the door.

"If he knew! Don't tell him, I beg you. First let me die. Give me something. I'll take it just like medicine, believing it *is* medicine you have given me. Only let it be quick! I haven't the courage. For two months I've struggled in despair without finding the strength or the way of putting an end to it. What help can you give me, Carlo?"

"Help?" D'Andrea repeated, aghast.

Eleonora once more stretched out her hands to take his arm and pleaded, "If you won't help me die, can't you . . . save me in some other way?"

At this suggestion d'Andrea withdrew more than ever and frowned severely.

"I beg you, Carlo!" she insisted. "Not for myself, but so that Giorgio won't find out. If I've ever done anything for you, help me now. Save me! Is this the way I must end, after having tried so hard, and suffered so much? Dishonored, at my age? What misery! What horror!"

"But, Eleonora, how did it happen? Who did it?" d'Andrea blurted out in appalled curiosity, finding nothing else to say in the face of the depth of her despair.

Eleonora again pointed to the door, covering her face with her hands. "Don't remind me! I don't want to think about it. But won't you spare Giorgio this shame?"

"How?" asked d'Andrea. "It's a crime! It would be a double crime! Think of something else."

"No!" she replied curtly. "Enough! I understand. Leave me now. I can't bear any more."

Her head fell back on the chair and she collapsed, exhausted.

Carlo d'Andrea, his eyes popping behind the thick lenses of his glasses, waited awhile in silence, unable to believe what he had heard or to imagine how this woman—a shining example of virtue and self-denial—could have been led astray. Impossible! Eleonora Bandi? In her youth she had had many proposals of marriage, one more attractive than the other, but she had refused them all out of love for her little brother. Why, then, now that her youth was gone—or was it perhaps just because of that?

He looked at her voluminous body and the suspicion in his eyes suddenly took on a lewd, ugly glint.

"Go, then," she said abruptly.

Without lifting her head, Eleonora could feel the change in his expression.

"Go! Go and tell Giorgio so that he can do as he likes with me and get it over with. Go!" she repeated.

D'Andrea went out stiffly. She raised her head a little to watch him leave. Then, as soon as the door had closed, she fell back into her former position.

II

After two months of mental torture, this confession of her plight gave her unexpected relief. It seemed to her that the worst was over. She no longer had the strength to struggle against this humiliation. She would have to abandon herself to her fate, whatever it would be.

Would her brother kill her when he came in? Well, all the better. She had no right to expect consideration or sympathy. Although she had done more than her duty for him and for that other ungrateful one, now all the hard-won fruits of her sacrifice were swept away.

She closed her eyes tight in a fit of revulsion.

In her conscience, she blamed herself. Yes, she who had found the strength to resist the impulses of youth for so many years, she who had always had the purest, noblest sentiments, she who had given up everything for the sake of duty—now, in a moment, all was lost.

In self-defense she had only one explanation to give her brother, and what weight would that carry in his eyes? She could say, "Look, Giorgio, it was because of you that I fell." And yet that was the simple truth.

She had mothered her little brother with loving care, and in return for everything she had so willingly lavished on him, in reward for the dedication of her entire life, he had never given her the pleasure of even the slightest smile of satisfaction and neither had his friend. Their souls seemed poisoned by silence and boredom, weighed down by stupid restraint. As soon as they received their degrees, like work horses they threw themselves into harness with such relentless dedication that in no time they had managed to become self-supporting. This haste to be free of their obligation to her, as if they could hardly wait to see the end of it, wounded her deeply. Almost overnight she found herself with no purpose in life. What was there for her to do, now that the boys were grown and no longer needed her, now that her youth was forever lost?

Even his first professional earnings had not brought a smile to her brother's face. Did he consider what she had done for him as a dead weight? For the rest of his life, would he feel obliged to repay her sacrifice?

She tried to speak to him straight from the heart: "Don't worry about me, Giorgio. My only wish is to see you happy and contented. Understand?"

But he broke in: "Hush! What do you mean? I know what my duty is. From now on, I take the responsibility."

"But why take it like this?" she wanted to ask. But knowing his obstinacy, she did not insist. However, there were times when she felt that she could no longer endure this pall of gloom.

From day to day his professional earnings increased and he surrounded her with comforts, even insisting that she give up her music lessons. In the loneliness of this forced leisure, an unfortunate idea occurred to her which, at first, had only made her laugh: *What if I should find a husband?*

Since she was already thirty-nine, any candidate would really have to be made to order. Yet it was the only way to free both her brother and herself of this crushing debt of gratitude.

Unconsciously, she began to pay more attention to her appearance, taking on a certain air of eligibility which she had never assumed before. The several young men who had proposed to her had long since married and had children. Although this had never mattered to her, she now felt resentful and envious of the lives her friends had made for themselves.

She alone was left like this.

But maybe there was still time; who could tell? Was her busy life to drag itself out in emptiness? Was the bright flame of her passionate spirit to be quenched under this shadow?

She was overcome with longing and bitterness which gradually altered her natural charm, her voice, her smile. She became biting, even aggressive, in conversation, and hated herself for this change in her disposition. Her body was repulsive to her and she was harassed by unsuspected desires which deeply troubled her.

Her brother, meanwhile, had saved enough money to buy a farm and build a charming little villa. At his insistence, she first went there for a month's vacation. Then, assuming that he had bought the farm in order to be rid of her occasionally, she decided to live there altogether. He would be left free, no longer burdened by her company or the sight of her, while she would slowly rid herself of this foolish idea of marrying at her age.

The first days went very well and she saw no reason why this new life should not continue. She would rise at dawn and take long walks across country, stopping here and there to listen, enchanted, to the cocks crowing, calling from one farmyard to another in the surprising silence of the open meadows where the grass shivered in the coolness of the early morning, or to admire the green moss striping a rock, or the velvety lichen on the twisted trunk of an ancient olive tree.

There, close to the earth, she would soon have recovered her good spirits, thinking and feeling differently. She would have become like the good wife of the tenant farmer who was always ready to keep her company and teach her so many things about nature, simple things which suddenly revealed a new, unexpected and deeper meaning to life.

But the tenant farmer was unbearable. He boasted of having "liberal" ideas, of having circled the world. He had been to South America too—eight years in *Benossary*—and he did not intend his only son, Gerlando, to be a lowly peasant. Consequently, he had kept him in school for thirteen years. He wanted to give him a little *lettering*, as he put it, so he could send him to America, where, no doubt, he would make a fortune.

Gerlando was nineteen and, for all his thirteen years of study, he had not yet finished the third year in trade school. He was a big, uncouth boy, all of a piece. His father's ambitions were a real martyrdom for him. The citified ways he picked up unconsciously from his school fellows only accentuated his boorishness.

By dousing his bristling head with water every morning, he managed to comb his hair and part it on one side, but, as soon as it dried, it rose stiffly as if sprouting from his scalp. Even his eyebrows shot out from under his low forehead, while the first hairs of a rough beard sprouted in little tufts beneath his lip and around his chin. Poor Gerlando! One could only pity him, so big, so dull-witted and so shaggy, sitting before an open book. Some mornings his father had a hard time rousing him from his leaden sleep and getting him off, still stunned, steps weaving, eyes dulled, to his purgatory in the nearby town.

When Eleonora came to the country, Gerlando, through his mother, addressed himself to the signorina to persuade his father to stop tormenting him with school, school, school! He could not stand it any longer. Eleonora tried to intervene, but the tenant farmer would have none of it. With all due respect and regard for the signorina, he would be obliged if she would not meddle in his affairs. So then, partly out of pity, partly to have something to do, Eleonora started to help the poor young man with his studies.

Every afternoon she had him come to the villa with his class books and notebooks. He arrived feeling ill at ease and ashamed because he noticed that the lady found his stupidity amusing, but what could he do? This was what his father wanted. He knew he could not learn from books, but, by golly, when it came to felling a tree or an ox . . . Gerlando raised his sinewy arm and a tender, proud look came into his eyes as he smiled, baring his strong white teeth.

Impulsively, from one day to the next, Eleonora stopped the lessons. She did not want to see him again! Her piano was sent out from the city and for a while she did nothing but play and sing and read. One evening she noticed that Gerlando, suddenly deprived of her help, her company and her little jokes, had come to spy on her, to listen to her playing and singing. Meaning to take him by surprise, she left the piano and quickly ran down the steps of the villa.

"What are you doing here?"

"I came to listen."

"Do you like it?"

"Very much, Signora. I'm in heaven!"

At this, she burst out laughing. Her laugh struck Gerlando like a slap across the face and he seized her, jumping on her in the darkness behind the villa, beyond the shaft of light shining from the open door across the balcony.

Overcome by surprise, she had not been able to push him off. She felt faint—she did not know why—under his brutal impact and had let herself go. She had yielded against her will.

That was how it had happened.

Next day Eleonora returned to the city.

Now why didn't Giorgio come in to humiliate her? Perhaps d'Andrea had not yet told him. Perhaps he was thinking of a way to spare her this shame. But how?

She hid her face in her hands to shut out the emptiness before her, but she found the same emptiness inside herself. There was no solution. Only death. When? How?

The door burst open and Giorgio appeared, pale, hysterical, his hair in disorder and his eyes red from weeping. D'Andrea held him by the arm.

"I want to know just one thing," he said between clenched teeth, stressing each word. "I want to know *who it was!*"

Eleonora, her head bowed, her eyes closed, slowly shook her head and began sobbing.

"I'll make you tell me!" screamed Bandi, going up to her while his friend tried to hold him back. "And whoever it may be, you'll marry!"

"No, Giorgio," she moaned, lowering her head still further and twisting her hands in her lap. "It's impossible, impossible!"

"Is he married?" he demanded, threatening her with clenched fists.

"No," she said quickly, "but it's out of the question."

"Who is it?" screamed Bandi, trembling all over. "Who is it? Out with it!"

Feeling her brother's fury towering over her, Eleonora withdrew still further and whispered under his murderous look, "Giorgio, I cannot tell you . . ."

"His name or I'll kill you!" roared Bandi, raising his fist.

But d'Andrea interceded, pushing his friend aside. "Go," he said severely. "She will tell me. Go . . . go!" And he pushed him out of the room.

III

Her brother was inflexible.

Before the wedding, during the few days required for the publication of the banns, he mercilessly pursued the scandal. To forestall the low jokes he anticipated from all sides, he deliberately set out to broadcast his shame in the crudest possible language. He appeared to be out of his head and everyone felt sorry for him.

But he had a tussle with the tenant farmer to get him to consent to this marriage.

For all his liberal ideas, the old man at first refused to believe such a thing possible. Then he said, "Don't worry, Your Honor; I'll stamp him underfoot as we crush the juice from the grapes. Better still, I'll hand him over to you, bound hand and foot, and Your Honor can do whatever you like with him. I'll provide the lash for the whipping myself, and I'll soak it three days beforehand so it will cut all the harder."

But when he understood that this was not the gentleman's intention and that Bandi had something else in mind—marriage—he was again taken aback.

"What? What is Your Honor saying? A lady of her standing marry the son of a common peasant?"

And he flatly refused.

"Begging your pardon, the signorina is old enough to know what she is up to. She knows right from wrong. She should never have done what she did with my son. Let me tell you: she had him come to her house every day! Your Honor can understand . . . a big fellow . . . and at that age, they don't reason or pay much attention. Now is this the way I'm going to lose my son who cost me I don't know how much to educate? The signorina, with all due respect, is old enough to be his mother!"

Bandi had to promise to turn over the farm as dowry and to provide his sister with an income. So the bargain was struck, and the wedding was a big event for the little town.

Everyone seemed to enjoy repudiating the admiration and respect they had formerly shown Eleonora Bandi. Between their esteem, which she had now lost, and the derision with which they accompanied her to this shameful wedding, there seemed no room for compassion.

All the sympathy was for the brother, who, of course, did not wish to take part in the ceremony. D'Andrea did not attend either, giving as his excuse that he must keep Giorgio company on this sad day.

An old friend of Eleonora's parents—a doctor from whom d'Andrea had managed to filch a large part of his practice—offered to serve as her witness. He brought another friend along as second witness.

Eleonora rode with them in a closed carriage to the Town

Hall. Later they would go on to a secluded little church for the religious ceremony.

The groom, sulking and gloomy, came in another carriage with his parents. They were all dressed up and feeling very superior because, after all, their son was marrying a real lady, the sister of a lawyer, whose dowry would provide them with a farm, a fine villa and an income to boot! To live up to his new status, Gerlando would now have to finish his studies. The bride was a little old? All the better! An heir was already on the way—and by the laws of nature, she would be the first to die, leaving Gerlando and his offspring rich and free.

These and similar considerations were being aired in a third carriage occupied by the groom's witnesses, peasant friends of his father, and two uncles on his mother's side. Numerous other friends and relatives of the groom waited at the villa, all in their best clothes—the men in dark-blue suits and the women in new caps and gaily colored aprons. The tenant farmer, with his "liberal" ideas, had ordered a fitting reception—everything first-class.

At the Town Hall, before entering the clerk's office, Eleonora had a crying spell. The groom stood to one side surrounded by relatives who urged him to go over to her, but the old doctor begged him to stay away for the moment.

Before she had entirely recovered Eleonora went into the office, and when she saw the boy beside her looking gawkier than ever because of his embarrassment, she had an impulse to rebel. "No! No!" And she gave him a look as if urging him to do the same. But a few minutes later they both said their "yes," accepting their inescapable punishment.

The second ceremony in the lonely little church was hurriedly dispatched and then the sad procession started off toward the villa. Eleonora did not want to part from her two friends, but she was obliged to climb into the carriage with the groom and her in-laws.

Not a word was exchanged between them the whole way. The tenant farmer and his wife seemed dismayed, occasionally stealing a glance at their daughter-in-law, then exchanging looks before lowering their eyes. Withdrawn and frowning, the groom stared out the window.

They were greeted at the villa by a loud salvo of firecrackers and by shouts of joy and applause. But the bride's expression and behavior chilled the guests though she tried to smile at these simple folk who were celebrating a wedding in their own way, according to tradition.

She soon begged to be excused, but stopped short on the threshold of her former bedroom when she saw that a nuptial bed had been prepared for them there. "Here, with him! Never! Never!" Filled with disgust, she fled into another room, turned the key in the lock and fell into a big chair, covering her face with her hands.

The voices of the jubilant guests reached her through the closed door. They were baiting Gerlando, congratulating him not so much on his wife as on the family he had married into and the beautiful property he had acquired.

Filled with shame, Gerlando leaned over the balcony, replying to their boisterous taunts with an occasional shrug of his heavy shoulders.

Yes, he was ashamed to be married to that woman. It was all his father's fault, he and his cursed ideas about school. The signorina had treated him like a big dunce, making fun of him and hurting his feelings. Then this had to happen! All his father thought about was the piece of property. But he—how was he going to live with this woman who made him feel so uncomfortable and who certainly blamed him for her shame and dishonor? What was worse, his father now claimed he would have to finish school! Imagine what fair game he would make for his schoolmates with a wife twenty years older than himself, a wife who looked like a mountain besides.

While Gerlando was tormenting himself with such thoughts, his mother and father were putting the final touches to the banquet. At last, triumphant, they came into the room where the table was spread. The table service, hired for the occasion, came from a restaurant in the city, which also provided a cook and two waiters to serve.

The tenant farmer came out on the balcony and said to Gerlando, "Go and tell your wife the banquet will be ready in a moment."

"Nothing doing. I won't go!" Gerlando grunted, stamping his foot. "Tell her yourself!"

"It's your place, jackass!" cried his father. "You're the husband! Go!"

"No, thanks! I refuse!" Gerlando repeated obstinately, protecting his head against an anticipated blow with his raised arm.

In a rage, his father grabbed him by his coat collar and gave him a big shove.

"Blockhead! You got yourself into this mess in the first place and now you're ashamed! She's your wife!"

The guests came running to make peace and to coax Gerlando to go upstairs.

"What harm is there in that? Just tell her to come down and have a bite."

"But I don't even know what to call her!" cried Gerlando, exasperated.

Some of the guests burst out laughing while others were quick to restrain the farmer, who wanted to strike his stupid son for spoiling the fine party he had prepared at so much expense!

"Call her by her baptismal name," his mother suggested softly. "Her name is Eleonora, isn't it? Call her Eleonora. She's your wife. Go, my son, go," she said, leading him toward the nuptial suite.

Gerlando rapped on the door. He rapped softly the first time and waited. Silence. What should he say to her? What a predicament! Why didn't she answer? Maybe she hadn't heard. He rapped again more loudly and waited. Silence.

Then, uneasily, he tried calling her by name in a low voice as his mother had suggested. But what came out was an Eleonora which sounded so ridiculous that quickly, as if to wipe it out, he said very loudly, "Eleonora!"

At last her voice, coming from another room, asked, "Who is it?"

Frightened and stammering, he went to the other door. "I," he said, "I, Ger . . . Gerlando. It's all ready."

"I cannot come down," she answered. "Go ahead without me."

Gerlando returned to the dining room with a feeling of relief.

"She's not coming. She said she won't come . . . she can't come."

"Hurrah for the blockhead!" exclaimed his father, who called him nothing else. "Did you tell her we were all at the table? Why didn't you *make* her come down?"

His wife interposed, trying to explain to her husband that it was perhaps best to leave the bride alone for the moment. The guests agreed: "The emotion . . . the discomfort . . . you understand."

But the farmer, who wanted to show his daughter-in-law that he knew how to do things right, sulked and gruffly ordered the waiters to serve dinner.

Although the guests were looking forward to the mouthwatering delicacies to come, they all felt ill at ease and dazzled by the extravagant number of glittering objects on the new tablecloth: four glasses of different sizes and shapes at each place, big and little forks, big and little knives, and then there were strange-looking feathers sticking out of small rolls of fringed paper.

Seated well back from the table, they perspired in their heavy Sunday clothes and stared at one another's hard, sunburned and uncommonly clean faces. They dared not lift their big hands, gnarled by hard work in the fields, to pick up a fork (the small one or the large?) or a knife, they were so intimidated by the waiters, who moved deftly around the table serving in white cotton gloves.

As the farmer ate, he looked at his son and shook his head, an expression of contempt on his face.

"Look at him! Look at him!" he muttered to himself. "What does he look like there all alone at the head of the table? How could a bride respect a big ape like that? She's right to feel ashamed of him! Ah, if I were only in his place!"

The meal ended in an atmosphere of general gloom, and the guests, with one excuse or another, soon took their leave. It was already evening.

"Now," said his father, when the two waiters had cleared the table and quiet descended on the villa, "what are you going to do? You'll have to get out of this by yourself."

And he ordered his wife to follow him to their farmhouse not far from the villa.

Left alone, Gerlando looked around him, frowning uncertainly.

He was conscious of her presence up there in that locked room. Maybe, now that all was quiet, she would come out. Then what was he supposed to do? Ah, how gladly he would have run back to the farmhouse to be near his mother, or would God he could sleep out in the open under a tree!

Suppose she was waiting for him to call her again? If she was resigned to the punishment her brother had inflicted on her, maybe she considered herself at her husband's disposal and was now waiting for him to—yes, to invite her to . . .

He listened: all was silent. Perhaps she was already asleep. It was dark. The moon shone into the room through the open door of the balcony. Without bothering to turn on a light, Gerlando took a chair and sat out on the balcony overlooking the open country which sloped away toward the far-distant sea.

Large, bright stars shone in the clear night and the moon cut a swath of silver across the water. From the vast fields of yellow grain the tremulous chant of crickets rose in a prolonged threnody. Suddenly, close by, an owl uttered a doleful "keewhoo" and from far off, like an echo, another replied.

Resting his arms on the railing of the balcony, he instinctively covered his ears to shut out those "keewhoos" calling to each other across the enchanted silence under the moon, and to escape from the wretchedness of his own uncertainty. Then, noticing the corner of a wall below which circled the entire farm, he thought that now all this land was his and the trees were his, olive, almond, carob, fig and mulberry. His too the vines.

His father had every reason to feel content because, from now on, his son would be subject to no one. And, after all, it was not such a bad idea to continue with his studies. He was better off there in school than here all day long in his wife's company. He'd take care of any of his school fellows who tried to make fun of him. Now he was a gentleman, and it no longer mattered to him if he were expelled from school. But this would not happen. He proposed to study hard from now on, so that one day he

could take his place among the gentry in town with no embarrassment, talking and discussing with them on equal terms. He
needed only four more years to get his certificate from trade
school, and then he would be an expert agronomist or an ac-
countant. Then his brother-in-law, the lawyer—who seemed to
think he had thrown his sister to the dogs—would have to tip his
hat to him! Yes, indeed! And he would have every right to say,
"What do you think you've given me? An old woman, that's
what! I've completed my studies and now have a gentleman's
profession. I can win a beautiful, rich young girl with a family
just as good as yours."

With these thoughts he fell asleep, his head cradled in his
arms, leaning on the balcony railing.

The two "keewhoos," one near, the other far, continued their
voluptuous lament. The luminous night seemed to trail a rippling moon-veil over the earth, the fields trilled with crickets,
and from afar a deep murmur arose from the sea.

Late that night Eleonora appeared, like a shadow, in the
doorway of the balcony. She had not expected to find the young
man asleep there. It both pained and frightened her. For a moment she paused, wondering if she should wake him to tell him
what she had decided to do and ask him to withdraw from the
balcony. But, on the point of shaking him, of calling his name,
her courage failed her and she herself withdrew softly, returning
to the room from which she had come.

IV

An agreement was easily reached.

The next morning Eleonora had a motherly talk with Gerlando. He would take charge of everything and would be free to
do whatever he wished, as if no tie existed between them. She
asked him only to leave her in peace, alone in that small room,
waited on by the old family servant who had seen her grow up.

Gerlando, aching all over from the dampness, had come in
from the balcony at an early hour and had fallen asleep on the
couch in the dining room. Roused from sleep thus suddenly, he

had a great desire to rub his eyes with his fists. His mouth hung open as he tried to knit his brows, not so much to show that he understood as to indicate his approval, and he kept nodding his head—yes, yes—to everything. But when his father and mother heard of the pact, they were furious and Gerlando tried in vain to make them understand that it suited him perfectly, that he was more than happy with this arrangement.

To calm his father, he solemnly promised to return to school early in October. But out of pique his mother insisted that he take the finest room to sleep in, the best room to study in, the nicest room to eat in—all the best rooms in the villa.

"And *you* give the orders, understand? Crack the whip, or I will come myself to see that you are obeyed and respected!"

She swore she would never speak to that wheedler again, a woman who had slighted her son like that, and such a handsome young man, too, far too good for the likes of her!

Starting that very day Gerlando began to study for his examinations in October. It was already late, with only twenty-four days ahead of him, but, by applying himself, who knows? Perhaps after all he would get that certificate he had been struggling for the past three years.

When the anxious bewilderment of the first few days was past, Eleonora, on the advice of Gesa, her servant, began to prepare a layette for the coming baby. It made her cry that she had not even thought of it.

Gesa, who excelled at this work, helped her and gave her the measurements for the first little shirts, the first cap. Fate has reserved this consolation for me, Eleonora thought, and she had not realized it. She would have a little boy or girl to care for, to devote herself to entirely. She hoped that God would send her a boy. She was not young and it would be difficult to leave a little girl in the hands of such a father were she to die—a little girl to whom she had imparted all her own feelings, her own thoughts. A boy would suffer less under the conditions which misfortune had brought him.

Tortured by such considerations and tired of working, she would pick up a book to divert her thoughts—one of the books her brother had sent her when she first came here. Every now and then, with a gesture of the head, she would ask the servant, "What's he up to?"

Gesa would hunch her shoulders, purse her lips, and reply, "Umph! His head's in a book. Who knows if he's sleeping or trying to think?"

Gerlando was thinking, all right. He thought that, all in all, his life wasn't very entertaining.

Here he was: he had a farm and he didn't have it; he had a wife and he didn't have her; he was on bad terms with his parents; he was furious with himself because he could remember nothing at all that he studied. Meantime his indolence left him prey to sneaking desires—among others, a longing for his wife because she kept apart from him. True, the woman was no longer desirable, but what kind of pact was this? He was the husband and, if anyone, he should be the one to decide!

He got up and went out of the room. As he passed her door, he caught sight of her and all his vexation vanished. Snorting so as not to admit his lack of courage, he told himself that she was not worth it.

Then, one day in October, he came back from town defeated, having once more failed his examination for the first technical certificate. Now, enough! He was through! He didn't want to hear another word about it. He took his books, notebooks, drawing squares, boxes, pencils and carried them down in front of the villa to make a bonfire. His father ran up to stop him, but Gerlando was vicious.

"Let me be! Here, I'm the boss!"

His mother came running too, and several farmers who were working in the fields. Wisps of smoke gradually thickened and rose from the heap of papers, amid the cries of the onlookers. Then, with a flash, flames crackled and blazed. The screams brought Eleonora out onto the balcony with her servant.

Livid, in his shirt sleeves, and strutting about like a turkey gobbler, Gerlando wildly hurled in the last books he was holding under his arm—the unwitting instruments of his long, futile torture.

Eleonora could hardly refrain from laughing at the scene and quickly withdrew from the balcony. But her mother-in-law had spied her and said to her son, "Your lady finds it amusing, eh? It makes her laugh."

"It will make her cry!" Gerlando shouted menacingly, going white as he glanced up at the balcony.

Eleonora heard his threat and paled also. She understood that the dreary peace she had enjoyed until now was over. It had been no more than a respite accorded by fate. What could that brute want of her? She was already spent. Another blow, however light, would finish her.

A moment later, dark and panting, Gerlando appeared.

"As of today, things are going to change around here!" he announced. "I'm fed up. I'm going to be a farmer like my father and you will stop playing the lady. Away with all these baby clothes. This child is going to be born a farmer too and will not need these fancy frills. Dismiss the servant. Do the cooking and clean the house yourself, the same as my mother does. Understand?"

Eleonora rose, trembling with indignation.

"Your mother is your mother," she said, looking him proudly in the eyes. "I am myself, and your being a peasant does not change me."

"You are my wife!" screamed Gerlando, seizing her violently by the arm. "You will do as I say. I give the orders here! Is that clear?"

Then he turned to the old servant and pointed to the door. "Get out! Leave immediately. I won't have any servants in this house!"

"I go with you, Gesa!" cried Eleonora, trying to free her arm from his grasp.

But Gerlando would not let go. He held her even more tightly and forced her to sit down.

"No, you stay here! You are chained to me, understand? I've been the laughingstock of the countryside because of you. Now that's over and done with! You come out of your lair, see. I'm not going to be left alone to weep over my shame." He turned to Gesa once more. "Out with you!" And he shoved her toward the door.

"What have you to complain of?" Eleonora asked, her eyes brimming with tears. "What have I ever asked of you?"

"What have you asked? Not to touch you, not to have any contact with you, as if I were . . . as if I were not good enough for an old woman like you! And you pay a servant to wait on me at the table instead of waiting on me yourself as a wife should."

"What difference can all this make to you?" Eleonora asked, disheartened. "I will serve you with my own hands from now on. Is that better?"

As she said this she burst into sobs and her legs gave way under her. Frightened, bewildered, Gerlando supported her with Gesa's help, and between them they put her into the big chair.

Toward evening her pains started.

Gerlando, repentant and scared, ran to call his mother. A farmhand was sent to town to get the midwife. Meanwhile, the tenant farmer, foreseeing the danger of losing his farm if his daughter-in-law should have a miscarriage, scolded his son:

"Blockhead! What have you done now? What if the baby dies? Suppose you don't have any more children? You'll be out in the street! What are you going to do? You left school and you don't even know how to handle a shovel. You're ruined!"

"What do I care?" cried Gerlando. "Just so long as nothing happens to her!"

His mother came running, her arms in the air. "A doctor! A doctor is needed right away! She's taken bad!"

"What's wrong?" asked Gerlando, white as a sheet.

But his father pushed him. "Run! Run!"

On the way Gerlando, trembling with apprehension, started to cry, but forced himself to keep on running. Halfway, he met the midwife returning with the farmhand in the carriage.

"Hurry! Hurry!" he cried. "I'm going for the doctor. She's dying."

He stumbled and fell heavily. Covered with dirt, he got up and ran on desperately, sucking at his bleeding hand.

When he returned to the villa with the doctor, Eleonora had almost bled to death.

"Murderer! Murderer!" muttered Gesa as she looked after her mistress. "It's all his fault! He dared lay a hand on her!"

But Eleonora shook her head. She felt herself slipping away little by little, her strength waning. Already cold, she was not sorry to die. It was sweet to die like this—a great relief after the torment she had endured. Her face like wax, staring up at the ceiling, she waited for her eyes to close softly of themselves, forever. She could no longer distinguish anything clearly. As if in a dream she saw the old doctor who had served as her marriage witness and smiled at him.

V

While Eleonora lay between life and death Gerlando never left her bedside day or night.

When she was at last able to get up and sit in a big chair, she seemed like another woman, transparent, almost bloodless. She saw Gerlando beside her, looking as if he too had come through a critical illness, and his parents next to him, full of kind attentions. Looking at them with those beautiful black eyes of hers, large and sad in her pale, thin face, she no longer felt any bond with them whatever. It was as if she had come back, new and different, from a remote place where every tie was severed—not only with them but with all her former life.

She breathed with difficulty, and her heart, beating wildly, jumped at the slightest sound.

Her head lolling on the back of the chair, her eyes closed, she regretted bitterly that she had not died. What had she to do here? Why was she condemned to see these faces around her again and look at all these things from which she felt so remote? Why this reconciliation with the depressing, sickening apparition of her past? A reconciliation which was more painful at times than others, as if someone had pushed her in the back, forcing her to see and feel the presence, the living, breathing reality of the odious life which was no longer hers.

She was convinced that she would never rise from that chair. She believed that at any moment she must die of heart failure. However, a few days later, she got up and was able to take a few steps around the room. Then, with time, she even went downstairs and out of doors, supported by Gerlando and the faithful Gesa. She formed the habit of going at sunset to the edge of the embankment which was the southern boundary of her property. From this plateau a magnificent vista opened out over the sloping fields all the way down to the sea. At first Gerlando and Gesa accompanied her, as usual; then she went with her old servant; finally she was able to go alone.

Seated on a stone at the foot of a century-old olive tree, she looked along the whole coast, slightly curving in the distance. Its little inlets and bays seemed to be cut out of the sea which changed with the shifting winds. She saw the sun, like a great disk of fire, slowly drown in the slimy sea moss resting on the gray water to the west, and fall in triumph behind the glowing waves, in a marvelous pageant of blazing clouds. She saw the evening star appear, glowing softly and serenely in the vaporous sky; then came the limpid moon, barely lit. Her eyes drank in the melancholy sweetness of the impending dark, and she breathed deeply, accepting the still, the quiet, as a superhuman consolation penetrating to the depths of her being.

Meantime in the nearby farmhouse, the old tenant farmer and his wife had resumed their conspiracy against her, goading their son to look after his own interests.

"Why do you leave her alone?" his father asked craftily. "Don't you realize that, after her illness, she's grateful for all the affection you showed her? Don't leave her for a moment. Always try to get closer to her heart. Then . . . then arrange it so that the servant doesn't sleep in the same room with her. She is well now and certainly can't need Gesa during the night."

Irritated, Gerlando shook his head at these suggestions.

"It's out of the question. It would never enter her head that I might . . . Not at all! She treats me like a son. You should hear the things she says to me! She considers herself old, finished, done with insofar as this world is concerned."

"Old?" put in his mother. "Certainly she's no longer a child, but she's not old either. You wait and see."

"They'll take away the land!" pursued his father. "I've already told you: you'll be dispossessed, out in the street! If your wife dies and there are no children, her dowry goes back to her family. Then what will you have? You'll have lost out at school and wasted all that time, without getting a thing out of it. Not so much as a fistful of flies! Think it over! Think it over while there's still time. Too much has been lost already. What else can you hope for?"

"Be gentle," his mother said sweetly. "You must win her over with kindness; talk to her like this: 'After all, what have you given me? I respected you as you wished, but now you should think about me a little. What am I to do? What can I do, if you leave me like this?' After all, dear God, there's no need to fight a war!"

"Then you can say in passing," his father pressed, " 'Do you want to please your brother who treated you the way he did and let him kick me out of here like a dog?' It's gospel truth. Just you wait and see. You'll be kicked out lock, stock and barrel, and your mother and I, poor old folks that we are, will go with you!"

Gerlando did not answer. His mother's words were almost a relief but, in their way, irritating too. His father's forecasts stirred his bile. What was he to do? He saw the difficulty of the undertaking, and he also recognized its urgency. In any case, he would try.

Now Eleonora ate at table with him. One evening at dinner, seeing him staring at the tablecloth deep in thought, she asked, "You're not eating. What is the matter?"

Although he had been expecting this question for several days because of the way he was behaving, he did not remember for the moment what he had planned to say, and made a vague gesture with his hand.

"What's the matter?" Eleonora insisted.

"Nothing," Gerlando replied impatiently. "My father, as usual . . ."

"School again?" she asked, smiling to get him to talk.

"No, worse!" he said. "He . . . he raises so many doubts in my mind . . . he worries me with thoughts of my future because he is old, he says, and here am I without a trade or profession. As long as you're here, it's all right, but then . . . then . . . nothing says . . ."

"Tell your father," Eleonora replied gravely, half closing her eyes as if to shut out his blushing face, "tell your father that he does not have to worry about it. I have provided for everything, tell him, so he can be at rest. Since we are talking about this, listen: if I should die suddenly—after all, one is here today and gone tomorrow—you will find a yellow envelope in the second drawer of the bureau in my room. There is a document in it for you."

"A document?" Gerlando repeated, not knowing what else to say in his embarrassment.

Eleonora nodded and added, "Don't worry about it any more."

Relieved, Gerlando told his parents the next morning everything Eleonora had said. But they, especially his father, were not at all convinced.

"A document? Tricks!"

What could that document be? A will leaving the farm to her husband? And if it were not drawn up in accordance with all the rules and regulations? It would be easily suspect, considering it was in a woman's handwriting and not drawn with the help of a notary. Then the following day wouldn't they have to deal with the brother, a man of law, a swindler?

"Lawsuits, my son! May God preserve you! Justice is not for the poor. And that one there—in his rage he would be capable of making black white and white black.

"Besides, who knows if this document is really there in that drawer of the bureau? Or did she just say that to get you to leave her in peace?

"Have you seen it? No. Well, even supposing she showed it to you, would you understand what it was all about? For that matter, what would we make out of it ourselves? Whereas if you had a son, there'd be no need of documents! Don't let her make a fool of you. Listen to us. Flesh! Flesh and blood! Not paper!"

And so one day as she sat under the olive tree on the hill, Eleonora saw Gerlando before her. He had come up stealthily.

She was wrapped in a large black shawl, for she felt cold, although the month of February was so mild that it seemed like spring. The vast slopes below were green with the new crops. The placid sea as well as the sky was rose-tinted, faded, but very soft, and the countryside looked like enamel as it lay dappled with shade.

Wearied by her admiration of that marvelous harmony of colors, Eleonora rested her head against the trunk of the tree. The black shawl was pulled up over her head and only her face was revealed, even paler than usual.

"What are you doing?" Gerlando asked. "You look like Our Lady of Sorrows."

"Just looking," she said with a sigh, half closing her eyes.

"If you could see how . . . how well you look in that black shawl," he added.

"Well?" said Eleonora, smiling sadly. "I feel cold."

"No, I mean well in . . . in . . . in the face," he stammered, sitting down on the ground.

Eleonora, her head against the tree, closed her eyes and smiled to keep from crying, assailed by a wave of regret for her lost youth so miserably spent. Yes, at eighteen she had been very beautiful.

Suddenly, absorbed in thought, she felt herself shaken gently.

"Give me your hand," begged Gerlando, looking up at her with feverish eyes.

She pretended not to understand.

"My hand? Why?" she asked him. "I cannot pull you up. I haven't enough strength even for myself. . . . It's almost dark; let us go in." And she stood up.

"I didn't mean you to pull me up," Gerlando explained. "Let's stay here in the dark. It is so beautiful . . ."

As he spoke he quickly grabbed her around the knees, smiling nervously, his lips dry.

"No!" she cried. "Are you mad? Leave me alone!"

To keep from falling, she braced herself against his shoulders, trying to push him back. But as she moved her arms and leaned over him kneeling there, the shawl came loose and covered him completely.

"I want you! I want you!" he cried, wrapped in the odor of her body, clasping her tightly with one arm as he sought to slip the other up to her waist.

But with a great effort she managed to wrench herself free

and ran to the edge of the bank. She turned to cry, "Don't move or I'll jump!"

At that she saw him rush headlong toward her and, leaning back, she threw herself over the cliff.

He caught himself with difficulty on the brink, his face white, his arms upraised. There was a sickening thud and, looking down, he saw a heap of black clothing lying on the green field beneath. The shawl, opening in the wind, fell softly a little farther on.

His hands in his hair, he turned to look toward the farm-house, but his eyes met the large, pale face of the moon just risen above the dense grove of olive trees. He hung there terrified, staring as if he had been seen from the heavens and stood accused.

SUCH IS LIFE

Reflective silence, floors smelling of wax, spick-and-span muslin curtains at the windows: Signora Leuca's house had been like that for the past eleven years. But now a strange suspense hung over those rooms. Was it possible that Signora Leuca had agreed after a separation of eleven years to let her husband return to live with her?

The measured ticking of the big clock in the dining room was disturbing as it echoed through those voiceless rooms—as if time itself could continue to flow as evenly and serenely as before.

Yesterday, in the little sitting room with the highly sensitive floor, the small silver and crystal objects had tinkled. It was almost as if the teardrops of the gilded candelabra over the mantelpiece and the little liquor glasses on the tea table were shuddering with fear and indignation after Lawyer Arico's visit—"the old cricket," Signora Leuca called him to her friends.

"Ah, life . . . life . . ." he kept repeating after his long harangue, hunching his shoulders, half closing his large eyes in his sallow face, and painfully stretching his thin neck.

All those crystal and silver objects hung there in suspense, waiting for Signora Leuca to protest at least by a shake of her head. But no, she stood tall and erect, fresh and pink-and-white as ever, her spectacles high on her aquiline nose, as she faced the little man who twisted all over at one more leave-taking and went on repeating in the doorway: "Life . . . Ah! Life. . . ."

Was life really like that—a burning shame too great to confess, an agony to be suffered by hunching one's shoulders and squinting one's eyes, or a hard, bitter pill to be swallowed by stretching the neck? Was it not life, after all, that Signora Leuca had spent here in this spotless, demure house for eleven years, receiving occasional visits from her good friends, the ladies of the Charity Society, the learned priest of Sant' Agnese or the organist, Signor Ildebrando? Had she not enjoyed a life of unending peace, spotless order, and silence marked only by the slow, even ticking of the big clock indolently striking the hours and half-hours inside its glass case?

Signorina Trecke, an old maid, ran like a frightened dove to the parish house of Sant' Agnese to sound the alarm.

"Signora Leuca . . . Signora Leuca and her husband . . ." she panted.

Her anxiety turned to amazement, her amazement dissolved into a vague smile before the unruffled nod with which the priest received her news, which he already knew.

Long-legged, short-waisted and stooped, Signorina Trecke was still blond at sixty-six. She was half Russian, half German, yet perhaps more Russian than German. She had been converted to Catholicism by her brother-in-law, God rest his soul, and was most zealous. Her eyes in her pale, flabby face were as blue as when she was eighteen, like two clear lakes obstinately reflecting the smiling, innocent skies of her youth, though who knows how many storm clouds had since passed to darken them. But Signorina Trecke went on feigning ignorance. She did not wish the gall of dismal experience to eat away at the fixity of her new faith, so she appeared completely naïve, to the great annoyance of her friends.

Melting into that empty smile of hers, she asked uneasily if Signor Marco Leuca really deserved to be forgiven, something she had never questioned because—perhaps it was slander, since His Reverence approved a reconciliation—but didn't Signora Leuca's husband have three children, three little girls with a . . . how do you say it? . . . by another woman? And what now? Would he abandon them to become reconciled with his wife? No? Then what? The wife here, another woman there, with three— how do you say it?—three *natural* daughters?

"Nothing of the kind!" the priest tried to reassure her, his usual serenity tinged with a mildly protective air.

Though there were catacombs under Sant' Agnese and even a gloomy, solemn, subterranean church, the parish house stood in the open, surrounded by soft, leafy green amid plenty of air and sunlight. One could see in the priest's limpid eyes and hear in his warm voice the good effects of this environment not only on the body but the soul!

"My dear Signorina Trecke, it is not a question of two households or of abandonment either; it is not even a question of an out-and-out reconciliation. We will have, God willing, a simple, friendly relationship, a few brief visits from time to time, and that is all . . . to bring a little comfort."

"To him?" asked Signorina Trecke.

"Of course to *him!*" the priest said. "To relieve the burden of his guilt, a kind word to soothe his gnawing remorse. He asks nothing more and, for that matter, our excellent Signora Leuca could not grant anything less. Now, don't worry!"

The priest placed his words like beautiful little porcelain vases on the table before him, there, there and there—each one graced with an artificial flower with green tissue paper twisted around the wire stem, charmingly effective at no cost whatsoever. But the organist, that good Signor Ildebrando who also acted as secretary, should have been told not to approve every word the priest said with honeyed smiles and little nods. It virtually turned Signorina Trecke's stomach.

Signor Ildebrando had never been able to forgive his long-dead parents for imposing such a sonorous name on him, most unsuitable for his slender, frail body as well as his temperament. He disliked ruddy, aggressive, noisy men who cocked an eye, hanging one thumb in the armhole of their vests like the great

I am! His nature was tepid, mediocre, colorless, and whenever possible he hung back, clinging to the shadows. He thought that Signorina Trecke, drab as she was, should do the same, instead of putting herself forward in the thick of things, meddling where she was not directly concerned.

"Well, in that case," she was now saying to the priest, "I could invite him to my house for supper, couldn't I?"

"Of course not!" said the priest, taken aback. "What have you to do with it, Signorina Trecke?"

"Well, if he is to be pitied—my niece says she knows him," she haggled, widening her mouth in a bland smile.

"You will do well, my dear signorina," the priest replied severely, "to keep closer watch over your niece."

"I? But how can I, Father? I really don't understand these things, as I've just proved to you . . . absolutely nothing," she said, opening her arms wide and bowing to take her leave, with a stupid smile still on her face and her childlike eyes clouded because of the hopeless ignorance with which she was afflicted.

Three days later Signor Marco Leuca, accompanied by Arico, the lawyer, paid his first visit.

Disheveled, shabby, blushing for shame, he looked bewildered in that impeccable house so delicately furnished, so jealously chaste. Trembling all over like a wounded animal, he could not utter a word. Then, in desperation, he dropped mutely to his knees before her. Signora Leuca was distressed and frightened by his appearance, aged and shockingly coarsened after eleven years, and she backed away in panic before his helpless gesture although her first impulse had been to help him up.

"Oh, no. God! No!" she moaned.

Then when he almost came to blows with the lawyer who turned on him angrily, loudly commanding him to be calm and not to make a scene, she wanted to run out of the room. He made a furious lunge to shove Arico aside, determined to present himself before her in all his abjection and despair. Hanging his head, he was mortified that his theatrical gesture had misfired; he had fervently hoped she would place her hand tenderly on his hair, not as a caress, but in forgiveness.

How in heaven's name could Signora Leuca have done that? He might have known it was impossible. Pity, patience, even compassion she had, not only for him but for all poor wretches with the same insatiable penchant for vice.

Ah! Life . . .

It was violently marked on his loose face with the telltale sag of the lower lip and the dark pouches around his sad, troubled eyes. But, as the lawyer said, he could at last perhaps enjoy the peace and sweetness of a home—now that his hair was gray and hers completely white . . .

"The sweetness of a home, did you say, Lawyer Arico?"

Signora Leuca knew very well that her house no longer had sweetness, only great calm. She did not say it depressed her, only that she was accustomed to it. She read, busied herself working for the poor, took up collections with the other ladies of the Charity Society, went to church or to the dressmaker—for she liked to dress well—and, when necessary, made calls on Arico, the lawyer, who was in charge of her affairs. All in all, she never had an idle moment. She was content this way, since God had not blessed her life with more intimate joys. At times, in the silence between one stitch and the next on the little shirt she was knitting for a poor child of the neighborhood, or between one line and the next of the book she was reading, she would suddenly sink into a timeless mood where thought seemed vain and comfortless. She would stare, then, at a familiar object in the room as if seeing it for the first time and as if it had no significance for her. She regretted the things she had never known and suffered that her own heart should have deceived her into supposing she could have been happy by marrying a man who—well, a man. Now Signora Leuca did not even despise him any more.

Yes, life.

It was not as her young girl's heart had dreamed. It was even wrong perhaps for her to speak of her revulsion for that physical contact which sullied one. Although difficult, it was also to be pitied since the price of pleasure had later to be paid in bitter tears.

It was in answer to the priest's exclamation, "In God's name, whoever said compassion was easy?" that she had let herself be persuaded to receive her husband briefly from time to time.

Her charity work, she knew, was really another way of passing the time. True, she did more than she really was able to do and exhausted herself going up and down stairs, or working late into the night for the poor. She threw off this fatigue by sheer will power. A good part of her income went to the needy, and she deprived herself of many things which, for her, were not entirely superfluous. But she could not say that she had ever made a real sacrifice, such as overcoming the recoil of her flesh at the thought of an insufferable contact, or risking the harmony of her neat, orderly life. She was afraid she could never do it.

The same impulses sprang up in her as in everyone else, but where others surrendered blindly she was wary. Her natural instincts were too guarded, her life too hushed, rarefied to a point where ordinary things no longer had substance. She would suddenly notice new, strange aspects of them which disturbed her, as if for the fraction of a second she could penetrate a hidden reality different from that commonly attributed to them. At such times, she feared she was losing her mind.

It should have annoyed her, therefore, that others thought her life so undisturbed and considered her the picture of serenity. Instead it pleased her. She wanted to believe it, convinced that she rejected every longing as soon as it arose within her because of her instinctive aversion for a soiled life. To be sure, she worked at her charities in the midst of sordidness, but she could not have mingled freely with the poor had she not felt herself immune. The only sacrifice she could make, after all, was to expose and eventually to conquer her own squeamishness. It was little enough. She did even more in subduing her own body, her own flesh and all that takes place in intimacy—even involuntarily— and which one never dares confess.

Meanwhile Signorina Trecke, with her usual air of feckless innocence, brought her niece to call and to hear the latest news. Other friends, Signora Marzorati, her daughter, and Signora Mielli, were already there. Urged to talk, Signora Leuca tried to say as little as possible about her husband's first visit.

Signorina Trecke exclaimed, "Ah, so he did come!"

Annoyed, her niece snapped back, "Why pretend not to know it, when you do?"

"I knew? I knew only that he was coming, not that he had come."

Her niece shrugged and turned away to talk to young Signorina Marzorati. The girl's mother bridled, not at all pleased to see her daughter talking with Signorina Trecke's niece, who was a scandal, not only because of her manner of dress, but because of all the gossip that raged around her.

Only Signora Leuca understood that it was not entirely the niece's fault but was partly due to what went on every day between her aunt and herself. They were engaged in a dangerous conflict, the aunt refusing to see any harm in the younger woman's behavior, and the niece doing her utmost to shock her aunt out of her hypocritical pretense. There was no telling where this might lead. What was to be done when Signorina Trecke, who saw harm in the most harmless things, refused to recognize evil when it was flung in her face?

Here, for example, she had expected Signora Leuca to be distraught after her ordeal and instead found her calmly discussing her husband's visit as if nothing out of the ordinary had happened.

"But really nothing did happen," Signora Leuca said, smiling. "He stayed for about fifteen minutes with Lawyer Arico."

"Ah! I'm glad it was with the lawyer!" sighed Signorina Trecke. "I was so afraid he would come alone."

"But why were you afraid?" asked Signora Leuca.

"My niece told me he was so fiery. Nella teaches in the school where he brings the oldest child every morning—goodness, even though they're not legitimate, I suppose they should be called his daughters, shouldn't they? Although they don't bear his name! Nella, what did you say their name was?" she asked.

"Smacca!" replied her niece sharply.

"Probably their mother's name," observed Signora Mielli, who always seemed to have dropped from the clouds when she did happen to say a few words.

"Yes, probably," Signorina Trecke went on. "Imagine! Right in front of my niece, he gave his daughter a—a slap one morning, and so hard it knocked the poor child down. Her cheek was quite scratched by his fingernail. When he saw how he had hurt her, my niece says he started to cry. Oh, I suppose he did some crying here too!"

As the other two ladies turned, expecting a reply, Signora Leuca felt obliged to say yes, that he had cried.

Although the niece was deep in conversation with Signorina Marzorati, she followed every word the women were saying and now she flashed out at her aunt, "No harm done! Her husband's tears never hurt Signora Leuca at all. I'm telling you this so you won't pretend to be shocked!"

Signora Leuca could not help noting the contemptuous tone of the girl's voice but she did not quite understand the reason for it, unless the niece meant to offend her aunt by ridiculing her attitude. A look of chilled amazement passed between her other two friends, Signora Mielli and Signora Marzorati. She herself smiled sadly, trying to enlist their sympathy for poor Signorina Trecke, who, as usual, chose to find nothing amiss.

"He must have changed a lot," Nella Trecke confided in Signorina Marzorati's ear, "but I'll wager Signora Leuca's husband was *something* in his day!"

Signora Marzorati was obviously more and more upset by her daughter's interest in whatever it was that that terrible girl was saying to her. The daughter wore glasses and had bulging breasts; her alarming naïveté was sometimes stormed by secret thoughts which made her blush crimson, because she feared she would no longer be taken for the overgrown child everyone considered her.

All this was clear to Signora Leuca but it gave her no satisfaction that her eyes could see through things so plainly, completely aware that she was not deceived. Then there was Signora Mielli with that air of never knowing what she was doing or saying, as though in a dream, so that in a pinch she might always exclaim, "Really? Did I do this? Did I say that?"

When her five friends finally left, Signora Leuca felt tired and depressed. She looked at the empty, displaced chairs in the sitting room whose disorder seemed to ask what had been the reason for this visit and whether or not it had been really necessary. Yes, it seemed so, for one must look into others' lives, to see what was going on in them, what others thought and what they had to say. This curiosity satisfied a desire in human beings to see beyond themselves, to vary the monotony of every day. It was a diversion from the irritations and difficulties of life. It helped pass the time. A misfortune? A scandal? And they would all run to see and hear about it. Who? Why? No, really? Impossible! When nothing happened, there was boredom and the agony of watching daylight slowly fade and die, as Signora Leuca was now doing through the windowpane.

The priest and the lawyer arranged that Marco Leuca would never come alone to visit his wife, that his visits would always be short and that they would not exceed two a month. However, a few days after the first visit he returned, alone this time and with the pitiful look of an unwanted dog expecting a kick.

Signora Leuca was annoyed, but concealed her agitation as she led him into the little dining room. He buried his face in his big hands and started to sob as soon as he sat down, but without dramatics this time. She looked at him and realized that it would take no more than an understanding word from her to dry his tears.

And then?

No. No. It was already too much that he had returned so soon and alone. Were she to encourage him with kind words, it would be tantamount to accepting his visits every day and asking for who knows what else, then farewell to the conditions of their agreement. No. He would have to stop crying of his own accord and find enough courage to say why he had come, giving a specific reason if he had one.

Dear God! After two hours of torture, Signora Leuca sat there stunned, trembling in every fiber of her body. He had come, he said, to confess. In vain she had reiterated that it was unnecessary, that she already knew everything, that Lawyer Arico had told her all. He had still wanted to confess.

He found the courage ruthlessly to expose his life, and seemed to enjoy debasing himself more and more, that she might trample on him and that her foot might be sullied in the mire with him.

Signora Leuca was stupefied by certain unheard-of obscenities. The outrage of it all held her gaze fixed on his clear portrayal of every loathsome detail. Her cheeks burned. She was conscious of the queasiness with which she held a hundred-lire note between her fingers, which he quickly snatched out of her furtive hand as if to hide it from himself also.

Although she had given him the money to rid herself of him, afterward she wondered whether this had been the real motive of his visit. Perhaps not. In all conscience, she had to admit that he had not asked for it, at least not directly. He had said, to move her, no doubt, that he had turned over to Lawyer Arico for his children the small sum remaining from his inheritance and had instructed him to pay that woman only the interest for household expenses. She was so stingy, he said, that she did not give him a cent to buy a cigar or even a cup of coffee if he felt like standing at a café bar. How could he possibly have asked his wife for anything after that confession, accusing himself of a weak character, a prey to all temptations, dumping all the blame on that woman's back? He had beseeched her, with hands joined as if in prayer, to help him overcome his weakness if only by letting him see her.

After that, it was evil of her to have given him money just to get rid of him. She had played on the very weakness he had implored her to combat. Signora Leuca's humiliation only increased as she thought that perhaps he had felt no compunction whatsoever in accepting the money.

She turned to the window to look out at the bright green of the vacant lots for sale across the way. A row of cypress trees and a few pines were the sole survivors of the princely old villa which had fallen into decay and disappeared. The azure sky on that clear day filled the silent house with light.

"Dear Lord," Signora Leuca cried, covering her face with her hands. "The evil we do . . . the evil that is done unto us!"

Her face still hidden, she recalled the candid look of an old English minister that summer in Ari at a boardinghouse which stood on top of the hill like a castle. How green! How sunny! And that swarm of young girls flocking around her every time she stopped to admire the broad valley!

"Marzietta di Lama . . ."

That was her name . . . the girl with the piercing eyes . . . the one with the rippling laugh as she raised her arm to show the Signora a little scratch on her nose. If only she could have been a mother, how much it would have meant . . . but even that joy had been denied her.

Glancing at her hands, she saw her wedding ring and felt an impulse to throw it out the window. A symbol of her married state, it now reflected all the ignominy of that man's confession, she thought, as she twisted her hands in her lap.

Still, if she had been governed by her flesh, fascinated and led astray by insatiable desires, she too would probably have fallen headlong.

As she glanced about the dining room, the furniture seemed to draw back as if waiting for her to return to the quiet of her orderly life. But in her turmoil she hardly noticed; the disturbing violence of that man's body had entered here to challenge the stability of all she had sought to build around and within herself—her conscience, her whole house.

But who had advised and influenced her, and how far was her charity supposed to go, sinking into contact with such hidden shame? Everyone's shame, perhaps more so for those who did not show it because they managed to hide it from themselves than for that poor fiend who wore it blazoned across his face.

Was this, then, her punishment? Punishment for what? Did they suppose that she was to blame for not knowing how to hold him when he left the house eleven years ago to wind up in such degradation?

It was not true: she had never denied him anything which, as her husband, he had the right to expect—and not only out of duty. No. She had always tried to be honest with herself, however painful the truth might be, so that now she was forced to consider how her body had consented, knowing full well that duty would be no excuse to ease her conscience when it later awoke with disgust after all love and respect for the man had gone.

No, she had not sent him away; he left her when she no longer satisfied him.

Having succeeded in freeing herself of all desire, Signora

Leuca wanted indignantly to ask those who advised her to show this "difficult proof of a charitable spirit" if that were not a bit too simple. If, on the contrary, it were not more mandatory to pity those who had struggled to resist passion? She wanted the proud satisfaction of being pitied, but in quite a different way. She wanted pity, not admiration! After all, she was not made of marble and was tired of insipid admiration. What did they think, that her deliverance had cost her nothing?

For the first time, the shining order of her house annoyed her. She was bored with it all and, jumping to her feet, she shook her head and cried, "Hypocrisy!"

Marco Leuca walked away from his wife's house reeling with satisfaction. It seemed to him, as he swelled out his chest to breathe, that the road opened before him, making a way between the houses and the trees. By God, he was free! And to prove it he had only to thrust one hand into his pants pocket and crumple that note between his fingers. He was free of all those tiresome restrictions laid down by the priest and the lawyer who boosted him up the stairs of redemption to his wife's house.

She had placed a barrier between them when she had slipped him that hundred-lire note *—she stood on one side, he on the other, and there would be no more passing over. On his side he could befoul himself as much as he pleased. What a relief! What joy! And let her not dare presume, with her grand manner, that he no longer needed charity.

A hundred lire! Drink! Drink yourself drunk!

He laughed and glanced around, a mad gleam in his eyes.

How well he had played his part! In return—one hundred lire! Almost a lira for every tear. He had enjoyed seeing her blench at certain descriptions; her eyes were troubled but gaping wide behind those glasses set on the bridge of her nose. When one hits on a way to reveal certain secret things, although they may be shocking, they also magnetize. Revulsion itself, shrinking like meat over a fire, with alarmed "whys," thirsts for more de-

---

* When this story was written, around 1930, one hundred lire were equivalent to about $12.50. [Translator's note.]

tail—but always from a distance, not close enough to touch! Here, come here and risk one little touch—it will not hurt. It will entice you . . .

He let out a loud guffaw and people turned to stare at him. Nice, those girls over there by the fountain of Sant' Agnese! Cute! If only he could stroke them, under the pretense of taking a drink of water. But no, he wanted wine—and in a first-class place, like a gentleman! Besides, those girls lacked zest. It was the others, with flanks like mares and caverns which so completely seized one with pleasure, from whom it was impossible to break away.

[The revision begun by the author in the autumn of 1936 comes to an end here, although he intended to continue the development of this, his favorite work. In fact, among his papers, notes were found outlining three new chapters:

(I) *Coming out after the visit and the confession with one hundred lire to spend for a spree.*

Degradation, wine, women, the bodies of women with flanks like mares.

It was no good any more.

(II) *This woman:*

She ran away once and then came back. Doubts about the last child.

The mediocrity of Sandrina and Lauretta. Elodina, the musician's orphan . . . a delicate stem, a rare flower.

(III) *Nella Trecke at home, seduction before our eyes.*]

She said that whether they cried or not, the children's hair had to be combed; or else with all the dust and filth . . .

Or else, what?

Lice! That's what. Then every morning there would be more tears getting rid of them with a fine-tooth comb—if that would suffice! Sometimes it was necessary to take a razor and shave off all the hair . . . then wouldn't they look pretty, the three of them, with shaved heads!

Oh, God! Why did she have to pull their hair so hard? Plaited that tightly, it curled against their necks like little pigs' tails, the ends tied off with string. It hardly looked as if they had any hair, soaked with oil as it was and parted clear down the back, just two pigtails, and yet Sandrina's hair was very thick.

Walking past the Villa Borghese, he glanced back at the tight little braids on her shoulders and felt tempted to stop and undo them. They took the short cut through the park to save time, also because he wanted to prepare his daughter for the visit they were about to make. It was a long way from Via Flaminia to Sant' Agnese where his wife lived, and he wondered if it was not too far for the child to walk.

Poor Sandrina! It wasn't only her hair. With that dress on, that hat and those wretched little drawers showing below her petticoat, she seemed to feel ungraceful and walked along like a little old woman. But lately, whenever he had complained at home about the way the children were dressed or tried to loosen their braids, *she* had threatened, "Beware, or I'll kiss them!"

For a few months now she had had a swelling on her lip which had grown until it was as round and hard as a pea and almost black.

It could not amount to much because, even when she pressed it, it did not hurt her. They advised her to see a doctor but she said that was nothing compared to other things: headaches, constant fatigue, and always a little fever toward evening. She did not need a doctor to tell her what was wrong—it was the terrible life she had to lead.

However, she stopped kissing the children. But she kissed him at night all right, laughing wildly and holding his head between her hands so that he could not move. She planted those kisses on his mouth . . . there . . . there . . . and there because, just in case what the neighbors said was true, she wanted him to catch it in the same place. It was a wicked joke, but a joke nevertheless because she knew what they said was not true.

He didn't believe it either, or rather it seemed unlikely anyone could die from a little lump which was not even painful. Also he dared not believe it, because it would be such a wonderful stroke of luck. So he laughed resentfully under those kisses she intended as poisonous stings. But one day he stopped before a mirror in a shop window to examine his lips carefully, passing a finger slowly across them and stretching the skin to make sure there was no crack. He, too, now refrained from kissing the children or, at most, he kissed the hair of the smallest one whose adorable little ways and sayings were hard to resist.

The other two, Sandrina and Lauretta, always had a dazed look on their faces as if in constant fear of something. The violent quarrels they witnessed almost every day had left them terrified. But when their father and mother locked themselves in their room it was even worse. Screams came through the door, crying, slaps, blows, kicks, running and falling and the noise of flying objects crashing to bits.

There had been a fight last night and he was now wearing a handkerchief wound around his right hand to hide a long scratch—if it was not a bite. There was another long scratch on his neck.

"Are you tired, Sandrina?"

"No, Papa."

"Would you like to sit over there on that bench to rest a little while?"

"No, Papa."

"Well, we'll take the streetcar on Via Veneto. Tell me . . . would you like to go to a beautiful house?"

Sandrina looked up from under her hat with an uncertain smile. She had already noticed that he spoke in a different tone of voice. It pleased her though she did not know what to make of it. She nodded her head.

"To see a lady . . . whom I know," he went on. "But you . . ."

He stopped, not knowing how to put it. Sandrina quietly grew very attentive, waiting for him to go on, but as he said nothing more, she risked a question.

"What is her name?"

"She's . . . your aunt," he told her. "But be careful not to mention this at home to your mamma, and not to Lauretta or Rosina either. Nobody at all, understand?"

He stopped to look at her. Sandrina glanced up at him but quickly lowered her eyes.

"You understand?" he repeated roughly, leaning down to look squarely in her eyes.

Sandrina hurriedly nodded her head several times.

"To no one!"

"No one."

"Do you know why I don't want you to tell?" he asked, walking on. "Because your mamma . . . and this . . . this aunt have quarreled. If she ever found out I'd taken you there . . . well, you saw what happened yesterday? It would be even worse! Do you understand?"

"Yes, Papa."

"Don't say a word to anyone . . . or there will be trouble."

After all these instructions and threats, Sandrina stole a look at her father's gloomy face and no longer felt any pleasure at going to the aunt's beautiful house. She understood that her father was not going there to please her, after all, but because he wanted to go even at the risk of another fight if his visit were found out—certainly not through her . . . but suppose her mother asked her where they had gone? Frightened, Sandrina immediately turned to her father.

"Papa . . ."

"What is it?"

"What shall I tell Mama?"

He jerked her hand violently and pulled her arm.

"Nothing . . . nothing, I said. You mustn't say anything at all!"

"I know, but if she asks me where we've been . . ." Sandrina pointed out, more dismayed than ever.

He regretted his roughness and leaned down to caress her.

"Sweet, my little sweet," he murmured. "I didn't understand . . . of course I'll tell you. I'll tell you just what to say if she asks where you've been. Now, perk up! Show me one of your pretty smiles. Quick, a little smile like the one you had when I took you to the puppet show."

His tenderness was more for himself than for the child. It made him feel he was being *good*. His heart swelled with joy as he caught the approving smile of a lady who happened to be passing as he bent solicitously over his daughter. He wanted Sandrina to give him a better reward, but although she tried obediently to smile, her cold, sad little face seemed to plead with him to accept it: the smile was the best she could do.

Sandrina was hardly ten but she knew she would have to protect herself first from her father, then from her mother and sisters as well. Her face was pale and too thin to be pretty; the perky little nose did not match her eyes, which were grim and serious and, when fixed attentively or glancing slyly to either side, did not have a sweet expression.

He sensed his daughter's secret hostility and straightened up resentfully, thinking that he was a fool to expect anything from the children of such a mother.

For quite a while, Signor Leuca had been thinking that it would be a good thing if his wife were to agree to raise his three children. Should their mother die—although he did not believe it likely—or should he take off one day, his rich wife could help these children as she did so many others. If it was not right to bring children into the world and then cast them off, at least he would have taken a step to insure their future. So this time Signora Leuca's husband came to visit her with a little girl.

He was afraid his wife would see through his scheme, as she had before when she suspected his visits of another motive than the need for moral comfort. Also he was not quite sure if, in her eyes, it would not seem brazen to bring this living proof of infidelity into her house.

He came in very doubtfully but brightened when he noticed her delight at sight of the child. He opened his arms wide and quietly let out a huge sigh of relief, smiling tremulously.

Signora Leuca welcomed the little girl tenderly, and Sandrina looked up at her with wide, bewildered eyes.

"Ah, look who is here! What is your name? Sandrina? That's a lovely name. You're the oldest, aren't you? And do you go to school? Oh, already in the fourth grade! Would you like to take off your little hat? We will put it here. Come, sit down beside me."

"Perhaps she doesn't know who I am?" she asked, turning to her husband who stood there tearfully looking on.

"My aunt," Sandrina supplied promptly.

"Yes, darling, your aunt," Signora Leuca agreed; surprised and touched by this answer, she leaned down to kiss the little girl's hand.

Many little children called her "aunt," affectionately prompted by their mothers to show their gratitude. But she felt especially pleased that he had suggested it, even though certainly for a different reason.

Very well, since she was her aunt, this little niece was to have a special treat: chocolate, cookies, and bread-and-butter spread with jam. Seating the child on a cushion at the table, nice and high like a grownup, she tied a little napkin around her neck.

"Ummm, it's good like this," Signora Leuca said as she prepared a slice of bread, first with butter, then with jam. "Now a spoonful of jam all by itself, to put in your mouth! Would you like that? Yes, I think you would."

Sandrina looked at her and smiled happily as though it were all too good to be true.

When she smiled, that ugly little dress and the way her hair was skinned back distressed Signora Leuca. Poor little thing! As soon as she had finished eating, they went into the bedroom to undo those miserable braids and make one large loose plait, tied halfway down with a satin bow. She then arranged Sandrina's hair becomingly over her forehead to soften her thin face, now pink with pleasure. How her eyes shone! Sandrina looked so entirely different that, seeing her own image in the mirror surrounded by the reflection of all the beautiful things in the bedroom, she did not know herself.

Signora Leuca was mystified by her husband's worried frown

when she brought the child back, her face glowing and looking so changed.

Possibly this transformation in his daughter gave him the same feeling she herself had had while she combed the little girl's hair, but she did not want him to mistake her affection for regret that this little girl was not her own. Why, she had even forgotten he was waiting there in the next room while she was busy fussing over the child!

When they left, Signora Leuca went to the window to watch that lovely tassel of hair hanging down her back. After waiting for a while and not seeing them come out the door, she tiptoed to the head of the stairs, curious to see what was keeping them. Then she understood why he had been so dismayed. Her mind at ease, she could not help smiling.

There he was sitting on the steps below, intently trying to do up those two horrible little pigtails again. He had slipped the handkerchief off his hand and from above Signora Leuca saw the long scratch, and an even worse one on his neck.

She was sorry that she had so thoughtlessly put him in this predicament and, remembering the two pieces of dirty string lying on her dressing table, she realized he could never tie off the ends without them, or manage to pull the hair tightly enough with his clumsy hands. If that horrid woman who scratched him like that was not to know about this visit, the child must go home with the same pieces of string. Quickly she ran back to her room and then hurried down the stairs.

"Wait, wait!" she called out. "Let me do it. I'm sorry. I didn't think. You're perfectly right."

As he got up, very embarrassed, she quickly took his place and plaited the braids. Then she bent over Sandrina to kiss her. He slyly took her hand and, before she could snatch it back, she felt the revolting contact of his lips upon it.

A long time afterward, in her little dining room, Signora Leuca sat, still rubbing her hand.

Three weeks, a month went by and her husband did not return. Signora Leuca had expected him to come with the other two children as he had said he would. Maybe that woman had found out about the last visit and had made a scene, or perhaps after his promise he was ashamed to come alone. She supposed he was ill, or possibly one of the children was sick or even the woman herself. Maybe he was still embarrassed because she had discovered him on the stairs . . . and she smiled over that. Or had he perhaps noticed her disgust when she had pulled her hand away?

Signora Leuca supposed so many things. Her friends of the Charity Society, stopping in to see her at that time, observed in a roundabout way that she supposed too much: if it was painful to receive her husband occasionally for short visits, then she should be happy that of himself he had spaced them out. To tell the truth, they said, those visits had grown rather frequent and were not, it would seem, any too brief either.

Finally she agreed that she did suppose too much but that she was still curious to know why he had not returned. It never occurred to her to question the reason for her concern. She said that she wanted to know if something had happened to him— not that it made any difference to her if he no longer came to see her.

Finally it no longer mattered. Everything seemed remote, even the closest things; as soon as she was conscious of them for an instant, they vanished. Curiosity was a thing of the past. She accepted, even welcomed, suffering, but it never touched her deeply. She seemed now to be immune to all the unhappiness life had to offer.

Then one day, instead of her husband, Lawyer Arico and the old priest came to see her. There could be no more doubt: something had happened. But what?

It was difficult to say whether the news was good or bad. The woman was dead . . . that woman.

"Dead?"

She had died suddenly of pneumonia. But the doctor who treated her said she had a cancer on her mouth and would not have lived very long in any case.

At this, Signora Leuca became suspicious. She asked the lawyer and the priest if they had known about the woman's condi-

tion when they suggested her husband's visits. Both protested—
the priest before God, and the lawyer on his word of honor.

"And did he?" Signora Leuca questioned.

"Did he what?"

"Did he know it?"

"Ah, that, yes," the little lawyer had to confess, twisting on
his chair. "He said that . . . he had vaguely . . . vaguely suspected it, he said."

Seeing Signora Leuca frown, the old priest asked, "Do you
suppose he foresaw her death? I don't think so."

"Oh, Father," Signora Leuca burst out, "for pity's sake, don't
misunderstand me. If you only knew how humiliated I feel! Believe me, my charity does not depend on the washing of a dirty
child's face. I'm afraid you do not think very highly of me, Father."

"Not at all! Not at all!" the old priest protested, smiling and
blushing a little.

"I'm sorry, but it is true," Signora Leuca insisted.

Seeing how deeply upset she was, the priest grew serious.

"Let us take care not to sin out of spiritual pride, my dear
signora."

"I?"

"Yes, you. One sins through pride in many ways. If, for example, you disparage the object of your charity by a suspicion
of this kind and so make your act more commendable before
God, or rather before your own conscience, your charity changes
and becomes something different."

"My own conscience?"

"Yes, Signora."

"Away from God."

"Yes, Signora. I am warning you: for some time now I have
noticed this tendency of yours and I am sorry to have to say it.
I mean this searching for reasons . . . this suspicious questioning
of every motive. You must guard against it."

Signora Leuca bowed her head sadly and covered her face
with her hands, regretting her outburst.

"Yes, it's true," she murmured. "I am like that."

Then Lawyer Arico, always impatient of discussions that did

not come straight to the point, ventured to say, "So now, Signora . . ."

"No, wait, Signor Arico," she looked up and quickly cut him off. "It is bad, very bad, what you reproach me of, Father, and I thank you. But believe me, it is not out of pride. Quite the contrary . . ."

"To disparage the object of one's charity?"

"No, myself, myself, Father! I would be more prone to disparage myself if I have had a wicked thought. In that case, I think he would be helped by someone worse off than he—if it is true that he had no ulterior motive. Perhaps I don't express myself clearly. I mean that, even though he became reconciled with me knowing this woman might die, I would still have done all I could for his children and for him. Wait! Wait! Let me finish. Because it seems more natural to me that way, more humane, even more merciful, without any appearance of . . . of exaltation or false grandeur . . . because, well, we are like that . . . and if he is not, then all the better. That is all I wanted to say."

"Well, now . . ." the lawyer quickly put in, seeing that the priest was satisfied with this explanation, smiling and nodding his approval.

But he had no luck with the blessed woman—very noble and all that, but a nuisance for a man with a lot of work to do. There she was, turning around again.

"No, please wait, Lawyer Arico."

What more could she have to say? Now she wanted to strip herself of all merit for her charity. Ah, dear God! Whatever had made that priest talk of spiritual pride? Just listen to that! She said it would not be charity but a real pleasure for her to take three children into her home, educate them and look after them like a mother. Fine! Now, that was that. If it was a pleasure for her . . . That was more than they had ever hoped to achieve by this visit. There was nothing left to do but thank her and go.

But that was not all . . . no, indeed! It could not be that simple! Now she wanted to know what price they thought she would have to pay for the joy of being a mother to those three little ones.

Lawyer Arico stared at the priest and felt annoyed when he

appeared to understand the hidden meaning of that question—
he even appeared to be confronted by a case of conscience which
had never occurred to him: Yes, with those three little ones there
was also the question of the husband . . . If he were to come back
again to live under the same roof with her . . .

"Oh, so that's it!" exclaimed Arico, scratching his neck with
one finger. "Never mind, Signora, I'll speak to him myself. His
Reverence will speak to him too. He certainly can't expect the
impossible."

"And then?" she asked curtly.

"Then what?"

"Signor Arico, you can speak to him as much as you like, but
you will never change him. We know him, dear God, and we
must accept him as he is. He will promise, he will swear to both
of you, and then . . . then the moment will come when he will
forget his promises. Well, given the inevitable outcome . . . I
say this for *me*, mind you, not for him!"

"How do you mean . . . for you?"

"For my responsibility in this, Signor Arico. I must foresee
what is bound to happen, knowing as I do the man I am taking
back! You will see. He will leave the children and go off, blam-
ing me again and saying that I opened the door with my own
hands to throw him back into his former life."

"But, not at all, Signora . . ."

"Don't be so quick to deny it. Wait and see if it does not turn
out just as I have said."

"Well, in that case it'll be just too bad for him! You're already doing too much taking in those children. If he wants to
behave like a—forgive me, it almost slipped out—that's his responsibility, not yours by a long shot."

But Signora Leuca was not looking at the indignant little
lawyer but at the silent priest. She knew from his silence that he
no longer thought her conscience had strayed away from God.
It meant that she must look to Him for inspiration—that the
final issue was up to life, life as it is and always shall be.

Farewell, reflective silence, spotless order, calm.

Signora Leuca's house was turned inside out to allow for more guests than it could hold: four must be accommodated by pulling all the rooms apart and putting them together again—eliminating the little sitting room and the dressing room, piling up furniture, and carrying pieces off to the basement to make space for three little beds and other new furnishings yet to be bought.

Signora Leuca would give up her own room to the three little girls and she would sleep in what had been the sitting room, relinquishing her wardrobe with its three-way mirror because it would not fit. Her husband would have to make do with the dressing room, large enough but rather dark.

She did not regret her comforts or all the beloved objects which now had to be discarded. She was gay in the midst of these scrambled rooms—so lonely before in their undisturbed order and now seemingly full of life because of their very confusion.

The new arrangement of the rooms, more practical than beautiful, nevertheless gave her pleasure. It represented another way of life to her. With old things in new places and new things arriving little by little, all her former uncertainty disappeared.

Meanwhile she saw herself going about these unfamiliar rooms, meeting her responsibilities and problems as they arose.

She wanted everything to be new for the children's room and spent whole mornings shopping: three little iron beds, enameled white—if there had been only one to buy she would have preferred to have it in wood, but three wooden beds were out of the question now that she had to economize. Everything must be white: chests of drawers, chairs, the little wardrobe with its mirror and the writing tables with shelves to one side. Perhaps it was not practical to have white desks, with the risk of spilled ink, but she wanted to teach them to take care of their things, and when they did their homework, she would supervise—not to protect the desks but to see to it that the girls worked well. Beside each bed was a little pink rug, and the curtains at the windows were pink, as well as the coverlets on the beds. The whole room was pink and white.

That nasty old cricket, Arico, said she spent too much and that it would have been a saving to bring the beds, chairs and tables from the other house for their use. She would not hear of it. She wanted nothing from there, not so much as a nail. But what if she were the only one to feel this aversion? What if he and the little ones wanted something familiar to keep? Without more ado, she decided to visit the house on Via Flaminia.

"What!" cried Arico. "After you've gone and spent all that money?"

The neighbors in the house, friends and acquaintances of the dead woman, all leaned out of their windows or ran to stand in the old, dilapidated doorway to see her step down from the carriage—tall, erect and elegantly dressed, a veil over her face. And what comments there were as soon as she walked into the vestibule and turned to the right, up the steps leading to a kind of terrace where two French doors opened out.

"Did you see her white hair?"

"Yes, but she looks young. What age would you say . . . forty?"

"A real lady . . ."

"And all for that old brute in there!"

"Still, it looks as if she's come to take him back!"

"Yes, he's probably good for something after all."

"Say what you like, for me a woman with glasses . . ."

Whether it was because the day was overcast, or because she had just come from outside, at first Signora Leuca could not make out a thing. Then, as she began to discern the poverty and filth around her, her heart ached that he had been reduced to living in such a place. A rank odor of stale flowers and medicines still lingered about the room.

"Where is he?"

Sandrina came in her petticoat to open the door. Her thin arms were bare, her hair uncombed. She was surprised by this unexpected visit of her beautiful aunt with the rich shining house, and said that her father was lying down and that the dressmaker had come.

"Ah, good!" Signora Leuca smiled and lifted her veil to kiss the little girl. "The dressmaker, did you say? We'll go in. Are you glad to see your aunt, dear? My poor child. Now that I am here . . . perhaps it would be best if I spoke to the dressmaker. Has she taken your measurements?"

"Everything is finished."

"What! Already?"

Holding the child's hand, Signora Leuca started toward the back room—and there he was, disheveled, his shirt open on his hairy chest, hurriedly pulling on an old black coat.

"You—here! Come in. The dressmaker . . . for . . . for their mourning clothes . . ."

His voice betrayed his distress and he seemed to be hurrying her, either in an effort to hide his emotion or because he was ashamed of his dirty surroundings.

But before looking at the mourning clothes, she wanted to get acquainted with the other two children. Oh, just look at that little one, what a love! Her chubby legs were bare under her little skirt and her arms were raised to lift the rumpled mass of jet-black curls at her neck. What eyes! Wasn't she a little headstrong, Signora Leuca wondered?

"Rosetta? Is that her name? What a darling!"

"No, Rosina," corrected Sandrina.

Rosina? Rosetta would be better suited to her roundness. But neither Rosina nor Rosetta really, with that black hair and those black eyes—dear God, how penetrating they were—and that bud of a mouth, a fiery bud, and a little nose that was hardly a nose at all . . .

Was she five or not quite? Certainly one of those black dresses could not be meant for her. She should have a white one with a black satin sash. But later on she would attend to all that . . .

"And this is Lauretta?"

Try as she might to sound affectionate, her voice was cold. It seemed as if she had already met this child in Sandrina—the same afflicted look, the same set, serious eyes in a long, pale face, the same miserably straight hair.

It was clear at a glance that the two older sisters had nothing in common with this little one, born a few years later. Lauretta was already over eight, fourteen months younger than Sandrina.

Signora Leuca checked a suspicion which rose in her mind, knowing about her husband's jealous fights with that woman. But now she was dead, and it was obvious the littlest one . . .

To conceal her doubt, she quickly turned to the dressmaker and exchanged a few words about the horrid dresses; then she told her husband the purpose of her visit. He agreed with her that nothing need be taken from the house. He would sell whatever he could and distribute the rest among the neighbors. He only wanted to take his clothes and whatever the children could still wear.

Signora Leuca had turned toward the bureau to look at the children's clothes when she spied her husband's gesture to restrain her and immediately saw the reason for it. On top of the dresser stood a photograph in a cheap copper frame. She realized it must be of that woman and pretended not to notice it. She told him there was no hurry about the girls' clothes; whatever they could not use should be given to the needy.

Then she asked Sandrina if she would like to go with her. Sandrina clapped her hands with delight, and Lauretta wanted to go too. Why not the little one, then? They could all go with her this evening because their room was ready.

But the baby refused to budge. She would not be separated from her father. Without her father she would not leave, and he had to stay on a few more days to liquidate his sorry past.

That evening Signora Leuca returned home with two little girls dressed in black.

"This is your room. Do you like it?"

Sandrina and Lauretta were spellbound.

"You will sleep here," she told Sandrina, "and Lauretta there. Rosina will sleep in the smaller bed between you."

Then she showed them the little desks where they would do their homework, assigning a desk to each one.

"Both desks are exactly alike," she pointed out, "each one has a little shelf."

She explained that they would attend another school, close by in Via Novara, and that she hoped they would study well, behave nicely and be neat. As for their clothing, for the moment they would keep the things they had until new frocks could be bought, pretty dresses to go walking in and others to wear at home with protective pinafores.

Meanwhile she bathed them, combed their hair and showed them through the house—where their father would sleep, where she would sleep. Finally she seated them at the table with her for supper.

There were so many things the little girls needed to be taught, but for this evening it was best to allow them to do everything their own way. They were in a trance. They didn't know how to take up a glass or hold the small-scale knives and forks bought especially for them, but they would learn in time. And she too must learn not to spoil them by overindulgence.

She kept them with her after supper, talking, although she was careful not to let her curiosity about many things lead her into questioning them. However, nothing would induce Lauretta to speak; she sat watching her sister Sandrina who was at ease, having been there before.

When Signora Leuca put them in bed, she discovered that they had not been taught to make the sign of the cross before going to sleep. She explained this to them as best she could and persuaded them to repeat a short prayer after her. Then, for the first time, she heard the sound of Lauretta's voice.

A little later, listening at their door to find out if they were asleep, she heard a terrible fight going on. They sounded like cats, pulling each other's hair, kicking and clawing. What was she to do? Open the door? Surprise them? If they kept their voices so low it must be because they had misgivings and did not want her to hear them. Then Lauretta tiptoed back to bed and there was silence, except for Sandrina's sobs half muffled under the covers.

That night Signora Leuca stayed awake a long time. She wondered what these children had for her that the others she had helped before did not have—all those children she could no longer afford to comfort. She had never before spent so much money for charitable work nor gone to so much trouble, and never once had she dreamed of taking one of the others into her home.

Was it because they were her husband's children? And for that matter, who knew if they really were, even one of them? No, that was not it. She had taken them in to fill the emptiness of her life, in spite of all the worry and difficulty this would mean for her . . . and certainly not only because of the children themselves.

So this was what it amounted to: She was the object of her own charity, to the detriment of those poor unfortunates whom she would no longer have time to care for and think about. It hardly seemed right. Even though it was impossible to do as much for them as for the two sleeping in there, already in a sense her own, she would feel conscience-stricken if she did nothing at all—at least for some of them: that little sick girl in Via Reggio, and—oh God!—the little orphan, Elodina, in Via Alessandria! She could not abandon them to their wretched fate when everything here was pink and white—beds, rugs, coverlets, and when she considered the pleasure she found in just thinking of things she wanted to buy for them—dainty underclothes, pretty shoes—and all the pains she would take to have them becomingly dressed. No! No! It was too unfair. And why, after all? Who were these children, really?

Tomorrow would she feel gratified to be praised for her generosity because she was taking in her husband's three children by another woman? And by a woman like that one? No. The very thought that such praise was inevitable made her regret what she had done. Were these children to be rewarded for their mother's shame and their father's guilt, "generously" forgiven by her? She had nothing to forgive, having suffered no more from her husband's actions than she suffered from so many other wrongs—for instance, the wrong she herself was now doing by excluding so many poor children because these three were more vital to her.

Ah! She would atone for her wrongdoing!

Suddenly she was aware of the slow, distinct ticking of the clock across the same gaping silence as before. It must be very late. Hovering and forlorn, she saw all her thoughts, her deeds, every feature of her life, more painfully than ever before.

And there, peering through the shadows in the luster of its cheap copper frame, sat the picture of the dead woman on the dresser. What was he doing alone at this hour in that horrible house? And why did she imagine him standing in front of the dresser with the child, looking intently at that photograph?

Her fault lay in having climbed all the way to the top of a high mountain—not for the vainglory of climbing. What glory was there in that? Or should she consider it a punishment . . . or fate . . . rather than a fault?

She well knew the chill, the silence of the summit, from which everything appears small and distant, blurred by a mist of solitary sorrow which perhaps does not exist below, at close range, but which here, aloof and apart, forms a cloud between the viewer and day-to-day reality.

Three days later her husband arrived, the little one clinging around his neck like a wild, scared kitten. Exasperated by this untamed child and the weight of the two heavy suitcases he carried, one in each hand, he was indifferent to the happy, affectionate greetings of Lauretta and Sandrina and blind to their completely new appearance.

The two little girls, who were expecting their father to admire their good behavior, their rosy cleanliness, their well-combed hair, their new black pinafores with white lace collars and cuffs, their dainty stockings and shoes, were disappointed and hurt.

It was a miracle that he did not curse, strangled as he was by Rosina's plump arms viciously gripping him tighter and tighter. Finally, unable to make her let go, he wrenched her off violently and threw her into a chair.

"There, be quiet or I'll let you have it!"

At this the frantic child rolled over on the floor, screaming and kicking, hiding her face in her arms, her hands clutching her hair. Infuriated, he turned his back and strode to the window.

"I can't stand any more!" he cried, facing his wife. "For sixteen days I have been shackled like this!"

As the baby crawled after him, howling like a wild thing, he added, "There! You see! You see!"

And just as Rosina was about to grab his leg, he lifted it up. Sandrina and Lauretta began to laugh.

"Oh, don't laugh!" Signora Leuca admonished them. "Shame on you, when your little sister is crying like that! Go, bring the toys we bought yesterday."

"Toys! Do you hear?" said her father, picking up the child. The little one was somewhat mollified in his arms, although still convulsed with sobs. But as soon as Sandrina and Lauretta came back with the toys and she heard the tinkle of tiny cymbals struck by a mechanical clown, she buried her face in her father's neck, not to see or hear.

Signora Leuca had the impression that this clinging child was a bedevilment of the dead woman, tethering him to all she had represented for him in life: misery, vulgarity and bondage.

She realized the impossibility of taming the little creature, who was as dark as if impregnated with the vice from which she had sprung, and whose blood, she sensed, was a savage mixture. Signora Leuca did not even attempt to take her from her father or persuade her to play with her sisters. She knew it was useless and might even make things worse.

She showed her husband to his room as if apologizing because it was not better, but immediately realized that this was the wrong attitude. In fact his reply, synchronizing with her thoughts, affected her strangely.

"Not at all! What are you trying to say?"

He frowned when he saw the single bed, having slept in a double bed until now, and asked, pointing to the child, "What about this nuisance?"

"She has her own bed in the girls' room," Signora Leuca told him. "Come, I'll show you."

He stood in the doorway admiring the lovely pink-and-white room with its three little beds. He was pleased and touched but ill at ease because he found it difficult to tell her that, since the death of that woman, the baby had taken her mother's place at night and might now refuse to sleep alone.

"Well, we shall see this evening," Signora Leuca replied. "If we manage to put her to bed in here, you might stay with her until she goes to sleep. Otherwise, we can move her little bed into your room and she can sleep there."

As she spoke, she saw that Sandrina and Lauretta would be only too happy to have this lovely room all to themselves. They had quickly adopted an air of well-brought-up little girls since they had come into her house, but their little sister clearly did not want to change. Their father was not too welcome either in the older girls' room in this lovely house where they were so happy, enjoying a new life with their "aunt."

In truth, their gloomy, unkempt father did not look as if he would ever adjust to these surroundings but must always feel a stranger, not daring to look about him, not knowing what to say, confused, embarrassed, repeating hoarsely, "It's too much, too much!"

He now asked permission to go to his room to unpack his bags, as though he were afraid someone might do it for him.

"Auntie, why are we in mourning for Mama, when Papa isn't?"

Signora Leuca, who had not noticed the color of her husband's clothes, stared at the child and did not know what to reply; not that it was so difficult to think up an answer but she suddenly realized that he was not wearing black out of regard for her, unwilling to parade his mourning for another woman before her eyes.

It saddened and upset her. How he must have wept for that woman! The horrible things he had confessed were still vivid in her mind and she knew that, although he might have hated her for enslaving him, he probably would give much to have her back, now that she was gone, and who knew how deep and lasting his grief would be. Unless . . .

Signora Leuca broke off this supposition which had troubled her for many days. She was more than ever convinced that her prediction would come to pass, if not today or tomorrow, then as soon as his first embarrassment had passed and he regained his old self-confidence.

Her agitation mounted as she began to notice ways of his, familiar gestures and expressions which should, on the contrary, have reassured her. His humility and the patience and the affection he had for the children were all but unbelievable . . . so many things which aroused her sympathy for him in his position —sympathy more real than she had been prepared, out of duty, to show him.

She was impressed at dinner, as they were discussing the little lawyer, to see him lift one eyebrow and contract the other in an intelligent frown—an all-but-forgotten trait of his which had always pleased her. His natural good manners at table impressed her also. He was self-concious only when she looked at him; then he would glance aside. His air of quiet good breeding came as a surprise to the two older girls who stared as if they did not recognize him. However, Signora Leuca, to her delight, saw him fall into the spontaneous, charming manner she had known long ago.

Wine! What torture! She had to wrench her eyes from the bottle every time, though it remained almost untouched. Her eyes betrayed her and it was useless to try to hide the fact that she knew about his habit of getting drunk every night. It must be hard on him now to drink hardly anything, yet he did not show it. Tonight was the first time in many years that they had sat together at table. Who knew if tomorrow, at lunch or at dinner, he would still be able to control himself?

After dinner, a tender, paternal smile moved his discolored lips under the graying mustache as he silently called her attention to the sleeping child in his lap. He asked quietly if it would not be better to undress her there before putting her to bed in the room where the other children were sleeping.

As she leaned over the child, her shoulder brushed his chest and she felt his breath on her hair. She touched him several times as she undressed the little one on his lap, but her apprehension disturbed her more than the actual contact. She was anxious lest her hands betray her nervousness.

Finally, when the child had been carefully put to bed and they both had tiptoed from the room, the dangerous moment was at hand, the moment when they were alone together in the intimacy of the house.

Yet, nothing happened. The door of the children's room was hardly closed before he sighed with relief and smilingly told her that he would now have peace until morning because Rosina never waked during the night. Then humbly and quietly he wished her good night and went to his room.

Signora Leuca lay in her bed turning many things over in her mind. She was especially irritated with herself because of her apprehension, the more unjustified when confronted by his withdrawn attitude. He dared not look at her and certainly never dreamed of drawing closer than she would allow, for the moment.

What was it she feared then? She had locked the door behind her as soon as she entered her own room. This precaution now made her angry. She was tempted to jump out of bed and unlock the door.

The priest noticed it, he said, after the last meeting of the Charity Society in the parish house. Her friends, Signora Mielli and Signora Marzorati, had of course noticed it; and so had good Signorina Trecke, impossible as it might seem.

Signora Leuca's zeal had cooled: she had not attended the meetings of the Charity Society for two months now. Not only that but she had skipped Mass for several weeks. And she treated her friends with indifference as if she suspected them of being partly responsible for the state in which she now found herself—with those three children in the house and that man who, for all the respect he showed her, must weigh like a stone around her neck.

There could be no question that the three children gave her a lot of work, but if this was so—and no doubt it was, since they had not even known how to make the sign of the cross when they first came to her—then all the more reason to attend Mass regularly every Sunday. Her attitude was incomprehensible, especially at the very time of the Novena in preparation for the Feast of the Immaculate Conception of the Blessed Virgin Mary.

Signora Mielli remarked that their friend, always so careful about her appearance, had begun to neglect herself. Her hair was badly combed, if at all, as if she no longer looked at herself in the mirror. Of course, she had *four* children to care for, not three, and all the worry of the house, but she could still have found time to groom herself properly had she wanted to. Evidently, with the serene, unruffled life she had led before, she did not know what a struggle it was to bring up children. But merit lay in conquering difficulties, not in going slack under their weight.

Too bad she had had to part with the devoted servant who had been with her so many years. But it was only natural. She should have taken in someone to help, for one person alone could not possibly do all the work now with three children and a man in the house.

"She hired another maid, yes, she certainly did!" said Signorina Trecke. "But she had to discharge her on the spot, because it seems that her husband . . . well, I don't know . . ."

"What? Her husband!" exclaimed Signora Marzorati making a wry face.

Signorina Trecke opened her mouth in one of her usual smiles. She didn't quite understand what it was Signora Leuca had discovered, but her niece had laughed her head off when she heard it.

"She laughed like a fool. I can't think why."

"Of course," mused Signora Mielli with a faraway look in her eyes, "Now surely, that man . . ."

"Dear God!" cried Signora Marzorati. "If Signora Leuca . . . of course she's right, poor woman. In her place as a wife, I'd rather put up with . . . I don't know what! I mean, you understand, Signora Mielli . . . well, *out*side the house, at least!"

When the two ladies had exchanged a few words, heavy with innuendoes, Signorina Trecke remarked angelically that Signor Leuca did go outside the house—every evening, as a matter of fact.

"I happen to know this," she said, "because he comes to my house."

Surprised, Signora Marzorati scowled at her.

"To *your* house! What for?"

"To see my niece," replied Signorina Trecke.

There could be no harm in Signor Leuca's visits now that he was reconciled with Signora Leuca and the priest himself had favored this reconciliation.

"What reconciliation?" Signora Marzorati exploded. "Do you know, at least, what your niece and Signor Leuca talk about when they are together?"

Signorina Trecke lowered her aging eyelids with roguish cunning over her cloudless blue eyes.

"They talk about the Republic of Ecuador," she said.

"About the Republic of Ecuador!" gasped Signora Mielli, not so far off for once.

"Yes," explained Signorina Trecke. "Because an expedition of big industrialists has left for the Republic of Ecuador. Everything is still to be done there: bridges, roads, railroads, electricity, schools . . . My niece knows a member of the expedition. She says that soon an even larger group will go: workmen, farmers, engineers, even lawyers and teachers. She says that she will go too—my niece, that is—to this Republic of Ecuador! That's all they talk about."

Signorina Trecke looked so stupid as she told them this news that Signora Marzorati and Signora Mielli were annoyed and, restraining their curiosity, changed the subject, turning away to discuss other things between themselves.

It was all over.

Signora Leuca, contrary to all her expectations, was hurt not so much by what had actually happened as by what she suffered within. It was because the harm she had foreseen, feared and awaited had failed to materialize that she now endured this torment.

She was certain, despite the scorn she felt for her own flesh, that she would not have yielded if her husband had seized her one of those nights in the silence of the house, but would have pushed him away. She would have been deaf to the promptings of her conscience which made her realize that if she rejected him she only gave him a fresh excuse to fall back once more into that horrible life. She had to admit that she would never have relented even though later her remorse would not be denied.

Yes, but it was equally certain that, if this had happened, her suffering would have been less cruel than what she now endured because it had not occurred.

For little by little her horror of his body, aroused by all those indelible images with which his confession had seeded her mind, had become a horror of her own flesh. Every evening when she closed her door—without locking it—she looked at her body in the mirror and wondered if it was really so undesirable that it did not even merit a sidelong glance from a man like that, who had found pleasure until recently in such a vulgar woman.

She was still beautiful and she knew it, thanks to the glances of men who turned to look at her in the street when she least expected it. Her hair, turned white as snow before the age of thirty, brought out the youthful freshness of her skin, and gave an ambiguous grace, like an innocent lie, to her smile every time she said, "Now, I am old . . ."

Her smooth throat rising like an unblemished column from her shapely bosom, her . . . God! How frightful this intimate analysis of her whole body was in its vain attempt to reassure herself that she was still beautiful, still desirable! Her former assurance was, after all, the reason why she had so clearly forecast for the lawyer and the priest what demands her husband was sure to make on her, in consequence of which she would have been obliged to put him out of the house.

She had lost interest in her appearance as she became progressively convinced of her husband's indifference—although he continued to show her every polite consideration. Refusing to admit the reason to herself, she pretended she had no time to dress her hair properly, what with the two older girls to look after and get off early to school.

And when, by accident, she had found that awful woman's picture in his dresser drawer, how greedily her eyes had devoured it! What a disappointment it was, after having imagined that she was so beautiful! Provocative, yes, but in fact quite ugly with a mad look in her eyes, and she was common. But it was only natural that he would have been attracted to that type of woman.

However, Nella, the vivacious niece of Signorina Trecke, certainly was not common in appearance and she clearly pleased and attracted him. Sandrina had been in her class two years ago when she first began to teach near the Porta del Popolo. What a coincidence that she should find her former pupil at the school in Via Novara where she was now teaching! She had walked home with her after class, Sandrina's father holding one hand and she the other. But now that it was all over, Signora Leuca did not want to complain even about the Trecke girl's betrayal. She had always felt an instinctive aversion for her and had recognized her as an enemy.

Considering his past reputation there should have been little need to seduce him, yet that is what Nella Trecke did under Signora Leuca's eyes, using her pupil as an excuse to come to the house nearly every day. She felt, no doubt, that a lady like Signora Leuca would not deign to notice, or would at most feel a little more scorn for that wretched man she had taken in—along with his daughters—out of charity.

Signora Leuca had accepted the challenge at first and closed her eyes to the young girl's smiles and blandishments, not wanting to admit the obscure, hidden jealousy they awakened in her. However, when she could bear it no longer, she had forbidden the girl to come to the house. But, afraid of betraying her own distress, she had not warned Nella's stupid aunt or the old priest, and thus had abetted their scheme.

Then the scandal broke.

The priest and the ladies of the Charity Society blamed Signorina Trecke for having given the pair the opportunity to meet every evening at her house and plan their flight together to the Republic of Ecuador.

Signorina Trecke wept inconsolably not so much over the disgrace that her niece had brought on her as over the fact that she was still quite unable to see the evil she had fostered and which had now brought down so many reproaches on her head—all well deserved, of course. Unfortunately, no healthy suspicions were ever to cloud her childlike eyes, which would now be red from crying because her ungrateful niece had left her.

To crown it all, even Signora Leuca found herself accused of doing things by halves, always, of course, because of that overniceness which had so often hindered her from giving free rein to her charitable instincts, especially in the difficult task she had attempted this time.

Heavens! Having taken her husband back into her house, why could she not have accepted the role of a wife in every sense? One has crosses to bear, but virtue lies in resignation.

Signora Leuca let them talk; she even let them think it was her fault. The wound was too deep: let their words fall into it like so many drops of acid. She did not mind—the more it stung, the better.

She smilingly received Lawyer Arico's compliments—which he saw fit to present to her privately—on having freed herself of that lecherous brute, an offensive encumbrance in her house, no matter what the priest said about it. She herself had only objected to *his* return, the lawyer recalled, but hadn't she said that the children would be a pleasure? Well, now he was gone, and what's more she had not had to drive him out; and she had the children.

"What could be better?" he concluded.

In fact, what could be better?

Was she to confide to Lawyer Arico that suddenly, as soon as she had heard of her husband's flight, the pleasure of having the children in the house had vanished as if by magic and a heavy burden of responsibility had settled on her shoulders, making the children seem strangers to her?

Signora Leuca did not even want to admit this to herself. She showered more attention and more affection on the three abandoned orphans than ever—but Signora Leuca felt a change come over her feelings for the little one, that savage little creature. She knew why only too well, but would not name the reason.

"Do you love me?"

"Ess!"

Kneeling in her lap, Rosina would stretch her little clawlike hands up to her neck, wrinkle her tiny nose, and purse that rosebud of a mouth.

"Oh! Not like that! My goodness! You look ugly that way!"

"*You* ugly!"

Signora Leuca had won her over to the extent that she now allowed herself to be picked up and cared for—but at the price of scratches, kicks and even spittings in the face!

The other two stood by, watching a little enviously. They thought it unfair for their aunt to take such trouble with Rosina in front of them—Rosina, who was downright naughty while they were always good as gold.

Only once had Sandrina, evidently speaking for Lauretta too, asked her, "Where is Papa?"

They must have understood something vaguely either from gossip at school or from the priest's words when he had come, very upset, to announce the elopement; or perhaps the copious tears Signorina Trecke had shed the following day, when she begged forgiveness for her niece, had told them more clearly than words.

"Papa has gone away but he will come back," Signora Leuca answered calmly, and they were satisfied.

But would he come back? Signora Leuca was certain that he never would. In any case, even if he did turn up one day or another, what could it now matter to her?

It was all over.

Her spirit sadly on guard under its mask of candid serenity, Signora Leuca was inwardly torn by a distress no one suspected; she was left with the three children to care for and bring up, but what was more, she bore an ever-present torment, not for herself alone, who was perhaps better off than many others, but for all things, all earthly creatures as she saw them in the infinite anguish of her love and pity, in that constant painful awareness— assuaged only by fleeting peaceful moments which brought relief and consolation—of the futility of living like this . . .

THE WREATH

Dr. Cima paused before the entrance to the public gardens which rose on a hill on the outskirts of town. He lingered a moment, looking at the rustic gate, an iron bar suspended between columns. Two melancholy cypress trees loomed behind them, melancholy despite the rambler roses twining in and out of their dark branches. A steep path led from the gate to the top of the hill where a pergola stood out among the trees.

Enjoying the warmth of the early sun, he waited lazily for his inertia to pass so that he could stroll in that old deserted garden. In the cool shade of the northern slope of the hill the air was heavy with the mingled fragrance of mint, sage and wild plum; the birds twittered incessantly in the nearby trees, welcoming the return of spring. The doctor gratefully breathed in the scented air, then started slowly up the path. New green bursting from all the plants, white butterflies fluttering over the flower beds—all gave a misty, dreamlike turn to his unhappy thoughts. How beautiful it was, this peaceful garden where few if any ever came to stroll!

If it were only mine, he thought, and this yearning was echoed by a prolonged sigh.

How many, like himself, had come here to walk and to sigh, If it were only mine? It is fate that whatever belongs to everyone never belongs to anyone in particular. At every turn a sign was posted: DON'T WALK ON THE FLOWER BEDS. DON'T DAMAGE THE PLANTS. DON'T PICK THE FLOWERS. You could take a look in passing! Ownership means "I" not "we," and only one person could say "I" here: the gardener. In a sense, he was the true proprietor and for this he was paid, given a house to live in and allowed to pick the flowers which belonged to everybody and to no one, some of which he sold for his own profit.

The singing notes of one particular bird, soaring high above the others, suddenly reminded the doctor of a long-ago vacation he had spent on a dairy farm lost among trees in open country near the sea. He had been only a small boy, but how he loved hunting! Who could remember how many little birds he had shot and killed that summer!

The everyday cares and problems of his profession were set aside for the moment, but not the fact that he had turned forty his last birthday. For him, he thought, the better part of life was over and, unfortunately, he could not say he had ever really enjoyed being young. There were so many wonderful things in life! It could be so beautiful. A radiant morning like this made up for many sorrows, many disappointments.

An idea suddenly occurred to him and he paused: Should he run back to the house for his young wife? They had been married seven months now, and he would have liked to share this enchanting walk with her. But after a moment's indecision, he continued slowly along the path. No. This enchantment must be for him alone.

His wife might have felt it, had she come here to walk by herself and without his having suggested it. Together, the charm would be lost. Even now, as he thought about it, some of the radiance had faded. A bitter taste of sorrow, vaguely sensed before, rose in his throat.

He could not reproach his wife for anything, poor dear; certainly she was not to blame for the gray hair at his temples and streaking his beard. She was all goodness. But she was only twenty-two, eighteen years younger than he. He hoped the affectionate regard she had shown for him during their brief engagement would naturally turn to love once they were married and she realized how much he loved her—like a young man despite his gray head. She was the first; he had never loved another woman.

Idle dreams! Love, real love, he had never been able to awaken in his wife—and never would, perhaps. She smiled when he appeared and she showed in many thoughtful little ways that she liked him, but this was not love.

His pain might have been less poignant were it not aggravated by an incident in his wife's life which he was unable to treat with the same gentle indulgence he usually showed for most other things.

With all the fervor of her eighteen years, she had fallen in love with a young student who had died of typhus. He knew this because he had been the doctor called to the boy's bedside. And he also knew that she had almost lost her mind, locking herself in her room in the dark, refusing to see anyone and never leaving the house. She even wanted to become a nun. Everybody at the time talked of nothing else but the sad fate of those two young lovers parted by death. The boy had been popular for his easy wit and charming, polite manner, while she who wept unconsolably after him was considered one of the most beautiful girls in the town.

A year passed before her family was able to persuade her to attend a few gatherings. Everyone was moved by her demeanor, her sad expression and soft smile—especially the men. To be loved by her, to rouse her from her obsessive loss, to restore her to life, to youth, became the dream, the ambition of all of them.

But she clung to her mourning. Malicious rumors began to circulate that, for all her modesty and humility, she must take a certain pride in her grief, realizing the love and admiration it inspired. But this was idle talk, prompted by jealousy and resentment. That her feelings were genuine was proven when, within a few months, she refused four or five offers of marriage from the more eligible young men.

But two years after the tragedy, by which time no one dared

present himself because of the certainty of being refused, Dr. Francesco Cima proposed and was immediately accepted.

After the first surprise, however, everyone tried to explain his victory: she had said yes because the doctor was no longer young, and no one would imagine that she had married him for love, true love; she had said yes because, as a rational man, he would not expect to be loved like a young man and would be satisfied if she accorded him affection, devoted respect and gratitude.

He soon found out how true this was, and it hurt. He had to check himself constantly to keep from blurting out some remark which might betray his suffering. It was torture to feel young and not to be able to express his passion for fear of losing her esteem.

He had been young for only one woman: his old mother, who had died three years before. She would have shared his joy in this beautiful morning, and he would have run to get her without giving it a second thought. That blessed old woman! He would have found her huddled in a corner, rosary in hand, praying for all the sick under his care. Dr. Cima smiled wistfully, shaking his head as he climbed the path up the hill. In praying for his patients, his saintly old mother had shown little confidence in him or his training. Jokingly he accused her of this once and she was quick to reply that she was not praying for his patients at all but was simply asking God to help him care for them!

"So you think that without God's help . . ." he began, but she did not let him finish.

"What are you saying? We need God's help always, my son!"

And so she prayed from morning until night. He almost wished he had had fewer patients, so as not to tire her so much. His smile returned. Remembering his mother, his thoughts resumed the airy unreality of a dream, and the enchantment of the day was restored.

Suddenly his train of thought was interrupted by the new gardener, weeding up above in a grassy plot.

"I'm here, *Signor Dottore*. Have you been looking for me long?"

"I? No, really . . ."

"It's ready—ready and waiting ever since eight o'clock," the gardener said, stepping forward, cap in hand, his forehead pearled with sweat. "If you want to see it, it's right here in the pagoda. We can go there now."

"See what?" asked the doctor, halting. "I don't know . . ."

"But, Signor Doctor—the wreath!"

"Wreath?"

The gardener looked at him, equally astonished.

"Excuse me, but isn't today the twelfth?"

"Yes. What of it?"

"You sent your maid day before yesterday to order a wreath for today. Remember?"

"I? For the twelfth? Ah, yes, yes," said the doctor, pretending to remember. "I . . . yes, I sent the maid, of course."

"Violets and roses, don't you remember?" the gardener said, smiling at the doctor's absent-mindedness. "It's been ready since eight this morning. Come and see it."

Fortunately the gardener walked ahead, so he was unaware of the sudden change in Francesco Cima's face as he followed along mechanically, dazed and distressed.

A wreath? His wife must have secretly ordered a wreath. The twelfth, of course—the anniversary of that boy's death. Still such grieving, after three years? She wanted to send a wreath in secret, even now that she was married to him! She who was so timid, so modest, and yet so bold! So she still loved that boy! Would she carry his memory in her heart for life? Why had she ever married him? Why, if her heart belonged to that dead boy and always would? Why? Why? Why?

He raged inwardly as he walked along. He wanted to see the wreath, yes, see it with his own eyes before he was willing to believe his wife capable of such deception, such treachery.

When he saw it on an iron table propped against the wall, it seemed as though it were intended for him and he stood there a long, long time gazing at it.

The gardener, in his own way, mistook his silence for admiration.

"Beautiful, huh? All fresh roses and violets, you know, picked at dawn. A hundred lire, Doctor. Do you know how much work it is to put all those little violets together one by one? And the roses. They're scarce in winter and as soon as the season comes on everybody wants them. A hundred lire is very little. It's really worth at least another twenty."

The doctor tried to speak, but he had no voice left. His lips parted in a pitiful smile and finally he managed to get out, "I'll pay you for it. A hundred lire—too little. Roses and violets, yes. Here are a hundred and twenty."

"Thank you, Signor Doctor," said the gardener, quickly taking the money. "I think it's well worth it."

"Keep it here," the doctor said, putting his wallet back into his pocket. "If the maid comes, don't give it to her. I will return for it myself."

He went out of the pagoda and down the winding path. As soon as he was alone and unseen, he stopped and clenched his fists, his face twisting into a sobbing laugh. "And I'm the one who paid for it!"

What should he do now? Take his wife back to her father's house without, of course, saying anything to hurt her? That was what she deserved. Let her go off and cry for that dead boy at a distance without playing unfairly with the heart of an honest man whom it was her duty to respect, if nothing else. Neither love nor respect? She refused the younger men and accepted him because to her he seemed old, and she was sure he would not dream of claiming her love. With that grizzled beard, he would shut an eye, even both eyes, on her consuming sorrow. An old man couldn't object to anything. So she had planned to send a wreath on the sly. Now that she was married, at least she had not thought it fitting to go herself. Yet, however old her husband might be in her eyes, this was carrying things too far. She had sent the maid to order the wreath in proof of her undying love, and the maid would then have taken it to the boy's tomb.

How unjust the death of that boy had been! Had he lived, had he grown to be a man and become familiar with all the little deceits of life and had married his dear, loving girl, she would soon have discovered that it is one thing to make love from a window at eighteen and quite another to face stern, everyday realities when the first ardor cools and the tedium of daily living leads to quarrels. That's when a young husband grows bored and first considers being unfaithful to his wife. Ah, if only she had known such an experience with that young man, then, perhaps, this "old" one . . .

He clenched his hands so hard that the nails dug into his palms. Looking down at his white, trembling hands, he got hold of himself. The first shock had passed. He stood there staring; then, seeing a bench not far off, he went over stiffly and sat down.

After all, wasn't this "old" man proposing to act like any young blood—make a scene, create a situation? And all those who had so readily pieced together her reasons for accepting him would then exclaim, "For shame! What on earth for? A wreath of flowers? Why not? She always sent a wreath to the cemetery on the twelfth, but the new gardener didn't know that. This year too she remembered, naturally, because the doctor has not been able to make her forget. It was wrong of her, no doubt, but one cannot reason with the heart. And after all the boy is dead!"

That is about what it would amount to.

Then what should he do? Let it go? Pretend to know nothing about it? Go back to the gardener and tell him to give the wreath to the maid, the wreath Cima had intended to keep there to confront her with?

No. Not that. He would then have to get his money back from the man and take him into his confidence.

Well, what then? Go back to the house and demand useless explanations? Face his wife with her poor subterfuge? Punish her? How contemptible all that was! How distasteful!

It was serious, and it went deep—serious because of the ridicule it would cause were his wife's true feelings for him to become known. He must control himself and realize that it did no good to feel young as long as everyone considered you mature, almost on the shelf. A very young man might have made a scene, but at his age he must win his wife's respect another way.

He got up, perfectly calm now, yet with a feeling of listlessness. The birds continued to twitter gaily in the garden, but where was the enchantment of a moment ago?

Francesco Cima walked out of the garden and started home. When he came to his own front door his calm vanished. Suddenly breathless, he wondered how he had ever managed the steps on such shaky legs. The idea of seeing his wife again now . . . She must be feeling sadder than usual today, but she would probably know how to conceal her sorrow. He loved her—oh, how he loved her! And deep within himself he knew that she deserved to be loved because she was good, just as good as the perfection of her delicate features showed her to be, and the depth of her velvety black eyes, the pallor of her lovely face.

The maid opened the door. The sight of her disconcerted him, for the old woman was in on the secret, a sort of accomplice. She had served his wife's parents for many years and was now devoted to her, so it was likely she would not talk. And certainly she would not be able to assess, nor even to understand, what he was about to do. In any case, she was an outsider. He wanted this to be a secret between his wife and himself.

He went straight to her room and found her combing her hair before the mirror. Between her raised arms he caught sight of her face, reflecting a look of surprise to see him home at this hour.

"I came back," he said, "to invite you to come out with me."

"Now?" she asked, turning around without lowering her arms, smiling faintly, with that lovely mass of soft black hair piled loosely on her head.

Her pale smile upset him almost to the point of tears. He imagined it held a profound pity for him, for his love of her, as well as her own sorrow.

"Yes, now," he replied. "It is so beautiful out of doors. Hurry. We'll go to the little garden, then farther on, into the country. We'll take a carriage."

"Why?" she asked almost unconsciously. "Why today?"

At that question, he feared his expression would surely betray him. It was already a struggle to keep his voice calm.

"Wouldn't you like to go today?" he said. "It will do you good. Hurry! I want you to come with me." He went to the door and turned. "I'll wait for you in the office."

In a short time she was ready. For that matter, she always did as he wished except where her heart was concerned, and there he had no power. She had put up that timid opposition: *Why today?* Yet even today, despite the sadness she must be feeling, she had obeyed him and was ready to go for a ride in the country, wherever he wished.

They went out and walked awhile through the small town; then he hired a carriage and ordered the driver to stop at the little garden. He went up alone, asking his wife gently to wait for him there a moment.

Dismayed when she saw him coming down the path followed by the gardener with the wreath, she almost fainted. But he encouraged her with a look.

"To the cemetery!" he said to the driver, jumping into the carriage.

As soon as they started off, she burst into tears and covered her face with her handkerchief.

"Don't cry," he said softly. "I didn't want to speak about it at home, and I don't want to say anything now. Please don't cry. It came about by accident. I had gone for a walk in the garden and the gardener, thinking I had ordered the wreath, mentioned it. Don't cry any more. We will go and leave it there together."

She kept her eyes hidden in the handkerchief until the carriage came to a stop at the gate of the cemetery.

He helped her down, then picked up the wreath and walked in with her.

"Come," he said, taking the first path to the left and looking at the graves, one by one, along the row.

It was the next to the last grave along that path. He took off his hat to lay the wreath at the foot of the grave, then stepped back quietly and withdrew to give her time to say a prayer. But she stayed there, silent, with the handkerchief still pressed to her eyes. She had not a thought, not a tear, for the dead boy. As though lost, she suddenly turned and looked at her husband as she had never looked at him before.

"Forgive me! Forgive me, Francesco! Take me home," she cried, clinging to his arm.

CHRONOLOGY

with Italian Titles and Sources

Stories published for the first time in newspapers or magazines:

1924	Mortal Remains	*Resti mortali*	*Il Corriere della Sera,* July 26
1932	Cinci	*Cinci*	*La Lettura,* June
1934	The Soft Touch of Grass	*I piedi sull'erba*	*Il Corriere della Sera,* April 20

Stories published for the first time in book form:

1902	The Examination	*Concorso per referendario al consiglio di stato*	*Quand'ero matto,* Streglio, Turin
1904	The Black Shawl	*Lo scialle nero*	*Bianche e nere,* Streglio, Turin
1904	A Mere Formality	*Formalità*	*Bianche e nere,* Streglio, Turin
1904	Fumes	*Il "fumo"*	*Bianche e nere,* Streglio, Turin
1906	The Footwarmer	*Lo scaldino*	*Erma Bifronte,* Treves, Milan
1911	Watch and Ward	*Di guardia*	*La vita nuda,* Treves, Milan
1914	The Wreath	*La corona*	*Le due maschere,* Quattrini, Florence
1917	Candelora	*Candelora*	*E domani, lunedì ...* Treves, Milan

NOTE on Bibliography

The dates of the stories are from the Bibliography of Pirandello (Bibliografia di Pirandello) by Manlio Lo Vecchio-Musti. The official bibliography was first compiled in 1939 and was brought up to date in 1952. This second edition is published by Mondadori, Milan.

NOTE on Italian Pronunciation

Stress is on an accented syllable. Where there is no accent, stress is on the penultimate syllable. The consonants c and g are pronounced hard (as in English came and gate) before a, o and u. They are pronounced soft (as in English cheese and gesture) before e and i. To make a soft c or g hard, h is inserted; thus chi approximates the English key. The gli (Consiglio) is pronounced like the double l with i in English million.

ABOUT THE AUTHOR

LUIGI PIRANDELLO *was born June 28, 1867, at Agrigento in Sicily. After attending secondary schools in Girgenti and Palermo, he went, at eighteen, to Rome but stayed there only a year, transferring, in 1886, to the University of Bonn. In Germany he worked at romance philology and philosophy, started to write poetry and completed a translation of Goethe's* Roman Elegies.

On his return to Rome, Pirandello was urged by his fellow Sicilian, the novelist Capuana, to try his hand at prose writing. Here at last Pirandello's genius began to emerge. In the twenty years from 1894 to the outbreak of World War I, he published innumerable short stories and four novels, of which the deservedly best known is The Late Mattia Pascal.

Pirandello then turned to the stage, partly in an experimental mood and in an attempt to convey as vividly as possible the attitudes and speech of his native island. A couple of regional plays preceeded his first stage success, Right You Are If You Think You Are, *which had its premiere in 1917. From then on Pirandello wrote forty-odd plays in relatively quick succession, the majority of them full-length. He was fifty-four years old when his drama,* Six Characters in Search of an Author, *brought him international acclaim.*

European, then American, performances of his plays led Pirandello to move about the "great world." He took his own company, from his Art Theatre founded in Rome in 1925, and played the major capitals of western Europe, later visiting Argentina, Brazil and North America.

In 1934 he was awarded the Nobel Prize for Literature. He died a year and a half later, having contracted pneumonia during the filming of his most subjective work, The Late Mattia Pascal.

REPRESENTATIVE SIMON AND SCHUSTER PAPERBACKS

For people who want to know more about science, philosophy, the arts, and history in the making

Adler: *How to Read a Book*, $1.75
Ames: *What Shall We Name the Baby?*, $1.45
Bell: *Men of Mathematics*, $2.25
Berenson: *Rumor and Reflection*, $1.95
Berne: *A Layman's Guide to Psychiatry and Psychoanalysis*, $1.95
Brockway & Weinstock: *Men of Music*, $1.95
Burroughs: *Vasari's Lives of the Artists*, $1.95
Chayefsky: *Television Plays*, $1.75
Cooke: *Playing the Piano for Pleasure*, $1.45
Dreyfuss: *Designing for People*, $1.95
Durant:
  The Pleasures of Philosophy, $1.75
  The Story of Philosophy, $1.75
Eastman: *Enjoyment of Laughter*, $1.50
Egri: *The Art of Dramatic Writing*, $1.75
Einstein & Infeld: *The Evolution of Physics*, $1.45
Fadiman:
  Fantasia Mathematica, $1.45
  Reading I've Liked, $2.25
Fellner: *Opera Themes and Plots*, $1.95
Ginzberg: *The Legends of the Jews*, $2.45
Gleaves & Wertenbaker: *You and the Armed Services*, $1.25
Goren:
  Contract Bridge for Beginners, $1.00
  Point Count Bidding, $1.00
Harriman: *Peace with Russia?*, $1.00
Heilbroner: *The Worldly Philosophers*, $1.50
Horowitz: *Chess for Beginners*, $1.75
Horowitz & Reinfeld: *Chess Traps, Pitfalls and Swindles*, $1.45
Kazantzakis:
  Freedom or Death, $1.75
  The Greek Passion, $1.95
  Zorba the Greek, $1.75
Kerr: *How Not to Write a Play*, $1.45
Lerner: *America as a Civilization*—VOL. 1, *The Basic Frame*; VOL. 2, *Culture and Personality*, each $1.95

Lovejoy: *Lovejoy's College Guide*, $2.50
Mills: *The Causes of World War Three*, $1.50
Newman:
  What Is Science?, $1.95
  The World of Mathematics (4 vols., boxed), $9.95
Oppenheimer: *The Open Mind*, $1.00
Pearson & Anderson: *U.S.A.—Second-Class Power?*, $1.75
Perelman: *The Road to Miltown*, $1.45
Pirandello: *Short Stories*, $1.75
Rosten: *A Guide to the Religions of America*, $1.50
Russell:
  Common Sense and Nuclear Warfare, $1.00
  A History of Western Philosophy, $2.25
  Unpopular Essays, $1.00
Schuster: *A Treasury of the World's Great Letters*, $2.25
SCIENTIFIC AMERICAN BOOKS:
  Atomic Power, $1.45
  Automatic Control, $1.45
  Lives in Science, $1.45
  The New Astronomy, $1.45
  New Chemistry, $1.45
  The Physics and Chemistry of Life, $1.45
  The Planet Earth, $1.45
  Plant Life, $1.45
  The Scientific American Reader, $2.25
  A Twentieth-Century Bestiary, $1.45
  The Universe, $1.45
Seldes: *The Public Arts*, $1.50
Shanet: *Learn to Read Music*, $1.45
Szilard: *The Voice of the Dolphins*, $1.00
Thurber: *Thurber Country*, $1.45
Weinberg: *Attorney for the Damned*, $2.25
Whyte: *Is Anybody Listening?*, $1.25

PRICES SUBJECT TO CHANGE